EXPRESS WESTERNS *presents*

A FISTFUL OF LEGENDS

21 New tales of the Old West

Edited by

NIK MORTON

2009

A FISTFUL OF LEGENDS

Edited by Nik Morton
First Paperback Edition: December 2009

Dedicated to Robert Hale Ltd., publisher of the Black Horse Westerns imprint, for keeping the spirit of the Old West alive.

Publisher: Ian Parnham
Co-edited by Charles T Whipple
Introduction by James Reasoner
Express Westerns logo & colophon: Nik Morton
Cover Painting by David McAllister
Cover Design by Jennifer Smith-Mayo
Eagle-eyed proofreading: Ian Parnham, David Whitehead, Charles T Whipple

Names, characters and incidents in this book are fictional, and any resemblance to actual events, locales, organizations, or persons living or dead is purely coincidental

All rights reserved. No part of this book may be reproduced or transmitted in any form or by any means, electronic or mechanical, including photocopying, recording, or by any information or storage and retrieval system, without the written permission of the author, except where permitted by law.

ISBN 978-0-557-19954-9

Copyright © 2009 by Express Westerns.
All stories copyright © 2009 by their respective authors have not appeared elsewhere previously, and are used by permission.

An EXPRESS WESTERNS Publication

A note about the excellent cover painting: The gun in the artwork is an 1858 Remington .44 conversion. After the Civil War, many cap & ball pistols were converted to take the cartridge and were in use throughout the 1800s. They were either a 'drop in' conversion, or a 'fixed and ported' conversion. The 'drop in' conversion simply replaces the original cylinder with one that takes cartridges. After that, the gunman installs a loaded cylinder, fires the cartridges, removes the cylinder, dumps the spent brass, loads more cartridges, and snaps the cylinder back into the revolver's frame. The Remington 1858 .44 cylinder could be quickly removed and replaced with very little effort; probably faster than ejecting brass and reloading a pistol with a loading gate. In the picture, the gunman has removed the cylinder, dumped the brass, and is resting it against the frame to reload it.

EXPRESS WESTERNS presents

A FISTFUL OF LEGENDS

Discover what it's like to ride with damaged men and sinister night stalkers, tragic doves, plucky homemakers and gun-toting belles. Experience for yourself the harsh reality of birth and death, love and hate, revenge, retribution and robbery. You'll find it all here, penned by a whole posse-full of Western writers old and new. So what are you waiting for? Saddle up for action and adventure ... and grab yourself *A Fistful of Legends*!

Acclaim for our authors in **Where Legends Ride**:
From *Meridian Bridge*:
One of the very best tales is 'Bubbles,' by *Ross Morton*. Within a handful of pages Morton presents three-dimensional characters that live and breathe and wander through the years like real people, and we're treated to a heartfelt overview of a friendship that spans the decades.
Gillian F. Taylor too offers more than a routine reworking of old formulas in 'Easier Than Working' as bank robbers Irish and Tomcat Billy come across a homesteader family in need. More than just a pair of good-hearted rogues, these two express a real range of emotion in their creator's hands.

From Ron Fortier, *Pulp Fiction Review*:
'The Prodigal' by *Chuck Tyrell* is a poignant, classic cowboy tale of right and wrong with a dedicated marshal having to hunt down his own son. Likewise 'The Man Who Tracked a River' by *Derek Rutherford* offered up a story of guilt and redemption that was steeped in the dust of the badlands. 'Desert Surrender' by *Kit Churchill* is a raw, grim adventure that had me turning the pages fast. These are all classic western gems. 'Once Upon A Time In Mirage' by *I.J. Parnham* and 'Snows of Montana' by the editor *Matthew P. Mayo* read like saddle-tramp sagas inspired by O'Henry, their twisty ends fun.

From *Pog's Literary Reviews*
Not only do *Lance Howard's* westerns contain enough action and traditional shoot 'em up for the most discriminating western novel reader, but they craft vivid characters and explore the vast panorama of human experience and emotion with situations relevant and immediate for a modern audience ...you'll find gunslingers and crooked lawmen right alongside battered wives and homeless outcasts...a western writer for the non-western reader and horse opera lover alike!

Contents

INTRODUCTION	James Reasoner	7
DEAD MAN TALKING	Derek Rutherford	9
BILLY	Lance Howard	22
LONIGAN MUST DIE!	Ben Bridges	31
THE MAN WHO SHOT GARFIELD DELANY	I J Parnham	46
HALF A PIG	Matthew P Mayo	53
BLOODHOUND	C. Courtney Joyner	58
MORE THAN MEETS THE EYE	Gillian F Taylor	68
BIG ENOUGH	Chuck Tyrell	80
ONE DAY IN LIBERTY	Jack Giles	93
SHADOWS ON THE HORIZON	Bobby Nash	106
ON THE RUN	Alfred Wallon	119
THE GIMP	Jack Martin	127
VISITORS	Ross Morton	136
THE NIGHTHAWK	Michael D George	149
THE PRIDE OF THE CROCKETTS	Evan Lewis	155
DARKE JUSTICE	Peter Avarillo	167
ANGELO AND THE STRONGBOX	Cody Wells	178
CRIB GIRLS	Kit Churchill	195
MAN OF IRON	Chuck Tyrell	208
CASH LARAMIE AND THE MASKED DEVIL	Edward A Grainger	217
DEAD MAN WALKING	Lee Walker	229
AFTERWORD	Nik Morton	242

INTRODUCTION

James Reasoner

It seems I was destined to be a Western writer. The first "grown-up" paperback I ever bought was a Western: *Bigger than Texas* by William R. Cox, published by Gold Medal in 1963. A year later, I discovered the work of Zane Grey, Max Brand, and Clarence E. Mulford. I still have vivid memories of that summer when I was eleven years old, reading *Hopalong Cassidy, Single Jack*, and *The Lost Wagon Train*. A few years later, I became a big fan of the Jim Hatfield novels from the pulp *Texas Rangers*, which were then being reprinted in paperback, as well as the Walt Slade paperback novels, written (although I didn't know this at the time) by one of the authors who had written Hatfield novels under the house-name Jackson Cole. I didn't know what a house-name was back then, either. All I knew was that I really, really enjoyed those Western novels.

But despite that, I didn't set out to be a Western writer. My goal was to be a mystery writer and, as it happens, I sold several hundred thousand words of mystery fiction before I ever wrote a Western. That came about because I'd gone to work for a book packaging company and the first job they gave me was to write a Western novel in their Stagecoach Station series. Luckily, I had continued to read Westerns all along and still thoroughly enjoyed them, so I was glad to give it a try.

I loved it.

Western fiction has a tremendous power to entertain.

Those who avoid it thinking that the Western is an outdated genre and has no relevance in today's world simply don't understand what they're missing.

The Western has a universality that is simply stunning.

You can tell any sort of story as a Western: comedy, tragedy, action, romance. You can pit man against nature, man against his fellow man, man against himself – or woman against herself, since strong female characters have been a tradition in Westerns going back decades and people who don't believe that just haven't read enough in the genre to know better.

Sure, there have been plenty of pulpish tales featuring more gunplay than character development, and sometimes that's just what the reader (and the writer) wants. But the Western has always featured much more moral complexity than its critics give it credit for, to go along with well-plotted stories that move at a pace guaranteed to keep the reader turning the pages to find out what happens next.

Nowhere can you find better examples of pure, powerful storytelling than in the pages of a good Western.

That's why, for many authors, the Western is as much fun to write as it is to read, and always has been.

Luckily for us as readers, there are still plenty of writers around who recognize the continuing appeal of the Western.

A while ago, a group of them put together a fine anthology of Western short stories called *Where Legends Ride*. Now, some of those authors are back with a second collection, joined this time around by a number of talented newcomers. Contributors range from Ben Bridges (David Whitehead), one of the deans of the Black Horse Western line published by Robert Hale, to sixteen-year-old Peter Avarillo (Chantel Foster), quite possibly the youngest professionally-published Western writer ever. Newer writers such as Evan Lewis, Jack Martin (Gary Dobbs), Matthew P. Mayo, and Edward A. Grainger (David Cranmer) contribute solid tales, along with top-notch professionals like Lance Howard (Howard Hopkins), Jack Giles (Ray Foster), Chuck Tyrell (Charles T. Whipple), and Ross Morton (Nik Morton).

As a reader, I count myself extremely fortunate that there are authors like these to spin such wonderful yarns and provide hours of solid entertainment. And as a Western author, I'm very pleased to count them among my friends and comrades who are upholding a long, proud tradition.

Now, go read the stories.

I guarantee you'll have a good time.

DEAD MAN TALKING

Derek Rutherford

Born and raised in Gloucester, UK, Derek grew up on a diet of spaghetti Westerns and hard-boiled heroes. He's the author of two published Black Horse Westerns – Vengeance At Tyburn Ridge *and* Yellow Town *– and numerous short stories. His latest western* The Bone Picker *has just been accepted by Robert Hale Limited. In his spare time, Derek plays and teaches rock'n'roll guitar and rides large motorcycles.*

The wall was sweating. Jared pressed his fingertips against the stone and they came away wet. He looked at the moisture for a moment and then touched his middle finger to his tongue.

"They say you killed three men," Mitchell said from the bunk below.

Jared licked his other fingers. There was barely enough moisture to taste.

"You awake?" Mitchell asked. "Heat got your tongue?"

Jared had been in the prison for three weeks, but this was his first day in the general population. He'd been beaten badly when arrested and had spent most of those three weeks shackled to an iron bedstead in the infirmary. Even now there were more parts of his body bruised than not.

"Four," Jared said. "It was four men."

"Four? You don't deny it, then?"

"No, I don't deny it."

Now he saw a trickle of water run down the crack between two blocks of stone. It looked like the constantly running water had worn away a half inch of the mortar between the stones. He stopped the droplet with a finger and then he ran it over his scabbed lips.

"Most people say how they shouldn't be here," Mitchell said. As if to reinforce the point, someone started shouting further along the cellblock, the words deadened by the stone walls.

"Uh-huh."

"Yet you admit to killing four men."

"I'd have killed five if they hadn't stopped me."

He dammed another dribble of water, and let his eyes follow the trail upwards. Towards the top the whole cell wall glistened.

"Five?"

"Yep."

"You're just a kid," Mitchell said. "You don't look like a killer."

"That's what one of them told me. Just before I pulled the trigger."

He heard Mitchell fidgeting on the lower bunk. The bed creaked. Mitchell cussed and groaned, then coughed. It sounded like his throat was blocked with phlegm. Jared could smell Mitchell, too. He stank like he hadn't washed for weeks. It didn't help that late May had turned loose a blistering day upon them.

"Someone said they're going to hang you," Mitchell said.

"That they are."

Now he felt Mitchell getting up, saw the shadows in the room change, Mitchell's craggy and bearded face appearing almost level with his own.

"There's people here killed a whole lot more men than that. And *they* ain't due to hang."

"I guess it depends on who you kill."

Mitchell was looking at him like he was an exhibit in a traveling show. The dead man that talks, Jared thought.

"You don't seem bothered."

"I'm bothered," Jared said. "But I did what I promised myself I'd do, and if I had the chance I'd do it all again." He wondered if Mitchell could see the water running down the wall. He longed to reach up and trap more of it – maybe five hundred fingertips of water would equal a cupful – but he didn't want Mitchell pressing his filthy fingers against the wall, so he held his cellmate's gaze instead.

"They weren't outlaws," Mitchell said. "That's what I heard, anyway."

"You've heard a lot."

"People talk. There's nothing else to do."

"You got that right."

High up on one wall a small rectangle of intense blue sky, divided up by three iron bars, hinted at freedom and wide-open spaces. Jared figured if he looked at it long enough, he might catch sight of a bird flying by.

"They were businessmen," Mitchell said. "So the talk goes."

Jared pulled his gaze away from the sky, refusing to allow himself the pleasure – and the pain – of thinking about freedom. "Yes. They were businessmen."

"Which is why you're going to hang. You'd shot a rustler or a bunch of robbers, you'd have been a hero."

Jared stared up at the ceiling. His scalp itched from all those hours resting on a thin gray pillow infested with God knew what.

He sighed, looked at Mitchell again. There was an eagerness in the man's eyes, maybe some perverse pleasure in the knowledge that the kid he was sharing his cell with was as good as dead. He wondered, should he tell Mitchell his story? If he did, he knew that within days, hours maybe, it would be all around the prison. Wouldn't that be cheapening the memory somehow?

Or would it be perpetuating those memories? Especially after they'd hanged him. At least then the knowledge would live on.

Mitchell licked his dirty lips as if he somehow sensed what was coming.

"You want to hear about heroes," Jared said, eventually. "*Real* heroes?"

"Is this to do with why they're going to hang you?"

"Uh-huh."

"Then sure, tell me all about your heroes."

Life for all of them would have been different had they not lived in the house halfway up the hill beyond the end of Main Street. Jared, eight years old at the time, had nicknamed the road "Only Street" on account of that's exactly what it was. There were a few alleyways leading off Main Street and there were a few gaps between buildings, but, whichever way you looked at it, Main Street was the only street in town.

They lived on the hill because Jared's father had a second cousin in Boston, or at least some place back east. Wherever it was, the cousin lived up on a hill. And that was, apparently, a good thing. "The best people live on hills," Jared's pa said. And when the chance came to put up his own house he chose a place close enough to town that he could still walk down to the livery stables of a morning, but high enough that, when the town spread – as it surely would, so his pa said – they would be with the best people.

The day that changed all of their lives was a Wednesday in August. Jared never knew the exact date. But he knew the time: suppertime. He was working his way back up towards the rear of their house, a pail of spring water in his hand. Every ten yards he'd change arms because of the weight. A warm westerly wind blew across the hill and he could feel grains of sand sticking to the sweat on his face. He'd just put the bucket down for a moment's rest before tackling the last – steepest – section of the path, and was pondering, for perhaps the thousandth time, on how anyone could think that living on a hill was a good thing, when Jim came scooting around the side of the house, a finger over his lips, and half-ran, half-stumbled down the steep path.

"Don't make a sound," he whispered. Then he grabbed Jared and pulled him flat against the ground. The pail caught on the edge of a large flat stone and tipped up. Cool water spilled all over Jared's pants and onto the dry ground.

"Look what you –"

Jim clamped his hand across Jared's mouth.

"Don't bite," he said. "*Listen.*"

The way Jim was lying against him, Jared could feel his brother's heartbeat. It was coming as fast as his breath, and the two things together made Jared tense and scared.

But there was nothing to hear. Not even a dog barking down the hill in town.

He nodded, hoping that Jim would understand he meant he wouldn't shout out. Jim took his hand away from Jared's mouth.

"What's happening?" Jared whispered.

"Three men came and – "

Their mother's screaming interrupted Jim's explanation. The scream was cut off abruptly but it seemed to roll down from the house and echo inside Jared's head.

"*Down*," Jim whispered, and pressed Jared harder into the dirt. A flint cut into his cheek. His brother's arm was heavy over his shoulders, holding him flat.

A man's voice – a stranger's voice – drifted on the wind.

"So you understand, mister? You understand *good*?"

"Get your hands off me," his pa said.

Jared had no idea what was happening, but when he heard the defiance in his father's voice he wanted to scramble to his feet, stand shoulder to shoulder with his pa, and take on whoever these men were. But Jim's arm held him firmly against the ground.

"And you, ma'am, you understand, too." It was a different voice, a little softer. "You scream again, and I'll kill you. I promise."

There was a long pause then Jared heard his ma say, "You're Hell bound. And I hope God has *no* mercy on your soul."

Jared could hear little Jay crying. He pictured the baby in his mother's arms.

"I'll talk to God when the time comes," the man said. "Meanwhile, you just sit inside and when this job is done you'll never see us again. I promise you that."

There was the sharp metallic sound of a revolver hammer being cocked.

"Get right inside the house, ma'am. *Now*. You don't want to see this."

Then his mother used language Jared had never heard her use in his life. There was a catch in her voice, as if she was on the edge of crying. He could feel Jim shaking.

What's going on?

He didn't know if he said the words aloud, whispering them into the dry earth, or whether they were only in his mind.

"I'll be all right, Mary," his father said. "I love you. Look after the…the baby."

Jared's mother said she loved him, too. But the words were almost unintelligible through her sobbing. Jared felt Jim opening and closing his fists.

What's going on?

"Let's go," one of the men said. "You understand, you just walk right into the jailhouse. You be inside and you be talking to Cole – maybe offer him a cigarette – then you light the fuse. You make sure he dies. Do that and your woman and kid get to live. You do anything else and they both die. Eventually."

"You understand?" someone else said. "We can see all the way to the jailhouse from here."

There was a pause, then Jared heard his father say, "I understand."

"They tied dynamite around his waist," Jim said, still whispering. He let go of Jared and they lay with their faces almost touching. There were tear tracks running through the dirt and dust on Jim's cheeks.

"What?"

"I saw them," Jim said. "One had a gun pointing at pa, another tied a belt of dynamite around his waist."

"What d'you mean, a *belt* of dynamite?"

"There were three of them," Jim said. "I was just coming in from feeding the chickens when I heard them. Ma was crying. Jay was crying. They were hitting pa. Beating him up good."

Air exploded from Jared's mouth. "We got to kill 'em!"

"Shushh! Then they tied dynamite around his waist," Jay said. He still had an arm locked around his brother's shoulders, not letting him do anything stupid.

Jared didn't speak for a moment. He was trying to work it out, to add what Jim had told him to what he'd overheard. Eventually it came together in his mind. His throat was so dry he could barely speak. "And he's got to go down to the jailhouse and... blow up."

Jim looked at him, his eyes wet, his lips trembling.

"You heard pa covering for us?" Jim said. "He mentioned Jay but he never mentioned us."

"We've got to do something," Jared said. "That's why he...He was giving us a chance."

"Listen, stay here," Jim said. "I'm going to look to see where they are, what they're doing."

"Let me come."

"No! Stay here. Don't let them see you. I'll be right back." He reached out and placed his hand on Jared's shoulder. "We ain't gonna let 'em do it, Jar. Don't you worry none."

Then his brother was scrabbling across the ground on his stomach, aiming for the dry gully that ran adjacent to the path up towards the side of the house.

Jared lay still for a few seconds. It was unreal. Just a few minutes before, they'd all been in the house: him, pa, ma, and Jim, talking and laughing, and little Jay gurgling away. Ma had the stove lit and a pie baking – boy it had smelled good – pa was making some candles out of horse fat. And now somebody was forcing him to walk into the jailhouse and blow a man up.

Blow himself up, too.

Jared eased around and raised his head slightly so he could see down the hill.

There was pa, already halfway to town, his big coat on, walking real slow, shuffling almost like he was an old man, glancing over his shoulder now, his eyes looking right at Jared. It was all Jared could do not to stand up and run down to him, hug him, have his pa lift him up and swing him round.

About a third of the way down the hill, also watching Jared's pa, a man sat on a rock. The man was wearing guns and had a hat pulled low over his face.

Suddenly it all seemed *too* real. Three men had come into their home whilst he was down at the spring and now pa was going to die.

But not without a fight, he wasn't. The men didn't know about him or Jim, so there was still a chance. He had a shotgun in the cabin – pa had started to take him rabbit hunting. If he could get to that and sneak up behind the guy down there... A sob escaped from his lips. By the time he'd got up to the cabin, somehow got in, it would be too late. And there must still have been two of them up there, anyway. Trying to get the gun was hopeless.

It had to be something else.

The bucket.

It was a heavy iron bucket. Every day he cursed the weight of it empty, and every day he cursed the weight more when it was full. Now he imagined swinging it with all his might against the man's head and he was suddenly glad of that weight.

All he had to do was get across the trail unseen, circle round behind the man, and... and save pa.

He started scrabbling uphill. The only place he could sneak across the trail was above the house. There were big rocks up there; sometimes ma dried their clothes on them.

He cast a look over his shoulder.

Pa had paused right outside the church now. The man watching him had lit up a cigarette. The man didn't look scared or bothered in the least.

Jared moved faster. The stones he knocked loose with his fingers, his feet, and the pail sounded like a thunderous landslide to him, and he willed himself to slow down. But no sooner had he slowed than he was telling himself he needed to go quicker. The church was way out on the edge of town, but his father didn't have *that* far to go to get to the jailhouse.

Jared eased himself into the dry gully. One time, when it had rained for three days, the gully had run with water. But now it had been dry for over a year. He followed the gully up and around the house. At the far side he paused, listening. He could hear his mother weeping. He could hear two men talking, one of them laughing. He could smell cigarette smoke.

Just as he wondered where Jim might be, what he might be doing, he heard the creak of the house door being eased open.

Jared raised his head. Jim was standing by the door with a shotgun in his hand. Later, Jared figured that Jim must have taken the shotgun to the chicken pen with him earlier, maybe on account of coyotes, and had dropped it when he'd seen the men arrive and had rushed down to warn his brother. But now all Jared saw was the chance for Jim to save them all. He felt his heartbeat quicken, the breath come in short excited snorts from his nose.

"Go Jim," he whispered, his own mission forgotten for a second.

Jim eased the door open another inch.

It creaked again.

One more inch, one more creak, and this time the barrel of a gun came through the door and pressed itself against Jim's forehead.

Jared had to fight not to cry out in terror and disappointment. He braced himself for the explosion that would end his brother's life. Instead, he heard the man growl, "We've got a little bit more company. Figured it was strange there was another cot in the corner."

Then a hand grabbed the shotgun and pulled it from Jim's grasp. Almost in the same movement the shotgun seemed to kick out with a life of its own and the stock slammed into Jim's belly. Jim screamed and fell to the ground, curling into a ball. The man stepped outside and brought the butt of the gun down on Jim's head. Now their ma was screaming, too, trying to drag the man off. The other man wrapped his arms around her and pulled her away.

The first man brought the gun crashing down again and again and again. Jim whimpered and sobbed. Jared was on the verge of getting up and taking a run at the man, swinging his bucket straight into his face, when the man said, "So how many more of you are there? Come on, speak. How many more?"

Another blow.

"Just me," Jim said, blood all over his face. "There's just me and ma and Jay and pa."

The gun's stock smashed down one more time with a force that Jared was sure must have knocked his brother out cold. But Jim looked up at the man. "I swear. There's just me and ma and Jay and – "

The sound of the explosion from down on Only Street arrived a second before the shockwaves trembled the ground. Afterward there was a long silence.

"– and pa," Jim said.

"Lordy," Mitchell said. He and Jared sat on Mitchell's bunk. Somewhere around the time that he had been describing crawling through the dirt trying to get around the house without being seen, Jared had eased himself off his own bunk and sat alongside his cellmate. He hadn't even been aware of his physical movements in the cell, only that for one brief moment, inside his head, it felt like his whole family had still been alive.

"Pa covered for me. Jim covered for me," Jared said. "Ma, too. She never let on."

Mitchell opened his mouth to speak, but ended up just shaking his head.

"Pa went into that jailhouse and blew himself and Cole up and –"

"Who *was* Cole?"

"He was one of *them*. They were scared to death he was going to talk when the circuit judge came by. Well, he *was* going to talk. That's why they got pa to do it. It had to be a townsperson, someone the sheriff would let inside the jailhouse. They had that place locked up real good waiting for the judge."

Mitchell was staring at Jared now, and Jared could tell that the story was taking on its own momentum inside the man's head. "They killed your family, didn't they?"

Jared nodded.

"Soon as that jail went up they shot ma and Jim and Jay like they were sick dogs. They didn't even say anything. Just drew their guns and shot them. And I lay in the gully and cried without making a sound."

"And those were the men *you* shot?"

"Those were the men I shot. It took me fifteen years to track 'em down. Them, and one more who I hadn't seen but who was down in the town, by the jailhouse, making sure pa never backed out. But in those fifteen years they'd changed their names and become respectable."

"And that's why they're going to hang you?"

"Uh–huh."

"You told the judge this story?"

"No one believed a word. Maybe the judge had even been bought. That town ain't even there anymore. Seemed like the whole place died that day."

"And the fifth man?"

"The fifth man?"

"You mentioned a fifth man earlier?"

"Yeah. The one who got away."

"Who was he?"

"He was the one who planned it all. He was the one who was *always* respectable. Their leader. If the judge was bought, he was the one who did it. He is, I guess, the one who's hanged me."

"They caught you before you got to him." It was a statement, not a question.

"I didn't take enough care. I made a mistake. Not killing him is my only regret."

Mitchell was silent for a long time. Then he said, "I've got a plan. I think you might like it."

"That water you were drinking earlier," Mitchell said.

Jared hadn't realized Mitchell had seen what he was doing. He felt a moment's shame that he'd tried to keep the trickling water to himself. "I wouldn't exactly call it drinking."

"No, maybe not. But it feels good on cracked lips, don't it?"

"Uh-huh."

"See, what's happening is this. They got a tank up on the roof here. There's a prisoner detail that no one likes. It involves carrying bucket after bucket from the well down in the yard, all the way up to the roof, and pouring it into the tank."

For a second Jared pictured himself at eight years of age, iron bucket swinging from his thin arms.

"The idea is," Mitchell said, "they can then pipe it around the prison and we can have showers and drinking water on tap. Just like those fancy houses back east do."

"Showers?" Jared said.

"I never had one," Mitchell said, as if this might be news to Jared. "But I think the governor does. Thing is, the pipe up here is leaking, best I can guess. It's been leaking for months. That's why I gave you the top bunk. Some days it drips off the ceiling onto the bunk."

"Thanks."

"You might have noticed where I worked away some of the cement."

"*You* did that?"

"It comes away real easy where it's wet."

"What are you saying?"

"I'm saying we bring back a knife or two from the chow hall I reckon two of us could easily pull out enough stones in one night, maybe two, to get through."

Jared stood up and looked at the soaking wall. "What's on the other side?"

"If you're asking what's on the other side of those stones, then it's just a passageway, a stone channel where the pipes run. It's big enough to crawl along. I know. I seen it when I was on rat duty. But if you're asking what's on the other side of *that,* then it's the whole of Mexico, my friend. You get to the border and you're home and dry."

Jared climbed up on to his bunk and pressed a fingernail into the mortar. Chunks of it came away, like tiny landslides on a hillside from long ago.

He looked down at Mitchell. "It might be Mexico for you. For me there's someone I want to see."

Mitchell was nodding, smiling. "I figured as much."

The Citizen Gentlemen's Club was tucked away between the Royale Hotel and the newspaper office in Tulane Junction. Both institutions were owned by Art Sherman. He'd made a fortune in his early days by arranging to have his own banks robbed, buying whichever judges he could with sums of money that they wouldn't normally earn in three years and then receiving lifetime kickbacks from the men he saved from the noose. Later, he invested in the railways – maybe, Jared thought, he even owned the Green Valley and the East Arizona lines that met just a quarter of mile away and gave Tulane Junction its name. In his time Sherman had been mayor of Tulane and there was talk of him supposedly running for the state.

All built on blood, Jared thought, and stepped into the club foyer.

"Sir. Sir! No guns in here, sir." The man hurried out of a small office to the right of the foyer. He was dressed in a maroon jacket, white shirt, and expensive black trousers. "Sir, this is a members only club. I don't believe – "

Jared hit the man on the side of the jaw. A sharp hard punch, with all of his shoulder and more than fifteen years of frustration behind it. The man fell to the floor and never moved.

Jared walked into the bar.

Oil lamps burning on the walls illuminated flock wallpaper. Fancy plaster patterns radiated from the base of the candle chandeliers like ripples in a still lake. There was carpet and there were leather chairs, a long mahogany bar and paintings on the wall.

A man behind the counter polished a glass and another – wearing two guns – stood at the end of the bar.

And there was Art Sherman sitting in a leather chair, reading his own newspaper, and drinking brandy.

Jared had chosen late morning, knowing that the club would be very quiet, but also knowing from his observations that Sherman would already be in here.

Sherman looked up. He smiled. A face used to good living and full of the confidence that such good living breeds. "Jared Walker. I heard you'd broken out of prison. I've been expecting you."

The man with the two guns pushed himself away from the bar, right hand resting on the butt of one of his revolvers.

"Why would *you* be expecting me?" Jared said. Sherman had never admitted to having any part in what had happened.

Sherman smiled. "I must say, you have guts. You know you'll never get out of here alive."

"That's two of us, then."

The man with the double guns had one of them drawn now. "Boss?" he said.

Sherman raised a hand, as if to say, *Hold on just a moment, it's all under control.*

"You could have run," Sherman said. "Saved your own skin."

The bartender was very still, his cloth motionless inside a glass.

"Here's the deal," Jared said.

Sherman laughed, a loud and raucous laugh.

"A deal? You come to offer me a deal?"

"Uh-huh."

"Kid, you *do* have guts. You should come and work for me. If I thought you wouldn't cut my throat the first chance you'd get, I'd employ you."

"Here's the deal," Jared said again.

"Listen, son. Maxwell there has already got a bullet aimed at the base of your spine. *Here's* the deal." Sherman put down his brandy glass, and raised his right hand, thumb and middle finger pressed together as if ready to click his fingers. "I snap my fingers, you're dead. How's that for a deal?"

Jared smiled. "Dynamite," he said.

"Dynamite." Just for a second something flickered across Sherman's face.

A warmth flared in Jared's belly. Until that moment, he'd felt nothing; no fear, no tension, just a knowledge that what he was doing would lead to vengeance and then death. But that flash of puzzlement – maybe even fear – gave him a feeling the like he hadn't experienced since he'd pulled the trigger on the last of Sherman's original gang.

"You built your empire on it," Jared said. "Selling it to the railways and the mines and the army."

"Your point?" Sherman sounded irritated now.

"You blew my father up with your railroad dynamite."

"You have no – "

"You think I'm doing this alone?"

Sherman leant forward. The fingers of his right hand relaxed, no longer one snap away from ordering Jared's death. Jared could see the man thinking it through.

"You're bluffing."

Jared raised his hands as if to surrender. He flashed a quick glance at Sherman's gunman, Maxwell. "I'm not drawing my gun," he said. "Let me just show you something." He pulled out a silver pocket watch, flicked it open. "Five minutes to midday," he said.

"I don't believe you," Sherman said. "Whatever it is you're saying." He raised his fingers again. "You're a dead man."

"I've been a dead man for a long time. But if I don't walk out of this club by midday your wife, your children, and your expensive house out on Sherman Street – Sherman Street, how modest is that? If I don't walk outside by then you'll hear an explosion that will make what you did to my father seem like a lucifer fizzling into life."

"You bastard. You wouldn't hurt – "

"An innocent family? I learned it from the best, Mr Sherman."

"What do you want?"

Jared glanced at the watch. "Four minutes to. I want a minute alone with you. No barman. No… bodyguard." Jared said the last word with a sneer.

"Let me kill him, boss," the gunman said.

Jared smiled. "You had a robbery at your explosives factory three days ago, Mr Sherman. Have they told you yet? You *know* this is real."

"You won't get out of – "

"Time's ticking."

"We can talk about this. How much money –? "

"We can talk if you want, Mr Sherman. We'll be interrupted by the explosion, but we can talk if you want."

Jared looked down at the watch again. He didn't say anything, just nodded.

"I think you're bluffing." There were red patches flaring on Sherman's cheeks.

Jared smiled again.

The hiss of burning oil and the ticking from the pocket watch were very loud in the still room.

"You're not a poker player," Sherman said. "I know a bluff when I s– "

Jared snapped the cover closed on the watch.

Sherman jumped. "Jesus!" he said.

"I guess we're rapidly running out of time," Jared said. "I made a mistake. I thought you might have cared for your family more than you did."

There was sweat running down Sherman's face. He snatched a handkerchief from his jacket pocket and dabbed at his forehead.

"It's you or them," Jared said, matter-of-factly. "And I assume you've chosen them?"

"You bastard," Sherman said.

And clicked his fingers.

In the confined space, the gunshot sounded like a stick of dynamite exploding. The second gunshot wasn't so loud against eardrums already deafened by the first.

Mitchell stood in the doorway, smoke curling up from the barrel of his Colt .45. Sherman's man lay on the floor, dead; Maxwell's bullet, fired by reflex as he died, smashed into the base of a ceiling chandelier. The chandelier fell and shattered on the boards. Several of the candles went out. Several continued to burn.

The bartender was fumbling beneath a counter.

Mitchell turned the gun towards him, shook his head. "Hold it, buddy," he said.

Jared, staring at Sherman, eased open the pocket watch cover. "Midday," he said. He noticed that one of the legs of Sherman's chair was starting to burn. The carpet, too.

Sweat rolled down Sherman's face like tears. His hands were shaking.

There was no distant explosion.

"You were right," Jared said. "I was bluffing. I could no more blow up a woman and her children than I could shoot an innocent man."

"Please…" Sherman begged.

Jared eased his own gun slowly from his holster. "This is for my father," he said.

And shot Sherman through the heart.

They paused on top of the ridge overlooking Tulane Junction. The fire, exacerbated by the bottles of brandy that Mitchell had smashed and thrown into the flames, had spread to the newspaper office and the hotel. From up here, the human chain of men and boys, women and girls, all rushing to fill buckets of water from the well in the square and throw them into the flames, looked like a column of termites fleeing a smoke filled nest.

Jared looked across at Mitchell, the man's face still as dirty and as unshaven as when they'd first met in the cellblock.

"I never said it before," Jared said. "But I appreciate the help. I mean, I could've done it without you…"

"Sure," Mitchell said, smiling. "But you wouldn't have got out alive… And –"

"And, what?"

"You wouldn't have seen him…seen the fear in his eyes. That was important to you, wasn't it?"

"It was everything."

Mitchell nodded. "I never heard nothing like what they did to your folks. It was an honour to help."

"I appreciate it."

"And now?"

"Now we ride to Mexico," Jared said. "And we start living again."

BILLY

Lance Howard

Writing as Lance Howard, Howard Hopkins has penned thirty-two Black Horse Westerns, the most recent being Coyote Deadly. *He writes horror under his own name, including the supernatural/mystery series* The Chloe Files *for adults and* The Nightmare Club *for kids. He also writes pulp adventure and was co-editor of Moonstone Books'* The Avenger Chronicles, *as well as writing graphic novels and comic books based on the 1930s pulp hero, The Spider. Soon, his work will be appearing in* The Green Hornet *and* Captain Midnight *short story anthologies. He lives in Maine, USA, and you can visit his website at: www.howardhopkins.com*

"Whatcha got there, Billy?" Bobby Ray Simpson asked, his tone sharp with ridicule. The young man of twenty with the prairie wolf features maneuvered to the front of the stocky boy ambling along the wide main street of Wendell, blocking his path. Cruelty painted Bobby Ray's face, meanness that bled from within. And with that cruelty, a vicious glint of joy gleamed in his dull gray eyes.

"Yeah, retard, what ya got?" Jimmy Bob echoed in the same provocative manner as his year older brother. Jimmy Bob's own face mirrored the meanness and lean, canine-like aspect of his brother's features, but he lacked the vindictive glint of eye. He was a follower, a product of emulation and lack of God-given smarts, to hear some of the townsfolk talk.

Billy didn't always heared others when they talked at him. In all his nineteen years he'd never heared quite right, anyhow. He reckoned that was just part of the way he was. But he heared others put a name to him, one that made his heart hurt and his almond-shaped eyes with their epicanthic inner skin folds well with tears. He wanted to cry, at the names, at the taunts, but forced himself not to. They would only make funner of him.

But he heared the two this time, saw them step to the front and side of him as he shuffled along, keeping his round face pointed towards the ground, his stubby fingers, drained white, clutching the folded paper object in his hand as if it were something precious. And to him it was. Nothing those boys would wanted, though he knew they planned to taked it from him just the same.

Billy, dressed in over-large canvas pants and a grime-coated heavy shirt, tried to walk to the side of Bobby Ray, but the brother shifted his position to block him and Billy stopped, his heart beginning to pound with fear.

He always feeled a-feared. He had good reason to in this town. Folks hereabouts didn't liked folks who was different from theirselfs. Miss Molly, the woman who runned the home where he lived, tolded him it was just because they were a-scared of him, that his difference made them think about their ownselves in a way they didn't like rightly. He didn't understand that. But there was lots of things Billy didn't understand. Sometimes he just couldn't think clear. It was only when he was reading about *The White Ranger* that he feeled better, feeled like maybe he could do some of the things the Ranger did. But in moments of clarity, he tolded himself that was all a lie. He was a nothing, way them other folks said he was. A nothing, and a retard.

"Look at the retard, Bobby Ray," Jimmy Bob said, pointing to Billy as the young man's face lifted. "Got a flat nose, jest like a piggy!"

Bobby Ray laughed, the mean glint in his eye sharpening. "Got himself no neck, neither, and a big ole round head stuck atop it." Bobby Ray speared Billy with his gaze.

Billy's heart beat a step faster. Why couldn't they just let him be? He never hurted no one. He just wanted to be left alone with the Ranger. He'd been minding his own business, just walking along the sunlit street and smelling the summer flowers in the air and thinking about his new book.

"His tongue's sticking out like some kinda dumb ole dog, too." Jimmy Bob snickered. "Got himself a phys-ee-cal deformity, I heard tell."

"Some kind of retard syndrome, Doc says," Bobby Ray put in. "Ain't fit to be livin', you ask me."

"Reckon he can rightly read that there book?" Jimmy Bob ducked his chin at the folded dime novel clenched in Billy's plump hand.

"Reckon he must jest lookit the pitchers," Bobby Ray said, making a grab for the book.

It was on rare occasions Billy exhibited any kind of co-ordination. He just hadn't been born that way. Movements came awkward and slow for him, like his speech, his tongue always in the way, as if his mouth were too small to contain it. But this time he managed to hold onto his dime novel. Miss Molly had boughted it for him. He could read enough of it to enjoy the adventure, to be a hero in his own mind for a few hours.

"Looks to me Billy here thinks he's the White Ranger again, don't it, Jim-Bob?" Bobby Ray let out a guffaw and tried to grab the book again. This time he got a piece of it, tearing a section from the cover. He flung it to the ground.

Billy made a guttural sound he could not hold back.

Jimmy Bob made a mocking face. "Gaw-damn, Bobby Ray, he's growlin' at ya! Told ya he was just some kinda animal."

"He's just some kind of *mistake*," Bobby Ray said. "His pa should have done took him out and shot him when he came out lookin' like a gimpy Chinaman." Bobby Ray speared Billy again with his gaze. "'Cept his pa done seen what he made and rode off for the hills, didn't he, Billy? Your pa didn't want nothin' to do with a retard like you."

The words hurt his heart. He heared them too well and something inside him wanted to give the boys just what they wanted, his death. He wished he could just die and then maybe the taunts would end.

"What…did…I…do to you?" he asked, his words slow, muffled. His speech worsed the more a-feared he became. Sometimes he could talked almost normal, espccially when he was with Miss Molly, but with these boys he could barely speak at all.

Jimmy Bob's brow narrowed as he looked to his older brother for the answer.

Bobby Ray uttered a nasty little scoff.

"You was done born, Billy. That's what you done to us. Ain't no call for your kind in this world. Yore jest a mistake and we can't stand lookin' at ya."

Tears welled in Billy's almond eyes, tears he fought desperately to hold back. He couldn't cry in front of them. It would only be worser for him. "I…not…a kind…I'm like you." He struggled to get the words out faster than they wanted to come.

Jimmy Bob let loose a bellowing laugh, and other folks sauntering along the boardwalks cast him a look, but didn't stop to see what the commotion was about. They wouldn't, Billy tolded himself. He repulseded them as much as he did these boys and no one would come to his aid, except Miss Molly and she was still in the general store where she'd boughted him the book. She hadn't even seen him wander out with it.

"He says he's just like us, Bobby Ray, can ya jest believe that?" Jimmy Bob laughed harder, slapped his knee in an exaggerated motion.

Bobby Ray grabbed two handfuls of Billy's shirt and jerked him close. "You ain't nothing like us, retard. You ain't normal, you hear me? Don't ever say you're a human being! Yore a nothin'." Bobby Ray spat in Billy's face.

Saliva dripped down the boy's round cheek and tears, which he could no longer hold back, trickled from his eyes.

"Haw-haw, baby's gonna cry now," Jimmy Bob said.

It was then it overwhelmed him for the first time. Anger. Bubbling up from within the hurt in his heart. He had not felt such a thing before. All he'd ever felt was a-feared, and shame for what he was. But now it was different. He was the Ranger in the book, angry at…at – what was the word that the hero had used? – in…injustice. That was it. Miss Molly tolded him it meant when something wrong happened and you felt angry over it, and you had to do something about it to make it right. *Injustice.* He feeled injustice. And anger.

So he kicked Bobby Ray in the shin.

It was a clumsy kick and Billy almost fell. The flash of shock on Bobby Ray's face erased the meanness for an instant and he jumped back as if his favorite puppy had just taken a bite out of his hand.

"Gaw-damn!" Bobby Ray said. "The retard done kicked me!"

Jimmy Bob chuckled, then suddenly shut his mouth as his brother cast him a fierce look.

Billy had been called dumb all his life but right now he knew he needed to runned back to the store or Bobby Ray was going to do something bad to him. He wasn't the Ranger in the book. Whatever made him think he could ever be someone special like that?

He ran sideways, the move catching the brothers off guard. His gait was a rambling zigzagging one, like a newborn colt finding its legs, though faster than anyone might have recalled him moving and not falling on his face.

Even so, he didn't make it very far. His mind became dazed and he lost his sense of direction. Where was the store? Where was Miss Molly?

He heared them, running up behind him. They were far faster, far more…normal.

The brothers caught up with him, each grabbing a shoulder, and shoved him into an alley. He stumbled forward, slammed into the wall of a building with a bone-jarring impact. Somehow, he managed to retain his hold on his book and his feet.

"Watch it, Jim-Bob," Bobby Ray said, then spat a stream of saliva into the dust. "Damn retard kicks like a dumb-ass mule."

Jimmy Bob laughed, then threw a punch at Billy's face.

It hurt. The feeling of those knuckles crashing into his face sent spikes of pain through his teeth and face, and more tears flowed from his eyes. The taste of metal filled his mouth.

Bobby Ray rammed a punch into Billy's gut, doubling him over, and Billy's fingers went limp. The book dropped from his grip, fell to the dust. Jimmy Bob swooped and grabbed it, tore pages free and scattered them across the ground.

As Billy tried to straighten, Bobby Ray kneed him in the face. Blood filled his mouth and leaked from his lips. His head spun and sickness climbed into his throat. He sank, back sliding down the wall, to sit in the dust.

Jimmy Bob jumped forward, tugged his brother's arm. "Hit the retard again, Bobby Ray! Teach him his kind is just God's mistakes. That's what pa says, God's mistakes."

Billy's head rose, and a quiet defiance washed into his eyes. "I…never…hurt you…" he said, words bubbly with blood.

Bobby Ray drew back his fist, but held it, something in his eyes overriding the meanness and replacing it with disgust.

"Ain't worth it. Ain't no fun no more...'Sides, I get any his blood on me I might catch his retard sickness." Bobby Ray whirled and stalked from the alley.

Jimmy Bob stamped on a page of the torn dime novel and followed his brother out into the street.

Those boys had hurt his heart. Hurt it bad. Blood dribbling from his lips, pain in his face and belly, he tried to crawl forward, gather the pages of his beloved book, but they had destroyed it. Tears rushed from his eyes again and he fell face forward into the dust. Sobs racked his body. Why couldn't they just leave him be? He'd never done nothing to them. He didn't hated them the way they hated him...

Another new feeling came, like the anger. He *did* hated them! He hated them for making fun of him. Hated them for calling him names and hurting him. For spoiling his book.

Hated them enough to do what the Ranger did to the outlaws he chased.

Hated them enough to kill them.

An agonized sound gargled from deep within his throat as he struggled to push himself up. Dirt clung to the blood and sweat and tears on his face. His legs trembled and he fell against the building as he struggled to stand. Using the wall for support, he tried to steady himself, draw himself up the rest of the way.

Near the general store, he recollected. A gun shop. He could getted a gun like the Ranger's gun.

He staggered from the alley and folks on the boardwalk cast him worried glances.

"You awright, Billy?" one woman asked.

He recognized her. She owneded the dress shop and sometimes she was kindly to him, gived him penny candy and talked sweet at him. He just hanged his head and walked on.

He reached the gun shop and stopped at the door. His round hand gripped the handle and the hate went through him again. He didn't like the feeling. It wasn't part of him. Those boys had putted it there. He wanted to get rid of it and there was only one way.

He went inside and down the aisle a man looked up from behind a counter as a bell over the door chimed. Billy liked the bell. It maked him think of happy things. It didn't hurt his heart.

"Billy?" the man asked, his brow furrowing. Mr Hepner. Old Mr Hepner, Miss Molly called him. Billy had seen him in church. "Lordamighty, what happened to you, Billy? Who did this?"

"Boys…" was all he managed to get out, then staggered up to the man. His eyes went to the guns and rifles displayed on the walls and on the counter. "I…want…" He had trouble forming the words.

"What do you want, Billy?" Mr Hepner asked, a worried light blinking on in his eyes.

"Gun…" he said. "I want gun…"

Mr Hepner cast him a wary eye and came around the counter. The gunsmith tried to lay a gentle hand on Billy's shoulder, but the young man jerked away.

"You have no use for a gun, Billy. You got no money, either."

Billy nodded rapidly, an odd motion with his lack of neck. "Need. Need…Ranger gun…"

Mr Hepner shook his head. "No, you don't need. You'll only get yourself killed. Bettin' I know which boys hurt you, Billy. I'll do somethin' about it. Where's Miss Molly?"

He kept his gaze focused on a Colt Peacemaker on display on the counter. "Store."

"General store next door?"

Billy gave his peculiar rabbit-like nod.

"I'll see to it somethin's done about those boys this time. Don't you worry none, Billy. Stay here. Don't go back outside." Mr Hepner sighed, disgust on his face, and went to the door.

Billy heard the bell chime as the shop owner departed. He smiled at the sound. Then his face turned serious and he tooked the gun from the display.

It weighed more than he had thought it would and he almost dropped it. It felt somehow wrong in his soft hands, and for a moment the hate almost went away.

But not quite.

They had hurt his heart.

He cradled the gun against his belly and staggered along the aisle to the door. Tears came from his eyes again and he stopped a minute after going back out onto the boardwalk.

They were there, across the street, tormenting a small dog tied to a hitch post.

The anger came back stronger. He hated them. He loved dogs. He was the Ranger now. The Ranger who fought…who fought…

In…injustice…

He let out a growl-like sound as he stumbled into the wide main street, trying to lift the gun and aim it at the two boys.

Bobby Ray turned his head as if some sixth sense had alerted him to the fact there was danger.

"Holy Christ on a crutch!" Jimmy Bob blurted, turning his head a beat behind his brother. "The retard's got himself a gun."

"You...you..." Billy couldn't get out the words, couldn't form them in his mind. He searched for them, wanting to say something the Ranger would say, but it wouldn't come.

"You gonna pull that trigger, Retard?" Bobby Ray said, straightening and moving away from the dog. Jimmy Bob followed him, as if he were attached by an invisible tether.

"I...hate..." Billy managed to say, the gun coming up, shaking in his hands. It was so heavy. So very heavy.

"Billy!" The yell came from behind him and his gaze swung backward.

Miss Molly had come out of the general store, and Mr Hepner stood behind her. Her eyes were wide with terror as she walked towards him.

She was so pretty, Miss Molly was. So pretty with her blonde hair and nice smile. She smelled good, too, like tea roses. He heared the fear in her voice and it surprised him he recognized it. He didn't like her sounding that way. It hurt his heart.

The commotion did not go unnoticed. A door opened across the street. A man stepped out onto the boardwalk, a tin star glinting on his breast. His gaze took in the situation in a heartbeat and his hand went for the Peacemaker at his hip.

"No!" Miss Molly yelled, thrusting out her hand towards the lawman. "Don't, please. Don't hurt him. He doesn't understand what he's doing. Those boys hurt him."

The marshal hesitated, hand on the butt of his gun.

"Please, Billy..." Miss Molly said, sounding as if she might cry. "Don't do this. I know those boys were mean to you, but this isn't you. You're not like them."

He shuddered with a sob, turned his gaze back to the boys, who stood motionless. A hopeful smile played on Bobby Ray's lips as his eyes cut from Billy to the marshal, who was easing the Peacemaker from the holster.

"They...they..."

"They what, Billy?" Miss Molly asked, stepping closer to him.

"They hurt...my...heart."

"I know they did, Billy, but you aren't like them. You aren't filled with hate for others who are different. They don't know any better, Billy. Please. Please, don't be like them. Don't let them take away your kindness."

He was unsure what she meant, his mind muddling again, having difficulty understanding her words. But he understooded her tone.

The marshal had his gun free and was edging it up, to aim on Billy.

Tears came from Miss Molly's eyes as she stepped in front of him, getting between the marshal's aim and Billy.

"You won't hurt them, Billy. I know you won't. You aren't like them. You're kind and loving. You're innocent."

"They hurt my book…" he mumbled, this time forming an entire sentence without hesitation. "They hurt my book."

"I'll get you another, Billy. I promise I will. Just drop the gun."

He looked at her, saw the kindness and worry in her eyes. She cared about him. She treated him like he was the same as the rest of the boys in town. It didn't matter to her he was a retard, and maybe it didn't even matter to Mr Hepner he wasn't like the rest.

"I want to be…the same…" he said, hands shaking more, his arms getting so tired holding up the gun.

The marshal stepped off the boardwalk, trying to angle around Miss Molly, to get a clear shot.

"The hell you do, Billy!" Mr Hepner said from the boardwalk. "They're the ones who are different, Billy. Born mean. They got no right treatin' you the way they do."

Billy glanced at the gunsmith, and some of the hate inside him went away. He dropped the gun, turned and flung himself into Miss Molly's arms. Tears rushed from his eyes and he sobbed into her shoulder, somewhere inside himself knowing he had almost lost something today; he had almost lost what made him special, the way Miss Molly tolded him he was.

"They hurt my heart…" he said, and she nodded, holding him closer.

"Marshal, we want him put in jail!" Bobby Ray said, as he and Jimmy Bob came running up to them. "He was gonna kill us. He's a dumb retard. Ain't safe havin' him out on the streets."

The marshal slid his Peacemaker back into his holster, a frown on his brow. He knelt, scooped up the gun Billy had taken from the store. Straightening, he checked the chambers. "Not with this gun, he wasn't. No bullets in it."

"Was on my counter," Mr Hepner said, coming up behind Miss Molly and Billy. "Don't keep them loaded."

The marshal's frown deepened and his gaze swept to the two brothers. "Didn't know that a few moments ago. I might have shot that boy, thinking he was going to kill you two no-goods. You've taunted him enough. Happens again and it'll be your asses sitting in a cell."

"But, Judas Priest, Marshal –" Bobby Ray started.

"I mean it." The marshal's face hardened. "You bother Billy again and you'll answer for it. Tell your idjit pa that goes for him, too."

Miss Molly led Billy away, her arms about his shoulders. He walked his awkward walk, the hate and anger inside him still there somewhere but not as powerful now.

"I…don't want to be…different…" he said.

"You aren't different, Billy," the young woman said. "You're special."

He heared her and this time he understood. But it didn't matter. "No…I'm…dif'rent. Always dif'rent…"

And it hurt his heart.

LONIGAN MUST DIE!

Ben Bridges

Under his own name and a number of pseudonyms, David Whitehead (Ben Bridges) has been writing westerns for more than twenty years. He founded a fan club devoted to the Piccadilly Cowboys in 1976 and three years later was appointed as a consultant to IPC Magazine's short-lived Western Magazine. *For more information check him out at www.benbridges.co.uk.*

Given that he'd once been called the most dangerous man in the territory, Jesse Rayne proved to be a model prisoner. He kept to himself, said *yes sir* and *no sir* and never, *ever* made trouble – which was odd, because Rayne had spent practically his entire *life* making trouble.

Thus, his willingness to toe the line in prison raised more than a few eyebrows ... until the authorities decided the injuries he'd sustained prior to his final arrest had finally taught him the error of his ways: that the near-constant pain of two broken ankles that never healed properly was a harsh lesson, and one he'd taken to heart.

Still, there was a method to Rayne's madness.

Even before he was delivered to the Pen he'd started planning his escape. But when he finally saw first-hand how things were, he'd had to think again. For what chance did a man have of escape when he spent most of his days chained to the floor of a dark, cramped cell that was oven-hot by day and colder than a pie-safe by night? And even supposing he *could* escape, if by some miracle he could breach whitewashed walls three feet thick, just how far could he get on two ruined legs?

So he came at it from a different direction, settled on just minding his manners and doing as he was told. He took everything they threw at him and the warden and his men slapped themselves on the back and told each other the system worked after all: they'd broken him, and he was no longer a threat to society.

How little they knew.

In one respect, however, they were right. They *had* broken him. For he no longer craved the pulse hammering thrill of a stage or train hold-up. The pleasure he'd once taken from seeing fear in his victims' eyes, the thrill of the chase, the dry rustle of stolen ten- or twenty-dollar bills between his callused fingers ... these things, once so vital to him, were as nothing. Now only one prospect offered that same heady thrill.

And so he thought about it hour after hour, day after day, night after night, and that was how he got through eight long years of prison life.
Lonigan must die.

The judge had sentenced him to twenty-five years. Given Rayne's track record, he said he'd have normally recommended hanging, but figured Rayne had already suffered enough, what with his ankles and all.

Rayne only shrugged when the sentence was passed. Arrogant as ever, the prospect of a quarter-century behind bars didn't scare him. There were ways and means to shorten a prison term, and eventually he employed them all. He attended church services regularly and spent hours whittling exquisitely detailed figurines for the authorities to sell at their public bazaars each Sunday, and with the help of the prison librarian he even learned to read and write.

Then the day he'd worked so hard for finally arrived.

He was called before the warden, who informed him that he was satisfied from the conversations he'd had with his staff that Rayne was a changed man. The warden used the word *reformed,* but what he really meant was *crushed.*

"But tell me, Jesse," he went on, "what have you learned from your time here?"

Rayne wanted to say, *Never get caught.* Instead, he said in a low, bubbly exhalation, "There's always a consequence to a man's actions, Warden. He makes a bad move, it's usually a bad consequence." Rayne could tell by the smile that spread across the warden's ruddy face that the answer pleased him.

The warden said, "You understand, of course, that I can make no promises?"

"Yes, sir."

"However, I truly believe in my heart that you have become a new and better man during your internment, and I would like to see you live out the remainder of your days in peace and freedom, and give something positive back to the society you terrorized for so long. That will be my recommendation to the parole board."

The warden was as good as his word. The parole board met and discussed the case the following week, after which Rayne was summoned again.

"We are of the opinion that you have paid your debt to society and learned important lessons about civilized conduct. It is therefore the recommendation of this board that you walk free ... on parole, of course."

Rayne strained to keep his expression neutral. It would be disastrous to allow anything other than humility and gratitude to show on his lean, prison-pale face now. At last, he said, "I'm beholden, gentlemen."

And he even managed a tear for them, just to prove it.

*

He left the Pen the following morning, limp-shuffled through the ornate adobe archway they called the sallyport, and there beneath the shadow of the guard tower and its big Hotchkiss gun, he drew in the first really *free* air he'd breathed in almost three thousand days.

In town, using some of the money the prison administrators had held for him, he bought a ticket for the first train north. Easing down onto a hard seat, he pulled his black hat low, crossed his arms and tried to sleep. But sleep at this late stage was impossible. After so many years of just minding his manners and following orders, his sluggish blood was finally starting to flow again with the anticipation of what was to come.

And why not? He *owed* Lonigan. Owed him *plenty*.

At the time of their encounter he'd been riding alone with a mad-as-hell posse dogging his back-trail. The robbery of a copper mine payroll at Organ Pipe Creek four weeks earlier had made things uncomfortably hot for him and his gang and, fearful of capture, the men had deserted him in ones and twos during the long chase west.

So he rode alone and on the dodge from a pursuit party that just wouldn't quit. But he was finally closing on the Colorado River. If he could make a safe crossing and lose himself in California, he could rest up for a while, spend his share of the payroll money and then set about putting a new gang together.

Thus, when he came down out of the Buckskins that cool September evening and rode into Apache Wells, it was simply to stock up on supplies before making one last push for the border.

The town was little more than two parallel streets between facing rows of false-fronted business premises, surrounded by a haphazard scattering of timbered houses and spindly shade trees.

It was a little after six and the sun was already starting to set. First Street was quiet, this being the supper hour, and the owner of Dean's Mercantile was just fixing to close up for the night when Rayne dismounted out front and threw a loop at the hitch-rail. A saloon sat almost directly across the street, and he was tempted to go grab a drink, but decided to get his provisions first.

He went inside and glanced around. The store smelled of leather, coffee, pickled fish and peppermint balls. Hams, pots and skillets hung from the low rafters.

Hearing the hollow thud of Rayne's boots on the worn floorboards, the storekeeper turned, set his broom aside and nodded tersely. He was tall and thin, with fine red-fair hair and lifeless green eyes behind small, round spectacles. "Help you?" he asked.

"Need a few things."

"Sure. What'll it be?"

He asked for plug tobacco and coffee, a handful of cheap cigars, some spruce gum, a selection of canned goods, some bacon and cheese. The storekeeper fetched everything and stacked it neatly on the counter. As an afterthought, Rayne added a couple of work-shirts to his order, some new socks, and a bottle of bald face whiskey that the storekeeper filled from the spigot of a barrel in the right-hand corner.

"That it?"

"That's it."

The storekeeper took a pencil from behind his ear and started to make a total on a scrap of paper beside the cash register. Rayne watched his lips work silently.

If he'd had any sense he would have paid for his supplies and rode on with no one the wiser that he'd ever passed through. But because it had always been Rayne's way to impose his will on others, he slipped his New Model Army .45 from leather and pointed it at the storekeeper's belly.

"If it's all the same to you," he said, "I'll just consider this as a gift."

He expected the storekeeper to raise his hands, take a backward pace and stammer something along the lines of, "S-sure, mister, just … just don't hurt me." But instead all pretence at civility leeched from the storekeeper's face and suddenly he looked old, worn down – and mad.

"The hell you will," he replied.

Rayne stiffened as if slapped.

"You know what I make from selling a strip of candy here, a few yards of cloth there?" the storekeeper demanded, speaking fast and low. "Pennies, mister, *pennies!* So if you think I'm gonna let you take what you want, just 'cause you've got a gun in your hand – "

Rayne slapped him across the face with the Colt. The sight opened a gash in the storekeeper's right cheek and his legs folded. He clung to the edge of the counter to keep from collapsing altogether.

Holstering his gun, Rayne reached for the provisions, but as he did so the storekeeper grabbed his wrists and clung tight.

"You'll have to kill me before I let you walk out of here without paying!" the storekeeper grated.

Rayne's temper flared. He tried to yank his hands free, but the storekeeper's grip was tight and all he did was pull the man forward, over the counter, taking the provisions with him. They crashed to the floor, and the storekeeper, damn him, started yelling.

Rayne had spent weeks dodging the law and was now so close to the border that he could almost taste freedom. He didn't need any more trouble at this late stage.

Deciding to cut his losses, he turned and started for the door, but the storekeeper, still sprawled on the floor and screaming at the top of his lungs, grabbed him around his left calf in an attempt to keep him from getting away. Rayne staggered, caught his balance, turned and stamped on the storekeeper's face, but that only made the storekeeper scream louder and hang on tighter.

Again, Rayne tried to drag his leg free.

Bleeding from the nose now, blood-smeared teeth bared in a determined grimace, the storekeeper clung on and yelled, *"Help! I'm being robbed!"*

Rayne drew his .45 again, thumbed back the hammer and shot him square in the face. Within the confines of the store, the gun-blast was deafening. The storekeeper's head disappeared in a red spray. His arms and legs twitched.

Pulling himself free at last, Rayne ran through the doorway, out into the lantern-lit evening – and straight into the man he eventually came to know as Lonigan.

The collision took both men by surprise. Rayne lost his grip on his Colt and it dropped with a thud to the boardwalk. Instinctively he bent to retrieve it, but Lonigan brought up a knee that slammed him backwards.

For the second time that evening Rayne saw red. He came up against one of the store's double doors and got his first real look at his opponent, a tall, slim man about his own age with dark eyes and short oiled black hair. The rest was just an impression: a creased black suit, a white shirt open at the throat, a gray vest; a townsman, unarmed.

Then Rayne threw himself forward, big fists rising and falling like billy clubs.

Lonigan wilted beneath the onslaught, and Rayne finally put him down with a heavy, downward swing that had every ounce of muscle behind it. As Lonigan crumpled, Rayne wheeled around and lurched toward his skittish horse. He tore the reins free, grabbed the saddle horn –

Lonigan slammed his palms down on Rayne's shoulders, dug into the folds of his box coat and wrenched him backwards.

Both men spilled to the hardpan, the horse reared up, flailed at the air a few times, then turned and ran.

Rayne elbowed Lonigan in the belly, heard him wheeze, then dragged himself free, pushed to his feet, turned and kicked him in the ribs, once, then again. Lonigan hunched up, his face, clean-shaven with long dark sideburns, screwed tight with pain.

Around them, the town was coming to life. Rayne heard shouting and turned. Men were silhouetted in the doorway of a saloon on the other side of the ill-lit street, and all at once he grew acutely aware that he was unarmed and afoot. Much as he wanted to keep kicking Lonigan, he knew he had to flee.

For one brief moment he debated stopping long enough to retrieve his gun, but that might cost him everything. Instead, he resolved to run, find someplace to hide, then come back later and steal a horse.

He leapt up onto the boardwalk and ran; he reached a corner and took it. A pounding similar to that of the blood thumping in his ears made him chance a quick backward glance.

A silhouette blurred into the shadow-filled alley behind him.

Lonigan.

Sweating hard, Rayne ran on. A yapping dog leapt out of nowhere, started nipping at his heels, and he wondered how everything could have gone so wrong so quickly.

Then he saw the far end of the alley fill with townsfolk and knew there'd be no escape that way.

With a curse he turned back to face Lonigan, and as he did so he realized that an outdoor staircase ran slantwise up the side of the store. If he could get into the premises above, find a gun, a knife, a hostage, he might turn his fortunes around yet.

He lurched toward the staircase, took the dried-out wooden steps three at a time.

Lonigan thundered up after him.

Rayne kept going, teeth clamped hard, reached the small landing, grabbed the door handle.

Locked.

No matter. He stepped back and shoulder-barged the door. It refused to yield, but he had an idea that the second blow might do it. He braced himself for another attempt, but –

All at once Lonigan was on the landing with him, fists windmilling, and then the door was forgotten as each tried to pummel the life from the other.

Rayne grabbed Lonigan by the face, squeezed tight and tried to push him off.

Lonigan shook his head free, hit Rayne in the stomach, said something like, "Give it up … "

Rayne managed to turn around and thrust Lonigan backwards off the landing, but before he could fall, Lonigan snatched at the rickety handrail and held on. He surged back, kicked Rayne in the shin and followed the move with a body check. Rayne stumbled backwards, hit the locked door.

Furious now, he launched a punch that would have taken Lonigan's head off had it connected. But it didn't. At the last moment, Lonigan dodged to one side, and Rayne's momentum carried him forward, past his opponent, over the railing and into thin air.

Rayne turned an ungainly somersault and came down hard, landing flat on his feet with a loud splintering of bone. Pain speared through him and he collapsed onto his face, squirming, mewling, his fingers clawing at the dirt.

A lifetime of pain later, big hands turned him roughly onto his back. Someone raised a lantern high. Although his vision was blurred, Rayne spotted a badge on the shirt of a big man with a horseshoe mustache.

A circle of faces stared down at him. He wanted to curse them but didn't have the strength. He heard someone say, "Look at his feet ... " And then another face appeared at the lawman's shoulder, the face of the man who'd brought him down.

"Is he still alive?" Lonigan asked anxiously.

The lawman nodded. "He's alive, all right, Reverend, though he'll be lucky if he ever walks again."

Rayne frowned.

Reverend?

He'd been beaten by a *preacher?*

For some reason the revelation brought with it an irrational, overwhelming sense of shame.

"But ... " said the lawman.

"What is it, marshal?"

"His face ... "

"What about it?"

The lawman said, "Do you know who you've bested, Reverend Lonigan?"

The priest shook his head.

"'Less I'm mistaken, you've just tangled with Jesse Rayne."

"Jesse Rayne?"

"Uh-huh. The most dangerous man in the territory."

When the train finally hauled into Apache Wells, Rayne climbed awkwardly down to the platform. The journey had been long and hard and he felt stiff and slow. He hobbled out of the depot and surveyed the town. Save for the recent arrival of the railroad, the years had hardly touched the place.

Stomach tight, he shuffled across First Street, afraid someone might recognize him from all those years ago and sound the alarm, but no one gave him a second glance. He stopped a woman in hoop skirt and bonnet, doffed his hat and asked her if Reverend Lonigan was still killing sin in those parts. When she confirmed that he was, and by all accounts doing a pretty fine job of it, he released a relieved sigh.

So far, then, so good.

At the nearby livery he dickered for a stocky Indian pony and a cheap eight-string stock saddle, then led the horse out into the street and swung astride. Cursing the pain the action brought to his damaged ankles, he walked the animal down to what had once been Dean's Mercantile.

A thin young man lounging on the boardwalk outside watched him come. He had blue eyes, straw-yellow hair and a bridge of freckles spanning his nose. He was eighteen, maybe a little younger. He wore a blue band-collar shirt and navy Crocker pants, and a brown leather cartridge belt hitched high around his skinny waist.

The kid quickly looked away. For some reason, Rayne's presence seemed to agitate him; he shuffled his feet, wiped his palms down his shirtfront and then turned on one run-down heel and wandered away.

Dismissing him from mind, Rayne dismounted and hobbled into the general store. The place was quiet. "Afternoon," said the clerk, coming through a curtained doorway in the back wall. "Help you?"

Knowing that he'd be moving hard for the border once he'd settled with Lonigan, Rayne ordered provisions for three or four days and asked the clerk to put them all in a gunnysack.

"Will that be all?" asked the clerk when he was finished.

Rayne's head filled with echoes from his past, the previous owner saying, "Is that it?" just before all hell broke loose.

He shook his head to be rid of the memory, glanced around, found what he was looking for and peered down through the long arc of pilfer-proof glass at the selection of guns beneath. "Want to buy one o' these," he said.

"Sure. Which one takes your fancy?"

"The .45," said Rayne.

The clerk picked up the Colt almost reverently, and cradling it in his palm, handed it over. Rayne closed his right fist around its walnut grips and hefted it. He liked its balance. He flipped open the loading gate, thumbed back the hammer, turned the cylinder, checked the chambers, then closed it back up, held it at arm's length, sighted along the short barrel. "I'll take it."

"You need a belt for it? We got – "

"No belt. But I'll need a box of ammunition."

He paid for his purchases, loaded the gun and stuffed it into his waistband, then left the store and tied the gunnysack around his saddle horn before remounting stiffly.

The freckle-faced kid watched him from the mouth of a nearby alley. Again their eyes met briefly. Then the kid turned away from Rayne, still unable to meet his gaze for any length of time.

Rayne's attention shuttled to the saloon across the street. He needed a drink to steady nerves that had never in the past needed steadying.

The church was a moderately sized frame building with white clap-board walls, gray shingles and a three-tiered bell-tower. It stood at the far end of

Main, just beyond the town, and was enclosed by a neat picket fence that separated it from the scrubby trail west. Rayne tied his horse to the fence and let himself inside, instinctively sweeping off his hat as he did so.

He paused beside the baptismal font and looked around. The building was empty. A narrow aisle led down between fifteen rows of Bible-strewn pews to an altar and an octagonal pulpit. Upon the altar sat a display of flowers; tamarisk mostly, mixed in with Indian hawthorn and desert willow. Bars of dusty late-afternoon sunshine slanted in through the tall, high windows to puddle like molten gold across the floor.

Turning his hat restlessly before him, Rayne shuffled slowly toward the altar. His footsteps echoed off the plain blue walls. There was a strange, throat-tightening sense of unreality to the moment. After eight long years he'd made it, and the vengeance he'd craved for so long was finally about to be his.

He was almost at the altar when a gentle voice behind him said, "Can I help you?"

He froze.

That voice. He remembered it so well, and to hear it again now left him light-headed.

He turned.

Lonigan stood in the open doorway and then came deeper into the church. Rayne was rocked by his appearance. In his mind, Lonigan hadn't changed a notch. The man he'd come to kill had been tall, lean, dark, about his own age. The man he faced now looked somehow shorter, heavier, grayer. It didn't seem possible that eight years could bring about such a change in a man, and yet –

He stopped then, as he realized what he'd just thought.

That he and Lonigan were about the same age.

Did *he* look that old? Had the years ravaged him the way they'd ravaged his target? The thought distracted him momentarily and he squinted at his hazy reflection in one of the church windows. He wondered when he'd last looked at himself, *really* looked at himself, and seen not the man he used to be but the old man he'd become.

"Are you all right?" asked Lonigan.

Rayne's eyes shuttled back to him and he said, "Don't you remember me, preacher?"

Lonigan's dark eyes, duller and heavier-lidded now, narrowed. "I'm sorry. Have we met before?"

Without warning, Rayne flung his hat aside and smashed a fist into Lonigan's face, and the preacher crashed against one of the pews, knocking it out of alignment. Bleeding from the mouth, he sank to the floor.

"Does *that* jog your memory?" spat Rayne, towering over him. "It ought to. Eight years ago you ruined my life."

The echoes of Rayne's voice died and the church went coffin-quiet. At last Lonigan's gaze sharpened and he said softly, "Is it *really* you, Rayne?"

"It's me."

"Did you *escape?*"

"No. They figured I'd served my time."

"And so you came here ...?"

"To settle accounts," said Rayne.

Lonigan considered that for a moment before releasing a trapped breath. "Then you've come for the wrong man," he said.

"Huh?"

"You ruined your *own* life, Rayne."

"The hell I did!"

Clutching the back of a pew, Lonigan dragged himself to his feet.

Rayne immediately took a backward pace and tore the .45 from his waistband.

Lonigan stared down at the gun. "Is this what you thought about while you were in prison?" he asked. "Killing me?"

"Uh-huh."

"Is it *all* you thought about?"

"Pretty much."

To Rayne's surprise, Lonigan snorted. "You're a liar. You served ... what was it, seven years? Eight? And you wasted them all just thinking about *me?* About *this?*"

"Don't flatter yourself. I thought about plenty else."

"Such as ... ?"

"What I could have had, if you hadn't taken my freedom away from me. A wife, maybe. Younkers. A *son.*"

"And what kind of husband do you suppose you'd have made? What kind of father?"

"A lousy one, most like. But I'll never know for sure, will I? Thanks to *you.*"

Lonigan reached into the pocket of his loose-fitting black jacket. Rayne stiffened, but the preacher only tugged out a handkerchief. He dabbed at his mouth. Some of the blood had dripped from his chin onto his white collar. He looked at Rayne over the square of cloth, shook his head and said, "I guess you'll never learn, will you?"

Rayne caught the tinge of bitterness in Lonigan's voice and said, grudgingly, "Learn what?"

"That life's all about choices. It always has been and it always will be. Some people make the right choices. Others, men like yourself, don't. They go for the easier option.

"Well, you face another choice right now. You can go ahead and kill me and spend the rest of your days in jail or on the run, or you can be *better* than that, stronger, set all your hatred aside and stop making the same mistakes over and over."

Rayne sneered. "No good appealin' to my better nature, Lonigan. I ain't got one."

"All men have one. But sometimes a man needs more strength to resist the beast within than to give it free rein." Unexpectedly, and with an odd, world-weary snort, he added, "I should know."

Something in his tone made Rayne say, "Oh?"

Lonigan took a breath. "That night we clashed? Did you ever wonder why I came after you the way I did? Why I just wouldn't quit?"

Rayne shook his head warily.

"I'll tell you. It's because I was in a mean mood and I welcomed the chance to take it out on someone."

"Better watch your mouth, preacher. Your halo's starting to slip."

"It slipped a long time ago," Lonigan said softly. "The first time I took a shot of good Kentucky bourbon."

He saw the surprise in Rayne's face and nodded. "Oh yes, I've made mistakes as well. My particular vice was whiskey, and eventually my need grew so bad I could hardly do without it. And yet I couldn't just go into a saloon like other men. As much as anything else I was a mean drunk, Rayne, *really* mean. So I had to drink alone, in shame, and always in fear that someone would discover my secret and drag my dark side into the light of day."

"I don't need to hear all this ..." Rayne muttered uneasily.

"I think you *do*," countered Lonigan. "No man can live that way, not forever. I got to the point where I had to make one of those hard choices I just mentioned. I could drink or I could preach, but I couldn't do both. It was a tough call. It would've been easy to tear this collar off and crawl into a bottle. But I didn't. I fought it. I *tried* to. God, how I tried ..."

"And that night ... ?"

"That night I wanted a drink so bad it felt like I had worms burrowing through my brain. It was such a torment that I could've *screamed.* So I went for a walk, to clear my head and get a grip, or so I told myself." There was a catch in Lonigan's voice. "Of course, I ended up outside the saloon, as I'd known I would, and I thought, the hell with it. I can live without this town and these people and the word of the Lord. I can live without all that. But I can't live another second without a drink."

Rayne was transfixed by the preacher's tone and manner. Whatever else he'd been expecting from their encounter, it hadn't been this.

Lonigan bowed his head, swallowed hard. "I had one hand on the batwings when I heard George Dean start yelling that he was being robbed. Then I heard a gunshot and I ran over, intending to help him. Instead, I ran smack into you."

Lonigan's mouth was a thin resentful line. "I was *hurting*, hurting bad for a drink, and if you hadn't come along when you did, I'd have gone right into that saloon and got one. You prevented me, Rayne. Because of you, I couldn't get that drink, and I was overcome with anger. And every bad thing I felt I took out on you."

"You sonofabitch," breathed Rayne, his eyes moving briefly to the pulpit. "You stand up there an' preach to others, but you're no better'n they are."

"I'm *human*," said Lonigan, simply. "But the point I'm trying to make – the *moral*, if you like – is that afterwards, I realized that I'd faced *another* choice that night – to obey my conscience and go to the aid of my fellow man, or to obey my craving and go get drunk. I figured it happened that way for a reason. I still do."

"So you quit the booze," said Rayne, wanting a drink himself right then.

"I quit it. But that doesn't mean I don't still *want* it. I do. Every hour of every day. But whiskey would satisfy me for a while, and then I'd sober up again and hate myself for my weakness, and go get another bottle so I could forget that self-hate. For that reason, I fight it, and take some small measure of comfort from winning each day's fight.

"So," he finished, squaring his shoulders. "What's it to be, Rayne? Do you shoot me? Or for once in your life do you make the harder choice instead, let go of all that spite and actually *make* something of your life? Which course would give *you* the greater satisfaction?"

Rayne made no immediate reply. He stared down at the floor, thinking.

Then he looked up again, thumbed back the Colt's hammer, *cli-cli-click*, and pointed the gun at Lonigan's paunchy stomach.

Lonigan's mouth twitched briefly in a sour smile. "I guess I was a fool to think I could destroy your life one day and try to save it the next," he said quietly. And slowly he lifted a Bible from the nearest pew and held it to his chest.

Hardly able to breathe now, Rayne took up the first pressure on the trigger and told himself this was going to feel so *good* ... When it came, when that report echoed around the church's high ceiling and Lonigan tumbled backwards, clutching himself, knowing he'd been gut-shot and it was going to take him a long hard time to die, the pain Rayne had nurtured for eight lost years would finally ease.

Wouldn't it?

His finger continued to tighten on the trigger.

Wouldn't it?

Lonigan's knuckles whitened over the Bible as he braced himself for the hammer-blow of the shot.

But now Rayne recalled what he'd told the warden a lifetime before. *There's always a consequence to a man's actions. He makes a bad move, it's usually a bad consequence.*

Wasn't that in so many words what Lonigan was saying, too?

He frowned. Had he unwittingly told the warden what he'd always secretly known to be true?

Gritting his teeth, he thought stubbornly, *Die, you sonofabitch.*

But his finger refused to pull the trigger, and a long ten seconds later he deflated, let the gun drop loosely to his side. And as he finally admitted to himself that Lonigan was right, he managed softly, "No, preacher. *I* was the fool."

It was dark when he left the church.

He'd come to kill a man but instead faced a truth he'd never previously cared to acknowledge. Now he felt washed-out and empty. He gathered his reins, set his teeth against the pain in his ankles and mounted up.

Drawing in a deep draught of fresh, free night air, he walked the pony back into town and drew rein outside what had once been Dean's Mercantile. He wanted to believe that this was where all his problems had started, but he understood now that they'd begun long before that night. He thought about all the choices he'd ever made and knew without doubt that, as Lonigan had said, he *had* ruined his own life.

He was just telling himself that things would look better in the morning when he suddenly became aware of the gun he'd bought earlier, digging into his side.

The gun.

It came to him then. A gun set him on the road to ruin. Maybe a gun could also end it for him.

Dry-mouthed, he heeled the horse over to the hitch-rack and dismounted. Fifteen feet away, a dark alley – the same alley in which he'd lost his fight with Lonigan all those years earlier – beckoned. He could vanish into its shadows, stick the gun up under his jaw and use the bullet he'd intended for Lonigan on himself. Just one squeeze of the trigger and no more of a life that wasn't a life at all and never really had been.

Oh Lord, it would be so *easy!*

The decision made, he limped up onto the boardwalk and made for the alley-mouth, pulling the gun as he went, and in that moment all further thought ceased for the simple reason that there was nothing left to think *about*.

But as he shuffled into the alley he sensed movement in the shadows ahead and abruptly came back to the here and now. Twenty feet away, a short skinny figure hurriedly stepped back from a lighted window just the other side of the external staircase.

It was the freckle-faced kid.

Seeing him, the kid turned and started to walk away.

Impulsively, Rayne brought the .45 to full-cock. "Don't you move a muscle!"

Hearing the sound, the kid froze and raised his hands.

Rayne shambled to the window. Beyond the smudged pane lay some sort of cluttered storeroom. The clerk who'd sold him the gun earlier that afternoon sat at a table in the center of the floor, totaling up the day's take. He had no idea he was being spied upon.

The kid murmured over a shoulder, "I wasn't doin' nothin'."

Rayne threw him a thoughtful look. "You ain't done nothin' *yet*," he corrected. "But it appears to me like you was planning to do some serious harm to the owner of that store. I reckon you've been trying to screw up the courage to do it all day."

"Where'd you get a fool notion like that?"

"It's written all over you, kid."

He glanced back through the window, at the money piled in coin and paper on the table. Time was he'd have been as tempted as this boy. But now ...

Again he thought about the life he'd thrown away, the family he'd never had, something the warden had said to him a week before, about giving something *back* to society.

"You ever been in trouble before?" he asked.

"No, sir," said the kid. "Honest."

"Then why start now?"

The kid turned to face him. "'Cause I'm at the end of my rope," he said bitterly. It fairly spilled out of him then: "I got no folks, no friends, no work, no money, just the clothes I stand in and my gun, an' that's just about the way it's always been for me."

"I've seen men make good from less than that."

"You?"

"No, not me. I never had the will or the wisdom. But ... " Rayne let the hammer down and stuffed the Colt back into his waistband. "What's your name, boy?"

"H-Hilton Gallagher."

"Figure on sticking around for a while?"

The kid shrugged. "I got no place else to go."

"Hungry?" asked Rayne.

Surprise crossed the boy's face. "Hungry so's my stomach's through to my backbone." Cautiously he added, "Why?"

"'Cause I think maybe you and me could stand to talk a while," said Rayne, as an idea occurred to him, a way to make amends. "That's if you're not too proud to listen to an old man's words?"

The boy looked at him. His Adam's apple bobbed nervously. "What do you care what happens to me? You don't know me."

"No. But I know your type. Thirty years ago I was pretty much where you are now, kid, and I made all the wrong choices. You still got the time to make all the right ones."

And he thought, *'Sides, I'm about as lonely as you are, boy, and right now I reckon I could use a son about as much as you could use a pa.*

"I figure I could stand to listen," Gallagher said at last.

A weight lifted from Rayne's shoulders. "Well, let's go get us that meal and somethin' to drink," he said. "Oh, and let's get one other thing straight."

"Sir?"

"You're wrong about having no-place to go, Hilt. From here on in, you're going *up* in the world." And surprising himself, Rayne actually smiled as he added thickly, "We *both* are."

THE MAN WHO SHOT GARFIELD DELANY

I. J. Parnham

Ian Parnham lives a long way from the Wild West in the misty glens and castle-strewn moors of the northeast of Scotland. He has written twenty Black Horse Westerns and five Avalon Westerns. You can visit him at http://ijparnham.blogspot.com.

"Go for your gun when you're ready to die," Frank Beckett said.

Garfield Delany gulped, his cocky attitude fading away faster than the dying rays of the sun at his back. "You won't get to ride out of Liberty, Marshal," he said, the tremor in his voice betraying his nervousness. "I've killed eleven men and I'm looking forward to making that a dozen."

Frank settled his stance, his hand dangling a few inches from his holster. His movement raised a gasp of anticipation from the people who lined the street to watch this showdown. "I'm not like you. I can't remember how many men I've killed, and I don't reckon I'll remember you."

The irony raised laughs from several men on the boardwalk. Garfield sought out those people and gave them a surly glare. "Once I've dealt with this lousy lawman," he muttered, "you'll be next."

More laughter sounded. Garfield firmed his jaw.

Frank still had several things to say, but before the laughter became too distracting his gun cleared leather in an instant. As if dazzled by the dull orb of the setting sun, he blinked and turned his head away then jerked his hand up too quickly. A single gunshot hurtled high in the air.

Luckily, Garfield was unusually slow on the draw, which gave Frank enough time to fling himself to the side. He hit the ground with his left shoulder and kept the roll going to land on his arm. He wasn't as sprightly as he once was and he flopped to the ground with an audible grinding of the bones in his back and shoulder that he knew he'd pay for later.

Then he levered himself up on his right elbow. Garfield followed his progress. With grinning confidence Garfield aimed at Frank's chest.

As his weight was on his gun arm, Frank scooped up a handful of dirt with his left hand and hurled it at Garfield. His shoulder protested and the dirt fell several feet short, but it still made Garfield flinch away, batting at his eyes.

A murmur of delight went up from the watching crowd.

Frank moved with calm precision, rolled off his gun hand, lifted the Colt and sighted Garfield down the barrel of his gun, only to raise the weapon and fire six feet over his opponent's head.

Garfield cried out in pain, his gun falling from his limp fingers, his other hand rising to clutch his chest. He took an uncertain pace forward then keeled over to bite the dirt.

Frank lay still for a moment. Then the applause started. Frank let it gather momentum before he stood and with a downward gesture of his hands that made his jarred shoulder complain, he called for quiet.

"And that," he said, "is an authentic account of how twenty years ago I shot the notorious outlaw Garfield Delany in Liberty."

A roar went up. Many of the watchers hurled hats in the air as the cheering grew, only for it to turn to catcalls when the shot man acting as Delany got to his feet to face them. He picked out the people who were jeering at him and delivered a shooting gesture with his fingers. His humor turned the good-natured catcalls to laughter.

Then the revived dead man raised his hat to reveal a shock of gray hair. "Samuel McCoy's Wild West show will now continue," he announced, "with a display of precision shooting."

As the sharpshooters burst from their covered wagon, the crowd craned their necks in eagerness to see the next act.

Frank didn't stay around to watch. His eyesight wasn't good enough these days to know whether anyone hit the targets. Besides, he had an appointment to keep.

An hour later, the appointment was dulling the ache in his shoulder, but he reckoned it'd take another hour before the whiskey blunted the other irritations. He sat on his own at the end of the bar and waited to be recognized. Tonight, he'd downed half a bottle before the inevitable questions started.

"Did you really once used to be Marshal Frank Beckett?"

"Did you really kill Garfield Delany like that?"

"Did you really round up the rest of the Delany Gang single-handed?"

"Did you really ride with Bat Masterson?"

Sure, he'd once been Marshal Frank Beckett, but not for fifteen years. He probably had killed Garfield Delany like that, but he could no longer remember exactly. He *had* tried to round up the rest of the gang, but he'd been so outnumbered he'd spent most of the time fleeing for his life. And he *had* ridden with Bat Masterson, but for only ten minutes and they hadn't spoken.

Nobody wanted to hear the truth, so he'd learned to provide the answers everyone wanted. When they finally left him alone, Samuel joined him at the bar.

"Another good day, Frank."

Frank shrugged. "Where to next, Samuel?"

"Carmon, two days' ride."

Frank poured himself another glass. "Sounds like we won't be anywhere interesting tomorrow night, so I'd better enjoy this."

"We won't be, but it'll give us time to practice. I've just come up with a great new idea for the show." Samuel waved the newspaper he'd been reading then leaned towards him, his eyes bright. "You'll love it."

Frank doubted that.

The Cowboy Olympics were in town. Carmon was enjoying the competition. Frank wasn't. It delayed his re-enactment until after sundown and that delayed his trip to the saloon.

From under a lowered hat at the back of the wagons he watched the shenanigans with a jaundiced eye.

Samuel had read that an event called the Olympics was to take place for the first time next year. His great new idea was to present the event as a competition between the showfolk and the townsfolk. He hadn't been sure his people would prevail, so no money was at stake, but clearly if the showfolk won easily there would be prize money next time.

So far, the shooting competition had been well received and ended in a tie. The steer wrestling earned a rowdy reception when the townsfolk won. But the fencing competition went badly when the showfolk built their fence the fastest.

Now Samuel's hazy understanding of the events led to the deciding game being a beef lottery, involving two cows, a grid and a shovel. Samuel came over to see what Frank thought of the new format for the show.

"It has potential," Frank said.

"It has," Samuel said, worrying at his mane of white hair. "But the crowd's growing restless. We need to work harder or we'll lose them."

"Oh?" Frank said, dreading what Samuel would say next.

"That means we need to liven up your re-enactment."

Frank shook his head. "We can't do that. It's an authentic account of how I –"

"I know, I know, and we all love it, but it's over with too quickly, even after I added the insults."

"It *happened* quickly. We faced each other in the street. We both went for our guns. I got dazzled, but so did he. He –"

"And that's the problem. Your story never quite rang true. I can't believe you'd face a notorious gunslinger with the setting sun in your face." Samuel looked at Frank until he gave an uncertain shrug. "So if you've remembered that bit wrong, who's to say what really happened?"

"Me. I was there. I'm the man who shot Garfield Delany."

"So you are." Samuel gave Frank a gentle pat on the shoulder, reminding him of his strongest argument. "But that shoulder of yours could do with a few days' rest."

Frank provided a reluctant nod. "What changes do you have in mind?"

That night he was late getting to the whiskey, but this time the questions were different.

"Did you really kill four men that day?"

"Did Garfield Delany really get shot three times and still fight back?"

"Did you really shoot the final man from one hundred yards away when he was fleeing on a horse?"

"Did Bat Masterson really congratulate you afterwards?"

Nobody was interested in the truth, so he provided the answers they wanted to hear. Finally, they left him alone with his bottle.

A while later, Samuel joined him at the bar.

"Another good day, Frank."

Frank frowned. "Where to next, Samuel?"

"Redemption City, four days' ride."

"Continuing with the Olympics?"

"We'll work on it, and on your re-enactment. We'll make them both even better."

Frank considered Samuel's firm gaze, which implied he wouldn't listen to reason. He sighed. "I already know how you can improve the fencing competition." Frank winked. "Make the fences higher."

Performances at Redemption City then Prudence then Beaver Ridge all amended the height of the fences and the complexity of the re-enactment. The audiences enjoyed the changes. Frank didn't, but at least the barroom questions became more interesting.

"Why did you face all those men on your own and not get help?"

"Did you really kill all ten men in the Delany Gang? I thought there were only six men in that outfit?"

"Why did Garfield Delany try to blow up Liberty with that wagon packed with dynamite when he lived there?"

"Did you really save Bat Masterson's life that night? I only ask because I thought he was working as an army scout when you shot Garfield?"

The additional thought he had to put into his answers reduced his drinking time and so when Samuel came over Frank was in a particularly sour mood.

"Another good day, Frank."

Frank scowled. "Where to next, Samuel?"

Samuel sighed. Then he leaned towards Frank and lowered his voice, as if relaying a secret. "Tomorrow night," he whispered, "Liberty."

Frank put down his glass, wondering if he'd heard him right, but Samuel had a pensive fixed smile that said he had and he knew what was on his mind.

"Then we have to take out your changes."

"We sure don't. This'll be our biggest audience this year. And that means we'll have to be bigger than ever." Samuel waved his arms, lost for words for once. "That means bigger prize money, bigger events, bigger–"

"Bigger fences?"

"Exactly, and that means you need to kill even more men in even more spectacular ways."

Frank fixed Samuel with a firm gaze and spoke in a deadly serious tone. "Liberty is the one place where someone might remember what really happened. We have to go back to the original version."

Samuel shrugged. "You've always claimed only you and Garfield were there, so nobody will know what really happened."

"I will," Frank murmured. Then he downed his whiskey and poured another.

Liberty wasn't how Frank remembered it. Twenty years ago it had been a festering boil in need of being lanced, but now it sprawled in all directions. It took him an hour to find the street where he'd shot Garfield Delany.

The remnants of the old mission around which the town had originally formed helped him to orient himself. And when he found the spot where he'd stood twenty years ago, the afternoon sun was at his back.

For a moment this fact worried him, but the old buildings were close by, so it was likely a reflection had dazzled him at the same time as the sun had blinded Garfield. This support of his memory of the events cheered him, and it kept him cheerful right up until the moment when Samuel arrived with news of tonight's changes.

That night the questions were predictable.

"Who was the woman?"

"Did you ever see her again?"

"Just how grateful was she after you saved her life?"

"Was Bat Masterson's sister really that pretty?"

For once Frank enjoyed himself, providing outlandish answers. That enjoyment died when he got the one comment he'd always feared: "That's not the way it happened."

The comment came late into the night. Frank thought he was the only person left in the saloon and he sat at the bar waiting for Samuel to collect him with news of their next destination and the next set of changes.

He'd already decided he'd try to persuade Samuel to paint the fences this time and so with a smile on his face he pushed his whiskey glass away from him and turned.

A young man faced him. His clear blue eyes and smooth chin that looked as if it'd never support a beard tapped at Frank's memory.

"I am the man who shot Garfield Delany," Frank said. "That was an authentic account of what happened here twenty years ago."

The young man shook his head slowly, sadly. "There were no wagons, or lassos, or dynamite, or people on the stable roof, or the whole gang facing you down. And there was definitely no saloon-girl needing rescue."

Frank conceded these points with a shrug. "As far as I can recollect, that is largely the way it happened."

"You and Garfield were out there." The young man pointed through the doorway, anger straining his voice. "That's the only thing that was accurate. But you didn't show the truth – that you shot him in the back while he was running away."

Frank reached for the comfort of the whiskey glass. A quick slug enlivened his memory; that wasn't what happened. But then again, he'd told the story so many times, he found it hard to remember anything other than the things he never talked about: the sweaty palms, the bowel-crunching fear, the pounding in his head that blanked his vision and dulled his hearing.

"We were the only ones there." Frank narrowed his eyes. "How do you know that?"

"Because I was there too. I was only a kid, but I was watching from the old stables across the road."

Frank frowned then provided the answer Samuel had given him on the night he'd persuaded him to join his show. "Garfield Delany was a killer who tried to destroy this town," he said. "I took him on and helped make Liberty into the quiet town everyone enjoys today. That's the important detail I remember, and that's what people want to see."

"Except that's not the way it was, either. Garfield Delany was a decent man who ran the saloon. He wasn't the leader of any outlaw gang and, besides, they never caused no real trouble. They were just a rowdy bunch that hung around his saloon. Garfield had already run them out of town when you shot him in the back."

Frank gulped. "How do you know all this?"

"Because I am Garfield Delany."

"What, his son?"

"That's right."

Garfield the younger settled his stance in a determined way that Frank hadn't seen for real in many years.

"There's no need for you to get yourself killed over this, kid."

"I won't, old man. I'm not like my father. He was no gunslinger, but I know how to use this gun. Now stand up and get what you deserve."

With a resigned sigh Frank stood up and pushed his stool back. The whiskey had its usual effect and he swayed before getting himself under control.

He faced Garfield, still wondering like every other time how he could avoid the gunfight. He doubted he could prevail. He doubted he could have prevailed even when he'd been the young Garfield's age. But the old feelings were still there: the sudden sweat, the churning loose guts, the pounding in his head that made it hard to concentrate.

"What can I say to change your mind?" he murmured.

"Nothing," Garfield said. His eyes narrowed, a sign he was about to draw.

A gunshot blasted, the sound echoing in the otherwise deserted saloon.

Frank winced, amazed at the speed Garfield had cleared leather, then drew and fired while awaiting the pain that would herald a long and welcome oblivion.

Garfield keeled over.

Samuel stood in the saloon doorway, a smoking gun out-thrust. "He talked too much," he said.

"Just like the other Garfield Delany," Frank said, gathering his composure by frantically mopping his brow with his jacket sleeve.

Samuel walked over to inspect the body. Then he looked up. His lips were set in a frown, but his eyes twinkled. "Just think how this'll improve the show. You're the man who shot Garfield Delany. Twice!"

"You shot him, and in the back. There was nothing heroic about it."

"Nobody ever said there was," Samuel said as the sounds of a gathering commotion grew outside. He looped an arm around Frank's shoulders and ushered him past the body and towards the door.

"If what he said was right," Frank mused, "the last time Garfield Delany got shot, it was in the back too."

Samuel flinched. "Are you sure that's what happened?"

A line of eager faces peered at Frank through the doorway. The murmuring went up, "Frank Beckett's done it again."

"Maybe so." Frank raised an eyebrow. "But then again, perhaps both times I had a trustworthy friend's help."

"That could work," Samuel said cautiously.

Frank nodded. "And if I remember it right, Bat Masterson helped me."

Samuel's eyes glazed as if he was picturing a new scene. Then he smiled and patted Frank on the back.

"Another good day, Frank."

Frank smiled. "Where to next, Samuel?"

HALF A PIG

Matthew P. Mayo

Matthew P. Mayo's novels include the Black Horse Westerns Winters' War, Wrong Town, *and* Hot Lead, Cold Heart. *His latest non-fiction book is* Cowboys, Mountain Men, and Grizzly Bears: The Fifty Grittiest Moments of the Wild West. *He and his wife, photographer Jennifer Smith-Mayo, divide their time between the coast of Maine and the mountains of Montana. Visit him at: www.matthewmayo.com.*

"You hung yourself, boy. You know that sure as road apples are ripe year round." Eamon Riggs stared at the sweaty, pocked face, but there was no sign that the boy heard him. His eyes kept that half-closed stare at nothing, as if he were bored and about to doze off. Like that his whole life, thought Riggs. It's the Mexican in him.

Riggs looked up at the ancient tree, the only one for miles. As a young man, he had made it his business, from books, to know all about trees. Curious about what he didn't have, he supposed. It was a big tree, dead a long time, as long as he could recall, and wind-stripped of anything that had been its skin. Now it was just silver and hard and good for one thing. Almost as if it had grown for that one purpose.

"You have anything to say at all?" Riggs waited.

The mule on which the boy sat, hands bound behind him, stepped in place and flicked one long ear, like a cupped leaf Riggs had read of long ago, when he had dreamed of travel south, deep into jungles.

The ear flicked again. As bored as the boy, thought Riggs. Ought to hang the damned mule, too. Just because I can.

A deerfly landed on the boy's temple. He didn't move.

Riggs took in a draught of air through his nose, his lower jaw canted as if he were considering how to answer a delicate question. His left hand struck out with his rawhide quirt and snapped at the beast's haunch. The mule lurched forward, digging hard, and all three men in attendance watched the boy's face finally show the light of interest, his eyes wide and pushing forward, his mouth stretched as if pulled from either side with fishhooks, his head and torso stiff and working back, then forward, like a pecking bird, black curls bouncing on his forehead.

Half-formed coughs rose and died in the boy's throat. One leg whipped wide, in arcs, and the curled boot flipped from it, landing upright ten feet away. In two minutes he stilled. An unfelt breeze spun him slowly and brown liquid like chew juice trailed over the bare foot in veins, dripping from the dirty toes.

"You boys come back with me. I'll send Parsons and Cunningham out to cut the bastard down and bury him." Riggs paused, then moved in the saddle and regarded the pair of cowhands staring at the sparse grass. "You hear me, Dilly?"

The taller of the two men looked at his boss, nodded.

Riggs turned and heeled the black he used for close chores. "And bring that damned mule with you," he said without looking back.

The two of them sat still for a few moments, then Dilly said, "That was too much for me, Pelt," in a voice barely loud enough for the shorter man on the dun beside him to hear. "I didn't think he'd do it. Thought for sure he was out to scare the fool kid, nothing more. Didn't think he'd do it."

"What do you mean?" said Pelt Simmons, the other, younger hand. "Fella had it coming, far as I can make out. Steal a half a pig and a horse to carry it on. Had it comin'." He pinched his lips tight and looked away. "Kid should of asked me. I'd of told him that. Might could have saved him."

Dilly looked at his companion. "You don't know, do you?"

"Know what?" Pelt, young and squat, sat slumped on his horse like he would someday melt into it. He was new to the Cross R and Dilly tried to ignore his hot-and-cold chatter.

Dilly looked ahead at the brown leather vest on the broad, far-off back of Riggs, and reined his buckskin to a stop by the old mule, a weal already puckering the dappled haunch. The beast's ears flicked back and it breathed hard, the man suspected from fright more than from the short run. He'd been around mules most of his life and he'd rarely seen one winded. They could work a horse under the table and still keep the wagon rolling.

Pelt stopped beside him, his horse fidgety. "What's wrong with you, Dilly?"

Dilly looked forward again. The last of his boss's hat disappeared beyond a rise far ahead. "Man we hung back there was the boss's nephew."

Pelt shifted his chaw to a cheek. "Naw." But his eyes remained on the tall man's face. "I thought he was Mexican help."

Dilly hooked a finger around the mule's rein, and it fell in behind his horse.

Pelt caught up with Dilly. "Why?"

"Why what?"

"Why'd he hang him? I mean, his own blood and all."

"Riggs is a hard man. He won't tolerate theft of any kind." The animals walked on. "But he pays well and is generous with time of a Sunday."

"It's cause he's a churchgoer, I suppose."

Dilly nodded. "Regular as a cow on sweetgrass."

Pelt sluiced a rope of juice, wiped his lips with a glove's cuff. "What made the boss so hard?"

Dilly looked up, squinting, as if watching a buzzard circle. "When I was new to this outfit, newer'n you are now, an old-timer by the name of Chick, on account of his last name ended with that sound, told me a few things about Riggs worth keepin'."

They rode in silence for some time, then Dilly said, "Riggs hates it here. Hates everything about it."

"Why does he stay?"

"Has to. Made a deathbed promise to his mother. Swore on the Bible and all."

"What did he promise?"

Dilly stopped his horse and looked back at the mule, then at the tree and the stilled body far behind them. He sighed and said, "To look after his younger sister. Family was everything to the old woman, so Chick said."

"I didn't know Riggs had a sister."

"Did. She's dead a long time now. Before I got here. The boy was hers."

Pelt twisted in his saddle and studied the tree and the body. Finally, he said, "He looked kind of Mexican to me."

"Part. Father, I reckon. He's dead, too."

"How?"

Dilly urged his horse into a walk. Eventually, he said, "Who, you mean."

"Riggs?"

Dilly said nothing.

"What about the boy back there?"

"You call him a boy? I reckon you two were close in age."

Pelt shrugged. "Was he fixing to run off? Seems like he'd a been better off not taking a half a pig with him. Odd thing to steal."

"He had his reasons."

"Like what?"

Dilly sighed again. "Had himself a girl, her folks. Mexican. Poor family, but they was good to him. Nice people. Not far from here. The boy let slip to me she was gonna have a baby. Had to tell someone, I suppose."

"Why didn't he just tell Riggs?"

"Bit of a hard case, like his uncle. Still, kid wasn't a bad sort."

"But he was Riggs's blood kin. Why would the boss do that? And over a pig?"

"Changed your tune, I see." Dilly looked back to the trail, then said, "I reckon Riggs weighed family with thievery and found family wanting. So he hung the boy."

The horses picked their way down the switchbacks of the big hill before the ranch came into view.

"Why'd he choose you and me for this, Dilly? I believe I could have lived out my days without seeing something like that. I swear."

Dilly half-smiled. "'Cause you're new and I ain't."

The young man nodded to himself. "I can handle it. I'm saving up for a place of my own. I'll have me a ranch, wife, kids." He looked at the older man.

"Boy," said Dilly, "if I had a gold piece for every time I heard that from a hand, I'd be richer'n Riggs."

Pelt worked more tobacco from the greasy knob he carried in his breast pocket. He packed it in his cheek. "You're older than Riggs, ain't you?"

Dilly felt heat in his cheeks and said, "By God, but you can be a rude pup."

"Sorry, Dilly. I only meant –"

Dilly rode ahead. "Just a kid," he said, tugging on the mule's reins.

Pelt leaned in the doorway of the barn. "So, what you going to do with your Sunday?"

Dilly looked up from sorting through his possessions laid out on the dirt floor. "Spend it, I reckon. Can't save it." He bent back to his task.

"That one's older'n you are, Dilly." The voice came from the shadows to Pelt's right. Parsons emerged, swinging a canvas feedbag half-filled with oats. He winked at Pelt as he passed outside, licking the length of a quirley and slipping it between his lips.

Pelt walked over to Dilly. "Parsons. Don't know how to take him."

"Aw, don't mind him. He's a decent sort. Just thinks he's smarter than everyone else."

Pelt looked down at the man's few things. "What you doin'? Leaving?" He snorted and reached for his chew.

Dilly didn't look up as he finished bundling his things and slipping them into his saddlebags.

"You *are* leaving." Pelt's jaws slowed. "But why would you leave, Dilly? You been here for a coon's age. This is your home."

"I reckon I've sucked all the goodness out of this bone, boy."

"But winter's coming."

Dilly flopped the bags onto his horse. Pelt hadn't noticed the saddled buckskin in the stall. The tall man knotted thongs tight, snugging his blanket behind the cantle, then heaved a child-size, canvas-wrapped bundle up onto the blanket. He doubled knots in the hemp wrappings, then rested his hand on the bundle and looked into the dark stall. "Time I did something, boy, instead of just sitting here growing old. Might be I'll regret it, might be it'll work out to my favor. Who can tell?"

There was a long silence, then he turned to Pelt and said, "Here." He forced a wad of folded bills and two gold coins into the young man's hand.

Pelt stiffened. "What's this?"

"Reckon it'll buy a half a pig, don't you?"

Pelt spit and nodded. "More than."

"I reckon we know who the pig was meant for," said Dilly. They were silent a moment, then he smiled at the young man and offered his hand. "You'll be just fine." Dilly gripped Pelt's hand tighter and his smile slipped. "You'd do well to figure out when it is you should leave. Find a woman, build up that spread. Somewhere aways from here. This land's less than dirt anyway." He smiled again, pumping the young man's hand.

Dilly led the buckskin toward the big door and raised one foot to the stirrup, then heaved himself up and into the saddle. "Now look, don't you forget to pay Riggs for this half a pig." He patted the canvas-wrapped shape snugged down behind him and winked. "Or else I'll end up decorating that tree just like the boy."

Pelt shook his head fast and stared at his boots. "No, no, Dilly. I wouldn't let that happen."

"I know it, Pelt. I know it. But don't pay him more than what's fair. The folding money will do. The rest is for your ranch."

Pelt looked up. "Dilly, you know I can't —"

But the tall man was already riding away, waving a hand. "I'll need a place to stay when I'm old, boy," he called. "Fix it up nice for me. I have high taste." He touched his hat's brim and heeled the horse into a gallop.

Before long, the only thing Pelt saw of his friend was a thin trail of dust rising up and over the hill. And then that, too, drifted off, leaving nothing to look at above the land but a blue sky.

BLOODHOUND

C. Courtney Joyner

> *Courtney Joyner is a screenwriter and director with over 25 produced movies, including the cult films* Prison, Class of 1999, *the TV movie* Distant Cousins, *and the new* Captain Nemo. *He's written extensively about the history of movies, and contributed chapters to the books* Lon Chaney, Jr., The Book of Lists: Horror *and* Duke: We're Glad We Knew You. The Westerners, *a collection of his interviews with western film makers, has just been published by McFarland. A member of the Horror Writers Association and the Western Writers of America, Courtney lives in Los Angeles.*

The footfall was light and delicate. It barely touched the ground. But Jim Bishop heard it; damn the devil's eyes, he heard it, he surely had. Jim steadied the Henry rifle against his bloody shoulder, letting the barrel search from outcrop to outcrop. He thought he saw something move in the shadows that butted against the light blue of the August moon. He thought...

Jim sipped the last drops from his water bag, but his mouth still felt like sandpaper. He'd been on this manhunt for five straight days and each one was worse than the last.

He'd started hot and eager, reading vague moccasin scuffs that led to a barranca under sharp limestone cliffs. Jim spent day two belly-crawling through the underbrush and eyeing horse biscuits. The hardening crust told him he was at least ten hours behind the mare and her outlaw rider, but he'd close their lead if he could keep up the pace. His prey was running like hell, so he had to run too.

The third day, a sidewinder spooked his pinto. The horse reared and stepped hard into a prairie dog hole. The leg snapped clean so Jim killed him clean, putting a single .44 slug behind the ear. He wiped his tears, and asked the open sky for forgiveness to feel better about killing his horse, but it didn't ease him none.

Days four and five saw Jim running hard on swollen feet, searching for his man from dawn until the sky started bleeding in the west.

Now Jim was bleeding too, and he didn't want to think how much blood he'd lost. Jammed against the rocks, he tried to ignore the red stream inching down his side. Hell, Sheriff Gus Beaudine took half a load of buckshot from a Greener to his guts, and still rode down on a gang of mail robbers and killed all three. That's what Gus always bragged, and if the old man could do that, then Jim figured he could bite through the pain that ripped at him now. Jim had a badge on his chest just like old Gus. Didn't that mean he was a damn tough lawman too? Wasn't that why Gus deputized him?

Questions swirled through Jim's mind, and he started to drift. His own breath and heartbeat offered comfort. They were there. Barely. But it was the sudden jolts of pain that reminded Jim he was still alive, which was more than could be said for the cot girl from Hondo. She was the deadest thing Jim had ever seen. Jim wanted her one-eyed face out of his memory, but she wouldn't budge. Her specter reminded Jim why he was here, and that he had to hang on, even with his life sticky on his fingers.

Jim's eyelids got heavy again. Behind them, he was sweeping out the two rusty jail cells and Sheriff Gus Beaudine was hollering, "Get out here, boy! I got somethin' real sweet for ya!"

Jim's breath caught in his throat and his knees wobbled with excitement as he charged from the cells and then stood at silly attention before the Sheriff's desk, arms cradling a broom like it was a Winchester.

Beaudine licked the last brown drop of breakfast bourbon from his bristle. He eyed Jim. "Boy, you're always cryin' about how you don't get to prove yo'self. Well, how'd you like to track me a killer?"

Jim tossed the broom and grinned wide as Beaudine pulled a bent tin star from the drawer and handed it to him. "You're already out the door and ya don't even know what I want done. Calm down, pin that on, and swear to uphold the law."

"I– I s– swear, sir," Jim said, pricking his finger on the back of the star. With the badge on his shirt, Jim snapped back to attention like he thought a good deputy should.

"Now if ya have to shoot somebody, there won't be hell to pay. You know anythin' about that Cowboy Paradise?"

Jim nodded. "I've heard some things, but I've never been."

"Well, Rayford's the fella who runs it, and he's a good... citizen. Takes care of folks. His best girl got butchered by some crazy sum'bitch and he wants his head." Beaudine looked out his barred window to the middle of the street. Jim followed his gaze. A pair of yellow dogs was tearing into each other. "I'll settle for the bastard markin' time in Yuma, but if ya have to kill him, go ahead and do it."

Jim choked. "I– I've never been so proud, I mean, y-you really think I can bring this murderer in?"

"I'm sendin' ya, ain't I? Get out there. Rayford'll give ya the details. Take one of the Henrys and a box of cartridges."

Jim pulled the rifle from the rack and checked the action. "Sheriff, I can't thank you enough for showing faith in me. And I promise I'll honor the badge. A fugitive who thinks he can out-run me, well sir, let me tell you – "

"I've heard it all before." Beaudine belched then poured his fourth Rosebud of the day. "You swear you can track a man better than a bloodhound, so go an' prove it. And don't make me look a damn fool."

The whiskey-soaked sheriff vanished from behind Jim's eyes as a fire of pain tore through his insides. The burning started low, then raced along the edge of his open wounds. Jim stuffed his fist in his mouth to stop from screaming. He wouldn't give away his position. No way. The fire eased as Jim huddled against the rock face, keeping his rifle low, so the moonlight couldn't dance off the barrel and show him up. He fingered the tin star. If he was going to die, then he'd take the crazy he'd tracked down with him, and that meant getting the killing shot. No matter what, this deputy was going to have his chance, and bring his prey down.

Jim tried to figure what he'd say to God. He knew he'd have to explain a few things, but at least he'd started this journey clean, wanting only to track his man and make a good job of it. He thought a capture was as good as a kill, but not anymore. Not after seeing what he'd seen inside Cowboy Paradise. God would understand that the animal that had done that violence had to be stopped cold. Yes sir, He'd understand.

The thought made Jim smile. His finger relaxed on the trigger. He felt like he had a sacred mission now, and anything he did was justified. If Noll Rayford could hear Jim say that, it'd be sweet music to his cauliflower ears. Jim didn't like Rayford at all, but now he and the flesh peddler had something in common.

The memory replayed easily for Jim: he was still a quarter of a mile away when Rayford began waving and shouting, his Dublin brogue boiling over. "*You're* the law? Gus leeches a hundred a month from me, and when I've got troubles he can't even come himself? Boy-o, you don't look old enough to shave!"

"Well, the sheriff of this county thinks I'm old enough to get the job done."

Jim dropped from the pinto. The horse nosed a water bucket hanging from the back of Cowboy Paradise. He drew his rifle from its leather shoe. "Paradise" was a wind-beaten prairie schooner with a purple bonnet and gold tassels fringing its sides. The wagon sat in a dry creek bed surrounded by acres of scrub that led to the foothills and then the mountains beyond. Some yards off, a red mule lazed in the shade next to Rayford's bedroll and coffeepot. Jim hid his surprise; he'd heard that men who traded in sin lived better than this.

Rayford bit the end off an unlit cigarillo. "I want one of them stakeout deals where the ants eat the killer's eyes, know what I'm talking about?"

Jim's response was a neutral shrug as he looked under the wagon at a crude faro table, a worm-eaten bathtub, and a tower of filthy shot glasses. After a month on the trail, Paradise would look damn sweet to a saddle-sore cowhand, eager to spend his pay. That's what Rayford was selling and he probably still had every dollar that ever crossed his sweaty palm.

The pimp grabbed Jim and spun him around. "You gotta send the right message! Bury that howling buck up to his neck and let the other Apaches see it! They understand that kind of punishment – treating them like they'd treat any white woman if ya gave 'em half the chance."

"You mean a Red Man hurt the lady who works for you?"

"A Red –? Sweet Christ on a crutch! Didn't Gus tell ya nothing? That wild one whose pa is some kind of horseshit medicine man, he done it. Claims to be a cousin to Geronimo. When he came out of them hills looking for Stella, I shoulda shot him on the spot. Nobody woulda blamed me!"

"Then you knew he was trouble?"

"Yeah. But he was a customer. So what?"

"Sir, it's illegal to sell whiskey to Indians."

Rayford poked Jim's chest with a stubby finger. "You better be kidding. Don't turn this around on me. I'm out a good whore! Maybe she was only worth fifty cents a ride, but she was mine! And she didn't deserve what she got. Take a look, boy-o. Stella's not going anywhere."

Jim climbed the whiskey-crate steps up to the wagon tailgate, parted the canvas cover and peered inside.

Stella's crinolines and flesh were shredded, so Jim couldn't tell skin from cloth, or raw muscle from store-bought finery.

Rayford laughed as Jim reeled, trying to steady himself with the rifle while fighting to keep his breakfast down.

The pimp settled on the bottom crate. "There's your noble savage for ya."

Jim was still doubled-over. "H-How? Did you see?"

"He must've had a long blade in his leathers." Rayford's words were flat and protested any responsibility. "I didn't see a damn thing! He paid and went in. I poured a hot cup and checked me moneybox. She didn't even yell. Apaches are pretty good at that, killing without making a sound. I hollered when his time was up, but he was long gone and she was like, well, what you saw."

Jim hefted himself onto his saddle, cradling the Henry .44. "You don't know me, Mr Rayford, but I'm a true bloodhound. I can track this man. And I'll bring him in for trial."

"What the hell are you going on about? No Apache gives a damn about white man's law, and I'm still out a whore! I've got to bury what's left of Stella, wash down the wagon, and find me another crib girl who'll work this trail! I'm owed for all that! I want to see his head, ya hear me? I'm *owed*!"

Rayford kept bellowing, but Jim already had his pinto at a full gallop, pushing the little horse as hard as he could to get away from Rayford's words. Stella's mouth and tongue were gone but she was crying louder than Rayford ever could. That's what Jim was hearing as he snapped the reins, angling his horse toward a wide thicket.

Jim eased to a walk and eyed the dry scrub. There were two fresh breaks in the tangle, and the sun-browned grass had been flattened by someone falling. Jim could make out footprints in the loose dirt, but they were as indistinct as ghost's. No toes, only heel. He thought his quarry was wearing moccasins, which meant the rocks wouldn't slow him down. The bloodhound allowed himself to smile; he had the scent and he could follow it. He was doing all right. That was the first day.

Jim Bishop's mind snapped back to the present: it was now the fifth night and he was dying. The West Texas wind cut into him as he pulled his jacket tight with his one good hand. He was as ready as he'd ever be for another attack, provided it came while he could still see and had the strength to pull a trigger. Sure. No problem at all.

Less than an hour before, Jim chased a figure over the rocks. He had the scent and was closing in. Jim dropped into a granite V, took aim, and split the dark with two shots from the Henry. He missed, but the orange muzzle flashes illuminated his target: a young Apache brave who moved faster than any man Jim had ever seen.

Their eyes met for a moment before the brave leapt for an overhang, grabbed it with his fingers and swung easily on top of a steep rock face. He was gone before Jim could even draw a bead on him.

Feet slipping on gravel, Jim scrambled for a better position. He reached out to grab a twisted root above the entrance of a small cave, pulling himself onto a narrow ledge that ran the width of the cave's mouth. Jim perched and listened for his prey. Something moved, and he whipped his rifle toward a gray bat, fluttering in the shadows. The thing flew past the deputy, then spun into the night sky.

Jim let out his breath, but he didn't relax. The Apache was close and Jim's nerves were electric under his skin. He detected something in the slight breeze that almost made him shoot. Almost. But Jim didn't want to show-up his position again. Still scared as hell, Jim stood ready. His thoughts were clear: he'd bloodhounded the killer this far, and wasn't going to lose the Apache by being over eager. He'd vowed to bring his man in and that's what he was going to do, just like he told Gus he would. No brag, just fact.

Jim's side opened so fast he didn't even feel it.

A sharp edge sliced through his skin, skidded along his ribs and was gone. Red blurred Jim's eyes, blinding him as the edge cut him again, ripping his shoulder and right arm to the bone. Jim rolled, jabbed the rifle into the attacker and fired point-blank. As the gun-smoke cleared, he wiped the blood from his eyes and struggled to fire again. He did.

But his attacker was gone.

Jim lay dying, his mind washing in the memory of how he got here. Everything he did led him to this spot. He had a good position in the rocks, twelve shots in the magazine, plenty more in his ammo box, and a pool of blood spreading from his gut. It wasn't right. The deputy shouldn't be the one who was slipping away, and Jim kept whispering to himself that he was going to get his man.

He couldn't stand, but he was going to catch a killer. Nice thought. Another bolt of pain reminded Jim that he wasn't going anywhere, and he curled up on his wet side, listening to his own shallow breathing.

"God," Jim said, "you know I ain't never done nothing like this before in my whole life; I don't know what the hell I'm doing out here. I ain't no tracker, I'm just a sorry bullshitter, and I don't blame ya if you let me die–"

A woodsmoke-smelling hand clamped over Jim's mouth, killing his private talk.

"I am Whistle Fire," a voice whispered in Jim's ear. "I am here to save you. Do not make a sound."

Jim nodded and Whistle Fire removed his hand. Jim didn't cry out. It took all his strength to draw his next series of breaths, while he fought to focus on the figure before him. The full moon's light showed a massive silhouette, shoulders crowned with bearskin and the teeth of mountain lions shone around his neck and wrists. A large silver cross centered on the man's chest and captured broken pieces of Jim's own reflection.

Whistle Fire's voice was deep and quiet, "Lay down your gun, Deputy."

Jim held the rifle tight.

Whistle Fire stared into Jim's eyes. "You have not lost your mind. I am Apache, and I know your language. Some of us do."

"I know them b– beads and I kn– kn– know them colors. You gonna finish me off?"

"If you know that, then you know I am medicine. I can't help you while you keep your arms like that. Lay down the rifle."

Whistle Fire pulled a soft hide bundle from his belt and opened it. Jim watched him as he laid out his implements: Whistle Fire cut a peyote bud in half and threaded a needle with thin, stretched gut. His moves were sure and he didn't look at the deputy once. "If I wanted to kill you, I could have four sunrises ago. Why are you doing this? You're just a boy. Your life should end in a soft bed many years from now, surrounded by your children."

Before Jim could speak, Whistle Fire forced the peyote into his mouth and clenched his jaw. Jim bit into the bud. The dry plant broke apart and its bitterness made him gag.

"Let it fill your mouth," Whistle Fire said, "then swallow. Do not think of anything."

The pieces stuck to the roof and sides of Jim's mouth, drinking the last bit of moisture there. Jim chewed the bud, and his grip relaxed as the mescaline traveled warm down his back and arms, carrying him away. The feeling wasn't like being drunk on Old Kentuck, or like anything Jim had known before.

"You cannot kill him," Whistle Fire said and took the Henry.

Jim grabbed at the shadow of a root, thinking it was his rifle. "It's my duty...you don't know... what he's... done..."

Whistle Fire wiped the blood from Jim's side. His words were flat. "He has shamed my people. He has lain with white women and traded hides for whiskey. He kills for pleasure. This is not right."

"Sure ain't, Whistle F-Fire... That's why... I..."

"I know better than you. A white man cannot kill him."

Jim's words slurred. "I have to..."

"You have never killed a man."

"Never shot nothing but a jack rabbit...but I told everybody in town I could bring him in...dead or alive... I told 'em 'cause I got a way of findin' a man. And I can smell him; I'm a blood – bloodhound."

"You do not hear what I say. You cannot do any of these things."

"But I gotta ..."

Below the two men, a shadowy shape moved silently from the mouth of the cave, along the edge of the drop-off, to a foothold. It darted up the side of the rock face, moving quickly hand-over-hand. It stopped at a place where it could watch Jim and Whistle Fire. Just watch.

The needle pierced Jim's flesh. He smiled as Whistle Fire laced the wound, laying muscle against bone and cleaning it with a root poultice. "Who sent you? That fat sheriff?"

"Old Gus is the law..."

Whistle Fire snorted. "He is a drunken coward who sent you because he knew he would not survive. I watched you track. You lost your horse, your water. But you didn't stop. You followed into these hills when others would have quit. You did your duty as an Apache would. Be proud of that."

"See...that's why they call me bloodhound."

"Who calls you that?"

Jim swallowed quietly. "Well, only me..."

Jim stayed on the hazy, warm edge. The pain was somewhere out of reach now, in another existence, and the truth kept tumbling out, "I've never done no real tracking before. Just read about it, and played cards with a scout from Fort Smith who told me some things. You think I'm lying, but I got a sense; I know when there's blood in the air. Or fear. Fear sweats right out of a man, and I can follow him. That makes me a bloodhound. And an honest-to-God deputy, see that badge?"

Whistle Fire pulled the last stitch. "What did you do to earn it?"

"I sweep the cells. Clean the rifles. Once I put a summons in a guy's pocket while he was sleeping. And the sheriff sends me across the street when he needs a re-fill..." Jim struggled to stand. "Maybe I ain't the world's best lawman, but I still got something to do ..."

"No you don't." The medicine man laboriously jacked each remaining cartridge from of the Henry, letting them drop to the ground. The brass hit the rocks like a gentle rain.

Jim drew a deep breath. "He's here..."

And then an enraged animal's scream split the air. The shadowy shape leapt on Whistle Fire and pounded his head against the sharp stones of the outcrop. Red sprayed like a fountain from the medicine man's temple as he brought his knees up against the thing's chest, pushing it off with a burst of raw strength.

Jim lurched forward, trying to fight. To help. But his mind reeled. Was he seeing a peyote dream? Narrowed red eyes lanced him, but they seemed like distant stars. Time slowed as Jim grabbed the rifle and swung it wildly into line. He eared back the hammer and pulled the trigger. It clicked on an empty chamber as the deadly shape moved on him. Jim felt his heartbeat, but little else. He fell out of his body and watched it being torn, and could not prevent it. Teeth sliced Jim's face. Hot saliva soaked him. Long claws ripped his stitches apart. Jim's nostrils were filled with the familiar pungent scent – the scent he'd followed these last five days. Then pain erupted again, squashing the effects of the peyote. Jim fell like a rag doll to the ground.

The medicine man drew his bone-handled knife and swiped the blade across his temple, smearing it with his own blood.

Jim straightened to his knees and battled as best he could, reaching up and digging his fingers into what he hoped were the creature's eyes, or even the flesh of its throat.

The deputy screamed; he was nothing more than a prairie dog being shaken to death in the jaws of an enormous wolf.

Everything was spinning when Jim saw Whistle Fire climb a small ledge and jump onto the thing's back. The medicine man plunged the knife blade into the shape-shifter over and over. The shoulders. The arms. The neck. The thing twisted. A cry exploded from its open maw. The cry didn't stop as it thrashed, but gradually it transformed from something guttural to something human.

A young man's voice.

Whistle Fire spiraled away and landed hard.

The knife remained buried to the hilt in the thing's chest. The Apache medicine man caught his breath, as the thing's flesh folded in on itself, its bones shifting and muscles snaking into a different form. The long arms shortened and the lupine legs thickened at the calf. Silver hair receded under the taut, brown skin of a young Apache.

Tears glinted in Whistle Fire's eyes as he watched human jaw and eyes settle into place. The snout-like nose collapsed, revealing the noble one underneath. Blood trailed across the youth's naked body, but his face was peaceful. Dignified.

"I don't know what happened," Jim mumbled. "I don't know what I'm seeing..."

Whistle Fire's lungs heaved. "*Ba'cho.*" He looked at Jim and found the words. "It means wolf. *My son.* Shape-shifter. Had you shot him a thousand times, he would not die. Only his father's hand could kill him. Our gods decreed it and so it is." His voice trailed off.

"Your son? I'm sorry..." Jim groaned.

"You will not die," the medicine man said. "I will see to that."

Jim tried to take it all in. "So this is real...?"

"You'd take comfort if you'd been shot to pieces. That you can understand."

"I knew I was dying...that's why I fought back..."

"I said you will live. In town, you'll show your scars, but no one will believe your words. That is good. People will laugh at you, then forget everything. You will have dreams, but one day they will stop. Your life will go on – in another town, without a badge. But still, you will catch the scent when the need arises again. That is your duty, your curse."

Whistle Fire knelt beside his son's body. "There must always be a kill when the hunter finds its prey. Man, animal or both. If it was not my son, it would be you. You do not know what is out here. Beaudine did not know you were a bloodhound. He thought you were a lamb to be slaughtered."

Jim closed his eyes. "Mebbe that's all I am." A sob came from his gut and Jim waited for the curtain to close on his mind. Something like sleep overcame him, and he let it happen.

The first touch of sun wasn't warm, but the light forced Jim's eyes open. Clean bandages wrapped his arms, chest and neck, and dried leaves marked the cuts on his hands and legs. Nearby, a barebacked chestnut nickered as if waiting for him. Whistle Fire was gone.

The rocks were spattered with dark brown stains that the rains would eventually wash away. There was a single, deep footprint made by a man carrying something heavy. The bloodhound didn't follow that scent. Instead, he looked beyond it to the open land below, and saw a jack rabbit darting through the scrub.

Nothing else moved.

Deputy Jim Bishop wiped his wet eyes. He yanked the star from his shirt and let it drop. The bent blood-smeared tin clattered down a crevice and was lost.

The scent remained.

MORE THAN MEETS THE EYE

Gillian F Taylor

Gillian F Taylor grew up on the plains of the Wild East (Anglia). She liked horsey things, including cowboy toys, and read her first western because the title sounded like a pony book. Her twelfth BHW, Silver Express *is just out (September 2009) and the thirteenth is due early in 2010. She still has the same cowboy toys along with her collection of 90+ toy horses, 40+ action figures and hundreds of pony books. There are two cats as well. The protagonist of this story, Jonah Durrell, appeared in* Two-Gun Trouble. *You can find Gillian at http://www.gillian-f-taylor.co.uk/.*

A prolonged, rumbling belch filled the morning air. Parsons sighed and, as an afterthought, offered an apology to his companion, Brown. They sat on plain wooden chairs on the boardwalk outside the Shovel Saloon, enjoying the morning sun before the day got too hot. Both liked to watch the early morning bustle on Panhandle Street.

Panhandle was the main, and almost only, street of Motherlode, a young and flourishing mining town in the San Juan Mountains of Colorado. A mob of loose burros carrying supplies was herded past, heading up the valley toward Animas Forks. Two women with shopping baskets passed the drinkers on the boardwalk, and a wagon full of beer barrels moved slowly down the street. Opposite, the door to Miss Jenny's fancy parlor house opened and one of her girls stepped out. A sweet-faced blonde in an elegant dress of blue silk with lace trim, and a dainty blue hat with ribbons that fluttered in the breeze, she was like an exotic songbird that had flown into a city slum by mistake. She turned down the street, passing the meat market, and entered the post office.

Brown and Parsons watched until the door closed behind her. If she'd been a girl from one of the cheaper brothels, they might have cat-called across the street, but Miss Jenny's girls commanded respect from all but the most devoutly religious men in Motherlode, and their kind were firmly in the minority. It was unlikely that anyone would have taken Brown or Parsons for members of that group. Parsons's red-veined face and beer belly implied a devotion to alcohol, not God. Brown was a skinny, knobbly man with white-blond hair and skin that was always red and peeling from sunburn. His general appearance, from grubby ill-fitting clothes to lank hair, suggested he didn't practice the tenet that cleanliness was next to godliness.

The man who rode out from between the saloon and the Colorado Hotel next door was of a different kind altogether. Parsons and Brown watched him with a mixture of respect and envy. He was tall, broad-shouldered, athletic in build, and unusually handsome. Black hair and liquid brown eyes formed part of the vivid impression he made: confident and ready to smile. His clothing was expensive: glossy black boots, black trousers, jacket and hat, a white linen shirt and a double-breasted waistcoat of cream and gold brocade. The elegant turnout distracted attention from his gun-belt, which was of fine black leather. In spite of its style and gloss, the double gun-belt was obviously functional, as were the matched Smith & Wesson revolvers with pearl grips and engraved scrollwork.

"That's one mighty smart piece of work," Brown remarked. "Looks like some doctor, or law wrangler maybe."

Parsons turned his head to spit on the boardwalk. The wodge of saliva narrowly missed the skirts of a young woman who had stopped ostensibly to check the contents of her basket, though she kept glancing at the handsome rider.

"That there's Jonah Durrell," Parsons said bitterly.

Brown's pale blue eyes opened wider. "The manhunter?"

"That's what he likes to call himself: I call him a bounty killer." Parsons snarled. "All those dandy clothes, that horse, them fancy guns – all bought with blood money."

Brown studied Durrell as he turned his fine dapple-gray and rode on up the street. "I never saw no killer all gussied up like that."

The bounty hunter rode at an easy walk, studying the buildings either side as he passed them. He nodded politely and smiled at a plainly dressed woman outside the feedstore. Her eyes widened in surprise before she smiled back, her weather-roughened face lighting up.

"He can dress as fancy as he pleases," Parsons said. "But under them smart duds he's nothing but a low-down piece of scum who cares only about hisself and the dollars he gets for hunting down other scum. He ain't got the discipline to get hisself a regular job. All he cares about is getting dollars for fancy clothes and fancy women. A bounty killer like him don't know nothing about friends, or being a Good Samaritan, like it says in the Bible. I hope he's heading out of town for good."

Parsons took a long chug of his beer, and tilted his chair back against the wall of the saloon to watch as Durrell rode north out of town.

Even though Parsons had been careful not to speak too loud, Jonah Durrell heard every word he'd said. None of it bothered him in the slightest. He cared more about how the woman's face had lit up. A simple smile from him had brightened her day and he knew she'd feel just a little better about herself for a while. Jonah was as vain about his striking good looks as Parsons, and many other people, believed, but he also laughed at himself for being so. And as he genuinely liked people, especially women, he used his looks and charm to bring a little pleasure to other people's lives. If a smile from him cheered up a woman carrying a basket of heavy shopping, then Jonah was happy to give her that smile.

As he left the town behind, Jonah nudged his gray into a steady jog. "We've got to cover some ground today, Cirrus," he said. The gray flicked back an ear to listen. "I want to find Isaac Glover, who works up at the California Mine. Get hold of him and bring him back to Motherlode today if we can."

Cirrus snorted and tossed his head in answer, making Jonah laugh.

They quickly passed the mob of laden burros, the gray's easy stride leaving the long-ears behind. Soon, Jonah traveled in peace, able to enjoy the spectacular scenery as he rode. At some 10,000 feet up, the sun was already warm though it was still early morning. Even after some five years in Colorado, Jonah was still entranced by the way everything seemed so crisp and sharp in the thin air. The mountain peaks in the distance were as clear as those that rose steeply on either side of the river valley.

He followed the tumbling green waters of the Animas. Aspen, willow and buffaloberry bordered the river, with wild pink roses flaunting themselves among the greenery. The mountainsides that cradled the river valley were crowded with dark masses of firs that even clung precariously to stretches of bare rock. Jonah smiled: riding to work was pure pleasure.

Jonah reached the little town of Animas Forks by mid-morning. As the only diversions on offer here were the solitary saloon and the bar of the two-story hotel, it wasn't surprising that workers from the surrounding mines preferred to travel into Motherlode for their entertainment. That was what Isaac Glover had done. The miner had been drinking and gambling away his pay when he got into a fight over a dice game. Glover fatally stabbed his opponent, Dandy Danny Doyle, and fled town. It wasn't an uncommon happening in the mining towns, and Jonah thought of it as a bread-and-butter job. The reward for bringing Glover in was just $50 but Jonah figured that was a pretty good return on a day or two's work. Glover couldn't earn that much for a month's toil in the mines.

Leaving the north end of town, Jonah followed the West Fork of the Animas River up California Gulch. The gulch rose steadily and after a mile or so it turned south, revealing the splendid Hurricane Peak topped with snow that glittered in the noonday sun.

Jonah drew rein for a minute, narrowing his eyes as he admired the view, and let Cirrus take a breather.

After a while, he nudged the horse on again. Now his attention was on the mine high on the northern slope near the head of the valley. Smoke poured from its chimneys, whisked away into the stunning blue skies.

The incessant pounding of the machinery grew louder as he got closer to the mine, drowning birdsong and muffling the sound of the river. Jonah hadn't been to the California mine before, but he'd visited plenty of others and had no difficulty in identifying the main office building.

He slid gracefully from the saddle, patted Cirrus's hard neck and loosened the girth to let the horse stand comfortably while Jonah went about his business. Leaving Cirrus tethered, Jonah checked the set of his guns. He brushed travel dust from his clothes and tidied himself up before entering the office.

A short, stout man with a shock of thick dark hair sat behind a large desk. He glanced briefly at Jonah, frowned, then held up a hand, silently asking him to wait. Jonah seated himself opposite while the clerk finished adding columns of figures, his fat lips moving slightly as he did the mental arithmetic. He wrote down the last number and, after laying the pen neatly in its holder, finally looked up.

"What can I do for you?" the clerk asked, his eyes searching Jonah, as if adding up the value of his clothes.

"My name's Jonah Durrell; I'm hoping you can help me." Jonah took out the reward note that Motherlode's marshal had written and unfolded it. "I believe a man named Isaac Glover works here."

The clerk nodded briskly. "He works in our smelting shed."

Jonah handed over the reward note. "I've come to arrest him on a charge of murder."

The clerk snatched the paper from Jonah's hand and his eyes darted back and forth over the sheet. He looked up, fixing Jonah with a hard stare. "You're sure it's Glover did this? Are there witnesses who're sure it's him?"

"He's in the Golden Pan every payday," Jonah said. "Enough people there know him by sight, so the marshal's certain-sure who he wants."

The clerk made a disgruntled sound and handed the paper back. "Glover's one of our best smelters. It's not easy getting a skilled man like him; he'll be hard to replace."

"Colorado's plumb full of miners," Jonah said, folding the paper again. "You won't have to look too long to find another, and I'm darn sure you can find a smelter who doesn't make a habit of murdering folk over a ten dollar bet," he added tartly.

The clerk glowered, but merely said, "You'll find him in the smelting shed. Talk to Bezener, the foreman, first. Tell him Kershaw sent you."

Jonah nodded. "Thank you for your help."

Kershaw nodded in dismissal and bent over his figures.

Jonah found the smelting shed easily enough. He stepped into the blast of heat from the huge machines where the treated and ground silver ore was smelted down to extract it from the rock and other minerals. Men stripped to the waist shoveled coal into the furnaces while others studied brass dials, checking temperature and pressure. The broad-shouldered man wearing a shirt and low-crowned hat had to be Bezener, the supervisor. Jonah walked over and introduced himself.

"Kershaw said you might be able to help me," he said, raising his voice to be heard over the noise. "I'm looking for Isaac Glover."

Bezener grunted. "Well, be sure and let me know if you find him."

"He's not here?"

Bezener shook his head emphatically. "Never showed up for work this morning and he ain't in the boarding house. He done lit a shuck for someplace, and never gave no warning. Production's down because of that no good son-of-a-bitch."

Jonah bit back a curse. "What about his pals – do they know where he's gone?"

Bezener shrugged. "Iffen he's gone, he's gone. I ain't sending someone out to drag him back."

"It's my job to drag him back for the law," Jonah replied. "Who're his pals?"

The supervisor turned and pointed at one of the furnaces further along. "You want Schmidt there, the fellow with his hair all but shaved off."

Jonah saw the sweating muscular man indicated and nodded. "Thanks, I'm grateful for your help."

Bezener nodded, and promptly seemed to forget him to deal with a problematic valve.

Schmidt seemed glad for any excuse to step away from the furnace and take a few moments' break from his work. He shook his brutish head when Jonah asked after Glover. "I don't know where he went," he insisted, his accent changing the w's into v's.

Jonah wasn't satisfied with his answer. Schmidt spoke with a casualness that suggested he really didn't know where Glover was, but there was a hint of superiority in the way he looked at Jonah. He might be truthful in saying he didn't *know* where Glover was, but Jonah was willing to bet that Schmidt could take a good guess.

"Some friend," Jonah said, watching Schmidt's reactions closely. "To take off like that and not tell you where he was going."

"He told me he was in a fight," Schmidt said hotly, defending his friend. "And he reckoned he'd better clear out for a few weeks."

"A fight?" Jonah said. "He didn't happen to mention that he killed a man during this fight, did he?"

Schmidt looked genuinely shocked. "Why would Glover kill anyone?" He shook his head and glared at Jonah. "I don't believe it."

"It's true, and there're witnesses to prove it," Jonah told him coolly. He looked hard at the other man. "Where do you *think* Glover's gone?"

Schmidt gazed at the floor, rocking his weight from foot to foot. "I don't know…"

"But you have an idea, don't you?" Jonah said harshly. "Glover stabbed a man over a ten dollar bet; he killed for *ten* dollars. Where's he gone?"

Still looking at the floor, Schmidt answered. "He used to work at the Red Horse Mine. He could go there and work for a while."

Jonah knew the Red Horse Mine was in Placer Gulch, separated from this one by the ridge of California Mountain. Like many wrongdoers, Glover stayed close to his home territory. Few of the men Jonah hunted showed much imagination and he wasn't surprised at Glover's choice of hiding place.

"When did he leave here?" Jonah asked.

"Just before our shift started; nearly one hour back."

As Glover would have ridden down California Gulch to reach the entrance to Placer Gulch, Jonah had probably missed him on the trail by about fifteen minutes. Assuming he'd gone to Red Horse Mine.

"Anywhere else he might go?" Jonah asked.

Schmidt shrugged. "He might go to Ouray."

"I'm grateful for the information," Jonah said. "I'm sorry your friend's in a mess, but he killed someone and he's got to pay."

Schmidt looked up. "Will they hang him?"

"I don't know," Jonah said honestly. "Depends on the judge. He might swing, but if he's not done anything else wrong, he might get sent to jail with hard labor."

Leaving Schmidt to think about it, Jonah headed back to the fresh air and relative coolness outdoors. He tightened Cirrus's girth and looked thoughtfully at the mountains surrounding him.

Retracing Glover's route meant a five-mile ride back down the gulch and up the next one to reach Red Horse Mine. The bulk of California Mountain and Hanson Peak lay between the two gulches, impossible to ride over. Jonah turned to study the head of the valley. It was a stiff climb to reach the saddle between the peaks there, but he would be able to cross behind Hanson Peak and reach the head of Placer Gulch on the other side. It was a tougher route, but less than half the distance. If Jonah had been asked, he would have said that he saw no point in going the long way round, but the fact was that he loved the mountains, and relished any opportunity to ride higher and see new vistas. His mind made up, he mounted and rode out.

Cirrus tackled the steep head of the valley with a will. They zig-zagged back and forth, rising towards the blue sky until they came out onto the flatter plateau of land between the peaks. Jonah dismounted and let his horse blow for a few minutes.

The air was thin and clear but the sun was warm as Jonah looked across the open grassy land, dusted with a rainbow of wildflowers. Looking at such a view took his mind off the petty squabbles and viciousness he dealt with in his work.

When Cirrus had recovered from the climb, Jonah rode around the edge of the plateau at a brisk lope. They made a shorter climb over a saddle between two peaks, and Placer Gulch came into view on the other side. Jonah smiled to himself as he drank in the beauty of the wild winding valley.

Everything was lovely, with the exception of Red Horse Mine, which sat on the landscape like an industrial stain. Smoke rose from its chimneys and the ugly plain buildings sat starkly in their lush surroundings.

After studying the rest of the view, Jonah finally focused on the mine and sighed. "Why does ugliness have to be the price of civilization?" he asked his horse.

Cirrus stretched his neck out and shook his head, snorting gently. Jonah laughed, patted him and started the gray on the steep descent.

After making enquiries at the mine office, Jonah went to the bunkhouse, climbing two flights of wooden stairs to the top floor. There was only one person in the dormitory, a man who matched the description he had of Glover. He was busy shaving. A saddlebag lay on the bed to his right, with some of the contents scattered on the gray blanket.

Jonah casually unfastened his jacket as he walked between the rows of bunks, making sure he had free access to his guns. His unhurried approach didn't appear to disturb Glover, who concentrated on scraping at his bristles with an open razor.

Jonah halted a few feet behind the man. "Isaac Glover?" he asked casually.

"Yep?" Glover stared at Jonah's reflection in the mirror. Slightly more than half of his somewhat jowly face was now shaved and devoid of soap.

Jonah drew his right-hand Colt in a slick move as he spoke. "I'm taking you in for the murder of Dandy Danny Doyle."

Glover scowled. "That low-down skunk cheated!"

"Tell it to the jury."

Glover continued to stare into the mirror, his body tense.

Jonah had no trouble reading the thoughts reflected in the light blue eyes. "Don't bother trying to jump me," Jonah warned. "I don't know if you've heard of Jonah Durrell, but if you haven't, I'll tell you myself that I'm an excellent shot and damn quick. Your shoulder's a plenty big enough target. I hit that and you'll be too hurt to fight me but not so hurt you'll die before I haul your sorry ass back to Motherlode. I did three years in medical school before I came west, so I can patch you up if I need to."

Glover stayed sullenly silent.

"Close the razor and toss it on the bed to your left, then you can wipe off your face," Jonah ordered.

Moving slowly and deliberately, Glover did as he was told. He wiped the remains of the shaving lather from his face and dropped the grayish towel onto the bed without turning around.

Watching Glover carefully, Jonah fished a pair of handcuffs from his jacket pocket. "Hands together behind your back," he said.

Glover obeyed and Jonah moved closer to fix the handcuffs.

Alert for trouble, Jonah saw Glover's shoulders tense and was already reacting when the miner stepped back towards him and started to turn. Glover flung up his right arm as he twisted, intending to knock Jonah's gun aside. Jonah swung his own arm out of the way and delivered a sharp jab to Glover's jaw with his left fist. Glover's momentum turned him into the blow. The steel cuffs in Jonah's hand hit Glover's jaw and he reeled back. Moving fast, Jonah cracked the butt of his gun into Glover's temple then smashed the handcuffs into his mouth.

Glover stumbled back and collapsed to sit on the floor, dazed and bleeding from a split lip.

Jonah looked down at him. "I guess I should also have mentioned that I'm pretty good with my fists."

Half an hour later, Jonah and his prisoner were on the trail to Motherlode. Rather than head north through Animas Forks before turning back south, Jonah opted to go up the side of Placer Gulch again. He climbed to a pass on the southeast end and headed down a narrow, steep-sided valley. It was getting on for late morning now and the sun was hot. The horses made their way steadily down the grassy valley, their coats dark with sweat.

Unlike Glover, whose handcuffed hands were tied to his saddle-horn, Jonah could drink from his canteen whenever he wanted, but the water was warm and not refreshing. When he spotted a shack with smoke rising from the chimney, he turned up the side of the valley towards it, thinking of coffee and maybe some food.

Jonah glanced back at Glover, who had been sullen and silent all the way. Halting at a polite distance from the shack, Jonah called to announce his presence.

There was an answering shout from within and, a few seconds later, an agitated man appeared in the doorway. The sleeves of his stained check shirt were rolled up and he clutched a damp cloth in one hand. His eyes were shadowed with fatigue.

"Praise the Lord," he exclaimed. "I need someone to ride to Silverton pronto and get the doc."

"What's wrong?" Jonah asked, glancing warily at the shack.

A wail of pain from within the shack answered his question. It was a woman's voice, tired and despairing.

"My wife went into labor last night," the man explained, absently wiping his face with the cloth. "She's been trying for hours. I think the baby's stuck. She needs a doctor. Please, you can take my saddle horse and spell it off with your own."

"There may not be time to fetch a doctor," Jonah replied. He prepared to dismount, then realized he was holding the reins of Glover's horse.

Jonah turned and looked Glover straight in the eyes. "You heard all that," he said; it wasn't a question. "There's a woman in there needs my help. I know how to deliver a baby and if I don't help her, she could die before a doctor gets here. I can't concentrate on her if I'm worrying about you too. Will you give me your word not to try anything while I'm working with that woman and her baby?"

Glover met his gaze directly. "I'm no saint when it comes to cheatin' skunk, but I ain't never hurt a lady. I swear to God I won't try anything so long as she needs your help."

Jonah considered for a moment. "You give your word?"

Glover straightened in his saddle. "I give you my word afore God," he said solemnly.

Jonah knew in his heart he had no choice but to risk Glover's pledge. He swung down from his saddle and got the small bag of medical instruments he always carried out from his saddlebag. Drawing his rifle from the saddle scabbard, he approached his prisoner. As he unlocked the handcuffs and unfastened Glover's hands, he told him, "See to the horses and stay out here. If you cause or allow any harm to that woman, I'll hunt you down and kill you myself."

Glover just nodded.

Jonah turned his back on Glover and entered the shack. He followed the husband to the bedroom in the back of the two-room cabin. Inside, he propped the Winchester against the wall. He took off his hat, jacket, and gunbelt, arranging the last so one revolver was readily accessible. The furnishings were plain: a homemade bed and chair, and two packing crates serving to hold clothes. But the room was warmed by a pink and green rag rug by the bed and green and white calico curtains at the small window.

The woman in the bed was small and slender. The hands resting on the quilt were reddened from rough work, but delicately made. Light-brown hair was caught back in a simple braid that left a few strands loose around her face. Her shadowed eyes widened as she got a good look at Jonah and her pale cheeks colored becomingly.

Approaching the bed, the manhunter introduced himself. "I'm Jonah Durrell: I'm a doctor."

"The name's Dawson," the man replied, taking his wife's hand.

Sweat stuck strands of hair to her pinched face. She looked pleadingly at Jonah. "Please," she said softly, "help me."

"I aim to," Jonah said, smiling at her as he set his bag on one of the crates.

The woman started to smile back, then her face contorted as another contraction took her. The hay mattress with its stained sheets crackled as she strained and moaned.

"Excuse me; I need to look," Jonah said gently as he lifted the quilt.

He hadn't been entirely truthful in calling himself a doctor, since he'd left medical college before taking his final exams, but Mrs Dawson needed the reassurance. Jonah's father was also a doctor, and Jonah learned a lot from him before studying formally for three years. He'd quit college for the freedom and excitement of life out west, but had discovered that his knowledge of treating wounds, setting bones and delivering babies was invaluable in a land where qualified doctors were few and far between. He always carried a bag with instruments and drugs for emergencies like this.

"Bring hot water, soap and a clean towel, Mr Dawson," he said. "I need to wash my hands."

With another brilliant smile for Mrs Dawson, Jonah opened his bag. He took out the jar of chloroform. He suspected this was going to be a difficult job, but he was determined to do the best he could.

It was mid-afternoon when Jonah walked out of the stuffy shack into the fresh mountain air again. Mrs Dawson had fallen asleep, exhausted. Cradled in a wooden box beside the bed was a baby girl with wispy fair hair. The baby was all but dead when finally delivered and Jonah had worked hard to coax her to life. At last the baby was sleeping, breathing steadily, its once-pallid skin now with a soft pink tone. Mr Dawson sat in a rocker and watched over his wife and daughter as they recovered from their ordeal.

While Jonah buckled on his gun-belt, he took a deep breath and released it, suddenly feeling deflated after the anxiety of the birth.

"Is she, that woman, alright?" Glover asked, jerking his head towards the door of the shack. He slouched towards Jonah.

Jonah nodded, smiling proudly. "They got a baby girl. Mrs Dawson's lost some blood, but I reckon she'll be fine now. She needs rest and good food more than anything. I'll fetch her an iron tonic and some supplies from Motherlode."

"That's real good," Glover replied. "I guess you're done helping her then." On the last word, he lashed out with a chunk of firewood he'd been hiding behind his back.

Distracted by thoughts of his patient, Jonah wasn't alert for trouble. Startled at the sudden movement, he instinctively threw up his arm to protect his head. The wood hit him just behind the point of his elbow – the funny bone. Jonah yelped at the shock and stumbled backwards, trying to regain his balance. Glover swung again and again, driving Jonah back as he defended himself and struggled to stay on his feet. His right arm was numb and didn't work properly. Glover gave him no chance to grab a six-gun with his left hand; it was all he could do to block the blows with both arms.

Lurching backwards once more, Jonah crashed against the wall of the shack.

"Ha!" Glover exclaimed as he closed in again, swinging the log at Jonah's head.

Jonah couldn't back away, but with the wall to lean on, he'd caught his balance at last. As Glover swung, Jonah ducked his head and threw himself forward into the miner. Glover went over backwards, hitting the ground with Jonah on top. Momentum carried Jonah on and he rolled free of Glover, righting himself and scrambling to hands and knees.

He turned to face his opponent. Glover was already halfway up and lunging at him. Ignoring the last twinges from the hit to his elbow, Jonah began to fight back. He blocked Glover's attack with his left arm and struck with his right, landing a punch on Glover's eye. Surprised, Glover cried out and made a wild swing with the log. Jonah caught it with both hands and twisted it from the miner's grasp.

"Son-of-a-..." Glover threw himself at Jonah.

Jonah dodged and clouted Glover on the ear with the firewood. As Glover staggered, Jonah struck again, splitting Glover's lips against his teeth.

Glover dropped to his knees and held out his hands. "Stop," he begged, blood running from his mouth. "Pull in your horns."

"Had enough?"

Glover nodded, wiping blood from his face with the back of his hand.

Jonah tossed the firewood back to the pile. He nodded to Dawson, who was standing in the door of the shanty. "Sorry for creating a fuss," he said. "We'll be on our way now. I'll bring you the supplies and tonic tomorrow."

"Thank you, sir," Dawson answered. "I'm mighty grateful to you." He paused, taking a deep breath, then looked straight at Jonah and said. "You never said what your fees are."

Jonah smiled and shook his head. "No charge. I make my living bringing folks like Glover here back for the law to deal with. Doctor work, especially delivering babies, makes a plumb decent change from fighting and shooting folk."

"You're surely a Christian soul," Dawson replied.

Jonah glanced at the unhappy sore Glover and repressed a smile.

Parsons's belch was lengthy, resonant, and expertly delivered just as a faded woman carrying a heavy basket of groceries, and with two small children clinging to her skirts, passed him on the boardwalk. His pleasure in watching her expression was interrupted by Brown digging a sharp elbow into his ribs.

"Look there. Ain't that the manhunter we saw this morning?"

Parsons looked at where Brown was pointing, and saw the distinctive figure of the manhunter on his gray horse approaching from the north. He was leading another horse, its rider slumped in the saddle.

The drinking buddies watched as Durrell rode past them on his way to the marshal's office.

It was almost evening now, but Durrell looked damn near as smart and fresh as when he'd left first thing that morning. His miserable prisoner sported a ripe black eye and a swollen lip; part of his face was unshaven, adding to his air of defeat.

"Ain't that jest like I told you?" Parsons drawled. "See how the manhunter done beat up that feller what ain't even been properly arrested yet, let alone proved guilty."

"I can see that for sure," Brown agreed, absently rubbing peeling skin from his sunburned nose.

Parsons took another swallow of his beer. "Like I done said, Durrell ain't nothing but a bounty killer. He beats folk up or shoots them, just so as he can have a few more dollars to spend on his fancy duds and fancy women. No siree; that there Jonah Durrell don't care about nobody except Jonah Durrell. Kin you picture a feller as wears two guns like him lifting a finger to help anyone?" He paused to spit onto the boardwalk. "Ain't never gonna happen. Never."

"I guess you're right." Brown agreed with his friend, as usual. He took a chug of his beer and looked up and down the street for a new topic.

"Say, there's Miss Jenny. I wonder where she's going?"

"Off to put last night's takings in the bank," Parsons said knowledgeably. "I bet that fancy parlor house brings in a few dollars. That Durrell goes there regular. I'd sure be ashamed to be a man like him, I tell you…"

BIG ENOUGH

Chuck Tyrell

Born in a small town on the Great Colorado Plateau above the Mogollon Rim, Charles T. Whipple (writing as Chuck Tyrell) grew up on stories of the Hashknife Outfit, the Pleasant Valley War, Chief P'tone, and Geronimo. A student of Western history for decades, he brings the hardy people of early Arizona to life in his fiction. His novels include Vulture Gold, Revenge at Wolf Mountain, *and* Trail of a Hard Man, *all released by Robert Hale's Black Horse Westerns imprint, with* Guns of Ponderosa, The Killing Trail, *and* Hell Fire in Paradise *scheduled for release in 2010 and 2011 by the same imprint.*

Everyone around here just calls me Kid because I'm the youngest of the four McCullough brats. The other three are Kane, who's oldest, tall as a ponderosa pine and thick through the chest. Then comes Kenigan, tall as Kane but slender and wiry as a red willow tree. The third one is Kris – middling size, but tougher than a basket full of wildcats.

Pa came west as a teamster with Amiel Whipple's survey party. He returned to the Blue Mountains of Arizona when the survey was finished and set up a rawhide ranch below the alpine divide in the Blues. Ma was a Spanish girl, third daughter of Miguel Rodriguez Diaz y Rojas, who owned a ranch across the line in New Mexico. Spanish she was, Amanda Rodriguez, with flashing black eyes and ivory skin just like mine, Pa says. But I remember her little because she died in the winter of '66 when I was just three years old. Now I'm seventeen, and big enough to take care of myself, mostly.

Early on, we farmed some and hunted a lot and our clothing tended to be buckskin as cash money for store-bought clothes was hard to come by. Then the army set up camp at Fort Apache and Wells Fargo doubled its run through Navajo Springs. That brought lots of people into the territory and all of a sudden ranchers and the cavalry wanted to buy the horses we caught from the wild and tamed at our spread, using the Flying M brand.

We were hunting mustangs when I first saw the filly. I knew she could run the minute I laid eyes on her. She was just a young 'un, pushing two years old maybe; one of the bunch that followed the tough old strawberry stallion we called Big Red. No one had ever caught Big Red but, once in a while, we got some of his mares and their colts.

"The black filly with the white socks's mine," I said, and Kane laughed.

"You catch her, Kid, and she's yours."

Big Red always led his bunch down Sycamore Canyon to water so we decided to make a horse trap just south of their watering hole. I didn't care if we never caught Big Red, so long as I trapped that black filly with the socks. My, but she was fine.

Me and my brothers went to work, and in two weeks we'd set up brush walls along the trail into water, with one gate at Sheep Creek and one at the mouth of the canyon. Two more weeks and Big Red's bunch got used to going through the two gates to water. Kane and I stood by the gates as the sun rose, waiting for Big Red to lead his mares and colts into our trap. But that old stallion was a canny one. He must have smelled us, because he kept the mares from coming in that day, and the next. All we could do was wait for the old strawberry stud to decide we were just part of the scenery.

Three days later, the mares wanted to drink, Big Red or no. We sat still and let the horses water. They'd come back, and next time, or the time after that, we'd shut the gates and take our pick of Big Red's herd.

The horses catfooted over the brow of the saddleback and headed single-file down the trail to water. Just inside the far gate, Big Red stopped and stood off to one side, head high and nostrils flared. He still didn't like the smell, I'd guess.

I counted forty-eight as they filed past, headed for water. The fine black filly kept to the middle of the herd, tossing her head and testing the wind. She didn't like the smell any more than Big Red did.

When the filly got half way to water, I slammed my gate shut. "Hit it, Kane," I hollered, and my big brother slid poles into the far gate to close it off.

Big Red led a rush toward Kane's gate and a dozen horses, including the stallion, leaped the two bars Kane got up and escaped before he could get the third bar in place. But the filly with the socks was caught, and that's all I really cared about.

Kenigan rode his lineback buckskin down to have a look at the thirty-six we'd caught – mares, colts, yearlings, and two-year-olds. "That old red stallion sure sires a fine colt," he said. "Almost too good to sell to the army." He broke a twig off an aspen to chew at. "What ideas you got in that head of yours about the filly with the socks?"

I tried to sound like I knew what I was doing. "Oh, I'll see how she trains up. I reckon she'll be faster than any horse you've got, big brother."

He laughed. "Don't get uppity, Kid," he said. "You and that filly've got a long way to go yet."

My brothers spent the days getting the horses we'd caught used to having men on horseback keeping them in a bunch and moving in the right direction, so they could haze the herd back to the ranch. I built myself a little camp down by Sheep Creek. I'd be up here a while, getting used to the black filly and letting her get used to me.

Before my brothers left, they helped me build a holding pen for the filly and my three-color paint. Patches the paint was a pet. I hoped some of her gentle ways would rub off on the filly.

The day they took off with the new horses, Kane rode by my camp on his way out. "You keep an eye out, Kid. Pa'd spit horseshoe nails if anything happened to you, Ma dead and all. You're the only McCullough woman we have."

"I been out on my own more'n once, Kane. I've got my Winchester and a bunch of cartridges, and I've got the Army Colt you gave me. Nothing's gonna sneak up on me without getting a slug through its hide, man or beast. Don't you figure I'm soft, just because I'm female."

Kane grinned. "You're female all right," he said. "You got bumps and hollows in all the right places, but you're so tough there ain't nobody in Arizona who'd get sweet on you." His face took on a serious look. "Kid, any man coming down the pike's gonna be some bigger than you. I figure you oughta shoot first and ask questions after. You hear?"

I scuffed a moccasin toe in the dirt. "I'll take care, Kane. Never you worry."

"Soon as we make the ranch, I'll send Kris up with grub and such." He neck-reined his long-legged dun gelding away, raising a hand in farewell. Made me feel good to have brothers who cared after me like that.

The men and horses moved out, and that left us females. Me, Patches, and the black filly.

I could let Patches out to graze because she came when I whistled, but the little filly with the white socks had to stay in the pen until she and I could get to know each other and she learned how to behave.

I had a bag of oats and a gunnysack nosebag that Patches loved. She could hear me rustle oats in the nosebag from half a mile away, and she'd come on the trot. After a couple of days, the little filly decided Patches was her herd, and she began to watch what Patches did. On the third morning, when Patches ate her bait of oats from the nosebag, the filly came up on her off side and had a good smell of the bag. She nipped at it; she wanted to get to the good grain inside. Before long, she'd be hooked.

Mustangers break horses. My brothers do it. Everybody does it. They ear a horse down, slap a saddle on his back, and rough-ride him until he gives up. A broke horse may be right for a cowpoke hired for the roundup or a green cavalry recruit, but I prefer horses like Patches. She likes me. She does what I ask because she thinks I'm one of her herd. Oh, she comes looking for treats and she can be stubborn, but at the end of the day, she's a friend.

I didn't want to break the black filly; I wanted to be her friend, too. I wanted her and me to be a team, and when the bets were on the table, I wanted her to give me all she had.

By the end of the week, the filly wore a halter and she'd let me move my hands over her face, into her mouth, and up around her ears. She'd lift whichever foot I stood by when I said "lift it," and I'd already started cleaning her frogs and trimming and rasping her hoofs so they'd be nearly ready to shoe when we got to the Flying M.

"Hey, Kid. You look like a gun with legs."

I reached back, grabbed hold of the Colt's butt while thumbing back the hammer, turned and crouched, spraddle-legged, gun held out with both hands, ready for whatever was on the way. "Don't like to be out in the holding pen working with the filly without protection," I said.

Kris held up both hands. "Don't shoot, Kid. I'm friendly."

I put the Colt away, then looked at his feet. He wore moccasins. No wonder I hadn't heard him. Kris could sneak up on a wildcat when he wore moccasins.

I slipped the lead rope off the halter and let the filly loose. "Did you bring me some grub? I'm down to a bit of bacon. Flour ran out yesterday. Hope you loaded some grain for my horses, too."

"Yeah, I got what you need. Say, that black filly's sure a little thing," he said. "Built nice, though. Kinda like you."

"I'll tell you, big brother, that filly's plenty big enough, and she'll outrun any horse you ride."

"Big enough, eh?" He laughed. "Big enough. That's good." And that became the filly's name. Big Enough.

Kris's face sobered down. "Kid," he said. "Two men busted a hardcase named Mort Eggertson outta jail in Saint Johns the other day. Sheriff Hubbell's out chasing them with a posse, but Pa'd just as soon you come home."

"I ain't ready. The filly ain't ready. I'll be back when I can ride her home."

"Kid, don't be stupid-ass dumb. Three men who'd have their way with you and then slit your throat are in these mountains. They ain't got food. They ain't got spare mounts. You got both. And you not weighing more'n a hundred pounds in wet buckskins. Now you listen to what Pa says. Come on home. You can finish up with the filly at the Flying M."

I may be the only female among the McCullough brats, but that doesn't mean I don't have my own streak of pure stubbornness. "The filly ain't ready," I said. "And I'll keep an eye out."

"Like you did with me? I could have had you two ways from sundown," he said.

Kris had a point. I'd not been aware of him until he spoke. "I'll be more careful." I could hear the pout in my own voice. "Not going home," I said. "Not yet."

Kris shrugged. "I'll tell Pa I tried. He won't be happy about it. You just may see him before long, so you'd better work your filly up good and fast." He slipped the panniers off the pack mule and rode away with the docile jack on a ten-foot lead.

I talk brave, but at heart I know I'm just a small woman: five foot and a smidgen in moccasins and, like Kris said, maybe a hundred pounds after Thanksgiving turkey.

When I turned back to the holding pen, Big Enough wanted to play. She loved to run and knew that when I put a long rope on her halter, she would be allowed to trot and gallop and flat-out run in circles within the pen. Patches grazed on the banks of Sheep Creek until I whistled that Big Enough and I were finished for the day. Both of them came begging for the nosebag, but I had to break out another sack of oats from the panniers before I could feed them. Patches ate first, as was her right for being my number one horse. But Big Enough pushed and shoved and tried to get me to pay more attention to her than to Patches.

Big Enough was a smart little horse, so by the time I finished rubbing her all over with a saddle blanket, flapping it around her legs and up under her tail, she'd learned that moving things were not necessarily dangerous and that I would never hurt her. In fact, I was the source of those good oats and a satisfying scratch around her ears and under her jaw, and she knew that a whistle from me meant something good for her. She'd come at the run and slide to a stop on stiff forelegs, her nose touching my stomach. And wasn't she a beauty when she ran?

I opened the panniers so see what Kris had hauled up the mountain for me. Flour and bacon and beans, along with salt and saleratus powder and coffee. The supplies fixed me for ten days to two weeks, but if need be, I could get trout from Sheep Creek, eat cattail hearts, steam clover, and maybe even plink a rabbit or two, though I didn't really want to shoot. The sound of a rifle carries almighty far in the thin mountain air.

I never built a fire I couldn't cover with my hat. For myself, three or four slices of sowbelly bacon and a couple of thick saleratus biscuits cooked in a frying pan was plenty for breakfast.

I'd just soaked a biscuit in bacon grease, slapped a thick slice of sowbelly on it, and taken a big bite when Patches whickered. She stood head high, ears pointed, facing west. Big Enough stood in the shadows almost out of sight. Her mustang blood told her to hide. Dropping the biscuit in the frying pan, I grabbed my Winchester, jacked a round into the chamber, and started to turn around.

"Lay the rifle down real slow, little lady. Real slow. If you don't, I'll shoot that beautiful black filly of yours."

I heard a hammer ratcheted back. I tried to keep my knees from shaking; I couldn't let anything happen to Big Enough. My rifle clattered to the ground.

"That's a good girl. That grub you've fixed up smells mighty good. Got enough for visitors?"

"Quit lollygagging around, Mort. All we need is a horse."

Taking a risk, I gulped a big breath and turned toward the voices.

Two horses in sore need of rest and feed stood on the bank of Sheep Creek at least fifty yards away, and three men who'd ridden far and fast. A tall broad-shouldered fellow with what looked like a three-day beard stood behind the right-hand horse. He held a Winchester across the saddle, aimed at me. The others had revolvers: a top-break Smith & Wesson and a Colt Peacemaker.

"You must be Mort Eggertson," I managed to say to the tall man without my voice trembling much.

"I am."

"Why was you in jail?"

"Killed a man."

I put on my stone face. "Then you deserved jail," I said.

"Ah, but he'd of killed me if I'd been a hair slower with my S 'n W." He indicated the top-break pistol at his side.

"Come on, Mort. Them guys with Hubbell cain't be all that far behind us. Let's git."

"I could whip up a bit more bacon and biscuits if you want," I said. The longer I could stall them here, the closer the sheriff's men would be, I reasoned.

I unbuckled my gun-belt and put it on the ground by the rifle. "Just so's you won't get any wrong ideas about me," I said.

"You don't seem all that scared of us, missy," Eggertson said.

I decided to bluff it out. "Mort Eggertson, you seem to be a better man than you make out. Were you all bad, my filly would be dead, and maybe me, too. I can see you don't like killing, and I reckon there's been times when you rode with the law." Still, I had a shaky feeling deep in my guts.

He smiled. Good-looking man, as men went. "You got me wrong, missy, all wrong."

I picked my biscuit and bacon out of the frying pan, put it on the grub box, then built another sandwich from the makings that was left. I handed it to Eggertson. He gave it to the man on the hindmost horse, and he piled into it like he'd not seen food for a couple or three days.

"Go ahead, missy." Eggertson kept his rifle on me. "Fix some grub."

I just nodded and set to stirring up some more biscuit dough. In two shakes of a dead lamb's tail, I had biscuit and bacon sandwiches for the other man and for Eggertson.

Without asking, I went ahead and set a pot of coffee on to brew. No man in this wide world can refuse a good cup of coffee.

Camping by myself, I had only one coffee cup. I filled it and handed it to Eggertson. "The others'll have to wait on you," I said.

He grinned and took a sip. "Strong enough to melt horseshoes," he said. "Just my style."

When he'd drained the cup, he passed it back and I filled it for the next man; then the next.

"What's your name, missy?" Eggertson asked.

"Kimberly," I said, "but everyone calls me Kid."

"Kid what?"

"Kid McCullough."

Eggertson took a half step back away from me. "You kin to the McCulloughs down below Alpine?"

"Family," I said. "You been around here long, you'd know of my brothers – Kane, Kenigan, and Kris. I bring up the rear. Oh, and my pa's Kieran McCullough."

"Mustangers."

"Among other pursuits," I said.

"Well, Kid," Eggertson said, "we're gonna have to borrow the paint mare."

I said nothing, but my displeasure must have showed.

"I'm not about to die when I've done nothing wrong."

I glared at him.

"If I didn't kill that man, I'd of been killed myself. A man has a right to protect himself."

One of the gunmen was only three or four inches taller than me, and looked all sinew and bone. The other had a full beard and a full belly, though he wasn't near as tall as Mort Eggertson.

"Hey, Mort," the skinny outlaw said. "She's not very big, but you can tell she's a growed woman. How 'bout we take a couple of minutes for a poke or two?"

I started. That's the kind of talk Kris told me about. I'd been good to them. Would they–? I began struggling for breath, striving to keep my panic under control.

"Posse's coming, fart face, and we don't molest women." Eggertson's voice held a steel edge. "You saddle the paint, Cy," Eggertson said to the little man. "I'll ride the bay, and Jess, you stay with the sorrel."

I didn't want those clodhoppers clomping around in my holding pen, upsetting Big Enough while they tried to catch Patches.

"I get the paint," I said.

At my whistle, Patches came trotting over, followed by Big Enough. I bridled the paint and led her out of the pen.

"Nice filly," Eggertson said.

"Use the girl's saddle," he said to Cy. "Get the mare ready to go."

The man called Cy scrambled to do what Eggertson commanded.

While Cy saddled Patches, Eggertson raided my stores. He took all the flour, the bacon, the beans, and the coffee. Then loaded the sack of grain behind the cantle of his bay's saddle. "This'll keep us going for a while, Kimberly," he said. "Maybe we can get out of that posse's way. We'll move on around Escudilla and into New Mexico. And if we have to, we'll run for El Paso and Ciudad Juarez.

"Now, if you'd please turn around and put your hands behind your back."

With all those guns pointing at me, there wasn't much else I could do. I turned around.

"Hate to do this. But we can't have you running for the posse and helping them find us." Eggertson tied my hands behind my back with a piggin' string and made me lie down. He rolled me onto my side and tied my ankles and looped them to my wrists. No way I could get up; just lay there like a calf hogtied for branding.

"Kimberly," he said.

I looked Bowie knives at him.

"We didn't take your black filly, and we never hurt you. Remember that, girl." His back was turned to the other hardcases, and damned if he didn't give me a wink. I'm sure he did.

"The filly ain't broke to ride," I said.

He shrugged. "Let's go," he said to the other men.

They took off over Sheep's Crossing and lit out like they were headed for Alpine, past Escudilla, and on to Alma in New Mexico. Those three men simply rode away and left me tied up on the ground.

For a while I just lay there, considering my situation. No food, no grain, a half-trained two-year-old filly...and if I couldn't get the piggin strings off my wrists and ankles, I'd be cougar bait by sunrise. I started to get mad.

I found there was a little play in the bindings around my ankles. If I bent my knees far enough, I could work at the knots with my fingers. Eggertson did me no favors. The knots were stone hard and done up tight. But it's not in a McCullough to give up. I kept on picking and pulling on those knots, and by late in the afternoon it felt like they'd loosened a little. My fingernails broke and the skin on my fingers got raw, but I worked at the knots until they finally came undone.

My eyes got hot and I really wanted to cry, but I still had to get the piggin strings off my hands; a mighty tough job with my hands tied behind me.

I struggled to my feet and stood for a moment, head down.

Big Enough whickered from the pen.

"I'm all right, baby," I said.

She blew, nodded her head, and scraped at the ground with a fore hoof.

The old knife I used to slice bacon still stuck upright in the log I sat on near the fire. Maybe Mort Eggertson wasn't as smart as he let on; maybe he was smarter.

I backed up to the knife so my tethers were against the blade, but the minute I started sawing, the knife fell out of the log. It wasn't an easy job to pick up that knife with my hands tied behind my back. Especially with the knife lying almost under the log. I laid myself down beside it and scrabbled around with the fingers of my right hand until I finally got a hold on the handle of the knife. I turned over, got my knees under me, lifted my torso, and at last was able to get to my feet.

I poked the knifepoint into the log and put all my weight on it, forcing it as deep into the wood as my hundred pounds could make it go.

Once more I tried to saw the piggin' string off my hands. I sawed and sawed, careful not to put too much pressure against the blade, and after what seemed like half a century, the piggin string parted. My hands were free, and the sun was down below the pines on the ridge beyond Sycamore Canyon.

Tears leaked from my eyes. I wiped them away with my dirty hands; probably made a mess of my face, but there was no one there to see it anyway. Damn that Mort Eggertson.

Once I'd freed myself, I couldn't help wondering where the Saint Johns posse was.

I built a hatful of fire. Nothing left to eat, but plenty of fresh water from Sheep Creek. Eggertson didn't take the nosebag either, and it had a double handful of oats in it. I spent the evening drinking stale coffee from what was left in the coffeepot, and warming myself by the fire. The night sounds all felt natural.

No use trying to start for home in the dark when I didn't even know if Big Enough would let me on her back. I crawled into my bedroll. Somehow I slept, but woke as the sky lightened with dawn.

All or nothing. Time to ride my filly.

I went to the holding pen gate with the nosebag.

"Big Enough," I cooed.

The black filly's head came up from the grass at the far edge of the holding pen. She looked so fine. Neck arched. Small nose with flaring nostrils. Broad forehead. Little perfectly shaped ears. Short-coupled body atop long slim legs. Four white stockings that reached just short of halfway to her knees.

"Come on, girl." I shook the nosebag.

Big Enough minced across the holding pen, head high and tail up.

I held the nosebag down by my leg. Big Enough lowered her head to sniff at the bag, and I leaned down to exchange breath with her in greeting. I scratched the place at the base of her neck where she loved it. Her neck arched again; she showed pure pleasure. I slipped the nosebag on and while she was munching oats, I ran my hands over her pleasure spots – along her flanks, around her hips, under her tail.

If she'd been a cat, she'd have purred.

With a leafy aspen branch, I tested her nerves. She didn't shy even half a step. I laid the branch across her back. She ignored it and sidled up to me, asking for more scratching.

All I had was a lead rope. That would have to do as reins. I took off the nosebag and tied the lead rope to the halter, looped it around Big Enough's neck and led her out the gate to the log I used as a seat. It would get me high enough to mount her without jumping.

She arched her neck and turned her head around to see what I was doing. I gave her a scratch-reward for being such a good girl.

"I'm going to get on, Big Enough." I pitched my voice low and loving.

I stood on the log and draped myself over Big Enough's back, stomach down. She side-stepped two or three times, but made no move to throw me off. I rewarded her with more of the petting and scratching she loved so well.

Before the sun came over the eastern pines, Big Enough and I were a team. She responded to the reins, to voice commands, and even to the pressure of my knees. We were ready to go home.

Our house was built with its back against a malpais ridge. It overlooked three miles of valley where we ranged our mustangs after they're gentled.

Kane saw me from half a mile away and came charging up to me on his favorite dun horse.

"Hey, Kid," he said. "What got you to riding bareback?"

I was a bit hot under the collar from riding all day and all night with no saddle. I knew I'd be walking bowlegged for a week. "Never you mind, big brother. Just be glad I'm home." I could've spit tenpenny nails at him.

"Whoa, whoa." He held both hands up in surrender.

"Beans on the stove?" I asked.

"Always are."

"I'll have some," I said, and kneed Big Enough into a run. That little girl horse dearly loved to run. And even though she'd been on the trail for more than twenty-four hours straight, she sped off and left Kane and his gelding trying to catch their breath in our dust.

By the time Kane got to the stable, I'd given Big Enough a bait of oats and was rubbing her down with a gunnysack. When she was good and dry, I left to find some food for myself.

A Franklin stove dominated our kitchen. At the back of the stove there's always a pot of coffee and another of *chili con carne y frijoles;* or, as white men say, chili beans.

I was on my second bowl when Kane sat down at the table.

"You all right?" he asked.

"Right as a woman can be after she's had her horse and all her food stole out from under her by Mort Eggertson and his gunsharps and left at the bottom of Sycamore Canyon all trussed up like a hog for market."

"Trussed up? You're using big words again. Eat your chili beans," he said. "And tell me what happened."

I told him in no uncertain words.

And he just sat there with a little smile on his face. Which ain't natural for one of my brothers. They get set to fight the minute any guy even looks at me sideways, and me, at seventeen, pushing at becoming an old maid.

"You know something I don't?" I asked.

"Leave it lie, Kid," he said. "You're home in one piece and you've got one hell of a filly. Ain't that enough?"

"Better than nothing, but I miss Patches." I finished up my beans, and poured a cup of coffee for me and Kane. "You're right," I said, "the filly's a whole lot better than nothing."

I watched Kane sipping hot coffee with that little smile on his face. "You know what, big brother," I said. "There's something funny going on around these parts."

Kane leaned his chair back on its hind legs. "What makes you think that?"

"Sheriff Hubbell and his posse never showed. The gunhand called Cy who rode with Eggertson seemed all fired worried about the Saint Johns posse catching up with them." I took a big gulp of my coffee.

"Eggertson took all the time in the world to eat but when Cy wanted to have a little 'fun' with me, Eggertson said they had to hurry. And you know what? That killer winked at me. *Winked* at me, I say. Then he all but wrote me a map of where they were headed, which means that ain't where they went, I know, but it's strange, real strange."

Kane grinned. "Don't worry your head about it, Kid," he said. "Just keep working with your filly."

"I will, but that don't bring my mare back."

And I did. Into the fall, all the winter, and through most of the spring. Big Enough was three years old. Just fifteen hands high, but faster than anything

I'd ever seen. I rode down to the Twenty-Four ranch one day, the one owned by an Englishman named Tullison, and bargained for one of those bitty foreign saddles. Just a little patch of leather with stirrups hanging on straps so thin they looked like they wouldn't even hold my weight. The whole thing couldn't have been more than a pound and a half, and it fit Big Enough just right.

We worked out every day. Down the valley at a dead run, round a clump of spruce near the end of the swale at a canter, then trot back to the start line. Big Enough loved it. She'd almost rather run than eat, except for the oats in the nosebag. We did the route at least four times a day.

On a bright May morning, I put the English saddle on Big Enough and led her out into the sunshine.

Kane and Kris were delivering mustangs to Fort Apache, and Kenigan had ridden off to Saint Johns.

Pa sat on the front porch with a pipe and a cup. "Horses coming," he said. "One man, two horses. The one on the lead rope looks like your paint mare."

I stepped over to where I could see down the valley.

The rider was Mort Eggertson.

I ran for the house and came out with a Winchester. I jacked a shell into the chamber and eared the hammer back.

Eggertson raised his hands shoulder high and kept on coming.

"Put the rifle down, Kid," Pa said.

"That's the man who tied me up and left me to rot in Sycamore Canyon! That's the man what stole my mare!"

"Do what I say, girl." Pa's voice was stern.

I lowered the rifle, but left it cocked.

Eggertson stopped about twenty-five feet away. "Morning, Mr McCullough," he said, his voice respectful.

"Hello, Russ."

"Russ? That's Mort Eggertson, a thief and a killer!" I shouted.

The man Pa called Russ crossed his hands atop his saddle-horn. "I apologize for what we did up on the mountain, Kimberly," he said. "My name is Russell Taklin. I work for the Pinkerton Agency. We had to set up the Saint Johns jailbreak so I could get in good with a bunch of rustlers working out of Alma, New Mexico." He took off his hat and ran a hand through his wavy hair.

"I found out they smuggled cattle through Canyon Diablo into Mexico, got word to Sheriff Slaughter in Coconino County," he said. "Slaughter and his men caught the gang on its way back across the border. Now ranchers around here in Apache County won't have to worry about the Wilkins gang."

He held out the lead rope. "I brought your mare back."

I scowled at him.

"Kimberly. Listen. You, too, if you please, Mr McCullough. This Arizona high country has got under my skin. I bought a couple of sections up on Big Diamond Creek. I'll be building a home there, Kimberly. I hope you won't mind if I come down here to visit once in a while."

I could feel my face turning red.

"You'll be welcome, Russ," my Pa said.

I swung up on Big Enough's back.

Russ Taklin dug in his pocket and came up with a gold eagle. He tossed it to me. "Rent on your horse," he said.

I tossed it right back. "Keep it. Or, if you want to double it, put it down on me and my filly. We're set on winning the Fourth of July race in Holbrook this year."

Russ smiled and raised an eyebrow. "You're going to win that big race with that little filly?"

"She's plenty big enough," I said, "and so am I!" We tore off down the valley at a dead run.

ONE DAY IN LIBERTY

Jack Giles

Black Horse Western writer Jack Giles is the pen-name of North London born Ray Foster. He now lives in Surrey with his wife, 'wolf' and granddaughter. Currently, he is working on his 10th western novel.

If anyone recognized Nathan Clarke as he rode into Liberty that cold day in February, 1866 they did not show it. The lower part of his face was covered in a thick layer of bristles and his hat brim was pulled low over his eyes. His breath came out in fine wisps like smoke on the cold wind. He had never expected the day to dawn when he would feel the same inner tension that he had experienced before a battle during the Civil War. Only this time it was different – no enemy to fight, just a bank to rob.

Alongside him rode Otis Riley, his body stiff in the saddle with military rigidity. This was more out of habit than with intention, for this had been the way that he had ridden with the Colonel during the war.

"Gabe's in place," Riley said, nodding towards old-timer Gabe Tremlett who was leaning against the hitch rail in front of the bank.

Clarke just nodded as he noticed Cyrus Rankin fiddling with some goods displayed at the mercantile store. Two more men were riding down the street as another emerged from the saloon to walk down towards Matthew Grey, who stood at the corner of the alley.

"Everybody's here," Riley commented, as he steered his mount towards the bank.

"Noticed that," Nathan acknowledged. He reached under his coat to pull a fob from his vest pocket. After a quick glance at the watch face, he put it away. "Could not have timed it better."

He glanced at Riley and smiled. Just over a week ago and with reluctance, they had set this up. But it needed doing. For Otis and all the others, it needed doing.

"Damn it, Colonel!" Burly ex-sergeant Otis Riley hammered his fists on the desk top with a force that made the office rattle. "You're the goddamn lawyer around here. Surely there's something you can do to stop them damn Yankees from taking our homes from under us!"

Calmly, Nathan Clarke, lawyer and one time colonel in the Confederate Army, looked around at the nine men piled into his office. Each face was expectant and angry. Clarke spoke softly yet in a way that demanded attention. "There is nothing I can do, gentlemen. The law is the law, and the way it stands now ties my hands. The Union won the war – it gives them the right to impose their laws on us."

"But it ain't right," Cyrus Rankin cut in. "My folks been raisin' hemp most their lives and now they got to go. It ain't right, Colonel, sir."

"I did not say the law was right," Clarke pointed out. "I could fight a case for you but it would take time and all the while every one of you would still be dispossessed."

"So what do we do?" Riley asked.

"Move on," Clarke stated, sadly. "There is nothing left for us here in Missouri. For myself, I plan to follow the trail to Texas and build a new life. I suggest you follow suit."

Riley stared at his former commanding officer in disbelief. He found it hard to accept that after everything they'd been through, the lawyer would be the kind to up and quit. "So that's it, is it?" He sighed deeply and raised his arms in surrender. "We just let them goddamn Yankees win again, huh? That's the best advice you can offer?" Riley turned to the others. "This is the man we followed right through that war and now he wants us to quit." He spun around to face the lawyer. "Well, Nathan Clarke, we rode out at your side back in '61 and lost some boys to them Yankee guns when they tried to stop us. We followed your lead when you chose to join up with that Atchison feller at Lexington."

"We taught them Yankees a lesson, didn't we, boys?" Rankin laughed. The others joined in but the lightness was short lived.

"Lexington was our only victory," Clarke said. "The Army hadn't a clue what to do with us – and when they made up their mind–"

"Shiloh," Otis Riley said, his voice hoarse. "Lost my brother there."

Clarke just nodded. "Lot of men died. I don't want to sound callous, but it was war and in war people die." Decisively, he stood up. "Now, you listen to me. I do not propose to leave here with my tail between my legs nor do I expect any of you to do so, either." He looked at each of the nine men. "Before I go anywhere, I mean to make the Union pay. What I have in mind is one big gamble but I do believe that with the right men it can be done. And it is downright illegal and the law and the Union could well be right on our tails when we pull it off." Clarke stepped around his desk to stand amongst them. "If any man here doesn't want a part in what I have in mind – then it would be best if he left now."

Riley glanced over his shoulder and, like the Colonel, noted the nods of assent from all those present. "We're all with you, Colonel," Riley commented.

Clarke nodded his gratitude then became formal again. "We are going to rob the Clay County Savings Association Bank in Liberty," he announced without any frills or dramatics – just a blunt statement of fact. "Missouri may have declared for the Union – but many of us did not. This particular bank favored the Union right through the war and the money in that bank belongs, as far as I am concerned, to Union sympathizers. Well, if the Union wants to steal from us – then we will get compensation from them."

"How are we going to do that?" Rankin blurted before Riley could form his own question.

"Simple." Clarke grinned. "We'll just walk in and tell them to hand over the money."

"What?" Riley gasped. "In broad daylight? Hell, Colonel, you can't do that – you'd get your goddamned head blown off."

"And ours with it," Rankin added.

"I do not think so." Clarke chuckled. "The trick will be in the surprise."

For a moment there was a stunned silence while the men thought about the proposal.

"And it's never been done." The speaker was slow and thoughtful. Everyone turned to look at the slight young man; throughout the proceedings, he'd kept silent, hunkered down on the floor with his back against the wall. "I think it could work."

"Thank you, Mister Warwick." Clarke grinned. "I wondered when you would join us."

Seth Warwick shrugged, slowly rising to his feet. "Takes some thought, is all."

Nathan Clarke held up his hand, silencing the younger man. "Before you start, Seth," Clarke stated, looking around at many expectant faces, "let me reiterate that now is the time for any man to walk away if he is not comfortable with what I have in mind. No one will think any less of him."

There was no hesitation; Matthew Grey stepped forward as a spokesman: "I figure there ain't a man here that ain't suffered at the hands of them Union fellas and them greedy carpetbaggin' sumbitches. You seen us through the war, Colonel, and we'll foller you through the peace."

Clarke nodded and smiled as he noticed the assenting heads behind Matthew Grey.

"Thank you, Matthew," Clarke stated, managing to keep the relief he felt from his tone. He gestured at Seth Warwick. "The floor is yours."

Warwick stepped behind the desk, while Clarke edged to one side so that he could concentrate on Seth and observe the reactions of the men at the same time.

"At the Colonel's request," Warwick said, "I've spent a few weeks in Liberty working in the mercantile store close to the bank. The bank is a solid structure with two tall arched windows to the left of which is a single street door. Inside, there's a counter for the tellers. Behind this is a steel vault, and they leave the door open. So much for security."

This last comment produced some low-key laughter.

"Mostly, the bank is busy," he went on, "but its slowest day's Tuesday; that's when the chief cashier tallies the books while his junior tends to the odd customer. Come the early afternoon, this area of the town gets a little dead – and I reckon this would be the best time to hit the bank."

"So why'd you need us?" Otis Riley questioned. "Seems to me, from what you say, anyone could pull this off on his lonesome."

"Maybe I've simplified things." Warwick shrugged. "Just opposite the bank is a saloon that's well attended. Those bank windows I mentioned are large and low enough for anyone across the street to see through. So, we'll need protective cover if the alarm's raised."

"Let me stress," Clarke interrupted, "in the event of discovery, I don't want any casualties. If it is necessary to return fire then shoot over the opposition's heads and force them to take cover."

There were a number of thoughtful looks and nods of understanding. They all knew the risks they were taking as well as being aware that many of the folk they might encounter would be of their own kind. Also, it could not be forgotten that with the war's end, allegiances could change.

"So when do we do this?" Otis Riley pressed.

"Before we do anything," Clarke stated, thoughtfully, "I need to know how soon you men can get your families ready to move out."

"Me and Matt there," Rankin offered, "we're camped out at Gabe Tremlett's place. Got a couple of wagons with all we could carry."

"What do you have in mind, Colonel?" Otis Riley queried.

"If it can be achieved," Clarke replied, "I want everyone ready to move out within the next seven days, and head for the City of Kansas. I would like to take the bank on the thirteenth and have our families on the Santa Fe Trail by that time."

Over the following hour, Clarke and his men went through each stage of the operation, with various tasks allocated. Finally, they agreed the sooner the small wagon train left, the better it would be. The consensus of opinion was that the City of Kansas was too close; they should be heading towards Council Bluffs before the men turned back to Liberty, which they would approach in groups of twos and threes from a number of directions.

With the plan settled, the men moved to the door. Otis Riley was at the back and lingered by the door for a moment, then he closed it behind him and walked back to the desk.

"Why are you doing this, Colonel?" he asked.

"Because it's there." Clarke shrugged. "Do you really need a reason?"

Riley shook his head. "I guess not, Colonel. Just can't figure out why you'd want to put your head on the block for us."

"And you have not been doing the same thing for me? Four years of war and you and the others have stood beside me – I cannot and will not walk away from that. Also, bear in mind that things will get worse for Missouri before they get better..."

Riley nodded. "I get the idea – but you ain't responsible for us no more. Hell, Nathan, you were the kid that did good – but you never let it go to your head like some. Come summer, you'd be down the creek fishin' and skinny dippin' like you'd never been away. And we went to war with you because you was one of us. But we're all growed now and we're men and – well, I figure that we have to take on that responsibility."

"You are right, Otis. We are all masters of our own destiny. So you and me – one last time – we will be the ones to go into the bank. Yes?"

Riley chuckled. "Why not? Be like old times. Nate and Otis – the first names folks came up with if there was mischief afoot." Then on a more sober note, he added, "What about your stuff?"

Nathan glanced grimly around the office before answering the question. "There is nothing that I need," he stated, decisively. "I am disillusioned with the law because there is neither justice nor balance in it anymore. I hear there is money to be made in cattle and that is what I intend to do."

"And by robbing a bank you get a stake," Otis said, then hastily added, "Well, I mean we all get a stake in our future."

"No, Otis," Nathan Clarke said with a fierceness that was reflected in his eyes. "For me, I get back what belongs to me."

Otis Riley stood there for a moment, his face registering shock at his friend's outburst. Then his features softened, as if some kind of understanding had dawned on him, and he quietly turned and left the office, closing the door softly behind him.

Nathan Clarke stood and turned to stare out of the window. He regretted his sharp response. Though he wanted to apologize, he knew that his outburst would have alerted Otis to his ulterior motive – a motive that he hoped would benefit many of those who had served with him.

He could not fully lay the blame on the Clay County Savings Association Bank for what they had done. They had done nothing illegal, but what rankled was the manner in which they'd used the law to repossess his home.

The Clarkes were not wealthy people – they just owned a considerable amount of land and made money from their crops, their herd of dairy cattle and pigs. Nathan's father Jebediah was respected in the community and by his neighbors. But Jebediah wanted more for his son; he wanted young Nathan to have an education and better himself.

With the help of a nearby preacher, Robert James, Jebediah had Nathan enrolled into a school and 'the farm boy' did better than anyone expected – so well that Nathan Clarke went on to law school before taking a job with a Pittsburgh law firm.

However, the education of Nathan Clarke did not come cheap and Old Jebediah had little choice but to travel to Liberty where he negotiated a loan on his property with Clay County Savings Association Bank. With his good standing and character, the bank was only too pleased to offer him assistance and Jebediah maintained his repayments.

Things changed with the declaration of the War Between the States. Missouri had declared for the Union but the people fought for the Confederacy – and amongst them was young Nathan Clarke who had taken a break from his job in Pittsburgh.

Within a year, the bank called in the loan, claiming that the repayments had not been met – but everyone knew that it was because Old Jebediah Clarke was a staunch Confederate.

Jebediah and his wife were taken in by the Rileys, their neighbors, but Nathan's father did not live down the shame. One day he wandered off by himself and never returned – he was found on his farm, hanging in the barn. Nathan's mother never recovered from the shock and, just before the war's end, she joined her husband.

After the war, Nathan returned home and opened up his own law office. He was determined to help those destined to lose their homes and livelihoods. But the laws kept changing and he soon became disillusioned.

Nor was his mind settled by the news that Henry Wirz, the Confederate commandant of the Andersonville prison camp, was tried, convicted and hanged for war crimes. He knew nothing about Andersonville; it was the execution of a Confederate officer that bothered him. He just wondered where this Union "revenge" was going to end and how many more Confederate officers would hang because they fought for what they believed in.

Rumors abounded of troops surrendering only to be gunned down by Union soldiers. Jayhawkers were crossing over from Kansas carrying out raids – the list seemed endless and Nathan feared for the future.

Already a friend from Pittsburgh had written to him with grim news that the Reconstructionists were looking for new laws to reclaim taxes from those who had fought for the Confederacy, and their property would be confiscated if they could not pay this additional levy. Nathan knew that the law would be passed sooner or later.

Things, Nathan Clarke decided, were going to get a lot worse before they got better and, although he could not fight it, he could do something. The raid on the bank would serve two purposes – he would reclaim what was his and, at the same time, he'd give a chance to those he had not been able to help by legal means.

Two days after the secret meeting, Nathan Clarke was visited by Gabe Tremlett. Between bouts of coughing that had the old man doubling over and spitting into a grubby handkerchief, Gabe said, "Everyone's parked on my land, Colonel, and ready to go just as soon as you give the word."

"No point in delaying things," Clarke mused. "We will move out tomorrow."

"Right, Colonel, I'll spread the word." Gabe seemed to pull himself together and licked his lips. "Colonel, Otis tole me what you're up to."

"Yes?"

"I want to be there – with all of you. I mean, you'll need some... someone to hold the horses."

"Gabe, that cough is not getting any better," Clarke said, kindly. "If you get a spasm during the raid..." He hesitated. Gabe must be sixty at least, yet he had been with them from the start. Clarke found sentimentality overruling his common sense: "And you are ready to go?"

The old man nodded.

"You get into trouble," Clarke warned, "no one can stop to help you."

"Just like the war – huh, Colonel?" Gabe grinned toothlessly. "Every man for hisself."

"That is correct, Gabe."

"Thanks, Colonel." Gabe nodded. "Be good to ride with the boys one last time."

Long after the old man had left, Nathan Clarke found himself dwelling on Gabe's words. It would be the last time that they would all ride again – together.

Now, Riley and Clarke drew up by the hitch rail where they dismounted and made a show of slipping the reins over the bar. Quickly, Gabe stepped in and gathered up the reins while around him the others moved to take up their stations.

"Are you ready for this?" Clarke asked of Gabe, concern in his tone.

"I'm fine, Colonel. Cold's got to the lungs – guess it's frozen them."

"Been smellin' snow on the wind," Riley commented. "Won't do to hang around."

"Then we had best get on with it." Clarke moved towards the door of the bank and opened it.

The warmth inside hit him as soon as he walked in with Riley by his side. Boldly, his nerves jangling, he strode over to the stove and warmed his hands. While there he flicked his eyes around and breathed a little easier. There were no other customers. He noticed the older cashier, Greenup Bird, was at his desk, writing in a ledger. A younger man, Bird's son William, was standing at the counter with a ready smile as Otis Riley approached him.

"Good afternoon, sir," William Bird greeted.

"Yeah," Riley growled, not interested in the pleasantries, as he flipped a ten-dollar bill on the counter. "Just need you to change that up."

"Yes, sir." William smiled, opening his drawer. "How would you like it changed up, sir?"

"Don't give a damn," Riley snapped, pulling out a sack from beneath his coat and slamming it down on the counter. "Just put all that cash in the sack, boy."

In an instant Greenup Bird was on his feet but before he could do anything, Nathan Clarke, moving with surprising agility, vaulted the counter, drew his six-gun and pointed it at the cashier.

"Make yourself useful," Clarke said with authority, producing a flour sack and thrusting it at the cashier. "Put the contents of that there vault of yours in here."

"You won't get away with this," the cashier said. "Someone'll see –" His voice faltered as he lifted his gaze to observe that there was a group of men outside the windows, their bulky frames preventing anyone looking in from the street or the saloon opposite.

Clarke tilted his head and jerked the barrel of the gun in the direction of the open vault. "I suggest you worry about the present," he suggested. "Do as you are told and you may have a future."

The remark made Otis Riley chuckle. Then he told the teller: "Best you give him a hand."

Reluctantly, William Bird joined his father where he continued to fill the sack that already contained the contents of the tills. When they were done, they handed the sacks to Clarke and Riley and stood there glaring at the robbers.

"You won't get very far," Greenup Bird protested angrily but said nothing more as it was clear that his futile protest fell on deaf ears.

"Close the door," Clarke said to Riley, who quickly obeyed. "All Birds should be caged."

For a moment Nathan Clarke stared at the vault door. He thought of locking them in but had no idea how long it would be before the imprisoned men would be discovered. They might even suffocate. He just hoped that fear would keep them caged until they felt that it was safe to emerge – at least long enough so he and his men could get out of town before the alarm was raised.

"Let's go," Clarke prompted.

Gabe Tremlett released the reins of the three horses as Clarke and Riley left the bank; the others moved towards their own mounts. That was when a coughing bout hit Gabe, the severity of it forcing him to his knees.

Clarke spun around and hauled the old man to his feet and virtually flung Gabe into the saddle. He lost precious seconds as he slammed Gabe's foot into a stirrup.

"Get going!" he roared, slapping the horse on the rear.

A handful of passers-by stopped to watch what was going on then gaped as guns appeared in the hands of the milling riders. Their attention was drawn to the bank where Greenup and William Bird were hammering on the window and yelling something, their voices muffled. Then the older Bird rushed to the door and opened it. "They've robbed the bank!" he wailed.

"Move out!" Clarke ordered his men, resisting the urge to fire a warning shot at the screaming cashier.

Across the street, Rankin sat astride his mount in the alley. He let loose with his six-gun, firing over the heads of the bystanders and forcing the cashier back inside the bank. As folk dashed for cover, Clarke and Riley urged their horses over the dusty hardpan, white clouds of air streaming from their mounts' flared nostrils.

Between them, Grey and Rankin created a crossfire, deliberately shooting at walls and windows rather than people. Hasty shots were returned but by then both men had turned their mounts, making good their escape by riding east and west.

On the outskirts of town, Clarke risked a glance over his shoulder and was grateful to see that he had not lost any men. It looked as though Rankin and Grey's covering fire had delayed any pursuit.

All that mattered to him was that they put as much distance as they could between any pursuers and their rendezvous point, for there was no doubt in his mind that there would be plenty of people who would hunt them down.

Nor was it long before they all became aware that there was a posse on their trail.

They were a few miles from Liberty when the first flecks of snow smacked into the hard riding band of fugitives. Flurries hurtled into them, carried on a fierce wind with a force that struck exposed skin like pellets. Within minutes, they rode heads down into a blizzard that wiped out their tracks.

Constantly coughing, Gabe rode alongside Clarke who kept a close eye on the old-timer and made sure that he remained in the saddle. He shuddered, feeling the cold bite into him, icy claws that sought their way into his bones.

He had never noticed it before – not in the winter fighting during the war. But he had been hardened then, not softened by the peace. And then he had not been on the wrong side of the law.

It was this act of nature that saved them as they veered eastwards and into the sanctuary of Matthew Grey's barn

The mood amongst the men was one of relief that quickly turned to a bout of joyous congratulations, all faces grinning. They had succeeded in their mission!

Inside the warm barn, they dismounted, heedless of the cold and the driving snow outside. Hands were thrust out towards Nathan Clarke but were met with a weak smile and a friendly clap on the shoulder before he drifted over to where Gabe Tremlett was slumped in a corner stall.

Nathan hunkered down beside the old man. "Close run thing, Gabe,"

Gabe shook his head in disbelief: "Just cain't get over it. Never thought we'd get clean away."

"Well, we did." Nathan smiled weakly. "And you earned your share."

"Forget it, Colonel. I don't want the money. It ain't a jot of use to me. Anywise, it was like I said – just one last ride."

Nathan began to protest but Gabe held up one hand to stop him while he delved into his coat pocket with the other. Slowly, he drew out a once white handkerchief and opened it. Seeing the thick mucus flecked with gobs of blood, Clarke drew back with horror on his face.

"See, Colonel," Gabe said. "The damn war already killed me. Just like it killed us all. None of us came back the way we was. War may be done but we ain't got peace – not a one of us." He thrust a finger at the others grouped around the barn. "And with them all gone, part of this – this community dies too."

The strain of all this talking caused Gabe to erupt in another coughing fit. Even though he was doubled up in pain, he climbed to his feet. "I'll get on my way." Gabe grinned, weakly. "Been nice ridin' with you."

"You take care, Gabe." Nathan Clarke smiled back but failed to hide the sadness in his eyes. As he stood and watched the old man mount up and ride away, he mulled over Gabe's words for a long while. He just stood there oblivious of the cold and what was going on around him until he was distracted by a gray shape emerging from the falling snow.

Seth Warwick reined in his mount and slid from the saddle. He led his horse inside and Clarke shut the door. Several seconds passed as Warwick slapped at his thick coat to dislodge a heap of snow.

"Well, Colonel, you did a fine job." Warwick grumbled out the words without praise. "You left a kid dead in the street. Least that's what folks are saying, but it could've been anyone with a gun in their hand."

"Anyone we know?" Clarke demanded with concern.

"A kid called George Wymore," Warwick stated pointedly.

"I know the family." Clarke eyed his men as their smiles vanished from their faces. "Damn it, I never wanted anything like that to happen."

Warwick nodded. "Yeah. But it happened and you had better get going. The way things are in town it looks like they're determined to hunt you down."

"They know who I am?" Clarke was worried now. "And the others?"

Warwick shook his head: "No one knows who robbed the bank. Questions are being asked but there's not a soul with a clue. Not that I'm saying any of you are safe."

"I take your point," Clarke conceded. "We had better get the money sorted and be on our way."

The division of the cash was easy with each man receiving over $2,000 apiece, but the bulk of the loot came in the shape of $40,000 in bearer bonds. Seth Warwick noted that many bore consecutive numbers and could lead to the discovery of the robbers' identities. Matthew Grey and one other were prepared to accept the risk and took their share while the remainder stayed with Seth Warwick who had "contacts" and ways to deal with the problem.

No one questioned this for they knew their lieutenant of old as a man who could procure anything and no one ever asked how.

Matthew Grey and his family traveled as far as Dodge City where he went into business with his brother-in-law who owned a feed and grain store.

Gabe Tremlett died of consumption three months after the robbery. His gravestone bore the legend: *He has gone on his last ride.*

Only Nathan Clarke, Otis Riley and Cyrus Rankin went to Texas. They rounded up a bunch of longhorns and drove them up to Abilene. On their return, they scouted for some land and made a deal with the Governor of Texas for the purchase that became the CR ranch.

Cyrus Rankin carved himself a chunk of land that he farmed, for he found that the ranch life was not for him.

Two years after the robbery, Seth Warwick paid a visit to the CR ranch. Nathan Clarke was sitting on the porch of his modest homestead. Warwick carried a bulky brown leather case that he plonked down beside the rancher.

"Mister Warwick," Clarke greeted him.

"Colonel," Warwick returned then pointed at the bag. "That's the last of it. Your share and Sergeant Riley's. Still got some of those bonds but they're mine."

"And the others?"

"Taken care of," Warwick confided, gazing out at the vastness.

"And you – how are you doing?" Clarke wondered, following the ex-lieutenant's gaze.

"Very well, as it happens." Warwick grinned. "You broke that damned Union bank, you know. Some businesses went under as well, including my employer. He had to sell up. Fortunately, I had the funds to buy him out. Pretty well set up now. I have shares in the railroad and a prosperous business all of which helped to have me appointed as a council member and a place on the board at the William Jewell College."

"Very impressive, Mister Warwick," Clarke observed as he pulled himself upright. "At least you made something of yourself without having to leave Liberty."

"Nothing to stop you coming back, Colonel," Warwick suggested, easily. "As far as folks are concerned, it was the James boys from Kearney who robbed the bank. Reckon they headed for Sibley over in Jackson County."

"They admit to it?"

Warwick shook his head: "They're not denying it either."

"As if they would." Clarke smiled.

"So what will you do with your money?" Warwick asked, waving his hand out at the landscape. "By the looks of things, it doesn't seem as though you need it."

"That is the thing, Mister Warwick," Nathan stated pointedly. "I – and I emphasise that – I never needed the money. Think well on that, Seth."

"So what will you do with that?" Warwick pointed at the case.

Nathan Clarke just smiled.

Nor did Seth Warwick get any insight into Clarke's plans during the few days that he spent on the ranch, but he was promised that things would be a lot different should he come by that way again.

Seth Warwick did return, and he found a thriving community had grown up in the small town of Ruskin. It had grown from a cluster of stores and a saloon to boast a bank, a school and a church, none of which could have happened without the injection of cash from an anonymous investor.

Warwick guessed at this investor's identity and when he asked the question *why?* – all he got was a knowing look and the cryptic comment: "When you next ride with Gabe Tremlett – you ask him why."

Author's note

The robbery at the Clay County Bank, Liberty, Missouri took place as described in this story. Generally, it is accepted that the first daylight bank robbery was carried out by Frank and Jesse James. Names were named and eyewitness accounts appeared long after the event. Despite a reward being offered by the bank for the capture of the bank robbers, it was never claimed. Who really robbed the bank remains a mystery and the only people who really knew what happened were the four men in the bank that day. This story is fiction but it offers a different slant to why the bank was robbed.

SHADOWS ON THE HORIZON

Bobby Nash

Bobby Nash writes prose (Evil Ways, Lance Star: Sky Ranger, Domino Lady, Sentinels, Full Throttle Space Tales, Green Hornet & Kato, Secret Agent X) *and comics* (Life In The Faster Lane, Fuzzy Bunnies From Hell, Demonslayer, Yin Yang, Bloody Olde Englund). *This is his first western. Find him at www.bobbynash.com.*

Doc Brand felt the rocks bite into his knees as he hit the ground.

Dust billowed around him as he slumped over onto his back. Eyes shut against the punishing bright glare of the sun, he lay there, contemplating whether or not it was even worth the effort to try and get back on his wobbly feet or if he should just keep his eyes closed and wait for the inevitable. He was bruised, battered, and the last coughing fit that racked his beaten body had brought up blood.

Doc had worked the county of Rock Creek for just a little under twenty years. There wasn't a man, woman, or child within a day's ride that he hadn't tended to in some fashion or another in all that time. He had always believed that his patients respected him for his years of devoted service.

Until today.

At best, he weighed a buck fifty on a good day. Of late, he'd been losing weight, despite continuing to eat normally. He had also noticed a slight tremor in his right hand that had not been there before. He wasn't sure when the shaking had started, but he felt it was disconcerting, to say the least.

After a while, he regained the strength to pull himself to his feet yet again. Every time he fell or simply stopped, swaying under the weight of his torment, he became disoriented.

Once the world stopped spinning wildly around him, he eyed the sun and the shadows of cactus and reckoned where he needed to go. On unsteady legs, he made his way across the hard land, the sun beating down on him and burning the back of his neck.

Despite his bruised knees and aching bloody body, Doc Brand set his chin and started walking again. Through cracked lips he cursed the vultures that circled above as well as the men who had left him in this predicament.

It started like any other day: he'd woken early. As was his routine, he walked up onto the hill at the edge of his property and watched the sun rise. Since he had been a young boy, he got a thrill out of watching the sun burn away the shadows on the horizon as the darkness retreated before the coming day. He never considered himself the literary type, but he found something about mornings to be almost poetic.

While the sun climbed, Doc fed the horses, checked the coop for a fresh collection of eggs, and filled the trough for the fat, lazy pig the Leonards had given him as payment for looking after old Pa Leonard when he fell ill last winter. After a breakfast of runny fried eggs, a fresh apple from the tree out back, and a couple cups of steamy black coffee, he felt ready for his final chore, sweeping the morning dust off the front porch. He'd only half completed this task, however, when he heard the unmistakable thunder of hoofs on dry earth that announced the approach of visitors. And from the sound of it, they were riding in fast.

It was rare that anyone stopped by to see him for any reason other than a medical emergency. Even those were few and far between since his semi-retirement. His replacement had a handle on things in town, but a few of his more stubborn patients didn't like being treated by someone as young as Doctor Thomas Porter, so they still came to him on occasion.

By the time two of the three riders dismounted by his front gate, he had already grabbed his medical bag from the bedroom closet and he was waiting on the top step of the porch.

"Doc!" a familiar voice shouted.

"Everett," he called back. "What's the matter?"

A young man, barely a day over eighteen, ran to the porch, kicking up a trail of dust in his wake. Doc knew the lad well. He had been there when the boy was born and had helped him through colds and a couple broken bones over the years. "Doc! It's my cousin Billy," Everett Gordon shouted. "He's been hurt!"

"Get him up here!"

Everett whistled and motioned toward the two young men to come closer. One man stayed on the horse while his friend walked the animal to the edge of the porch, using one hand to keep the horse reined in and the other to steady the swaying man in the saddle.

"This is Billy," Everett said as he helped the injured man off the horse. "An' this here is Jess Taylor."

Doc nodded a quick greeting while Billy's arms were supported on the shoulders of his two friends. As Doc checked Billy's belly wound, blood pooled on the porch and spilt on the ground. "Everett, this boy's been shot!"

"Yes, sir."

"Get him inside. That bullet has to come out."

The three men lifted the unconscious Billy and carried him through the doorway.

"What happened?" Doc asked as he cleared off his dining table and motioned for them to place the injured Billy there.

"Nothin' you need to worry about," Jess said before Everett could answer.

Doc immediately took a dislike to the stranger. He knew everyone in Rock Creek Valley, but he'd never met Billy or Jess before. Something about these two set off warning bells in his brain. He was good at reading people and these guys were trouble.

"Fair enough," he replied. "Everett, have your friend fetch some water from the well and you grab me some towels from the pantry over there." He pointed toward a shelf near the far wall where a stack of folded towels and washcloths lay.

The two men looked at one another for a moment, but did not move.

"Now!"

Once they were in motion, Doc pulled a sharp knife from his bag and cut open Billy's blood-soaked shirt. A small hole in the boy's abdomen oozed dark blood. The first order of business was to staunch the wound. Doc pulled a clamp from his bag and, with one of the towels Everett had brought to slow the flow of blood, he packed off the wound.

"We've got to get this bullet out before he loses any more blood. I need you to hold him steady!"

"O–okay," Everett stammered as he grabbed hold of his cousin's arms and held them fast.

"Where's that water?"

"Right here, old man. Keep your shirt on."

Doc's cheeks flushed, but he kept his anger in check. The needs of his patient were more important than putting Everett's friend in his place.

Doc went to the sink and washed his hands with carbolic soap. The last thing he wanted to do was cause an infection. From the cupboard he grabbed a bottle of carbolic acid solution, one of only a few remaining supplies he kept at his home. He returned to his patient to sterilize the wound.

He dug into the boy's gut. It took him a lot longer than it should have, partly because he kept an eye on Everett's friend and partly because his hands wouldn't stop shaking, but his forceps finally pulled out the .44 bullet.

"Is he gonna be alright, Doc?"

"I don't know, Everett. He's lost a lot of blood and there's still a big risk of infection. Luckily, the bullet didn't pierce the intestines. We need to get him into town so we can give him some proper treatment."

"Well, Doc," Everett said, "that might be a little tricky."

"Why? What did you do?"

Before Everett could answer, Jess interrupted, pointing a finger directly at the doctor. "All you need to worry about is patching Bill up so we can ride on out of here. You just patch him up good, old man, and keep your questions to yourself."

Doc bristled at being called *"Old man,"* but let it go. Something he never would have been able to do once upon a time. Before Sarah. At the moment, he had bigger problems than a bruised ego. "Ride out of here?" he said. "This kid can barely walk, much less rein a horse over uneven terrain. And something tells me you boys can't stick to the open trails."

"Well, that's not really your problem, is it?"

Doc stepped forward placing himself between the bleeding boy on his kitchen table and the stranger he'd let into his home. He didn't know Jess Taylor, but he knew his type very well. Men like him used intimidation as a weapon just as they might a pistol. In his youth, Doc had been very much like the man who stood before him. He did not like what he saw staring back at him.

The comparison was jarring, but he had laid the demons of his past behind him years ago. The man he had once been was long gone.

Right now, he needed to make sure this stranger knew he wasn't afraid of him. "Actually, it is very much my problem," Doc said coolly. "Once you brought him here he became my patient and that makes him my responsibility until he's recovered – or dead."

Jess huffed loudly and stomped off to the far end of the room, leaving Doc to tend to Everett. That's where the similarities between the doctor and the stranger ended. Unlike Jess Taylor, Doc Brand would never have backed down when challenged.

"Would you care to explain, Everett? Your Pa would be very upset if he could see you right now."

"I'm sorry, Doc," Everett said. "It wasn't supposed to happen like this."

"Like what? What did you d–?" Doc stopped short when he heard the creak of a floorboard behind him. He barely made the turn when Jess caught him on the chin with a haymaker.

Doc felt the splinters claw at his face after he dropped like a stone to the floor. He tried to lift himself back up, but a boot to the head made him reconsider.

After the second kick everything was dark and quiet.

The first thing Doc heard was the thunder.

It wasn't until he opened his eyes that he realized that it was the sound of three horses riding away from him across the hard terrain. His mouth was dry. He tried to spit, but tasted only the grit of dusty earth that had not seen rain in weeks.

He wasn't exactly sure where he was, but knew he wasn't at his home.

A quick survey told him the bad news. They'd left him in the wilds of the open country, far off the beaten tracks. So far out this way, it was doubtful he would run across anyone who could help him. It was a good half-day's walk, probably longer given his condition, to the nearest town, if he knew which direction town lay. It had been so long since he'd traveled beyond the confines of the county limits that nothing looked familiar. With no patients outside the county and no family to speak of anywhere, there never seemed to be a good reason to travel anymore, a decision he was quickly coming to regret. He had traveled extensively when he was younger, riding across the land wherever his horse would take him. Now, he found himself tiring far more easily than he had in those days of youthful adventure.

The sun was high in the midday sky and heat shimmered just above the ground as far as the eye could see. The only moisture in sight was the sweat that poured from his tired and bruised body.

Injured and without water, Doc knew the chances of getting out of this in one piece were slim. However, if there was one thing that had not changed with age, it was his stubborn streak. That, at least, he still had in common with the brash young man he had once been. He still didn't know how to back down from a challenge.

And he still hated to lose.

He hoped the town or his cabin lay not too far ahead, since he didn't know how long he could last out here without a hat.

Doc Brand started walking and, after what seemed an age, his steps faltered. The strength in his body was sapped away by the unremitting sun. Every bead of sweat was a little more of him, of his essence. He stumbled and fell, painfully hitting his knees on the hard ground.

Despite his bruised knees and aching body, Doc Brand regained the strength to pull himself to his feet, set his chin and started walking again.

Night fell on the town of Silver Springs.

Everett Gordon and Jess Taylor tied their horses outside of the new Silver Star hotel. Everett helped his cousin Billy off his mount and took the brunt of his weight.

Billy was weak from the surgery and now had a fever. Despite his claims to the contrary, Everett was worried.

Jess, on the other hand, didn't seem to care. He'd booked two rooms, one for Everett and Billy and a second for himself. Everett was concerned that spending the money so soon and in the same town where people knew him was a bad idea. When he voiced his concern, Jess lectured him on the tactics of hiding in plain sight.

"How's he doing?" Jess asked as Everett helped his wounded cousin into the bed.

"Not so good. He really needs a doctor."

"He's already had a doctor, remember? Do you really want to go through all those questions again? Questions we can't answer."

"I know. I know. But Billy's sick," Everett shouted. "I think he's dying!"

Jess grabbed the younger man by the shirt and jerked him close. "Now you listen to me, you little pissant. I'm about goddamned sick and tired of your complaining. It's not my fault your cousin was stupid enough to get himself shot, but I'll be damned if I'm gonna risk those federal marshals catching me because we took him to the town doctor. That's why we went to see the old man out in the country."

"Yeah," Everett said with only a slight tremble in his voice. "We didn't have to leave the doc out there to die – he's a good man."

"If I'd had my way, I'da shot him in his house. It's only your bellyaching made me take him part-way with us."

"But to die like that, when he tried to save Billy an' all…"

"He was old – past it. He'd be dead soon anyway."

"I still don't like it."

"Tough. I did what I had to. And you should take a lesson from that, Everett boy. I don't take none too kindly to people what irritate me." He smiled. "And right now, boy, you're starting to become an *irritant*." Jess pulled Everett closer until only a fly's width separated them. "Do I make my meaning clear?"

"Y – yes," Everett stammered.

Jess let go then pushed him away. "Good. Now I'm going to get a drink and maybe play some cards. You keep him quiet." Jess turned and left the room, closing the door behind him.

Trembling with shock, Everett sat on the edge of the bed and stared at his cousin's pale face. Beads of sweat had formed but, thank the Lord, Billy had drifted off to sleep. Or maybe he had simply passed out again from the pain. Everett could not be sure.

Everett sighed and whispered, "We've got to get out of here."

Billy did not answer.

Doc Brand walked through the night. More than once he wanted to lie down and sleep, but he would be damned if he was going to make it that easy for the coyotes that roamed these hills. If the notion of making a meal out of him crossed their minds, he was going to make them work for it.

The sun had just begun to rise over the mountains. It was a beautiful sight. As he walked on unsure legs, his thoughts turned to Sarah, much as they did every morning as he stood on the hill at the boundary of his land and watched the first rays of morning peek out over the mountains. Even after all these years, he missed her. When she left, the desire to witness the sunrise had almost gone with her.

The heat was already powerful and made his head throb. He doubted he'd be able to survive another full day in the beating sun without water.

Still, he trudged on.

An hour after sunup, he climbed up the slope of a hill that seemed oddly familiar. Heart pounding, he reached its crest and gazed down off to his right. Silver Springs sat in the distance, a white, red and gray checkerboard against the browns and greens of the countryside. His cracked parched lips twisted into a smile. Suddenly renewed, Doc Brand moved down towards the trail off to the left that led to his home.

It took a couple of hours to make it to his cabin fence and he was exhausted and dehydrated when he stumbled through the gate.

He noticed that his horse Stallion was all right in his corral, drinking from a trough. But his horse would have to wait. His first stop was the well. Lurching to its stone rim, he gulped handfuls of water from the pump before collapsing to the ground and letting the crisp, cool water splash over his body.

Finally, a sliver of strength returned to his battered form and he felt anger welling up in him. He raised his weary body and forced himself to stand.

Grimly, he turned and stepped up to the porch and went inside. Despite their violence against him, Everett and his friend had not damaged his house. Some provisions were missing, of course. Mostly food, but they had also taken the shotgun he kept by the front door to shoo off the occasionally over-curious bear or coyote. Thankfully, he realized they had not found his hidden cache of medicines.

He cleaned and bandaged his wounded and bleeding legs and knees. There were cuts and abrasions on his arms as well, but he paid them no mind. A split lip and cut on his face completed the checklist of injuries. Doc ingested some pain relief medication left over from the prescription he had filled for Emil Austin after his riding accident and made his way to the bedroom. Without even bothering to remove his wet muddy clothes, he collapsed onto the soft, hand-packed mattress. Sleep came quickly.

When Doc Brand woke, it was dark and his head pounded fit to burst. For the life of him, he could not remember going to bed or why he hurt so much in so many places. This wasn't old age, he felt sure. He lit the oil lamp by the bed and its buttery glow filled the bedroom. He swung his feet out and got up. It wasn't until he passed the small grooming mirror he used to shave that the fog shrouding his memory lifted. There was a sizeable cut above his left eye, which had turned a deep shade of purple since he bandaged it. Dried blood was caked to the left side of his face, obviously having poured from the cut on his forehead.

Slowly, carefully, he washed himself, checking to make sure he had not missed any of the cuts that littered his body. Once he was sure that he was no longer bleeding, he slowly and painfully put on clean clothes. Yet again, his body had betrayed him. This was not the first beating he'd ever taken, but never had it taken so much effort to perform so simple a thing as getting dressed.

Without too great an effort, he slid aside the small nightstand that for many years stood by his bed. Beneath it was a loose board that he lifted away. Reverently, he pulled out the box. He never expected to lay his hands on its contents again.

The pungent aroma of oil and gunpowder hit him as soon as he opened the lid. He lifted the first of two bundles from the box and carefully unwrapped it on his dining table, which was still coated with his patient's dried blood. That seemed a long time ago, too. Then he opened the second bundle.

It wasn't until he held them in his hands that he realized just how much he'd missed these twin revolvers. The walnut grip felt right pressed against the palm of his hands, which, he noted with some small satisfaction, were no longer trembling.

The material from a third bundle fell away and he strapped on the belt with its two leather holsters. The final bundle contained a box of fifty .45 cartridges.

Twenty years ago, he'd used these guns to kill a man he once called a friend. That one act was enough to make the gunfighter he had been surrender the lifestyle and move on. And he never looked back. He buried the man he was before and reinvented himself. One month after he laid down his guns, Doc Brand arrived in Rock Creek. Then he'd met Sarah, married and had eighteen wonderful years. She never knew about his past, though from time to time expressed curiosity. How could he explain he'd trained as a doctor only to find himself killing a man in self-defense, against his oath? He'd fled west and found he had an aptitude for killing and could live well as a hired gunman.

But that last killing changed him. He took up his old calling and swore never to hold a gun again. Being with Sarah made the promise easy to keep. And this cabin had been their home ever since.

And now three men violated it with an act of savagery.

Doc checked out the guns with care, wiping the preserving grease from their dark metal. He loaded five bullets into the cylinders that had been empty far too long. When he snapped the chamber closed, an electric thrill shot through his body. Suddenly, the bruises and cuts were forgotten. Age no longer mattered. Doc Brand faded to the background as the man he had once been resurfaced. He slid the guns smoothly into the holsters on his hips and made his way toward the door. With a swagger he had not felt in two decades, he stepped out onto the porch just as the sun began to peek over the horizon.

A new day dawned.

Doc Brand was no more.

Gentleman John Brand was back.

And death was never more than a few steps behind him.

John Brand rode Stallion into town as the morning sun cast long shadows. He did not know Jess Taylor well enough to second-guess him, but he had met plenty of men like him over the years. *He had been a man like him.* There were only a few places where they could go. He didn't know the particulars of whatever crime they committed, but it was a sure bet that theft was involved. Not to mention a gunfight with someone skilled with a rifle.

That narrowed the options. His first guess would be a stage carrying cash, probably to or from the local bank. Maybe the train, though he seriously doubted that the three of them could have pulled off a successful train heist.

As he rode past the bank, John slowed his horse's stride. Everything appeared normal, which only confirmed his suspicions. They had not robbed the bank. That left the stagecoach.

"Howdy, Doc," Mary Swan shouted as he rode past. Miss Swan ran the saloon. Though he hadn't taken a drink of the hard stuff in years, he'd gotten to know the lady when he patched up a few of her people after a few rough tussles. Most of the time, Miss Swan's saloon was a right friendly place, but every so often one of the local cowboys imbibed a few too many and decided he was ten foot tall and bullet-proof. That was usually when Miss Swan's muscle had to move in and cut said cowboy back down to size.

Plus, she made one helluva steak and potato dinner that he often took in trade for services rendered. Not that she couldn't afford to pay, but sometimes a home cooked meal went a lot farther than the two bits he normally charged.

"Miss Swan." He tipped his hat.

"You look like something one of my cats dragged in. You feeling alright?"

"A little rough around the edges, but none the worse for wear."

"If you say so." She gave a girlish laugh.

Not for the first time, he wished he were a younger man.

"Never seen you packing before," she said, nodding at his holsters. "What's the occasion?"

"I may be traveling down some unsavory country roads, Miss Swan. Never can be too careful."

"Well, take care, Doc."

He smiled and tugged gently and the horse stopped near the porch. The horse bent its neck and drank from the trough. "Have you seen Everett Gordon around today?"

"I don't think so," she said, thinking it over. "I'm pretty sure I saw him yesterday, though. He was with a couple other guys. New in town, I believe. I'd not seen them before. They were here playing cards for a few hours before they rode out of town."

"And you haven't seen them since?"

"One of the guys, I forget his name, a loud mouth, was here earlier. He'd drunk a bit too much and laid hands on one of my girls, roughed her up a bit. That's when James politely asked him to take his business elsewhere."

"You think your boy James saw where he went?"

"I can find out, I suppose," she said, concern now coloring her voice. "What's this all about, Doc?" She eyed his six-guns.

He forced a friendly smile. "Nothing to fret over. I just need to talk to them."

"Uh huh. Talk, eh? Doc, what did they...?"

"Just find out which way he went," John said in a tone he had never used in her presence before. "Now, please."

"Uh, sure," Miss Swan said. "I'll be right back."

"I'll be here," John Brand said. "I'm not going anywhere."

Miss Swan's enforcer, James, told him that the drunken boy whom he believed to be Jess Taylor had staggered toward the Silver Star Hotel.

Brand thanked the man and rode off, heading to the far end of Main Street. He noted that Miss Swan had not returned to the porch to bid him *adieu*, which seemed out of character in their relationship.

Perhaps she picked up on his intentions. The weapons were a dead giveaway, he reckoned.

It would not have surprised him if that were the case. He had noticed that women more often than not understood a man's intentions with little more than a look. It was damned unnerving, but was one of those little quirks that made women so irresistible. For the first time since he'd met her, Brand was glad he wasn't younger. Something told him that Miss Swan would not have liked him as much if he were.

It didn't take long to reach the hotel; he was in no hurry. His eyes scanned the street, keeping a wary glance for anything out of the ordinary. He had walked into an ambush once and the experience had taught him a very valuable lesson. Always know your surroundings. It was an education that had not lessened with time.

The lobby of the Silver Star Hotel was not that different from the saloon Miss Swan ran. Perhaps it was a bit classier to the untrained eye, but once the cowboys, ranchers, and gunslingers made themselves at home the two places became all but identical. They were loud, smoke-filled... and, well, very loud.

No one looked twice at him when he entered.

A piano stood in one corner of the lobby and a well-dressed man tapped at the ivories, his back to the room. John didn't recognize the tune. There were a few tables in the lobby where several spirited games of poker were being played. All in all, it appeared to be a nice quiet day.

"Hello, Jacob. Everett Gordon?" he asked a pudgy man behind the counter. Jacob Talmadge had a bum leg; Doc operated on it ten years back when Jacob was injured in an explosion while handling a crate of dynamite.

"Room Two, Doc."

"Second floor?"

"Yes." Jacob added, curious, "That boy with him looks in a mighty bad way, Doc. I bet he'll be glad to see you."

"No. He won't."

"He won't?" Then Jacob seemed to notice for the first time Doc's gun-belt. "Doc, can I ask what–?"

"No."

Without another word, John Brand made his way up the flight of stairs. By the time he reached the second floor landing, he was wheezing a little and his bruised body protested at the exertion. The hotel seemed less crowded once he'd escaped the noise of the lobby. As he reached the door to room number two, he had a pistol in his right hand.

He raised a fist to knock, but then thought better of it.

Carefully, he tried the knob with his left hand and was not too astonished when it opened. Everett had never been the smartest of young men, so he wasn't surprised that the boy had not thought to lock the door.

The door's hinges squeaked and alerted Everett, who was sitting at the side of the bed where his cousin lay quite still. From his pallor, the boy called Billy was beyond help. If the boy wasn't dead yet, he soon would be.

Everett looked at Doc as if he had seen a ghost.

"Hello, Everett."

"D– Doc... You're alive?"

"Where is he?"

"Doc?"

"Where's your friend, Everett? Jess, the swine who attacked me, where is he?"

"Right behind you, old man."

Brand stiffened slightly. He had not heard Jess Taylor's approach, which made him far angrier than the gun he heard being cocked behind him.

"You here to finish the job, Mr Taylor?"

"You're a tough old codger, I'll grant you that. Toss your gun."

Brand didn't move, still gripping the pistol.

"Are you *deaf* as well?" Jess asked angrily. He reached forward, his hand closing over the butt of the gun in the holster at the Brand's left hip. "I said–"

Before the younger man could get the words out, John Brand swiveled, knocking him off balance, his left fist delivering a wild punch that caught him on the side of the head.

Jess Taylor hit the floor awkwardly, losing grip on his pistol, which clattered across the floor, stopping just out of reach.

Gentleman John leveled his six-gun at the man on the floor and cocked back the hammer. "Now, what was it you were trying to tell me, youngster?" he said with a hint of sarcasm. "My hearing ain't what it used to be."

Jess Taylor trembled slightly, partly from rage, but mostly from fear. For all his bravado when facing a weak older man, as he had perceived the doctor to be when they met the day before, he had been as brash as they come. But against someone more than willing to fight back, that bravado dissipated.

"That's what I thought," Gentleman John said. "This is your lucky day, boys. Whether you realize it or not, you did me a big favor and I'm feeling generous. I do have a piece of advice for you."

"And what's that?"

"If you beat up a man and dump his body for the vultures, you should make sure he's actually dead." He kept the gun trained on Jess as he spoke. He had a feeling that the angry young man would not let this go so easily.

Everett was less of a concern.

Jess searched the room with his shifty eyes, doubtless seeking anything that could save him. The Spartan decor offered few options. Still on his knees, he raised his hands in surrender.

Brand's face twitched a grin.

Jess's eyes went wide.

"Don't."

Jess leapt for the pistol lying on the floor, scooping it up and turning it toward the man who had knocked him down.

He was not fast enough.

Brand squeezed the trigger and felt the hard steel buck in his hand as it fired.

The impact of the .45 bullet hit Jess in the chest and he folded backwards against the bed frame. Without a sound, he fell face down to the floor. Blood pooled beneath him, soaking into the large sheepskin rug that covered the center of the room.

Without blinking, Gentleman John Brand turned the gun on Everett. "What's it gonna be, Everett? Your call."

Trembling, the young man stood and walked away from the bed and headed toward the door.

Everett kept the gunman in sight and never turned his back on him. Once he made it to the hallway, the boy broke out into a run.

Brand listened to his footsteps clattering down the stairs. "Smart boy," he said as he holstered his pistol.

John Brand cinched his saddlebag tight. It surprised him that after twenty years in Rock Creek, the longest he'd ever put down roots in any place, he could still fit everything he owned of value inside his old leather saddlebag.

After the shooting in the hotel, Everett Gordon was arrested in the foyer. The marshal questioned the Doc but, after seeing the bruises and swelling on Doc's face and arms, coupled with Everett Gordon's confession, he decided the death was self-defense and considered the matter closed.

For a short while, Brand considered putting the guns back in their hiding place and settling once more into his routine. Rock Creek would always need a doctor. Even a semi-retired one.

But some small voice in the corner of his mind, an echo of the man he had once been, wouldn't let him put the guns back in the box. He understood. He had said as much to Jess Taylor before pulling the trigger. They had done him a favor.

John Brand remembered who he truly was.

Old Doc Brand had been a mask, one he had happily hidden behind for Sarah's sake, but now that she was gone, was there a reason to keep hiding?

The only answer that made sense was *no*.

This particular morning began as so many before it had. He woke early, as was his routine. Then he stood on the hill where they had watched the sun rise for eighteen years.

After a hearty breakfast of beans, ham and eggs, he packed a bag.

Mounting his horse, Brand cast one last look at his cabin. He rode past the grave and doffed his hat. "Be seeing you soon, honey," he said and moved his horse to the gate.

A letter was set to be delivered to Miss Swan. With it was the deed to his cabin and land. She'd been nice to him over the years and he wanted her to have it. A final thank you for being his friend. He also asked her occasionally to put fresh flowers on Sarah's grave. He suspected Miss Swan would be all too happy to do so. She'd been Sarah's friend as well, after all.

Brand knew he would never return to Rock Creek. There was so much of the new frontier that he had not seen, so many places yet to visit. He pointed his horse west.

"Time to move on, Stallion," he told the horse. Without looking back, Gentleman John Brand rode off toward the darkness as the sun rose behind him, pushing the shadows on the horizon farther and farther west.

ON THE RUN

Alfred Wallon

Alfred Wallon, born on May 20th 1957, is a native German and started to write professional western novels in 1981. He has written about 150 short brochure novels and 30 paperbacks and hardcovers in various genres. His favorite novel is the historical western. He is an active member of Western Writers of America. In early 2008 he started collaboration with David Whitehead, All Guns Blazing, *a western novel written under the pen-name Doug Thorne. Other projects with David Whitehead are in progress. Currently, Wallon concentrates on his western family saga* Rio Concho *in Germany and has planned other western novels for different publishers. His website is: http://www.alfred.realxxl.de*

"Damn it, he's dying!"

Ed Collins heard the fear in Bob Tolliver's shrill voice, but he rode on ahead without looking back.

"Ed, for God's sake!"

The urgency in Tolliver's voice finally stopped Collins.

He turned in the saddle, his shoulder-length blond hair flaring in the breeze. Not many men could hold Ed Collins's eyes; he was a tough-looking man of forty-five winters. He glanced at Fisher, who was now in such bad shape that he could hardly sit straight on his lathered horse.

Fisher was some five years younger, bald headed and pale-faced, and he had both hands pressed to his stomach. His eyes were screwed up tight and he was muttering words that Collins couldn't make out. He reckoned Fisher couldn't endure the hard ride any longer.

Collins took off his hat and wiped the sweat from his forehead. He cursed under his breath when he noticed Tolliver trembling. Normally, Tolliver was very cold, especially when push came to shove. But now sweat turned his dark hair black and he looked pallid beneath his suntan. Collins couldn't remember ever seeing Tolliver scared, but he was scared now.

Yet just a few hours earlier, everything had looked just dandy. They'd paid a short and sudden visit to a small bank in a remote cow-town. The hold-up was Fisher's idea, dreamed up when he found out most of the local farmers left their money in this bank. Trouble was, once they'd emptied the safe, the bank's manager, gun in hand, chased them out into the street. Collins shot him, but the bastard still managed to fire in return and nailed Fisher.

None of them were strangers to violence. And the robbery hadn't been the first hold-up for any of them. Wanted posters gave evidence to their careers as bank robbers and killers. But it was the first robbery that had ever gone so terribly wrong.

"We gotta stop now!" Tolliver said. Getting more and more nervous, Collins reckoned.

They'd worked their way through a rocky canyon for about half an hour. The sun bounced off the sheer sides, scorching. They lacked canteens. If they didn't find water soon, the heat would kill them before any posse caught them. They knew they were being followed. At least half the township was on their back-trail, looking to get their money and then dispense some good, old-fashioned hang-rope justice.

"Ed, you hear me?"

"I hear you!" snapped Collins. "Now you hear this! If we stop, we *all* die. Fisher, me, *you* – all of us!"

"Fisher's got to rest."

"Why? He's as good as dead right now. What difference is a ten-minute rest going to make?" Collins heard the fear in his own trembling voice. He expected the posse to catch up at any moment. They'd pushed their mounts hard to put as much distance as possible between them, but with the shape their horses were in now, the sheriff and his posse could be making up lost time. Collins had already spotted dust on the horizon. He knew their chances were fading by the minute.

"Look at him," Collins invited grimly. "You really think he'll make it? He's gut-shot. Sooner or later, he'll die." Collins rubbed at his whiskers. "Man, I wish we could turn back the clock. I'd never agree to do that job."

Fisher was doubled over with tremendous pain, but he heard what Collins said. He tried to speak, but no words came. With a grimace, he fell from his saddle. He grunted as he hit the hard stony ground.

Tolliver quickly dismounted at Fisher's side. He went pale when he looked into the fallen man's face. "Ed!" he cried. "Ed, he ain't breathin' – he's dead!"

Collins showed no reaction. That was Fisher's hard luck, he figured, and nobody could change it. Now there were only the two of them left. It meant that the money would divide easier: about ten grand each. "Come on," Collins growled. "Let's raise dust."

"What? You mean just *leave* him here?"

"Well, we ain't got time to bury him. We ain't even got time to say words over him."

Tolliver struggled to understand. "It's not Christian," he argued.

"No. It ain't. But it might just save us from joinin' him in Hell."

"Yeah, that's true enough, I guess. But what about his horse?"

"It'll just slow us down," said Collins. "Leave it."

Tolliver hesitated over the body of Fisher for a few seconds then nodded. "Alright." He quickly remounted, and when they rode out he didn't look back.

Collins's lips twitched in a half smile of satisfaction. Fisher's death brought it home, alright. They had to look to themselves now, to their own survival. The posse rode ever closer, and if they should catch up then it was over for them, *everything* was over.

Hoof-beats – a lot of them – sounded in the distance. Not a good sign.

The robbers rode hard and fast. They reached the end of the canyon and then turned west, over a saddleback and through a small creek.

Something wasn't quite right with Collins's horse. It began to favor its offside forefoot, and its normally steady gait gradually grew wayward. About fifteen minutes later, the horse wagged his head, snorted loudly and stopped dead.

"What's wrong, Ed?" Tolliver sounded like he already knew and dreaded the answer.

Collins dismounted and inspected the horse's offside leg. He cursed loudly. "Damn! Gone lame on me!" The horse's fetlock was badly swollen: he'd travel no further this day.

"We should've brought Fisher's mount..."

"Quit grousing about what we should've done, Bob. What's done is done."

"Yeah, right. We better get off this road," fretted Tolliver, throwing a glance over a shoulder. "Soon as we can. Come on!"

For once, Collins didn't argue but merely nodded. He gathered his reins and led the horse slowly forward. They had to find him a fresh horse, and fast, else they'd be at the mercy of that posse and finished for good.

The lame horse protested with a loud snort, but Collins kept a short rein and the animal had no choice but to obey. Collins wanted to let the horse take it easy, but he had no time. They had to find cover and hope the posse didn't spot the tracks leading to it.

God alone knew where they were now. Fisher had been the only one who knew the area, but he was dead. Collins and Tolliver came from Colorado and had never been in this county before. They had no idea where to go other than keep on pushing west.

His face burned and sweat stung his eyes. Collins was slowly but surely reaching the end of his reserves.

Tolliver fared no better. Forced to walk with Collins, he now constantly stumbled over his own feet.

The sun still hadn't reached its highest point when Collins stopped at the top of a hill, the horse's muzzle nudging his shoulder. A smile came to his cracked lips. "Bob! Come quick! Look at this!"

Tolliver hurried after him as best he could.

About a hundred yards below lay a small farmhouse with an adjoining stable. Nearby, a man was repairing a corral. No other living soul seemed to be around. Most important to Collins's mind were the half dozen horses within the corral.

"We'll go in, take two fresh mounts," Collins said, "and then we'll shake this damn' place from our heels once and for all!"

The farmer showed no surprise when the two weary trail-dusted men led their horses down the slope toward him. That struck Collins as odd: after all, they both had guns aimed at the farmer's belly.

"Just stay where you are, old man," Collins called when they were close enough. "Bob, you take a look around the house!"

The old man watched Tolliver inspect the house. He looked about sixty with deep wrinkles and gray hair, but still stood tall and straight. The look in his blue eyes underlined the fact that he was not really all that old. "I'm alone here, boy," muttered the oldster. His voice was deep, and his eyes mirrored something Collins did not like at all. "Why don't you put that gun away?"

Collins was still suspicious, but decided to lower his six-gun. The old man was no threat to him and Tolliver. If the old man dared to attack, Collins would kill him without a second thought.

A moment later, Tolliver reappeared in the yard. "No. No one else around, Ed."

Collins nodded and looked at the corral. A smile crossed his whiskered face. "We'll trade you our horses for two of yours, old man," he said. "The fastest two."

The old man shrugged. "You're the ones with the guns. Take your pick and get the hell out of here."

Tolliver frowned. "I don't like your tone, mister. Maybe I should teach you some manners. Whaddaya think, Ed?"

Collins shook his head. He thought of a scheme that might save him and Tolliver. "We'll take him with us," he said. "All the way to the state line."

Tolliver looked puzzled. "He'll just slow us down!"

"Nuh-uh. This way, he can't tell the posse which way we headed or how far ahead we are. And think about this. Even if they *do* catch up, there's nothin' they dare do while we got us a hostage!"

The farmer took the news placidly. "Well, best we get to it," he said in a mild voice.

"Bob," said Collins, "pick the three best horses." Tolliver knew horseflesh, and Collins had complete faith in his judgment.

After they'd saddled and bridled the horses, Collins gestured that the old man should mount up. "Do what I tell you, *when* I tell you, and you'll live through this," he said.

The old man merely shrugged and toed into leather.

Half an hour down the trail, Collins turned to the old man. "You got a name?"

"Jefferson Davis," the old man said.

Collins blustered, "Like hell you are!"

"Oh, I'm not in any way related to the former president of the Confederacy. No way." He doffed his hat and mopped his lined and wrinkled brow.

Collins laughed. "You don't say."

Tolliver grinned.

A while later, they came to a crossroads, where they stopped.

"I guess you fellers reckon you hold all the aces right now, don't you?" Davis said.

"I reckon – and why not?" said Tolliver, some of his usual braggadocio returning. "We just stole twenty grand from a bank in Cedar City."

Davis frowned. "I keep money in that bank. Two hundred dollars."

Collins gave an insolent grin. "Well, tell you what," he said. "We'll pay you back your two hundred right after we cross the – " Collins swallowed at the sound of hoofs coming, moving fast and getting nearer.

Collins eyed Tolliver. They both drew their weapons.

"Simmer down, boys," said Davis. Three riders approached from the south side of the crossroads. "I know these men. They don't mean you any harm. They work for the Broken T."

"You'd better be right, old man," snarled Collins, holstering his weapon. "'Cause if you're wrong, you'll be the first one to die." Tolliver tucked his six-gun in his waistband and hid it with his vest.

The three newcomers rode closer. As Davis said, they were cowboys. Plain honest workers, from the looks of them. When they saw Davis and his two companions, they reined in and nodded howdy.

"'Afternoon, Mr Davis."

"Howdy, Trent."

"You're a long ways from home," noted one of them, a guy about six feet tall with hair that showed the first signs of gray. "Where you headed?"

Without hesitation, Davis said, "The railhead at Willow Springs. This here's my nephew Alex and his friend Garrett. They need to be on the next train out, so if you'll excuse us –"

"Sure thing, Mr Davis. Well, boys, have a nice journey."

"Remember me to your boss," said Davis.

Seconds later, the cowboys rode on and disappeared out of sight behind a hill.

"You did good, Davis," muttered Collins.

Davis threw him a withering glance. "I'm not fond of riskin' my life and, believe it or not, I really love my farm. I want to make sure I live to see it again."

"You will, you keep playin' straight with us." Collins's eyes, however, told a different story.

About an hour later, the sun was well on its way toward the horizon when they came to a weathered sign. A grove of maple bordered the trail on either side. The sign told them the border was a mile ahead. Collins and Tolliver relaxed visibly. They'd made it, or as near as dammit.

Then Davis reined his horse in.

"What's up, old man?" Tolliver demanded.

"Don't rightly know," replied Davis. "Could be a thorn. I'd better check, anyway..." He slowly dismounted and moved round to the offside of his horse, so it was between him and the robbers.

"Well, hurry it up," said Collins, his palm on his gun-butt. "We're not out of the woods yet."

"Yup, it's a thorn. Won't be a minute."

While Davis checked his horse, Tolliver leaned over and whispered, "You really gonna kill the old man?"

A big black crow cawed and flew out of the trees, distracting them. Eyeing it, Collins said, "Sure. Never leave a witness behind, Bob. You never know when they might come back and bite you in the ass." He turned back to Davis – but the old man wasn't with his horse.

Branches moved among the trees along the road and a shape darted into the shadows.

"Damned sonofabitch!" cursed Collins. "He's got into those trees!"

Collins turned his horse to chase Davis.

"Ed!" Tolliver screamed. The shrill quality of his voice warned Collins that something bad was about to happen – or already had.

Sure enough, it had.

Up ahead, a group of armed men broke cover and slapped rifle-stocks to their shoulders or thrust handguns out to arms'-length. Collins's eyes went wide and he screamed, "Sonofa –"

The gunmen opened fire.

The fusillade tore through men and mounts. Tolliver took bullets in the face and stomach. He wheeled backwards off his horse. A moment later, the horse grunted and went down on top of him.

Collins fared little better. The first bullet cored through his left arm. As he clutched at the wound with his right hand, another bullet bored into his right leg. He hunched up and, through a red mist of pain, he saw Davis join the attackers. "You shot my dadblamed horse!" Davis shouted.

Then a third bullet caught Collins in the shoulder and threw him out of the saddle.

His world suddenly went very quiet and very black.

When he regained consciousness, Collins found himself looking into Jefferson Davis's grim face. Davis was surrounded by the men who'd ambushed him and Bob. They all wore deputy badges. The Cedar City posse, for sure.

"Decided to join us again, huh?" Davis's voice was hard now, not at all mild and reasonable, nothing like a gentle farmer.

Collins tried to answer, but couldn't. His throat was too tight, too dry.

He watched Davis draw something from his jacket pocket. It glistened in the afternoon sunshine. The old man carefully pinned it to his vest.

It was a tin star.

"Reckon maybe it's time I introduced myself properly," the old man said. "I'm Jefferson Davis, County Sheriff."

Collins managed, "Wha ...?"

"You boys ran out of luck when you crossed my path," Davis said. "Naturally, you weren't to know I always spend Sundays on my farm. It suits me. I'm a peaceable man who loves the quiet life."

Collins looked at the faces around him. One of the posse men held between his fists a coiled rope. A hangman's noose already dangled at its end.

"H– how ... how did the p-posse know where we went?" he asked, as if it really mattered at this late stage.

"Oh, that's easy," said Davis. "You remember the cowboys we met earlier?"

Collins nodded.

Sheriff Davis continued, "I told them you were my nephew and we were headed for the railhead at Willow Springs. Well, that's where we are now, boy. There *used to be* a railroad depot here, but it closed two years back. A little further east, you can still see the right-of-way, but not from here. So the cowboys knew right away what I was saying."

Collins swore.

"Never underestimate an old man," Davis said, "especially when he's the law."

Collins felt his face drain of blood. Much longer and all they'd have to hang was a corpse. He cursed loudly as they hauled him up and sat him on his horse. Pain from his wounds lanced into him. He eyed the noose in the deputy's hands.

Sheriff Davis spat on the ground. "As much as I'd like to string you up now, son, I'm taking you in. If you survive the journey back, you'll get a fair trial. *Then* we'll hang you."

THE GIMP

Jack Martin

Freelance writer, actor and novelist, Gary Dobbs writes as Jack Martin. As an actor he has appeared in Doctor Who, Torchwood, Gavin and Stacey, Moonmonkeys, Larkrise to Candleford *and* The Risen. *His début novel* The Tarnished Star *has been remarkably successful and his second western* Arkansas Smith *is due out in 2010. You can find him at his blog: http://tainted-archive.blogspot.com/.*

"Are you coming to the hanging?" his mother asked.

Jed looked across at her. She seemed impossibly old, her skin like leather, her back stooped from a life on the frontier. Only her eyes showed any sign of vivacity. He shook his head. On Sunday they were hanging Juan Sanchez. He'd been tried and found guilty of murder. Now he had an appointment with the hemp. Jed didn't much like hangings. He'd seen one as a child and still vividly remembered where the horse-thief's head was torn clean off by the fall.

"Whole town'll be there," she persisted and placed the plate of eggs, beans and bacon on the table in front of her son. "It's going to be right after church service. People like a good hanging after praying."

"No, Ma." Jed mouthed a whole egg in one go and swallowed noisily. "I won't be going to no hanging."

She clucked her tongue against the roof of her mouth. "Too soft by far," she said and went outside to smoke her corncob pipe.

All his life Jed Wilcox had wanted to be a lawman. That's what he always thought about, dreamt about. His father had been the sheriff over at Midas County and the old man claimed that his father before him had ridden with the Southern Regulators and what were they – if not special lawmen with jurisdiction across territories? 'Course the job had killed the old man; the Giles Gang gunned him down when he came between them and the bank they were trying to rob, but that grim fact did little to dissuade Jed from his ambitions to wear a tin star. Indeed if anything it strengthened his desire. Wearing a star would not only continue the family tradition, but would somehow give meaning to his father's death.

It was not likely to happen, though. A childhood bout of smallpox had left him with a permanent limp, a twisted left foot. People called him "Gimp" and laughed when he told them that one day he'd overcome his handicap and become a lawman, perhaps the most famous the West had ever known. He would be seventeen this next birthday, which hardly made him a boy anymore, and already the years were running out on him.

Sanchez, a small wiry man with eyes that appeared black in a certain light, waived counsel at his trial, which pleased Judge Berry no end since it was obvious the Mex was guilty so why waste time litigating. Several witnesses, a saloon-full in fact, saw Sanchez coldly gun down Forest Harper in an argument over a card game in The Golden Nugget.

The star witness, a man called Perkins, had been sitting next to Harper when Sanchez had blasted him. Indeed, Perkins had fainted clean away when a large portion of the unfortunate man's brains splattered warm and sticky across the side of his face. At the trial he had looked across the courtroom at Sanchez and said in a calm, clear voice that there was no doubt, he had seen the Mexican smile as he emptied the contents of a U.S. Model 1841 Mississippi Rifle into the gambler. 'Course Perkins hadn't been able to say what Sanchez had done directly after the shooting but there were plenty of men willing to take up the story from that point onwards.

Throughout the proceedings, Sanchez sat like a man untroubled by any burden. On occasion, he had in fact appeared mildly jaded and didn't seem to hold any animosity towards those who testified against him. At one point the judge felt obliged to stop the trial while someone woke the Mex who'd fallen asleep sometime during the last witness's testimony. Even when the judge read out the verdict – that Sanchez was to be hung by the neck until he was dead, dead, DEAD – Sanchez retained his composure, which seemed a curious mixture of amusement and boredom.

The hanging, as with all hangings in the territory – leastways those of a legal kind – would take place at noon on Sunday. The figuring behind this was that a man was closer to his Maker on a Sunday and would be more likely to find forgiveness in the after-life if he paid for his earthly transgressions on the Sabbath.

Once the trial was over, Sanchez calmly allowed himself to be led back to the jailhouse by Sheriff Morton and his deputy. All seemed to agree that the Mexican was one cool character and, in a strange way, rather likeable.

Jed crossed the street and headed towards the jailhouse.

It was cattle season and the smell of the hundreds upon hundreds of beeves that had earlier passed through towards the Cape Cattle Company stockyards hung heavy in the air. Jed sidestepped several times to avoid the calling cards the cattle had left behind. This wasn't particularly easy given that his left foot would twist and drag behind him. Stepping in shit was bad enough but Jed had to be extra careful because he'd end with it running all up the inside calf of his left pants leg. Which simply ruined his whole day because he couldn't wear boots since his misshapen leg wouldn't allow it. His soft moccasins offered scant protection.

"Howdy, Sheriff Morton," Jed said as he entered the sheriff's office. "Anything you want doing today?"

"Sit down before you fall down." Morton's words were harsh but his weathered face was kindly as he watched Jed walk over to a hard chair, his wayward left leg dragging, and perched on it.

Jed was eager to do whatever it was the sheriff had in mind for him today. Usually, he would run a few errands, pin up the odd wanted notice around town or more often than not fetch a pail of beer from the saloon and food for the prisoners. The sheriff and his deputy often joshed him, saying he was working up to becoming a lawman and that one day they'd deputize him for real. Jed didn't mind all that, though. Simply being around here made him feel something like a lawman.

Morton sucked on his pipe and allowed a fragrant cloud of smoke to escape between his teeth before speaking. "You ever handled a rifle?" he asked.

Jed looked at the sheriff in amazement. "Who won the turkey shoot last spring, Sheriff? I reckon there ain't many who use a long gun better than me," he said. The Sheriff should know well that Jed Wilcox was a crack shot with long gun or short, and practiced with his dad's old guns whenever he had the cash to buy cartridges. If he was fast and accurate with a gun, maybe that would help make up for his game leg.

The sheriff stood up and grabbed a Spencer from the cabinet beside the door. He ran a hand through his thinning gray hair and smiled then tossed the gun to Jed. "Careful," he said. "It's loaded."

Jed caught the rifle and gave the sheriff a look of sheer puzzlement.

Morton glanced towards the rear of the building where Sanchez slept in his cell. "D'you think you can handle it?" he asked.

"Handle what?"

The sheriff grinned but it was without humor. "I've got to go round up Deputy Richards," he said. "Damn fool's gone and gotten himself locked up over at Four Winds. The damn fool followed some rustlers across the town limits. He's been charged with operating outside his jurisdiction or some such nonsense. I'll clear it all up and be back before dark."

Jed looked first at the rifle and then at the sheriff. His face must have betrayed his confusion because the sheriff smiled and shook his head.

"I want you to keep an eye on our prisoner Sanchez back there," Morton said.

Jed stole another quick glance at Sanchez. The Mexican was asleep, oblivious of them both. "Really? No Joshing?" He realized how he must sound and he corrected himself. "Sure, I can do that." He limped to the rear of the building and satisfied himself that the outlaw was really sleeping. When Jed came back, the sheriff was buckling his gun-belt.

"I'll be back by sundown," the sheriff said. "Mary'll bring grub over from the eatery around four; other than that, don't let anyone in here."

"Sure," Jed said.

"Good." Morton tapped the cooled ashes from his pipe into his hand and rubbed them over his pants leg. "Good for the fabric," he explained. "Keeps it strong."

Jed nodded and then looked down at the rifle. He tested its weight in his hands and liked the balance. He jacked the lever halfway to make sure there was a cartridge in the chamber. He smiled. "Does this mean I'm a deputy now?" he asked.

The sheriff smiled. "Maybe," he said. "We'll talk later." The sheriff placed his battered Stetson on his head at a rakish slant and strode out the door. A moment later, Jed heard his horse moving away.

"Hey, kid," Sanchez called. "Come on over here."

Jed glanced at Sanchez and then pulled his father's fob watch from his pocket. It was a little after three. The watch was a constant reminder of his late father and Jed felt the old man's presence, like a ghost, as he stared at its worn face. "What do you want?"

"Some water," Sanchez said. "I'm dry." He banged his empty pitcher against the bars of his cell.

Jed nodded. He held the rifle in the crook of his arm while he hobbled and collected the empty pitcher from Sanchez. He took it over to the corner and filled it from the pot.

"Here you are," Jed said. He carefully maneuvered the pitcher back through the bars of the cell while balancing the rifle under his arm.

"*Gracias, amigo*," Sanchez said. He took a huge gulp before placing the pitcher back on the small table, which, except for the hard bunk, was the only other furniture in the small cell. He sat down on the edge of the bunk and rasped a hand over the stubble on his chin.

"You'll get some grub soon," Jed said.

"Don't figure they'd starve me before they hang me."

"You scared?"

Sanchez smiled so wide that every tooth in his head was visible, standing out in brilliant contrast against his swarthy face. "No."

"How come?"

"Ain't no point in being scared." His face clouded over for a moment but then he smiled again, shook his head and laughed. "If this is my time to go, then that's fine by me. *Gracias a Dios.*"

"I don't cotton much to the things you've done," Jed said. "But it sure looks like you've got sand."

"Ain't sand," Sanchez said. "But I ain't as bad as folks say. I made my confession to *el padre*. I am at peace. I do not fear death."

"Mighty fine sentiments," Jed said. He shifted the weight of his stance to relieve the numbness creeping into his bad leg. "You've killed people, though." It wasn't a question.

Sanchez grinned. "I have," he agreed. "But I never kill anyone who did not deserve it."

"Surely that's for the Almighty to decide?"

"Kid, when someone points a gun at me, I sure do not wait for *El Dios* to make a decision. I kill the son-of-a-bitch."

Jed smiled. "That's a very good point."

Presently, Sanchez asked, "You got a smoke? The one thing I could use right now is a smoke. I clean used up the last of my baccy yesterday and the sheriff is not too obliging with his."

"I don't–" Jed said and then hesitated. "I'll see if the sheriff's left any in his desk."

Jed limped as quickly as possible over to the sheriff's desk and opened the center drawer. Sure enough, wrapped in a sheet of waxpaper was at least an ounce of the sheriff's usual shag. He placed the rifle carefully on the desk and then rooted about until he found some brown rolling papers. He took several papers, matches and a clump of the tobacco, picked up the Spencer, and went back to the cells.

"Don't suppose it'll hurt none for you to have a little bit," Jed said and passed the makings through the cell bars. "What with you being a condemned man and all."

"Thanks for reminding me, kid." Sanchez skilfully rolled himself a smoke. "Light?" Sanchez pointed at the cigarette in his mouth.

Jed produced a sulfer match from his shirt pocket and struck it alight against the bars and lit the Mexican's cigarette. Then he watched as the man drew the smoke deeply into his lungs and blew it out through his nose.

"You see, kid," Sanchez said, "I am not bad by nature. I just took a wrong turn somewhere down the line or maybe life just dealt me a rotten hand. I am not afraid to die. I will go to that rope with a smile."

"That takes courage."

"Or blind stupid pride." Sanchez drew hard on his cigarette, threw it on the floor and ground it out under his heel. He picked up the pitcher of water and tossed it through the bars of the cell.

Out of instinct Jed stumbled backwards and lifted his hands to shield his face as the water soaked him. The rifle clattered to the floor. Instantly, he realized his mistake, but it was too late. Sanchez had already hit the floor, reached through the bars and grabbed the weapon. Jed felt a horrible sinking feeling in his stomach.

Sanchez, whose easy smile had turned feral, pointed the rifle directly at Jed.

"Best you let me out now," Sanchez said.

"I can't." Jed wiped the water from his eyes.

"I do not want to kill you, kid," Sanchez said. "Do not make me do it."

"Kill me and you still won't get out." Jed's voice rasped, his voice cracking. He'd been a fool, sucked in by Sanchez's deceptive manner and soft words. He'd let his guard down.

"I might as well hang for two as one," Sanchez threatened.

"I can't let you go," Jed insisted. "I'll die first."

"Get the keys off the hook on the wall." Sanchez pointed with the rifle. "Do it now. Nice and slowly. No sudden moves or I will kill you. I swear to *El Dios*, I'll kill you."

Jed locked eyes with the Mexican and if he had any doubt that the man wasn't serious then it vanished in that instant and he saw the very real threat of death in those eyes. They were cold, evil, and darted like those of a feral animal.

"Now!" Sanchez snarled.

"You might as well kill me," Jed said and bowed his head.

An impasse had been reached and neither of them would yield.

At that moment, the door opened and Mary came in carrying a tray of food. She closed the door behind her, turned around, and gasped as she took in the situation. Her large blue eyes stared in shock.

Sanchez swung his rifle at her. "Don't scream." His voice was filled with menace. "See those keys there?"

Mary nodded and the tray things rattled.

"Bring them over and I'll let your one legged friend here live. Do it, girl."

Mary looked first at Jed and then at Sanchez. She lowered the tray to the sheriff's desk and reached for the keys.

Jed hung his head. Whatever chance he'd had of being a deputy, no matter how slim, was gone forever. How many more deaths would Sanchez be responsible for if he escaped? How many would that make Jed responsible for? That was assuming, of course, he survived the current situation.

"Good girl." Sanchez all but purred. "Now come over here and open this cage. Then I will leave the two of you in peace."

"You won't hurt us?" Mary's voice held a fearful tremor.

"Not without reason," Sanchez said. Then he lifted the rifle and aimed it directly at Jed's head. "Quickly, or he dies."

Mary walked to the cells and slid the key into the locking mechanism. With a turn of the key she unlocked the cell door and Sanchez swung it inwards. He lunged out of the cell and grabbed Mary and held her tightly with his arm under her jaw. He looked at Jed and smiled. There was no humor in the gesture, though.

"Now go get me a horse, all saddled up."

Defeated, Jed turned to the door.

"And do not think of raising the alarm. You do and I will make sure *la chica bonita* here gets it first."

Jed nodded and walked slowly out of the jailhouse, his game leg dragging behind him.

Once outside, Jed stood in the pale afternoon sunshine and cursed his stupidity. He should never have allowed this to happen! His stomach churned and his heart pounded against his rib cage. There was nothing to do now but get a horse for Sanchez. He couldn't make a move or raise the alarm until Mary was safe.

He looked back over his shoulder at the jailhouse window and then Mary's face appeared briefly. Bitterly, Jed realized Sanchez was reminding him who called the shots.

Moving as quickly as he could, Jed made his way to the livery stable but found that Gabby, the manager, was not around. That was good. Jed looked through the stalls and found the horse he was looking for. A black stallion named Blaze for the flame-shaped patch on his rump. Gabby had won the beast in a card game and said he couldn't sell such a magnificent creature. The old man often allowed Jed to ride the animal, so Jed and Blaze knew each other well.

With some difficulty, Jed saddled the horse and led it out of its stall. He tethered Blaze to a post and then went back into the livery office and located Gabby's gun, an ancient Dragoon Colt that the old man seldom used but kept in the top drawer of his desk. Jed checked it was loaded and stuffed the revolver into his waistband, covering it with his shirttail. He dropped a handful of shells into his pocket and made his way outside and led the horse across to the sheriff's office.

Jed tied the horse to the hitching rail and after making sure that his gun was out of sight, he went into the jailhouse. He had to wait for a moment for his eyes to adjust to the gloom but then he saw Sanchez, still holding Mary, step out of the shadows at the rear of the building.

"The horse outside?" Sanchez asked.

Jed simply nodded.

"Good. I will let the girl go when I get it."

"I'll wait," Jed said.

"Good." Sanchez smiled. "It was nice to know you, kid. Now stand aside."

Taking a step backwards, Jed watched helplessly.

Slowly, holding Mary in front of him, the rifle's muzzle shoved into the soft flesh under her jaw, Sanchez walked to the door.

"*Adios,*" Sanchez said. Taking the girl with him, he stepped outside.

Jed stood, impassive until he heard the sound of Blaze breaking into a gallop, then he went outside.

He was relieved to see Mary was unharmed, kneeling on the boardwalk. Her auburn hair was mussed but she seemed unharmed. She was sobbing but Jed had no time to tend to her at the moment and he quickly limped around her and down onto the street. He curled his tongue and placed a finger each side of his mouth and let out a shrill whistle.

At the end of the street, Blaze suddenly pulled to a stiff-legged stop. Sanchez flew over the horse's head and landed hard upon the ground.

Jed whistled again and the well-trained horse ran back towards him.

The horse came directly up to him and Jed rubbed Blaze's nose. "Well done, boy," he said and hitched the stallion to the rail and moved out to the middle of the street. He pulled the old Dragoon from his waistband and limped towards Sanchez. The big gun felt good in his hand.

Cursing, Sanchez got to his feet. His right hand hung limp from the wrist. As well as he could, he lifted the rifle and aimed at Jed. "*You want to fight me, gimp?*" he yelled and let off a shot that sent dust spitting up at Jed's feet.

Jed knew the outlaw was still out of pistol range and he calmly continued limping towards the man. Sweat ran down his back and his heart seemed to want to shake itself free, but he bit his lip and concentrated his attention on Sanchez.

"Crazy kid!" Sanchez screamed and let off another shot and once again the slug puffed up dust at Jed's feet.

The street started to fill with onlookers. A man ran over to Mary but no one made any effort to come between Jed and Sanchez.

"*Kid,*" Sanchez screamed, "one more step and I will kill you!"

Jed stopped. He figured he was now in range and when he spoke it was with a calm and clear voice. "Make your play," he said.

"You loco son-of-a-bitch!" Sanchez lifted the rifle to deliver the killing shot.

The Mexican didn't get a chance though. Jed raised the Dragoon in a move he'd practiced thousands of times and triggered the weapon as it centered on Sanchez's chest.

The slug struck the action of the Spencer, jerking the stock upward and smashing it into Sanchez's nose, nearly tearing it from the Mexican's face. The man screamed and fell to his knees, the now useless weapon on the street beside him.

"Looks like you missed your lunch," Jed said and held the Colt steady in his hand. "Get up and walk back to the jailhouse."

"Thon of a bitch," Sanchez mumbled, trying to stem the flow of blood from his smashed nose. Groggily, Sanchez got to his feet and walked back to the jailhouse, Jed's Dragoon Colt pushed firmly into the small of his back.

Jed looked up as Sheriff Morton came into the office. The lawman was alone and had a look like thunder on his face. He went through and looked into Sanchez's cell. The Mexican was sleeping but even in the half-light the bruising was visible on his face.

"You been beating up on our guest?" the sheriff asked.

Jed said nothing and merely shrugged. Then, after a moment, he asked, "Where's Deputy Richards?"

"Ex-Deputy Richards. Damn fool's been involved in stirring up trouble in the Indian Nations. That's why they've got him locked up and I don't suppose he'll ever wear a badge again."

"I see," Jed said but didn't push it any further. He figured the sheriff would tell him the details if he felt a need to.

"Now you go on home," the sheriff said. "It's getting late and your ma'll be wondering where you got to."

"Sure." Jed got to his feet. He considered telling the sheriff what had happened today but decided against it. The sheriff would find out soon enough in any case. Too many people had witnessed the escape and recapture of Sanchez for it to stay quiet.

Jed crossed the office and was almost through the door when the sheriff spoke. "I heard what happened today," he said.

"You did?" Jed shrugged his shoulders. "Sorry."

"We'll talk about it some more tomorrow." Sheriff Morton reached into his pocket, pulled out a tin star and tossed it across the room.

Jed caught it and looked at it in his hand.

The sheriff sat in his chair, yawned and pulled his hat down over his eyes. "Be early in the morning, Deputy."

VISITORS

Ross Morton

Writing as Ross Morton, Nik Morton has three Black Horse Western novels published – Death at Bethesda Falls, Last Chance Saloon *and* The $300 Man. *He was the co-editor of the Express Westerns' anthology* Where Legends Ride *and his story 'Bubbles' is featured among its 14 tales of the Old West. Nik Morton's crime thriller* Pain Wears No Mask *and his psychic spy Cold War thrillers* The Prague Manuscript *and* The Tehran Transmission *(Libros International) have received good reviews. He lives in Spain, edits and writes books. His website is www.freewebs.com/nikmorton and his blog is at: http://nik-writealot.blogspot.com/.*

"**M**a, we've got company," Frank said, pointing beyond the picket fence, to the knoll a mile away that marked the southern skyline. A dust cloud announced the approach of riders.

Kate Bartlett stood still on the porch, the glass pitcher of lemonade poised to pour. Now this little reward to Alice and the boys for their efforts with the livestock would have to wait. When Bill was away, the children were happy to do his chores and milk their two cows and Wilhemina the goat. She brushed a stray wisp of gray-streaked auburn hair into place behind her ear.

A strange stillness settled on the land. A few seconds earlier, birds chirped. Now there was an eerie silence.

That amount of dust meant a fair number of horses and Kate didn't think it was a herd of wild mustangs. It could be a cavalry patrol, but she wasn't going to make that assumption. It could be a posse of lawmen or a group of desperadoes. While Kate prided herself on making strangers welcome, she was still very careful. Trading post gossip told of some terrible stories and she was certain some of them were not fanciful.

She lowered the pitcher to the table. "Move the animals into the barn, boys," she said, careful to keep her tone easy but firm.

"Right, Ma," Frank and his twin brother Ethan chorused. They ran down the porch steps, across the unkempt rose garden and vaulted over the white picket fence. The boys sped to the patch of scrubland where Wilhemina and the two cows grazed.

"Alice, fill the buckets and put the lid on the well."

"Yes, Ma." The well was to the right, just inside the fence, so Alice didn't have far to carry the buckets after she filled them.

The children knew the routine. "Be prepared" was the family's maxim.

Determined to show outward calm, Kate lifted her dress and walked through the open door into the house. But her stomach churned. Funny, how old fears resurfaced. Kate found that the older she got, the more she felt she had to lose. Or maybe age and experience just made her more cautious and less adventurous. Once inside, however, she found herself breathing easier.

Kate opened the gun cabinet. On the day they moved into their new home, Bill bought six 1873 Winchesters and fifty boxes of .44-40 rounds, enough for a small army. That was three years ago and every Saturday he trained the boys how to shoot. Without fail, they brought home meat for the pot, which suited Kate fine.

When the children returned, she shut the door but didn't bar it. The boys closed the thick oak window shutters while Alice placed the water buckets in front of the fireplace. Then they stood, waiting for her instructions.

"Alice, you and I will load the Winchesters," Kate said. She took the rifles from the cabinet one at a time, handing them to Alice. "Lean them against the wall by the mantel," she said. She filled her hands with boxes of bullets from the gun cabinet drawer, and then handed a box to Alice. "You sure you can handle the loading, honey?"

Alice screwed-up her nose and wrinkled her brow. "Ma, I've been doing this for Pa for at least a year. Of course I can do it!"

Kate smiled with pride at her daughter's plucky answer. *A bit like me at her age, I guess. My, I must have been a real trial to Ma, God rest her soul.*

Then Kate handed Ethan and Frank a Winchester apiece and they moved to the loopholes cut in the heavy oak shutters.

"They're coming, Ma!" Frank called from his station on the left.

Kate opened the door a crack.

Magnificent and threatening in buckskin and colorful war paint, the redskins rode up to the gate of the picket fence. She recognized them – Chiricahua Apache from the San Carlos reservation.

Her throat felt very dry.

Four Apaches on paint ponies faced her from the other side of the fence. They were stern looking men, with high foreheads, flat hard faces, wide cheekbones and square jaws. Long shining black hair draped to broad muscular shoulders. They wore blue and red cloth headbands.

Two of them wore open threadbare jackets that revealed wide chests, and both carried 'trapdoor' Springfield .45/70 rifles and Mills cartridge belts around their waists. One gripped a war club and incongruously appeared slightly absurd in an ill-fitting striped trade shirt and a shabby bowler hat. The fourth Apache was clad in a fringed buckskin shirt decorated with beadwork. All four wore cloth breechclouts and white cotton leggings; their moccasins were decorated buckskin.

Beyond, on the slight rise leading away towards the trail, eight more sat their horses, poised to charge, it seemed, some with lances, others with rifles. Waiting. The Apaches knew patience.

Kate wiped her sweating palms on her apron then grabbed the Winchester Alice handed her.

"There's a bullet in the chamber, Ma," Alice whispered.

"Stay here," Kate said, and stepped out onto the porch. She was glad she didn't wear breeches; she felt her legs tremble under her skirt, but took heart in the fact that the Apaches could not see the effect they had on her. Apaches were cruel and vicious fighters who put great store in bravery.

She descended the steps from the porch and walked steadily towards the Indians, making her way along the cinder path edged with white-painted stones and struggling rose bushes. She stopped at the gate.

"What do you want?" She hefted the rifle in the crook of her arm.

The Apache in a fringed buckskin shirt eased his pony forward; it snickered. "We ask for water for our tired horses," Fringed Buckskin said in reservation school English. He seemed a few years older than the other three. He was handsome and imposing with yellow paint smeared over his high cheekbones and his big broad nose. Her heart sank when she noticed that none of them wore their reservation identity tags.

Fringed Buckskin's dark penetrating eyes glanced left and right, scanning the barn and the vegetable patch. Then he leaned forward on his pony. "Where is your man?"

"My man is inside with our family." Kate spoke loudly. "In fact, his rifle aims at your heart right now." From the corner of her eye, Kate saw Ethan poke the rifle barrel out the shutter loophole on the left of the door. *Good boy*, she thought.

"I want to talk to your man."

Kate shook her head. "He doesn't want to talk to you." Normally, she'd have let them water their horses, but she didn't like the look of the other three. Something about their expressionless faces made her wary. She raised the rifle slightly, not a threat but definitely a message. "Sorry, but you are too many. We don't have enough water for all your horses. And I am not allowed to give anything to runaways from the reservation."

The Apache in the bowler hat spat on the ground and shook his buckskin-covered war club. The others shifted on their horses.

"We do not run away from San Carlos," said Fringed Buckskin. "Our children die. Strong men go to their graves before their time. All this happens because of the bad food the white man gives us. We leave San Carlos only to hunt fresh meat."

Nodding, Kate looked straight at him, knowing Ethan and Frank were covering the spokesman's three companions. "I understand. We have no say, but we don't think it's right, the way the government's treating your people."

"Then let our horses drink."

"Sorry." She raised the rifle. "I told you why. Besides, we cannot allow war-parties on our land!"

She didn't move her gaze from his eyes, even though she heard discontented murmurs from his three companions.

"We are not a war-party – yet," he said, his tone ominous.

"Why the paint?" she said. Her legs felt as wobbly as jelly.

"A reminder of the old days for these young men. Nothing more."

The Apache in the bowler hat broke away and trotted his horse forward, closer to their spokesman. Brandishing his club – buckskin covered wood handle and stone head – he spoke in his own tongue: "Nantan Lupan, why do you talk with this woman? We don't ask – we take!"

So Fringed Buckskin was called Nantan Lupan: Kate only caught the name but she recognized it – *Gray Wolf* in the Apache language.

Gray Wolf scowled at the youngster. "Eskaminzim, you know it is not this woman's fault the Major is a crook."

She managed to snatch the gist of his words. Kate said to Gray Wolf in English, "The young warrior is anxious to make war, I fear."

Sighing, Gray Wolf nodded. "He is well named."

Big Mouth. Kate smiled at the Apache's dry humor.

"He and the others want the glory of the days of Cochise." He shrugged. "I cannot blame them. Everything in San Carlos is rotten – food, clothing – and the white people."

Kate nodded, sympathizing. She'd visited the reservation a number of times and picked up some of their language, usually while helping the Indian women give birth. She'd had some experience herself at that. She'd borne five children, two of them stillborn, and knew what pain was about.

While at the reservation, she'd heard rumors that Mr Clum, the Major – a local title for the Indian Bureau's agent – had resigned. Something to do with his authority being usurped by the military. Apparently, his replacement was mostly absent, busy with his private mining venture, which used food and materials from the agency warehouse.

"They're all the same, the whites!" snarled Big Mouth. "*Hai-ya!*" he shrieked and leaned down, wielding his club.

Kate saw the blow coming and flinched away. The club hit the side of her head.

Big Mouth's horse reared and whinnied as Kate stumbled sideways, grimly maintaining her grip on the Winchester. Her dress billowed around her as she sank to one knee. Left eye blinking at the flow of blood from her head-wound, she saw Big Mouth raise his arm with the blood-tinged club ready to throw.

A rifle blasted behind her and Big Mouth grunted. He tumbled from his horse, his bowler hat flying into her rose bushes. Big Mouth fell onto the picket fence, which collapsed under his weight.

Ethan. Ethan made the shot! Kate regained her footing and stumbled back, the rifle aimed at the three mounted Apaches.

Gray Wolf dismounted and knelt beside Big Mouth. Pointed ends of the fence had pierced the young man's side and thigh and blood stained the broken white wood. Gray Wolf glanced up and for a fleeting second she thought she detected sadness in his gaze. He barked orders and signed to the other two. In that same instant, they charged, their horses trampling down the gate and the adjoining fence.

She backed away down the cinder path then braced herself, the stock of the rifle against her shoulder. She fired.

Her shoulder felt the familiar recoil and the bullet slammed into the chest of the foremost charging Apache. He jerked, fell back off his horse, and raised a small puff of dust as he sprawled amidst roses. Blood splattered the white petals and the rust-colored soil.

Kate jacked another cartridge into the chamber as the second Apache slung himself low behind the belly of his horse.

"Ma!" Alice called. "Hurry inside!"

Rifles blasted from the cabin and at least three bullets hit the oncoming horse.

Kate turned and ran, one hand hitching up her dress, the other holding the rifle. She shut her left eye, because its vision was blurred by blood from her head wound.

The Apache leapt from his dying horse, landed on his shoulder and rolled over and over in a swirl of dust. He jumped to his feet, pulled a long knife from its sheath and sped after Kate.

Tumbling onto the porch, Kate tripped on the hem of her dress and bowled into the small table and knocked over the pitcher of lemonade. It dropped to the porch boards, smashed into tiny shards and splashed its contents all over her shoes.

The Apache's long knife flew past her cheek and stuck deep in the oak door.

Someone opened the door and she fell through into the cabin.

"Oh, Ma, you're hurt!" Alice rushed to her mother.

Frank dropped the strong wooden bar into place across the door.

Ethan fired once. Then again.

Kate felt giddy and feared she'd faint. She sank onto a straight-backed chair and leaned her rifle against the table. Her hand trembled as she raised it to touch her temple. Her head throbbed. Her fingers came away sticky with blood. She gritted her teeth. She had to keep going or everything would be lost. "It's nothing, dear," she said. "Get a damp cloth and wipe the wound clean – the blood's getting in my eye."

"Ma," Ethan said, "I got the 'Pache who hit you."

"I got the other one," Frank said, his tone without triumph, simply stating a fact. "He won't be throwing any more knives."

Kate marveled at her sons – sturdy fifteen-year-olds and dead shots.

"They're going," said Ethan.

"For now at least," added Frank.

"Keep watch," Kate said. "We've killed three of them, so they'll want revenge at the very least. They'll be back."

With shaking fingers, Alice soaked a cloth in a bucket, squeezed the excess water out then carefully wiped at the dried blood on her mother's head-wound. "What started it, Ma? You seemed to be getting on all right with their leader. Then it all turned nasty."

"Male pride, I suppose." Kate forced a smile. *God knows*, she thought, *we women have enough to contend with out west.*

That brought back bitter memories of her time in the wagon train, when she was only one of eight women among fifty-two men. She and Bill were newly-weds on their way West. Then, they fought off Indian attacks with single shot rifles that overheated and misfired. They did a lot of killing in those days; they did it just to survive.

Now, the Apaches fired their Springfield rifles. Bullets pounded into the oak door and thick window shutters. But they didn't shoot often, probably because they had little ammunition, something that was hard to come by for an Apache on the reservation.

From the loophole in the window on the left of the door, she returned fire. This hard land made Kate a strong woman, but after a while she found it difficult to heft the nine pounds of weapon to her shoulder and fire. The recoil wasn't so bad yet she was sure that if they survived this raid, she'd have an almighty bruise to show for her efforts. Neither twin betrayed any sign of discomfort. Their father would be proud of them. Her heart lurched. If only Bill would come back soon!

The Indian Wars were supposed to be as good as over – the reservations filled to overflowing – when Bill insisted they build their homestead up against the mountain. "We ain't going to be surrounded, Kate Bartlett, no way!" he informed her. "If the few hostiles left take it into their heads to try for our scalps, they'll have to ride full into our Winchesters!" The cabin had windows on three sides – Frank covered the east, Kate the south and Ethan the west. The bedrooms were at the back of the house, and beyond them was a deep cavern that was once home to a bear. Now it housed their winter store of foodstuffs.

"Fire!" Kate screamed, her voice hoarse from the shouting and the black powder smoke from the Winchester. The cloying smell of gunpowder caught at the back of her throat. The fusillade from their three weapons thundered in the close confines of the cabin. Alice hadn't been given a rifle as she'd said she was a lousy shot. "Sure, I can hit a barn, but none of those 'Paches are that big."

"Yeah, but I reckon you could talk them to death," Ethan said.

"I cain't!" she snapped.

"Hey," Kate said, "let's think about the enemy – I mean the ones outside the family!"

Her children laughed, despite their predicament, which made her feel better.

Now, Alice handed her a freshly loaded rifle. "Here, Ma, swap."

Kate was proud of Alice too. She was thirteen and already filling out her dress so that the Henderson's boys had trouble taking their eyes off her. She took after her mother with her curves, and had her auburn hair and hazel eyes as well. Alice's eyes shone tears, long lashes blinking against the smoke.

"You okay, honey?" Kate asked.

Alice nodded. She brushed the back of her hand across a cheek, leaving a smudge of burnt gunpowder.

Kate carefully handed over her Winchester, which Alice took by the stock to avoid the hot barrel.

Alice moved to the center of the room, dipped a cloth in a water-bucket, and wrung it out. She cooled the barrel with the damp cloth; it hissed like a snake and steam fronds twirled.

Four more buckets of water stood in strategic places around the room ready to douse any fires that flaming arrows might cause. At least Bill had used slate cut from the mountain behind the cabin to cover the roof.

The Apaches fired flaming arrows at the roof, but the slate wouldn't light. They even used arrows with burning sagebrush attached. Some smoke leaked through the rafters, but the sagebrush soon burned out on the hard slate.

Kate glanced at the mantel clock as it chimed. The whooping and hollering of the Apaches had been going on for over two hours. Now everyone in the cabin sounded hoarse. They choked in the smoke and cordite that clogged the cabin. *Two hours pass very slowly when you're fighting for your life,* she thought. *You get accustomed to the fear, and then start taking it for granted after a while. And the close proximity of death becomes all too familiar.* She reckoned they'd killed one more Apache in those two hours.

Frank now had a ricochet wound on his cheek but that's all they'd suffered so far.

"Ma, look!" Frank called. "What d'you make of that?"

At the side of the barn, Gray Wolf was in a heated argument with one of the young Apaches. Abruptly, Gray Wolf turned away and leapt onto his pony. He barked something at the young warrior then urged his mount back the way the Apaches had come hours ago.

"Oh, shit," Frank said. "He's going for reinforcements!"

"Frank, I won't have that kind of language in our home, do you hear?"

Docilely, he nodded. "Yeah, Ma."

"That'll be a 'yes', I think."

"Yes, Ma."

"Oh, no – they've lit the barn!" Ethan triggered a shot, then another.

Kate's heart sank. She moved to Ethan's loophole. Flames already licked at the sides of their barn; gray-brown smoke curled slantwise in a slight breeze. But there were no Indians in sight. She put a hand on Ethan's shoulder. "Don't shoot unless you have a target, son."

"Our cows – and Wilhemina!" Alice sobbed.

"We can't do anything about them, honey," Kate said and gritted her teeth.

"Here they come again!" Ethan said.

Kate rushed to her window loophole and peered through.

Just in sight to her left were two Apaches, riding hard from the east side of the house. They were hiding behind the bodies of their mounts. A thin trail of smoke followed behind them, as if the horses' dark tails were peeling away.

"They're going to burn us out!" shouted Frank.

Mindful of the burning barn, Kate said, "Make your bullets count!"

Frank fired – once, twice, three times.

They were anxious moments, as Kate couldn't see what was happening. But she heard the pounding hoofs. Then a single horse came into view, with its rider's leg slung round its neck. She drew a bead on the animal and fired. The poor horse made a horrible sound and stumbled, but that didn't stop the Apache. He leapt over the falling animal and rolled to Kate's right, out of sight.

Abruptly, there was a double thudding sound at the base of the door.

"What was that?" Alice asked, her voice high-pitched with fright.

The sound of splintering came as the Apache used his ax on the door.

Hurrying to the center of the room, Kate braced herself and fired from her hip, four times, placing her shots low on the wooden door. Splinters flew and she heard a single howl and a grunt, then the sound of the Apache falling to the boards of the porch.

"I reckon you got him, Ma!" Ethan shouted.

"I got the other one," said Frank. "He ain't moving, neither."

Only five Apaches left – until Gray Wolf returned with more disgruntled runaways.

"There's smoke under the door!" Alice said, pointing.

"Use your bucket, quickly!"

"Yes, Ma." Alice hauled the bucket over to the door and threw water at its base.

A single shot rang out, but it wasn't from a Winchester.

Alice stumbled back and the empty bucket clattered on the floorboards. "Oh, my God," she whispered, "I've been shot!"

Gritting her teeth, Kate fired three more rounds at the door, lower down. She heard the warrior roll off the porch and thud to the ground.

"No more coming," Ethan said.

Kate laid her rifle on the table and rushed to Alice. "Let me see, honey," she said, hugging her daughter against her.

Alice sobbed but didn't cry out. Kate's heart pounded. "Please God," she whispered, "spare me any more heartache."

Kate moved Alice to a chair by the table and sat her in it. "Let's have a look," she said, her voice calm and gentle.

Alice nodded. She bit her lip against the pain.

Carefully, Kate tore away Alice's bloodstained dress to expose her shoulder.

The Apache must have fired a pistol through the door. The wood had slowed the bullet and it had lodged in Alice's shoulder, just against the bone.

"It'll hurt like Hell," Kate said, "but you'll be alright."

Alice let out a giggle. "Hey, Ma, you said 'Hell' –"

"So I did, honey," Kate said. "I'll have to dig the bullet out later. For now, I'll bandage it to stop the bleeding. Alright?"

"Yes, Ma. Whatever you say, but it does hurt… a lot."

"Be brave," Kate said, tearing a strip from Alice's white petticoat. "I know how it feels, honey. I was hit by an arrow – and I was breastfeeding Frank at the time – or was it Ethan?"

"Ma, d'you mind?" Ethan said.

Kate chuckled. "That's what mothers do, you know, embarrass their boys when they become young men."

Despite the pain she was in, Alice let out another little giggle.

But the humor was cut short by a solid thumping sound above them.

"That wasn't an arrow." Alice eyed the rafters.

"No," said Kate. "One of them must have climbed up the mountainside and jumped onto our roof."

"If one or two of them get in here, we're to Hell and gone, Ma."

"Ethan, I told Frank. And I'm telling you. We'll not have that kind of talk in our home."

"Yes, Ma."

"Nevertheless, you're right." Kate glanced up. The sound of slate tiles being bashed, pulled up and discarded to the ground disheartened her; she blamed her tears on the dust falling through the cracks.

Frank aimed his rifle at the ceiling between the rafters.

"No, don't shoot!" Kate warned. "There could be a ricochet from the stone."

"But, Ma, we can't–"

"We wait." Turning to Alice, she said, "Keep an eye out. If you see daylight, call me."

Alice swallowed and nodded.

The Apache above continued to bash at the slate tiles.

"Frank. Ethan. Back to your windows," Kate ordered.

Ethan poked his rifle barrel through the loophole when suddenly it was grabbed and jerked upwards, wrenching his trigger finger. "Ouch!" he cried. Hastily, he grabbed the stock and tugged but the Apache gripping the barrel wouldn't let go. "Ma, he's got my gun!"

Kate rushed to stand beside Ethan and aimed her rifle at the loophole where the barrel was still being held from outside. She fired through the wooden shutter twice.

Even above the sound of the Apache demolishing a portion of their roof, Kate heard the Apache's grunt as Ethan's rifle dropped back into the room. There was some shuffling on the other side of the window, and it didn't move away.

Now nobody wanted to poke a rifle barrel through the window loopholes for fear it'd be grabbed again. They could all hear the footfalls of Apaches along the porch boards. They seemed to be biding their time. Waiting for darkness, perhaps.

"Ma, I don't know if I can stand it much longer," Alice whispered. She sat at the table, reloading a Winchester. Her left arm rested on the tabletop so there was little movement to disturb her shoulder wound. She gave a wary glance up at the rafters. The Apache still pummeled away. "I wish Pa was home."

"Be brave, honey," Kate said soothingly. She was reluctant to leave her loophole.

"They don't know when to quit!" Ethan snapped.

"Would you – if your friends lay dying or wounded out there?" Frank said.

"Well, it ain't natural," Ethan said. "It's as if they have a death wish."

"Yeah, they wish for us to be dead," Frank said.

"That's enough of that talk," Kate told them. "You're upsetting your sister. As long as the Apaches are out there, we fight them. That's an end to it."

The sun sank towards the horizon on their right. The sky showed a full moon through Frank's loophole when the remaining Apaches made their final attack.

Alice stood at the table, watching the rafters. She said the onset of dusk made it difficult for her to see daylight. Loaded rifles and fresh ammunition lay on the table. An oil lamp hung from a rafter and cast its buttery light on Kate, Ethan and Frank who stood in the middle of the room and covered the windows and the doorway.

The Apache on the roof redoubled his efforts and bits of slate tile tumbled to the floor and shattered. Two Apaches used hatchets on the door while the east and west window shutters were also attacked by ax blades.

"Don't shoot till they're inside and make every shot count!" Kate ordered. Her body trembled, but not with fear. Anger burned in her chest. She'd spent the best years of her life bringing a family into this world and now they could be slaughtered because of a hothead's whim.

The look of joy on their faces as they learned to walk, the innocent pleasure they took in the smallest achievements. The sleepless nights nursing her ill children, the knocks and scrapes and tears from which they bounced back. Tears ran down Kate's cheeks but she ignored them.

Kate Bartlett braced herself for the onslaught.

A large section of the ceiling fell in with a rafter and chunks of adobe. The Apache tumbled into the cabin at the same time, shrieking his triumph.

The lantern swayed, light and shadow cavorting on the walls. It was utter chaos. The Apaches outside seemed to quicken their pace, chopping with axes.

As the Indian landed, Kate whirled and squeezed the trigger. She shot at point-blank range and the Apache crashed into her as the bullet bore through his chest. His dead weight pushed her backwards and she lost her footing and fell under him. His hand grasped a huge knife in a death grip and it stabbed into the floorboards an inch from her ear. He smelled of wood-smoke, grease and body odor.

The window shutters splintered.

"Ma," Alice screamed, "they're breaking in!"

The door crashed off its hinges, its thick oak eaten away by ax blades.

Hardly able to breathe with the dead man on top of her, Kate croaked, "Fire!"

*

"*No, don't fire!*" Gray Wolf shouted from the porch.

There was a blood-covered young Apache standing at the east and west windows and two in the doorway. Gray Wolf's voice stopped them in their tracks. All four of them gasped for breath. Blood, war paint and sweat glistened in the light of the swaying lantern.

The two men in the breached doorway stood aside and Gray Wolf stepped in. He gave the place a hasty glance, noting the three rifles levelled on him and the young Apaches at the windows. Purposefully, he strode over to Kate and heaved the dead Apache off her. He took her hand, helped her up, and said, "I have brought the reservation police to take these men away. They have been foolhardy and will be punished."

Kate nodded. Her voice croaked from a combination of smoke, anxiety and lack of water. "Foolhardy, but brave too."

He gestured at Ethan, Frank and Alice. "As were your children."

"I will protect them with my life," Kate said, steel in her voice.

"I do not doubt it," he said, eyeing her hand.

Then she realized she was still holding her rifle.

"But it is not necessary now," he said. He turned on his heel and walked outside, giving orders.

She followed him, gingerly crossing her once-lovely wooden floor that was now littered with spent cartridge cases and discolored by water- and bloodstains. She stepped over the broken door and stood on the porch.

Docilely, the remaining four reservation escapees shuffled towards the waiting Apache police who were dressed in ill-fitting five-button fatigue jackets.

Gray Wolf directed another Indian to bring a wagon for the dead and wounded.

Seeing an Apache lying face down about fifteen feet off, Kate turned away. So pointless, all of it. Her eyes filled with tears – relief or released tension, she didn't know which, or care which, for that matter. She breathed in, glad to be alive, and coughed on the stench of roasted animal flesh and the burnt wood of the barn. She glanced to her left: it was almost completely demolished, a few charred uprights all that remained. Poor Wilhemina, she thought, distracted.

Whooping and yelling, the corpse near her came to sudden and startling life. The Apache was wounded in the thigh but certainly not dead. He charged her with his hatchet held high.

She felt the color drain from her cheeks. Her arms ached as she lifted the Winchester. The blessed absence of punishing recoil made her loath to rest the butt against her shoulder. Reluctantly, she nestled the wood against her bruised body.

Even in the dusk she could see the snarl of his teeth and the gleam in his eyes as the young Apache ran limping towards her.

Suddenly, the Apache shrieked. Thrust sideways, he dropped the hatchet and knelt in the dust, clutching a bloody shoulder.

The sound of a big Henry rifle echoed from the mountain. Kate recognized its distinctive report. She lowered her rifle as Gray Wolf strode back, helped the wounded Apache to his feet, and led him to a wagon.

My God, Kate thought, *Bill only wounded him in the arm!*

Kate's children gathered around her.

"Did you see that, Ma?"

"I sure did, Ethan."

"Now, that's shootin'!" Frank said, eyes shining.

"I can still hit a barn with any gun," Alice declared. "Leastways, when my shoulder's better."

The wagon moved out with the wounded and dead. Gray Wolf smoothly mounted his pony and then waved a kind of salute to the crest of the hill, where Bill Bartlett sat astride his big black stallion, silhouetted by the rising moon.

Later, as Bill led a packed mule over the wrecked picket fence, he said, "You been partyin' while I was gone?"

"Heck, no," Kate said, brushing a stray strand of hair from her brow. "A social call is all. Just visitors."

THE NIGHTHAWK

Michael D George

Michael D George has written 60 Black Horse Westerns so far: several under his own name, but also the Iron Eyes books written as by Rory Black; Bar 10 Books written as Boyd Cassidy. His other pen-names include: Dean Edwards, Roy Patterson, Dale Mike Rogers, John Ladd, and Walt Keene.

As he recovered consciousness, Johnny Crimson choked on dust that filled his mouth and caked his eyes. For a nightmarish moment he feared he was blind, but no, he glimpsed daylight through narrow slits between his lids, though his vision was blurred.

It was all a blur. He had no idea what had happened to him and his fellow trail drivers.

He lay on his back and his chest felt crushed. He could barely breathe. A chill ran through him as he realized he was buried under Buck, his favorite buckskin quarterhorse. Not buried by the hands of men but by something else, something from his hazy past, something far more brutal than any man could devise.

With his gloved left hand he clawed at the ground around his agony-racked body.

Excruciating pain tore through him. Then he saw bone jutting from his left arm, a few inches above the wrist. He lowered the arm and labored to turn his head. He wanted to look for his right hand. He felt the fingers, moved them, but couldn't see them – most of his right arm was trapped between the buckskin's carcass and the dusty ground.

The stench of decay filled his nostrils. How long had the horse been dead?

What happened?

Questions screamed in his mind over and over as he fought to recall the events that brought him to this sorrowful state.

He blinked rapidly to clear his eyes and then peered through the swirling dust in a vain bid to get his bearings – to see something, anything that triggered a memory.

His mouth was dry – never been so dry before.

Maybe he was hurt worse than he feared. His heart hammered as he realized he could neither see nor feel the lower part of his body. He concentrated on moving his legs and feet, but there was no response. With cold reasoning, he decided if his legs were attached to his torso, then he just couldn't feel them. Maybe that was a good thing. He had more than enough pain racking the upper part of his bruised and broken body, which he could glimpse sticking out from beneath Buck.

What happened?

After what seemed like an eternity, he managed to lift his broken left arm and move it across to where his right arm was pinned. He started scraping at the ground beside the cantle with his fingers. It was a slow, tedious and painful fight against the dead quarterhorse and the crumbling ground that trapped his right arm.

But Crimson was used to fighting. His entire life had been one long fight. In the beginning, he'd fought just to survive the cruel plains where his parents tried to start a small farm. Of fifteen children, he alone reached maturity. Then he was dragged into a war he didn't want; a war he came through without a scratch. Then, for nearly eight years, he rode north on one trail after another, driving countless Texas longhorn steers to the distant railheads. All those drives, and he'd never so much as broken a fingernail. So, scraping handfuls of dirt away with a busted arm was one fight he was determined to win.

As he toiled beneath the horse, the sun moved across a cloudless blue sky. He sweated and grew thirsty.

Flashes of memory returned. Maybe he'd win this one last fight. The gap was growing and with it the thought that soon he'd be able to free his right arm. With two arms, surely he could get his sorry carcass out from under his dead horse.

Then he paused.

He vividly remembered when night replaced day – maybe it was only yesterday. Bill Baker, his trail boss, kicked his boots to wake him from an unsettled sleep. Baker was a solid man, a man Crimson trusted with his life.

He recalled now that he was one of three nighthawks. Men who nursed a herd of steers throughout the hours of darkness and made sure they didn't stampede. Anything could get a herd of longhorns on their feet running in blind panic. Sometimes, it was the howls of coyotes baying at the moon and stars – it only took the one scared steer to set them all off. Other times, it was the sound of a rifle or a six-gun. But the nighthawks feared thunder and lightning the most.

Crimson knew nothing more destructive than thousands of panicked steers in a blind stampede, trying to out-run their own terror.

So the nighthawks were to prevent that at all cost – and sometimes that cost was mighty high.

Crimson started to scratch at the loose earth again and remembered the graves and markers along the trail – the dead faces of dead trail drivers he'd ridden with over the years. There was no room for even one mistake for a nighthawk. Sadly, each one of those men had made a mistake and paid for it with his life.

The ground seemed to be getting damp and a little easier to claw away.

Then he realized the dampness wasn't water under the soil's surface. It was blood. He lifted the gloved hand free: it was stained red. He hoped the blood came from the horse and not him.

Scrabbling in this awkward position, Crimson found that his shoulder ached. He rested for a while then heaved in a big sigh that pained his chest. Slowly, he moved his right arm and he grinned, coughing on the dust, as he pulled it free.

The nighthawk then used both forearms for purchase and rolled over. A crippling pain, like a branding iron being thrust into his back, burned into him.

He yelled out, but there was no one to hear his pitiful croaking cries. His memory awoke from its slumber.

Last night, Baker handed Crimson his supper on a tin plate and hunkered down beside him. They'd talked and ate.

"A storm's brewing in the west and headed our way, I reckon,' his seasoned trail boss said.

"We've been through a few in our time," Crimson replied.

"Yeah, but remember I had to hire too many greenhorns. Beggars can't be choosers."

"Yeah, but they're learning fast."

"Maybe so, Johnny, but keep an eye out, will you?"

"Of course. We'll get to the railhead, don't you worry, Boss."

Baker eyed the night sky. "I'm not thinking about Sedalia right now."

And now Johnny Crimson had the dead weight of his horse on his back. He continued to dig himself free from under his top string mount. Flies swarmed on the carcass as the heat of day spread over the vast flat plain.

Crimson had ridden out to join his two fellow nighthawks, just like always. Skeet Peters and Tom McCoy had learned a lot in the five weeks since the herd set out, but they were still novices. They reckoned they knew their job, but they'd got it wrong. A true nighthawk gets good after many drives and plenty of incidents along the way. Both Baker and Crimson knew that, but sometimes luck was kind to beginners.

As Crimson's blood-soaked gloves reached his legs, he feared he was hurt far worse than he'd thought. With a sinking feeling he realized his legs were mangled. He now knew why. Questions no longer haunted him. He had the answers. All of them.

The memories crashed into his mind like an explosion. Maybe the pain when he'd freed his arm ignited the fuse and cleared his clouded thoughts, or maybe, like folks always say, your life flashes in front of you just before you die.

Crimson remembered. After supper, Bill Baker walked with him to his horse. Baker had been anxious about the storm and pointed up to the black sky as tempestuous clouds gathered. The cloud was alive with flashing venom. Lethal forks of twisted lightning crashed into the plains a few miles behind the herd. Getting closer with every heartbeat. He'd seen this type of storm before and knew it might prove deadly or it might change direction at the very last moment.

He recalled Baker's fatherly hand on his shoulder. "Nasty storm, Johnny. Heads up."

Crimson nodded, stepped into the stirrup and swung up on his buckskin, the best horse in the remuda on a night like this.

"Keep them calm, Johnny!" Baker said.

Gathering his reins, Crimson swung the quarterhorse around and galloped on to the herd where Peters and McCoy waited.

Those simple words echoed over and over in Crimson's head. The truth flooded over him as he lay pinned beneath his horse.

There was no more mystery. Crimson knew why he lay in this blood-filled hole.

Keep them calm, Johnny.

Crimson managed to keep them calm for nearly three hours. He'd conducted them as if they were a big city orchestra. Checked every move they made. Stopped every hint of alarm the massive longhorns showed, before anything even started. His eight years as nighthawk paid dividends that night.

It was almost midnight when Skeet Peters made a mistake.

One really bad mistake.

Crimson's heart pounded like a war drum inside his chest as he pulled both shattered legs from under the stricken horse. Even the leather chaps couldn't disguise the truth from his weary eyes. His legs were crushed and he couldn't feel his feet. But there was no pain.

Last night, the sky turned eerie dark blue just before lightning flashed directly over the heads of the longhorns. That image burned in his mind. He knew he would never forget that sight if he managed to live to be a hundred. Although right now, he reckoned he'd be lucky to see another hour out.

The lightning started to ripple in sheets. Peters drew his six-gun when he saw a few steers rise and break into a run.

Crimson screamed out, but his voice vanished in the sound of the pounding hoofs.

Peters fired and the herd turned, as if they were one living creature, not thousands.

Now, Crimson used his right hand and arm to pull himself up to the level of the surrounding plain. Time and again, pain hit him and he blacked out. When he regained consciousness, he sweated because the nightmare stayed with him. Each time, he crawled a little more. Every movement was agony.

It took what felt like forever to travel the five or six feet.

He lay on his chest then after a while he found the strength to raise his head and see where he was.

The sight before him knifed through his being with such pain, it dimmed all his combined injuries to dull aches.

Utter devastation lay all around. The chuck wagon in ruins. The supply wagon splintered, scattered. Canvas shredded and sideboards reduced to a million fragments scattered across the plains. Gruesome remnants of cowboys – trampled to death in their sleep as the longhorns ploughed through the camp.

Then Johnny Crimson saw him.

Ramrod Bill Baker – or what was left of the trail boss – lay less than twenty feet from Crimson's dead quarterhorse. Only Bill's neckerchief was recognizable.

"No!" Crimson screamed. "No!" he wailed as he tried to move his broken body. "No!"

Then, he felt what he'd never expected to feel again. Someone kicked the sole of his boot.

As the kicking became harder, he opened his eyes and the sun vanished from the sky and was replaced by stars amid darkness.

Crimson stared in disbelief.

"Having a bad dream, Johnny?" Bill Baker asked. He held out a tin plate of chow and grinned.

Johnny Crimson tossed his blanket aside and got to his feet. He stared down at his body. It was no longer broken. He looked into the troubled eyes of his trail boss. "Thanks, Boss," he said, accepting the plate of stew. As he slurped the warm food from a spoon, he gazed around the camp. It was intact.

He let out a big sigh as a sense of immense relief washed over him. "I must have been having a nightmare, Boss," Crimson admitted. A bead of sweat trailed down the side of his face. "Damn! It all seemed so real!"

"I get 'em after eating cheese," Baker said.

Crimson shook his head. "Worst I've ever had." He used a chunk of bread to soak up the last of the stew. "Time to circle the herd, I reckon."

"Yep." Baker walked with Crimson to the chuck wagon. The trail boss thumbed at the black sky. "I'm a tad leery of that storm that's coming, Johnny. It looks like a real mean one!"

Crimson put his plate in the dirty dishpan on the chuck wagon's tailgate. He turned to Baker and shoved his hat back on his head. He studied the bruised sky and felt his heart quicken. It was so vivid, the same as in his bad dream.

Lightning ripped across the dark clouds in flashes of blinding light. *Lethal forks of twisted lightning crashed into the plains a few miles behind the herd. Getting closer with every heartbeat.*

Crimson walked with Baker to the remuda and came to a stop in surprise: Buck, his quarterhorse was already saddled. He stared at Baker. He wanted to speak, but no words came.

"I got Peters to saddle Buck for you," Baker said. "Better check the cinches, though – he's still a greenhorn!"

Swallowing hard, Crimson nodded. The cinch was OK. He reached up and took hold of the saddle-horn. As he placed his boot into the stirrup, he felt the hand of the trail boss on his shoulder. "Nasty storm, Johnny. Heads up."

A chill traced Crimson's spine.

"Keep them calm, Johnny!" Baker said.

Crimson gathered his reins and quietly turned the buckskin to face the herd. He spurred Buck to join McCoy and Peters who were already circling the herd beneath the savage heavens.

As the quarterhorse gained pace, Crimson looked at the ferocious sky and sensed his pulse and heart quicken. He felt like a man headed toward his own gallows, but he kept on riding. He could not turn back. He was a nighthawk.

THE PRIDE OF THE CROCKETTS

Evan Lewis

Evan Lewis writes mysteries, westerns and historical fiction. He hangs his hat near the end of the Oregon Trail, but considers himself a spiritual Texan. He has a story in Ellery Queen's Mystery Magazine *(February 2010).*
Visit him at www.evanlewis.com

If Davy hadn't been nagging me so hard, I might have avoided that mountain falling on my head. I was rattling the Wells Fargo through Heartbreak Gap, trying to ignore his carping and whining, when he shouted at me to rein up.
 Stop, dang it! When'll you learn to listen?
 Trouble was, I'd been listening all the way from Santa Fe, about how I needed to find me a wife and turn respectable and start making a name for myself – the same applesauce he's always going on about – and I was in no mood to humor him.
 That's when I heard the explosions, and looked up to see trees, cougars and rocks big as houses come barreling down both sides of the gap.
 And that's all I knew for quite a spell.

I woke up to more of Davy's griping.
 You're the sorriest excuse for a Crockett I ever seen.
 I spit the blood and pebbles out of my mouth, pawed the dust from my eyes and surveyed my surroundings. Half the stage lay crushed under boulders, and the rest was splintered all over the landscape. I was covered in rubble and my left leg was pinned beneath a pine tree. The horses were missing, and the Wells Fargo strongbox lay next to me, its lid bashed open. The Army payroll I'd been toting was gone.
 Davy was more than right. I was a sorry excuse for a human being.
 We've knowed that for a coon's age, Davy said. *No use bellyachin' about it now.*
 I closed my eyes, wishing those rocks had killed me. Trouble is, Davy's not really a person. If he was, I'd have grabbed him by the neck and tossed him into a bed of scorpions. Davy's just this annoying little voice in my head, a voice that never shuts up. And if that weren't bad enough, he claims to be my grandfather, the famous Davy Crockett.
 Well, maybe he is, and maybe he ain't. I was born thirty years after he died at the Alamo, so I never heard him talk. But he's a cranky old cuss, and refusing to call him Davy is like poking him with a hot stick. He's been

badgering me since the summer of my thirteenth year, saying *do this, dang it,* and *don't never do that,* and *when the devil you gonna get hitched and start into politics?*

That sort of talk tends to wear on a man.

If I had my fiddle, I'd play 'The Cowboy's Lament'.

Seeing he was in one of his moods, I shoved that tree off my leg and got up to be on my way.

Luckily, the stage had no passengers. There'd been some, but on hearing of the brutal robberies taking place in these parts, they'd lit off at the last station with a sudden passion to see the East.

Feeling powerful thirsty, I reached for my flask of Apache lightning, and discovered it gone. Twice as thirsty now, I patted all my pockets, and things got worse. Some lowdown skunk had lifted the twenty dollars that comprised my entire life savings.

A fine pickle you've gotten us into.

What do you mean "us"? You can just flit back to the Hereafter and consort with the angels.

And desert you when you're down? Wouldn't be the Crockett way.

I shook my head, wishing I could shake him right out. I'd already tried that, of course – along with holding my head underwater, stuffing a dozen live horny toads in my mouth and setting my hair on fire – but he'd survived every assault.

Scowling down at the ground, I noticed a mess of footprints.

Seven of 'em. And looky there. One has a busted boot.

Sure enough, next to the dispatch box was a print with a crack across the heel.

Casting a wider loop, I saw hoofprints, and found where the gang had tethered their horses. From there, they'd ridden off into the brush. I turned back, dug my old Stetson from under a stunned cougar and started climbing the rubble that had once been Heartbreak Gap.

Ain't you goin' after them varmints?

That's a job for the law. Only thing I'm hunting is some whiskey, and maybe a horse.

It's your moral duty, Davy insisted. *It was you they robbed, and Crocketts stomp their own snakes.*

But I'd no interest in snakes, two-legged or otherwise, and marched off toward the next town with Davy's dire imprecations buzzing between my ears.

It was near twenty miles before I came to a watering hole and, having walked all night, I was almost thirsty enough to drink the stuff.

Whoa, Davy said as I strode by, *there amongst the horse tracks. That busted boot again.*

So?

So them stage robbers are follerin' this road. Maybe you can still catch 'em.

I snorted. The last thing I wanted was to catch stage robbers. That would mean notoriety, and somebody'd be bound to recognize me. Being descended from a legend is a great disadvantage. Soon as folks hear my name, they expect me to act like some sort of hero.

I'd once asked a college professor if there was anywhere folks hadn't heard of old Davy. He said China, maybe, or Persia, but the only place he was sure about was Zanzibar. Such places seemed like paradise to me, and I went there in my mind as I tramped along that road.

Two hours later, I came to the town of Lizard Gulch. And right away, I began to feel twitchy. Everywhere I looked were signs and banners with such messages as "McFarland for Sheriff" and "Re-elect Sheriff King" and "McFarland is a hoss-theef" and "Homer King wears bloomers."

Ah! The sweet scent of politickin's in the air!

I grimaced. Politicking was one of his particular peccadilloes, him having had some small success at it.

Small? Boy, you call the United States Congress small? If you had the gumption to try it yourself, you'd see it ain't no frolic.

I sighed. Now I'd set him off, and I'd be hearing about his famous "half-horse, half-alligator" speech and that blasted Indian Removal Bill and his squabbles with Old Hickory for the rest of the day.

Rest of the week, he said. *Or maybe the month. You got a heap of learnin' to do.*

I kept walking. Thus far, the only inhabitants I'd seen were a few sleeping hound dogs. There were guns banging and people yelling somewhere at the other end of town, but there was nothing unusual in that. Any time you get this many folk in close proximity, shouting and shooting is sure to commence.

All at once a beady-eyed hombre with a red bandana over his chin came busting around the corner with a sack on his back.

"Hey you," I said, friendly as could be, "I'm lookin' for the sheriff."

His eyes boogered out like he thought me a lunatic, and he tore right by without a howdy-do. I shook my head. Civilized folk had no proper manners.

A second man hove into sight, also carrying a sack, in as much a bustle as the first. Skipping the niceties, I wrapped a paw around his arm and hoisted him off the ground. "Where's the sheriff, dang you?"

This, too, produced a remarkable response. He seemed possessed by a conniption fit. When he finally got control of himself, he aimed a hogleg at my stomach. "Put me down before I ventilate your innards!"

I put him down, alright, flat on the ground, where I stepped on his neck and kicked his six-shooter across the street.

"Now," I said, ignoring his squalls, "let's try again."

While we were thus occupied, the beady-eyed man returned, riding a horse and leading another. He waved a sawed-off shotgun in my face. "Unloose him, you talkin' grizzly!"

Exasperated, I took hold of his gun, along with half his arm, and tossed him into the nearest horse trough.

Just then a whole passel of people came tearing around that corner, waving Winchesters and pitchforks and howling like their britches were on fire.

Catching sight of me with that one rascal wriggling under my boot and the other splashing in the horse trough, they all pulled up and stared in slack-jawed wonder.

A man in a bristly red beard and a green tweed suit emerged from the crowd and clapped me on the back. "What's your name, son?"

"Dave," I said, too flabbergasted to lie. But I found my wits and added, "Crocker. Dave Crocker."

The bristly fellow waved his hands above his head and shouted, "Ladies and gents of Lizard Gulch! Once I'm elected sheriff, my first act will be to appoint Mr Dave Crocker here, the man who single-handedly nabbed these bank robbers, as my number one deputy!"

The crowd hooted like Comanches and shot off their weapons.

Bank robbers? Deputy? As I fought to digest these statements, the would-be sheriff nodded to several hard-edged citizens, who began hauling that one hombre out of the horse trough and prying the other from under my boot.

A wide-shouldered man in a flat-brimmed hat and wearing an undertaker's suit rushed forth, shoving the other men aside and snatching up the sacks the robbers had carried. "Dog my cats!" he cried. "The money's all here!"

I turned to the green tweed candidate. "Look here," I said, "ain't no way I'm going to –"

But before the words were out the undertaker sprang up on my opposite side and grabbed my arm. I was about to squash him when I spied a tin star on his chest.

"Good citizens," he said, "unfortunately for my opponent, he'll have no chance to appoint this man deputy." With that, he dug a badge out of his vest pocket and stuck it onto my shirt. "For I have already done so!"

Hallelujah, Davy said, *my prayers have been answered.*

While the crowd hollered some more, the sheriff looked around, puzzled-like. "Curse you, McFarland, where'd those bank robbers get to?"

The candidate made a rude noise. "*That* for you, King. If you hadn't been so busy hornin' in on my play with this big hillbil—, I mean, this distinguished visitor here, you'd have corraled 'em."

I could take no more. Shaking free, I plucked that little star off my chest, bent it in half and flipped it into the horse trough. "I ain't nobody's deputy," I told all and sundry, "and don't plan to be. I just came to report a stage robbery."

Not long after, I'd parked my carcass in what Sheriff King called his office. In actuality, it was a big round table in a corner of The Alamo Saloon. I was none too pleased about being in a place called The Alamo, but the liquor was a durn sight better than I was used to, and the sheriff was buying, so I swallowed my complaints.

That saloon was the fanciest I'd ever seen. They had crystal chandeliers, a rail along the bar, shiny brass spittoons and portraits of high-collared swells lining the walls. Back behind the bar, instead of a mirror, hung a big picture of the Alamo, which I recognized right off because of its hump.

Hmph, Davy said. *Didn't have no hump when I was there.*

I smirked at that. Imagine the Alamo with no hump! It's such remarks that make me question the old coot's sanity.

Sheriff King was eyeing me in a peculiar fashion. "You know, Crocker, I got a feeling I've seen you somewhere before."

"I got three twin brothers," I said, "purt' near as handsome as me."

"Looks familiar to me too, Pop," said a silky feminine voice, "but if I'd seen a galoot this big, I surely wouldn't forget." The speaker stepped out from behind me, and I stared up at a buxom yellow-haired gal in a glittery purple dress. She ran a hand up my arm, squeezing muscles here and there as if judging horseflesh. "I'm Kassy. Kassy King."

The sheriff torched a cigar. "You say that stage job was over at Heartbreak Gap? That's in the next county. I'll get a wire off to the sheriff there straight away."

"But the tracks led here," I protested. "Those outlaws could be right under your nose."

He smiled patiently. "I got my own robbers to worry about. If only that monkey Hank McFarland hadn't helped 'em get away."

Kassy King said, "Can I keep him, Pop?"

"We'll see. You scoot along, Kass. I have a proposition for this fellow."

Miss Kassy pouted some, but blew me a kiss as she sidled away.

Davy said, *I'll wager she fries a mean flapjack.*

I gave King a stern eye. "If you're totin' more badges, just keep 'em in your pockets. I still ain't interested."

"I understand completely. Not every man is disposed to a career in law enforcement. I merely wished to discuss a short-term business arrangement."

"If you're talkin' money, talk away."

The sheriff smiled with all his teeth. "Due to your popularity, I believe your support could tip tomorrow's election in my favor. If you'd consent to wear a deputy's badge, just until the ballots are counted, I'd insist you accept a generous donation from my campaign fund."

I expected Davy to whoop at this, for it would result in my wearing a star, at least for a day. But he was strangely silent.

"How generous?" I asked, still needing a horse.

Reaching into his coat, King extracted a crisp stack of bills. He riffled through them, letting the aroma waft my way. "What would you say to a hundred dollars?" He studied me, eyebrows arched. "Heck, make it two hundred."

I whistled. Two hundred dollars would not only buy me a horse, but also keep me in whiskey and ammunition for months. I'd worked at many a job – ranch hand, trapper, trail driver, miner, wagon train scout, and other less glamorous pursuits – but I'd always steered wide of wearing a star. Not only would it scandalize my friends and family back in the canebrakes, but it would please Davy, and anything pleasing Davy was sure to displease me.

Still, fate had stranded me in this devil's den of politics and women. If I didn't escape, Davy'd be hatching one of his schemes to make me a respectable citizen.

"What would I have to do, exactly?"

A finger dipped into his vest and out came another badge. "Just wear this, and tell folks you're workin' for me. And should the opportunity arise, you might wax eloquent on my sterling qualities as a sheriff."

"And once you're elected, we're quits?"

"That's it. No strings."

I ruminated. Much as the notion of packing a star went against the grain, it was only for one day. And since Davy wasn't trying to nag me into it, he likely had something against the idea. That, of course, was the deciding factor.

"Got yourself a deputy." I pinned the badge onto my shirt. "Come tomorrow, I'll be in the market for a horse. Know where I can find one?"

"Happens I do. I own this saloon, you see. Had to shoot a trail bum here last week, and as he hadn't paid for his drinks, I sort of inherited his pie-biter."

"How much?"

King's smile got oily. "Well, seeing as how you're practically rich..."

I plucked the star off my shirt and spun it on the table like a top.

"...and also my favorite deputy, he's yours for twenty bucks."

"Done," I said, and re-pinned the star.

*

The weight of that badge made me thirstier than ever, but no amount of liquor seemed to satisfy me. I sat slumped at that table, feeling ever more sorrowful, while the sheriff went out to make his rounds. I was already regretting my decision. When word got out that the grandson of old You-Know-Who had become a lawdog, there'd be terror-stricken towns from Texas to California begging me to come tame them.

About then I noticed a little four-eyed specimen at the next table, scribbling words onto a tablet. He squinted over at me a time or two, chewing on his pencil. It made my scalp itch.

"Hey!" I said. "What you writing?"

The little dude blinked up at me. "I'm a traveling correspondent for the *Rocky Mountain News*. As it happens, I'm composing an account of a mysterious stranger – that's you – assisting the sheriff in recovering stolen funds. You gave your name as Dave Crocker, I believe. Is that spelled with one 't' or two?"

A moment passed before I took his meaning. Then my gizzard clenched up. "How should I know? Do I look like a goldurned schoolmarm?"

"You look," he said, "like a fellow I saw last month up in Durango. This man got into a tussle with eight or nine mule skinners, and by the time it was over, the doc could only find enough pieces to stitch six back together."

Ah, Davy said, *your fame precedes you.*

"That weren't my fault," I said, "they—"

"Fault's not the point. The point is that folks said this big fellow was the true-blooded grandson of old Davy Cro—"

In an instant, I was at his table with my hand over his mouth.

"Now I remember!" squealed Kassy King. That blamed shemale had snuck up behind me again. "You look just like that painting over there."

I swiveled my head, dreading what I'd see. The man in the nearest picture had reddish-gold hair, a wide forehead, bushy sideburns and a dimple in his chin. His eyes were dark and dangerous. He didn't look no more like me than a bullfrog. I said as much.

Miss Kassy giggled. "Not him, silly. That's Jim Bowie. I meant the other fellow." And she pointed at another painting further down the wall.

And sure enough, it was a dad-blasted portrait of old Davy, rosy-cheeked and pointy-nosed, from when he'd infested the U.S. Congress.

Miss Kassy clapped her hands. "Listen up, folks. We are in the presence of greatness. This distinguished gentleman, our newest deputy, is the genuine grandson of the immortal Davy Crockett!"

This here, Davy said, *is where you take a bow.*

I was out of there so fast I took the batwing doors with me. I meant to find

King and return that badge pronto. But I'd hardly reached the street when a tow-headed tyke came howling around the side of the saloon. "Mister Deputy! Mister Deputy! Please, you gotta help!" And before I could ask what ailed him he scurried back around the building.

Well, I didn't consider myself a real lawman, but if this young 'un was in trouble I felt bound to render aid. I hitched up my gun-belt and followed. He motioned me on as he rounded the corner behind The Alamo, and I threw up a fog of dust as I pounded after him.

"That's far enough!" barked a voice. I pulled up to find myself surrounded with shooting irons. Seven hard-eyed men formed a circle around me, and at their center was the bristly gent in the green tweed suit. Hank McFarland.

Just behind him stood the tow-headed boy, who stuck thumbs in his ears and waggled his fingers at me. McFarland flipped him a coin and the boy scampered off. There's seemingly no limit to the perfidy of town-bred humans.

"I hear you're working for Homer King," McFarland said. "I'm making you a better offer."

I examined McFarland's men. I knew their type, stone-cold killers with no more conscience than rattlesnakes. But two of them looked familiar, and I gave them a second squint. "Hey," I said. "Those are the bankrobbers I caught."

"They've joined my campaign committee," McFarland said, "and I trust you will too."

"Or what?"

"Or someone might swear you were behind that bank robbery – and the stage job too. We'd have to shoot you for resisting arrest."

"You can't arrest nobody. You ain't the sheriff."

"Will be by tomorrow," McFarland said. "One way or the other."

Best join this pack of wolves, Davy said. *You can't whup all seven.*

I frowned. Now he wanted me to play the coward. I didn't know what he was up to, but I wasn't falling for it.

"After due consideration," I said, "I've decided to endorse your candidacy." Smiling large, I stepped forward and put out a paw. "Let's shake on it."

McFarland grinned and grasped my hand.

And he was still grinning when I plucked him off his feet, cracked him overhead like a bullwhip and laid into his gang of cutthroats. His flailing legs were hard to aim, but equally hard to duck, and half his men had busted skulls or fractured jaws before they knew what hit them. They all started flinging lead free and generous, some of it nicking my anatomy, but more plowing into McFarland. Somehow, one of them got behind me and started carving my leg with a Bowie, so I cross-drawed my Navy Colt and brained him with the butt. My blood was up now, and I returned fire with equal enthusiasm, producing a most delightful chorus of howls.

All at once I heard cheering, and realized a powerful lot of people had gathered to watch. Meeting no further resistance, I paused to find my enemies scattered about me in blood and ruin. I tossed McFarland in among them and sought an escape route.

"Wait!" came a shout, and onto the battlefield rushed Sheriff King, leading a half-dozen men wearing deputy badges. As the deputies gathered up the wounded and the slain, King addressed the crowd.

"Fair citizens! My favorite deputy has done it again. And little wonder, for it's come to my attention that the blood of Davy Crockett flows strong in his veins!"

The crowd whistled and crowed until the sheriff motioned them to stop.

"If you look close," King said, "you'll see McFarland's gang includes this morning's bank bandits, and I'm betting the same bunch robbed the Wells Fargo. Considering that my unworthy opponent, if he's still among the living, is now under arrest, I declare the election cancelled."

This garnered only light applause, but King perked them up with, "Let's all retire to the saloon and toast Crockett's heroics. Drinks are on me!" And he pulled that thick wad of bills out of his coat, waving them over his head.

Folks started streaming through the rear of The Alamo, reaching high to clap me on the back as they passed.

Congratulations, Davy said. *You done it.*

Anytime he paid me a compliment, I was instantly suspicious.

Done what?

Caught the thieves plaguin' these parts. Half of 'em, leastways.

What do you mean, "half"? I got them all.

That so? You find the feller with the busted boot?

Dang. I'd forgotten that footprint, but there was still time to redeem myself. King's deputies had already dragged the bodies away, so I strolled about, keeping an eye on the dirt. I'd covered most of the area and was heading back toward the saloon when I spotted that print. I pointed, triumphant.

There! The rascal was standing right there!

Right enough. But which rascal?

I furrowed my brow, figuring who'd been where, and when.

Dang.

Exactly.

The last of the citizens were now crowding through the saloon doors, and I pushed in after them. The liquor was flowing free and everyone was looking jolly, particularly Homer King, who'd just claimed another term as sheriff. I made my way to his side.

"Sheriff King did a bang-up job catching those crooks," I said above the roar. And while King took a bow, I added, "And he's about to catch a few more."

This brought puzzled looks and cries of "Huh? Who?"

"Your illustrious Sheriff," I said, "is going to arrest himself, along with these sidewinders he calls deputies."

King's mouth flapped open. His men growled and laid hands on their gun butts. Everyone else gaped in astonishment.

I reached into his coat pocket, yanking out the wad of bills. "You've seen this stack of greenbacks he's so free and easy with. Well, I know where he got it – from the stage I was drivin' when these owlhoots dumped half a mountain on me."

King began to bluster, but his men's faces went dark with guilt, and there was no doubt my charge was true. Before King knew what was up, I snatched him off the floor and twirled him downside-up, exposing the bottom of his boots.

"This broken heel proves it! His prints were all over the ground next to the empty dispatch box."

King's language was scandalous to hear and, as there were ladies present, I popped his head into a brass cuspidor.

His deputies suddenly bristled with six-shooters, forming a tight group as they edged toward the door. "Don't nobody try and stop us," one gritted.

I stared, feeling helpless. I had King in one hand and that sheaf of bills in the other. Even if I could go for my gun, there'd be innocent folk slaughtered in the crossfire.

Nothin' dazzles outlaws, Davy said, *like the sight of greenbacks.*

If you got a suggestion, spit it out.

I just did.

And then the light dawned. "Ain't you forgettin' something?" I asked the deputies.

Their eyes narrowed. "Like what?" said one.

"Your money." And while they gawped, I tossed that stack of bills into the air above their heads, scattering them every whichaway.

They all looked up, transfixed, and some started snatching bills with their free hands. And while they were at it, I tilted the sheriff up horizontal and charged straight at them. That brass cuspidor, with King's head still inside, struck like a battering ram and bowled them over like nine-pins. Next thing they knew, my boots were doing a war dance on them.

When I stepped aside, the floor was littered with ex-deputies nursing busted ribs and shattered gun hands. I was about to drop King when I saw something glinting in his pants' pocket. I reached in, and out came my old silver flask, along with the twenty dollars I'd been carrying. I flung him to the floor and gave him a kick in the britches for good measure.

How's that, I asked Davy, for stomping my own snakes?

You're the pride of the Crocketts, boy. I knowed you wouldn't let us down.

You're the pride of the Crocketts, I replied. You got enough pride for every Crockett from here to Judgment Day.

All of a sudden Kassy King stood before me. I did my best to look sorrowful, but inside I was whooping for joy. "Sorry about your pa," I lied. "I expect you hate me now."

She looked at me a long while, and I braced myself for a slap. Instead, she flung an arm around my neck and jumped up so I was forced to catch her. "I've been waiting eighteen years for a man to do that. Now I'm finally free!" She swung her head to face the crowd. "We need a new sheriff, and who better than the reincarnation of Davy Crockett? I say we vote him in right now, by popular acclaim!"

Well, the whooping and hollering was painful to my ears, and before I knew it someone had stuck a sheriff's badge on my chest.

Just then that little newspaper dude appeared, scooting his pencil across a tablet. "What a story," he blurted. "Sheriff Davy Crockett cleans up Lizard Gulch. When the news hits Denver you'll be a sensation! Quick, somebody direct me to the telegraph office!"

As he sprang for the door, Miss Kassy planted a juicy smacker on my lips. "Isn't it wonderful, Dave? Now we can get hitched!"

My eyes bulged. My heart thundered. Frantic, I stuffed my life savings into her dainty hand. "Where's that horse your pa promised me?"

"Out to the side of the saloon," she cooed. "But why?"

I plopped her onto the bar and plowed through the crowd, hunting a side door. Not finding one, I lowered my shoulder and bulled through the wall in a shower of splinters.

I see it all now, I told Davy. You didn't push me toward that deputy job 'cause you knew I'd balk.

You're as predicable as a dog with a flea.

Spotting my new horse, I forked him and went fogging toward the nearest telegraph pole.

And you said not to fight McFarland, knowing I would.

Like a cat with a rat.

Bam! went my six-gun, parting the telegraph wire. I snagged the falling wire from the air and went streaking toward the next pole.

I'll bet you knew about King all along.

Only since you first met 'im, and I seen his prints in the street.

Passing that next pole, I gave the wire a yank, busting it free, and continued down the line until I had a nigh a mile of telegraph wire snaking in my wake.

How long you figure to keep that up? Davy wanted to know. *Word's gonna get out anyway.*

Not before I get clean out of the territory.

Won't make no difference. You're a lawman now.

Not for long. To even things out, I aim to rob the first bank I see. After that, I'm taking me a long vacation.

You know, he said, *I've always had a hankerin' to see San Francisco.*

I surely do. That's why I'm headin' for China, or Persia. Maybe even Zanzibar!

DARKE JUSTICE

Peter Averillo

Chantel Foster, writing as Peter Avarillo, is sixteen. She has been brought up on western literature and encouraged and mentored by her grandfather, Ray Foster, who is also represented in these pages.
This is her first published story.

As Joey Lavern stepped out of the saloon on to the rough wooden boardwalk, he paused long enough to stretch his slim nineteen-year-old frame. A slight, cool breeze wafted around him, spitting fine dust into his face, forcing him to squint. He gave a guilty start as Sheriff Rick Blaine walked out of his office and threw Joey a wave.

With a forced smile, Joey returned the gesture, thankful that the lawman had moved on towards the only eating-house in town.

Eyes watering, Joey looked around at Matlock's familiar buildings and felt an overwhelming sense of regret. Only two weeks ago he was satisfied that he was settled enough to call Matlock home. Well, not quite home, for that was back east in Philadelphia. The lure of the west he'd garnered from dime novels brought him to Matlock. A place that was now familiar – but worrisome.

Had Sheriff Blaine known what Joey had done, surely, he would have stormed across the hard packed dirt road to arrest him. At least the lawman's gesture was friendly and for that Joey was grateful.

He just wished he'd never volunteered to take part in that stagecoach robbery. The experience had terrified the life out of him. There'd been nothing romantic about it and it sure wasn't as easy as it seemed in dime novels. Even Tom Sly, one of the other two men involved besides him, expressed second thoughts.

"I don't like this," Tom Sly had said, watching the stage driver whip the horses up the steep incline towards the boulders where the three masked men hid. "Bad luck, they say, to rob the breed woman."

"Stories." Henry Stilwell dismissed the superstition. "No one's come up with any proof."

"Tell that to the Coker brothers," Tom Sly fired back. "They held up her stage and never got to spend a penny."

Stilwell snorted. "Yeah? The way I heard it, a bounty hunter called Morgan Darke took them boys out. Coincidence – nothin' more. So shut that mouth of yours before you spook the kid."

Joey was already spooked. By the time the stage crested the hill and came to a halt under the guns of Stilwell and Sly, they seemed to have control of the situation: they made their presence felt with ready shotguns.

Clad in a sheepskin-lined jacket against the chill of the high altitude, the driver sat as though carved from stone, her face impassive beneath a battered gray hat. Joey noticed that she was not looking directly at Stilwell and Sly and assumed she was doing it to avoid antagonizing them.

While Stilwell and Joey kept the driver covered, Tom Sly dismounted and opened the door of the stagecoach to rob the passengers.

The driver's green eyes slid in Joey's direction and he felt a shiver run down his spine. He reckoned her passive attitude was a deception. She covertly studied each of the robbers in turn, as if committing the visible parts of their faces to memory. She made Joey very uncomfortable.

Then it was over and the three bandits rode away with Joey uncertain of what had taken place, for his total concentration had been on the breed woman. Frantically, he tried to keep up until Stilwell called a halt several miles from the scene of the hold-up.

"Well, what we got?" Stilwell demanded.

"'Tweren't the normal stage," Sly grumbled. "Jus' three old biddies heading for Abilene. All they had was cases of dresses..." He handed Stillwell a battered brown valise. "And this."

Stilwell snapped open the valise, looked inside, and grinned. "Well, that weren't no waste of time," he said, holding up a wad of greenbacks.

"How much you reckon?" Sly asked.

"Enough, Tom, enough," Stilwell replied with a grin.

"You'll be able to pay off the bank, now, Mister Stilwell?" Joey asked, hopefully, for he did not want to go through that experience again.

"Enough," the older man assured him. "And then some. You done good, Joey, and you deserve a share."

"Yeah, I guess," Tom Sly agreed, but there was a doubt in his tone. "Still don' sit easy with me. I mean, we just stuck up the breed woman–"

"Stow it, Tom," Stilwell snapped. "I know what we just done. Figure it best if we split up. I'll pay off the bank and we'll meet back at the ranch in a week or so and divide up the rest. As far as folks'll be concerned, you two are off doing a piece of business for me."

"Why?" Tom Sly's tone carried suspicion.

"By the time a posse gets here," Stilwell explained, "they won't know which way the money went, and we need to be above suspicion."

Tom Sly grinned as the explanation seemed to put his mind at rest.

Joey said nothing. Despite the praise, he knew it was just a gesture to boost his low morale, and it didn't make him feel any better about himself.

That had been nearly two weeks ago.

Joey's nervousness slowly evaporated. If the law knew what he'd done, the sheriff wouldn't have just given him a friendly wave.

He forced a bounce into his step as he walked up the boardwalk towards the livery stable. It was about a two-hour ride to the dilapidated ranch where he'd worked for the past six months and called home. He'd always been grateful to Henry Stilwell for taking him on, despite his inexperience, and teaching him how to be a ranch hand. When he'd heard Mr Stilwell's explanation about the proposed robbery, he'd felt obliged to volunteer out of gratitude. Joey had no wish to see Mr Stilwell lose the place because of the bank's impatience over the old man's inability to repay his loan on time.

Maybe now that Mr Stilwell could use any extra money to make needed repairs on the house, little more than a shack, the barn, and the bunkhouse. Strange, how Mr Stilwell seemed to care more for his cattle and horses than he did for his buildings.

Joey passed the corral and stepped through the livery's large doors into the shadowy confines of the stable. There were two people near the stalls at the far end.

Jeb Summers, the middle-aged owner of the livery, was busy shoveling oats into a feedbag. He glanced up, gave Joey a welcoming smile, then bent to continue with his chore.

The other person was a stranger, hardly more than five feet five inches tall with long black hair that hung to the shoulder. Black seemed to be the dominant color: waist-length denim jacket, jeans, shiny leather boots and a low-crowned flat-brimmed hat varied from black to shades of gray through wear. A black moleskin glove covered the left hand like a second skin and a black leather gun-belt was cinched around the hips with a slanted, cutaway holster that held a Colt .45 angled for easy access.

Joey decided the stranger was a gunfighter, since the rig looked as though it was designed for the kind of fast draws he'd read about. Occupied with brushing down his roan, the man in black seemed unaware of Joey's presence.

Quickly, Joey ducked into the stall that held his horse. As he removed his saddle from the tree, he dislodged a scrap of paper that fell to the ground. Curious, Joey set everything to one side and bent down to pick up the folded sheet. As he opened it, the color faded from his face and beads of perspiration broke out on his brow.

His hands trembled and his stomach churned as he re-read the crudely printed poster.

WANTED
For
Stagecoach Robbery
JOEY LAVERN
$150
Reward

It wasn't just the poster that alarmed him. How was it possible? He couldn't remember anyone using his name during the robbery. Had the posse caught up with Tom Sly or Henry Stilwell? Had they given him away? Panic set in as he wondered what his mother would say if she heard that her only son was now a wanted man.

Joey was so wrapped up in himself that he was unaware that someone stood behind him – until he felt something cold and metallic touch his ear. In the same instant, his gun was smoothly removed from its holster.

"Hello, Joey," the voice in his ear was soft and firm.

For a moment he stood there frozen to the spot. Pounding, his heart seemed to be the sole moving muscle in his body. Letting out a deep sigh, he slowly turned to face the inevitable. He was surprised to find himself staring into the icy green eyes of the breed woman.

Close up, she was beautiful. She wasn't much older than he was. He couldn't drop his gaze from those almond-shaped eyes set above high cheekbones. Her flawless skin was dark with a suggestion of mixed blood.

The words blurted out of Joey's mouth: "I didn't do anything much."

"I know." The breed woman shrugged. "But you were still part of it. Didn't see you do a thing to stop it."

"What are you going to do?" Joey nervously lowered his eyes and took in her gun-belt, its silver buckle shaped like an eagle about to scoop up its prey. That was how Joey felt – her prey.

"Take you to the law, I guess," the breed woman informed him indifferently.

Joey glanced at the open doors: "I could make a run for it."

"You could try," she agreed lightly. "But, then I'd have to put a bullet in you."

"What? You'd shoot me in the back?"

"When a man's worth a hundred and fifty bucks to me," she said firmly, "then you can bet I'll do whatever is necessary."

"Got no choice, then," Joey said, resigned to his predicament.

"Never did have." The breed woman nodded at the open door as she slid Joey's gun behind her belt. "Let's get this done with."

With her gun leveled at his back, Joey began the humiliating walk down to the law office where Sheriff Rick Blaine was about to have his peace broken.

*

Matlock's lawman was in his mid thirties and happy with his lot. All he had to do for his pay was carry out his duty and maintain a visual presence. In the year he'd occupied the post, apart from dealing with the odd drunk and keeping order on Friday nights when the local hands came into town, nothing broke the peace. He sat at his desk, his belly full from his recent meal, content to enjoy a cigar.

The office door opened and Blaine's sandy eyebrows shot up and down in a combination of shock and surprise. The Lavern kid was pushed inside by a woman dressed in black. He sat mesmerized as the woman tossed Joey's gun onto the desk in front of him. There was something odd about the woman: she was wearing six-guns like a gunslinger.

"Just what's going on here?" he demanded, leaning forward in his seat.

The woman produced a poster from her pocket and held it out. When the lawman refused to accept it, she slammed the poster on the desk. "The kid's wanted for stage robbery."

Blaine unfolded the poster and studied it with an air of disbelief.

"Just need a receipt," the woman said.

Blaine patently ignored her. He glanced at Joey: "This is a joke, right? I don't have the time for pranks. Now you and your girlfriend had better get out of here before I get angry."

"No joke," the breed woman said coldly, as if stung by his jibe.

"Ain't talking to you, girl," Blaine responded sharply. "Joey, you want to tell me what this is all about?"

"Sorry, Sheriff Blaine," Joey said, his tone apologetic. He stared at the floor. "But, like it says there, I helped rob this lady's stage."

"Why, Joey?" Blaine wasn't totally convinced what he was hearing was true. He picked up the poster and waved it at Joey. "You in trouble? I can tell you this sure ain't the way to go about it. This dodger don't look right." He threw up his hands. "Look, just get the hell out of my sight, the pair of you, before I do something I might regret."

"No, sir. Honest," Joey blurted out. "Would never have done it but Henry – Mr Stilwell – he was getting so desperate. I mean, if the bank foreclosed on him he'd have lost everything. I had to help him out... after he took me in and –"

Blaine held up his hand. The gesture brought Joey's flood of words to an instant halt. "This ain't making sense to me. You're trying to tell me that Henry was going bust? You have to be kidding me. I think I'd have known about something like that."

Turning his attention away from Joey, the lawman glanced at the woman. "And you – you reckon this boy held you up. I don't recall anyone reporting a stage hold-up."

"I didn't report it. I'll deal with it myself," the woman said.

"So what did those fellers do, huh? Make introductions before they robbed you?"

"One of them thought it was a good idea to hole up in Abilene." She shrugged with an icy nonchalance. "Feller called Tom Sly. With me and my passengers pointing our fingers at him, guess he had no choice but to confess and name names."

"Oh, this gets better," spluttered Blaine. Then he slammed the palms of his hands down on the desk. "Now Tom Sly's involved as well? So, what I'm being asked to believe is that three respected people from this town went out and robbed a stage." He paused and pointed at the woman. "Your stage. Because Stilwell, who we all know has money stashed away at the bank, needed some pocket money. Give me a break, lady."

"Then, maybe, you'd like to have a word with Mister Hickock," the woman suggested. "He's the law in Abilene."

"I know who he is," Blaine roared, his anger on the surface now. "This joke's gone far enough. You really take me for an idiot?"

"You said it, not me," she stated lightly.

"It's true, Mr Blaine, it's true," Joey pleaded. He glanced at the woman then back at the sheriff. "I'm really sorry. I – I want to go home – to Philadelphia."

"Nobody's going anywhere just yet," the woman said. "Let's settle this problem another way." She reached down and withdrew a sheet of paper from her boot. Carefully, she opened it out; it was a poster. Then she folded it so only the likeness was visible as she laid it on the desk.

Joey leaned forward for a better look. He gasped: "That looks like Mr Stilwell."

"Sure does," Blaine agreed, puzzled. "Wait a minute..." He tugged open his desk drawer and pulled out a sheaf of flyers. He thumbed through them until he found a match to the one on his desk. He whistled through his teeth.

"Like you said – a man with a lot of money stashed in the bank," the breed woman reminded him. "Now you know how he came by it."

"Rustling, bank and stage robbery," Blaine read out, shaking his head in disbelief. "And living right under my nose."

"Who?" Joey asked.

"Stilwell's real name is Charles Pilbeam," she said gently. "He's wanted in three states and has a two thousand dollar reward on his head." Then, with a smile that failed to touch her eyes, she added, "Dead or alive."

"Lady," Blaine warned, "you'd best leave this to me. I'll give you a receipt for Joey – but Stilwell's *my* problem."

"That's so sweet of you." She smiled. "What a nice man you are – to think that I wouldn't be able to deal with old Charlie Pilbeam. Mind you, that's what a lot of people thought – until I brought in Bill and Pete Coker's corpses."

"Henry said something about that!" Joey recalled. "I think he said the Coker brothers were brought in by a man called Darke? Morgan Darke?"

"Morgana – there's an 'a' on the end of my name," the woman stressed. "It's Morgana Darke."

"Then why did they say it was a man?" Joey asked, perplexed.

Blaine smiled ruefully: "What man would admit to being taken by a woman?"

"When it's usually the other way around." Despite the banter, Morgana Darke's comment came with an icy, bitter tone.

Sheriff Blaine was fast regretting the way he'd handled this situation. From the moment he'd seen the armed woman with the pretty heart-shaped face, he should have realized she was dangerous. He cursed his lack of judgment. "So you drive a stage," he mused.

"Tom said she was known as the breed woman," Joey offered.

Blaine nodded: "Heard of her. It's said to be bad luck to hold her up. No wonder. Looks like the breed woman and Morgan, er – Morgana Darke are one and the same. Am I right?"

"Typical man." Morgana glanced beseechingly at the ceiling. "Takes a while, but they get there in the end."

"You got no cause to take umbrage," Blaine said.

She gave him a dark look.

He ignored it and stood up. He took Joey by the arm, ready to escort the prisoner to the cells.

But Joey held back, as if reluctant to take the first step toward the end of his freedom. "Why do they call you the 'breed woman'?" he asked.

"'Cause she's half Indian," Blaine growled, yanking Joey's arm and pushing him towards the cells.

"That's what folks say, Joey, but they're mistaken," Morgana replied. "I'm a *didikoi* – a half blood gypsy and proud of it."

"That right?" Blaine grunted as he locked the cell door. "Far as I'm concerned, a breed's a breed."

"*Shin bostaris*," she hissed under her breath.

Refusing to look at her, Blaine returned to sit behind his desk. After taking paper and pencil from his drawer, he scratched out a receipt and pushed it across the desk.

"I know that kid," he said. "I reckon he was tricked into this."

Morgana tucked the receipt into the top right pocket of her jacket. "I got that impression, too," she confirmed. "That don't make it right, though."

"No," Blaine conceded. "But –"

"Look, Joey Lavern is in your custody. So, you make the decisions about him from now on. He's not my responsibility."

"Lady, I know Joey," Blaine protested. "He's out of place here and he won't stand a chance in prison. He–"

"You don't get it, do you?" Morgana snapped. "The kid's in your custody. Do what you think is right."

"And Henry Stilwell?" Blaine queried.

"All mine," she said in a firm tone that brooked no argument.

"Dead or alive, huh?"

"It'll be his choice." Morgana shrugged.

"Looks like we won't meet again."

"Of course we will." Morgana grinned. "Who else will be handing over that two thousand dollar bounty?"

Blaine fired back, "You've got to be alive to collect."

"Be seeing you, then." Morgana Darke waved a cheery farewell, opened the door, and was gone.

As she strode down Main Street towards the livery, Morgana slipped Joey Lavern's wanted poster from an inside pocket of her jacket and ripped it up. It had served its purpose. She felt confident that the lawman would do the right thing. If he didn't, then either way the greenhorn would have learned his lesson. Even Tom Sly had pleaded with her to forget about the kid for Joey would have run at the slightest hint of trouble.

As far as Morgana was concerned, Joey Lavern and Tom Sly were small fry compared to Pilbeam. She wanted him most of all.

During the stage robbery, Pilbeam had sat leering at her, wanting her to make the slightest move for a weapon that would give him the excuse to fire his shotgun. Bill Coker had done the same, and he had paid for that mistake with his life.

Anyone who pointed a gun at Morgana Darke had no right to live to tell the tale.

Charlie Pilbeam glanced out the grimy window of the shack he called home. Darkness was encroaching and another day was sliding into the past. As each day passed, he came nearer to his fifty-eighth birthday, perhaps the only event he had to look forward to. His standing in town was so big now that he could drink as much as he liked at the saloon and not pay a cent.

Though neither Tom Sly nor Joey Lavern had turned up, Charlie wasn't too troubled. He glanced at his bed; underneath lay the valise with five thousand dollars stashed inside. In fact, the longer the other two remained absent, the more likely it became that Charlie would have all the money to himself.

Without lighting the lantern that sat in the middle of a scarred table, Charlie made his way to the bed. He sat down and removed his boots and slid them under the bed. Then he stood up, snapped his braces down and dropped his pants to the floor. He stepped out of them, all the time staring out the window at the darkness beyond. They weren't coming, he thought. The kid had probably skedaddled. Should never have taken him along. Hell, it was the kid's choice, but then again the kid mightn't have offered if Charlie hadn't lied about the bank foreclosure. Needed some excuse since the kid overheard Tom jawing about the planned robbery. Tom should be back by now. Probably stopped off in town for a drink or several. Maybe he'd turn up come the morning, Charlie decided as he unbuttoned his shirt.

Barefoot he crossed the planked floor of the room where he folded his clothes and laid them neatly on a chair.

Dressed only in pale red long johns, he returned to the bed. With this nightly routine completed, he lay back on the straw mattress and covered himself with a thin gray blanket. Within minutes, he was asleep.

A couple of hours later his eyes snapped open. He was sure he'd been disturbed by a scraping noise. He looked around, eyes straining to determine anything in the shadows that might have disturbed his sleep. Nothing.

Relaxing, he snuggled back down.

No sooner had he closed his eyes than he was wide-awake again. This time, he smelled burning. Alarmed, he sat up. The window reflected a fiery glow. Cautiously, he swung from his bed and grabbed the shotgun that rested against the nightstand. He always left it loaded; the heft of it gave him some reassurance.

He edged towards the door then paused when he noticed something had been poked under it. Maybe that accounted for the scraping noise he heard earlier? He bent down to pick it up. Straightening out the paper, he went back to the window and by the flickering light of the fire outside realized he was holding a wanted poster.

"Damn it to Hell," he grumbled, as he recalled what Tom Sly said about it being bad luck to rob the breed woman.

Superstitious nonsense! He looked through the window and breathed easy. It wasn't the barn or the bunkhouse. What the hell? Someone had built a fire – it looked like it was made of hay and some of his busted corral poles.

Damn it to Hell, he thought and tossed the poster to the floor, I ain't hanging around to be burned out.

He swung open the door and rushed out, shotgun held across his chest. Barefoot, he stepped across the warped boards of the porch. A splinter dug into his heel but went unheeded as he jumped to the hard packed ground. He moved cautiously towards the fire. All the time, his gaze flicked from side to side, searching for the fire starter. The twin barrels of the shotgun followed the movement of his eyes.

"Show yourself!" he yelled.

"Right by your side." The voice was soft, almost seductive, and definitely feminine.

He turned.

A woman emerged from the barn entrance.

"The breed woman!"

"The name's Darke, Morgana Darke," she told him casually. "You may have heard of me."

"Darke's a feller," Charlie snapped, glaring at her.

"So I've been told," Morgana said and jerked her Colt at him. "Be an idea if you let go of that shotgun. Hate you to have an accident."

"What's it matter?" Charlie grunted. "Poster said dead or alive."

"Your choice," Morgana replied.

Charlie swung his shotgun around and moved to one side.

In the same instant, she fired her Colt. The .45 bullet smashed into Charlie's left arm, destroying muscle and bone. Unable to maintain a grip on the shotgun with his nerveless hand, he staggered back and the barrels cracked against his shin. He tried to get a better grip on the shotgun but the combination of falling weight and his haste made him misjudge and his finger pulled the trigger. The full force of both barrels tore away Charlie's left leg from the knee down. For a second he just stood there on one leg. Then he let out a shrill scream and toppled over to one side.

He lay there, shuddering as shock took control of his body; the shaking was so great he couldn't prevent Morgana from lifting the empty shotgun from under him.

"Never got took by a woman before," Charlie mumbled. His body shook uncontrollably while his face twisted with pain.

"First time for everything, Charlie." Morgana shrugged. But she was talking to a corpse. Shock and blood loss killed him, she reckoned.

Leaving Charlie Pilbeam where he lay, Morgana strolled over to the shack and went inside. She lit the lantern. As she looked around she noticed how sparsely furnished the place was; the only thing that interested her was the valise poking out from beneath the bed.

She knelt and dragged out the valise and checked the money: it was all there. She smiled, satisfied, and stood up. She stripped the blanket from the bed, went outside and wrapped Charlie's body in it. With this chore completed, she strolled over to the barn and lay down on the straw. There was no point in going back to town this late at night. So she slept.

At first light, she was wide-awake. She washed her face at the pump, then saddled Charlie's horse and led it over to the corpse. She boosted the stiff blanket-wrapped body up and over the saddle; within her slim body were muscles toned from more activities than just driving a stage.

She'd just finished tying down the body when she heard someone riding up the trail leading to the shack. Quickly, she crossed the open space and took cover against a wall. Colt drawn and ready, she waited until the rider had pulled his horse to a halt.

"I know you're there, Miss Darke," Joey Lavern called out. He dismounted and tied the reins to a hitch post.

She stepped into the open, her gun pointing at him: "Sheriff let you go, then?"

"Yes." He hesitated. "Miss Darke, what did you say to Sheriff Blaine? I've never heard that before. Sounded like *Shin bostaris...*"

"Let's just say the last word sums him up. He's a bastard."

"Oh."

"But even he has common sense, since he let you go. Learned your lesson, huh?"

"That's right, Miss Darke. Just came by to pick up some things," he said. "Well, maybe not my dime novels. They're what got me into all this trouble in the first place."

"Do what you like, Joey. My business with you is done." Morgana slipped the receipt from her pocket and handed it to him. "People around here have nothing but good to say about you. Just don't come to my notice again – or you'll answer to me."

"Don't plan to," Joey confessed, crumpling up the receipt. "I'm going home. Guess the west isn't like what I read in those books."

"Joey – you just need to realize the difference between fact and fiction." Morgana smiled. "I know those writers – if they wrote about me, I'd be a man."

"I'd know different," Joey pointed out, eyes appraising her. "But why would they do that?"

"Simple, Joey." Morgana mounted and gathered up the reins of Charlie's horse, the man's corpse slung across the saddle. "Surely you must have realized by now. This is a man's world."

ANGELO AND THE STRONGBOX

Cody Wells

Malcolm Davey, writing as Cody Wells, resides in the Santa Rosa Valley of California with his wolf-hybrid, Duma. He likes nothing more than to watch a movie or read a good book about the Old West. His fascination with the Wild West started at a very early age and it has never left him. Visit him online at: http://stormwolf2.webs.com.

"Step out of the coach – and bring the strongbox with you!" demanded the masked gunman astride his piebald. He appeared short and wiry and wore a black Stetson decorated with silver conch shells. Travis the stagecoach driver watched, his hands tightly gripping the reins. Buckskin clutched a wounded arm, his shotgun lying on the ground some ways back.

"If you want the strongbox, you come in and get it!" Buckskin recognized the voice of the passenger called McAlister. The darned fool, he thought. "You'll get a belly full of lead for your trouble!" McAlister said.

"Is that so?" The bandit signed to two of his fellow road agents. They dismounted and approached the coach from the other side. Buckskin couldn't see, but he heard. They fired in through the leather window cover and the wood door. McAlister must have got off a couple of shots before they finished him, Buckskin reckoned, as one of the bandits screamed and stumbled back off the roadside.

The outlaw in the black hat opened the door on his side and a man cried out, "Don't shoot, for pity's sake! The fool's done for and I'm hit in the arm."

"Too bad," the gunman said and fired twice into the carriage.

Buckskin heard a body slump to the floor.

Then the gunman climbed into the coach and after a few minutes yanked the strongbox along the carriage floor. "Give me a hand, will ya?" he called.

The remaining four road agents rode round to that side and two of them dismounted.

Travis must have seen his chance. He let off the brake and gee'd up the horses, lashed his whip and the coach pulled away. "Let's git!" shouted Travis. "I reckon they won't be wantin' witnesses!"

Buckskin held onto his hat and glanced back and grinned. The leader of the bandits fell out of the carriage into the dust, the strongbox toppling on the man's left leg. The carriage door slammed shut and Buckskin's heart raced.

The two mounted road agents lit after the coach, firing their six-guns. Buckskin ducked instinctively, they were that close, darn it.

Suddenly, Travis was hit and he slumped forward in the boot and the reins fell away. The horses pounded on, regardless.

The trail wound along the mountainside, a sheer drop on the left. Buckskin's heart hammered and sweat poured. Wheels sent up dust, obscuring the two mounted men. Bullets hit the luggage rack behind Buckskin. He tried leaning forward to grasp the reins, but his wound made him weak and dizzy.

Buckskin's heart sank. Ahead was a rider and he was pulling out a rifle from the boot behind the saddle. *Another one of the bastards!*

The rider raised the rifle to his shoulder and fired.

Buckskin ducked. He was doing a lot of that today. Sumbitch, the man was shooting at his pursuers! Clamping his hands on the rail, Buckskin risked looking back down the trail. Yes! One of them was hit, fell off his horse – damned fine shooting! The other one came on, but reined in when the rifleman's shots got too close, spitting splinters of rock in the man's face.

The coach approached the mounted rifleman and, as it trundled past, Buckskin looked at his savior. He was about six two, in his mid-thirties. His shoulder-length, raven-dark hair, olive complexion, high cheekbones and strong jaw suggested some Mexican blood. He wore a wine-colored cotton shirt and faded buff canvas pants. The low-crowned Stetson was pulled down at the front to shield his hawk-like blue eyes from the glaring sun. He packed a sidearm too: a short-barreled .45 in a brown Mexican single-looped holster on his right hip.

The coach raced past the rider, its wheels very close to the edge. "I can't stop!" Buckskin wailed.

Riding at full gallop, Angelo shoved his Winchester back in its boot. He spurred his horse after the runaway stage. The thunder of hoofs and the rumbling of the wheels made it impossible for him to hear what the man in the driver's box was hollering. He looked scared, which wasn't surprising. As the wheels passed so close, the edge of the trail broke off and tumbled down the mountainside.

Angelo caught up with the coach and passed it. He reached out for the bridle of the spooked lead horse. He was only a fingertip away when his gray faltered, as if running out of steam. The poor critter had already shown signs of fatigue before he gave chase, and he was asking a lot now since the midday Texas sun was merciless to anyone fool enough to be caught out in it. But Angelo was used to the harsh elements, and expected his horse to be as sturdy. He heeled the gelding hard and leaned forward in the saddle. "C'mon fella, one last spurt, you can do it!"

The gray gave its all and Angelo edged his mount between the sheer rock and the four-horse-team with inches to spare. Level now, Angelo caught hold of the lead horse's bridle and yanked on it. Gently, not to alarm the animal, as he didn't want them plunging off the trail. Gradually, the horse responded, and in time so did the rest of them. It took him what seemed an age to bring the runaway stagecoach to a halt amidst swirling dust.

The man sitting in the driver's box yanked on the brake and clambered down, his knuckles white from clinging for dear life to the side-rail. He was middle-aged and heavy set, dressed in a buckskin shirt and wool pants. He took off his hat and wiped his brow with a neckerchief and ran a hand through receding golden hair. "I'm in your debt, mister." He had a well-groomed mustache and goatee. "I thought I was done for." He reached up and shook Angelo's hand. "Buckskin Pete Morgan, Buckskin to my friends."

"Angelo." He slid from the saddle. "What in tarnation happened?"

Buckskin frowned, putting his hat on. "Not a pretty sight, Mr Angelo. A few miles back, six masked bandits held us up. McAlister, one of the passengers, was carrying a lot of money in his own personal strongbox. That's what those sons-of-bitches were after."

Angelo moved up to the coach. He tugged back one of the leather curtains and peered through the window. Two men lay sprawled on the floor, blood oozing from bullet-holes. He pulled open the door and leaned in, checking the neck pulses of both shot men. "Get the canteen from my horse. We've got a live one here!"

Buckskin hastily reached for the canteen and, fingers fumbling, unwrapped the strap from the saddle horn. The canteen dropped to the ground. Buckskin's face twisted as his hand grabbed his wounded arm. "Damn!"

Angelo saw the distress in the man's face "You okay?"

"I'd be fine if this arm didn't hurt like Hell." Buckskin reached down and picked up the canteen.

"We won't be needing it now," Angelo said. "The guy's just died on us." He slammed the carriage door shut and walked the gelding to the rear of the coach where he tied the reins to a bootstrap.

Angelo took out the makings and rolled a smoke. He struck a match on the side of the coach and lit his cigarette. "I'll help you take the stage into town. How far is it?"

"Gatlin's about another five miles along this trail. I really appreciate your help, fella."

"I was planning on taking a couple of days to rest my horse and get a decent meal and all. Might as well be Gatlin as any place."

Buckskin climbed into the driver's seat. Angelo gathered the reins and jumped up alongside him. He drove at a steady pace giving the horses an easy haul after their exhausting scurry. Buckskin seemed in a somber mood. Not surprising, really, after all he'd been through. Angelo left the man with his thoughts.

As the coach approached Gatlin, Angelo reckoned it was a relatively small place. A row of buildings ran down either side of its single street. He pulled up at the rear of the stage depot and wrapped the reins around the brake lever.

Buckskin looked a little bewildered. "Why the back?"

"We don't want to alarm folks, do we?" Angelo jumped down from the box.

"I guess not," Buckskin said. "I'll inform the undertaker and the sheriff. If you need livery, it's across the street."

Angelo untied his horse. "You need to see the doc, mind."

"Oh, I'll live – but, yeah, once I've told the sheriff." Buckskin carefully clambered down.

"No doubt I'll be seeing you around."

"Where'll you be?"

"Not sure, Buckskin. Where can you recommend?"

Buckskin scratched his head. "Well … if you're wantin' a decent room and somewhere to get cleaned up, I reckon you try the Silver Dollar Saloon. It's a little more expensive than most, but the service is a lot better and you won't find any cockroaches 'tween the sheets. It's just past the café on your right."

"Obliged."

"Thanks once again, fella. I won't forget what you did for me."

After he'd taken care of his horse at the livery, Angelo stepped up onto the boardwalk and entered the Silver Dollar. It was just like any other saloon. To the left, a long polished bar ran almost the entire length of the room. At the far end, a flight of stairs led up to a balcony with an ornate balustrade. Several tables filled the floor in a disorderly fashion.

Only a handful of patrons were in the room. A small man was mumbling to himself at the end of the bar; he seemed to have had more than his share of whiskey. Just left of the stairwell sat a man hiding behind a newspaper. Four businessmen occupied the middle of the room, eating a meal of pork ribs and corn bread.

The large-framed barman in his forties was chatting over a drink with a woman at the bar. The barman had thin gray hair and wore a well-pressed white cotton shirt, wool vest and an askew necktie. His round face had a huge smile on it as Angelo approached the bar. "What'll it be, mister?" the barman asked, his small piggy eyes appraising Angelo.

"You serve a decent beer in this place? And I don't mean the kind that's made out back."

The woman smiled. "Give the man a glass of our best, Marty." She was in her mid-forties, small and slender and just starting to lose her good looks. Her auburn hair framed a fair skinned face dominated by large dark eyes. "I own this joint," she told Angelo. Her scarlet, tight fitting silken dress displayed a hint of cleavage. "Kathleen O'Connor's my name, most folk around here just call me Dixie."

"Dixie?"

"On account of where I came from, I guess."

"Angelo."

"You mind me asking what line of business you're in, Mr Angelo?"

"It's just Angelo. No mister about it. I can turn my hand to anything that's honest."

"You lookin' for work?"

"Nope, I'm just passing through."

Marty placed the beer in front of Angelo. "That'll be two bits, mister."

Angelo pulled a dollar bill from his shirt pocket and laid it on the counter. "I also need a room."

"No problem," Marty said and pulled a key from under the bar counter. "Room eight, last one down the hall. You plan on staying long?"

"Couple of days I reckon, and then I'll be on my way." Angelo lifted the glass and drank the beer down in one go, and then wiped his mouth with the back of his hand. "Well, if you'll excuse me, ma'am, I'll get cleaned up and have myself a —"

He was cut short as a young cowboy strolled up and grabbed Dixie's upper arm and yanked her away from the bar. He pushed back the black Stetson decorated with silver conch shells. "We need to talk, Dixie."

"Not now, Joe."

"Yes, now! Let's go out back. We've a little problem that needs takin' care of."

"Let go, you're hurting me!"

"You heard the lady," Angelo said. "Now let her be!" he added, towering over Joe's wiry frame.

As he fixed his gaze on Angelo, Joe scowled, his top lip twitched slightly, and beads of sweat started down his forehead. The fingers of his right hand tapped the butt of the Smith & Wesson Schofield holstered high on his hip.

Dixie tugged. "Joe!"

Joe shook his head as if he'd been in a trance and released his grip on Dixie. "I'll be back within the hour with the boys. Be sure to have the back door unlocked." He turned to Angelo and in a low voice said, "This ain't over, mister!"

"It is from where I'm standing."

Joe turned and sauntered out. The batwings swung noisily.

"You OK, ma'am?" he asked Dixie.

"Yes, thanks, Angelo. A private matter, is all."

Nodding at her, Angelo moved away and mounted the first step of the stairs.

At that moment one of the businessmen yelled across the room, "Hang on there, mister." He was a burly man with a large round face and bushy mustache.

Angelo stopped as the man approached. "Something on your mind?"

"Turner …Turner's the name. I couldn't help but notice your little, shall we say … disagreement with Joe Paxton."

"What of it?"

"Take my advice and stay well clear of him. He's a —"

"Listen, I've been in the saddle for five days near as damn it. I'm tired, dirty and hungry. I aim to get me a bath, something to eat and then get my head down. When I want advice, I'll let you know."

"I—I was just trying to be friendly, mister."

Angelo turned and climbed the stairs without saying another word.

"Who the hell do you think you are?" Turner demanded.

"Someone you don't want to mess with!"

It was early evening when Angelo sat down to a meal Dixie had prepared. The medium rare steak, corn and freshly baked biscuits made his mouth water. It was a pleasant change from the beef jerky and dried beans he ate on the trail. And with a long haul ahead of him, he was going to make the most of this stopover.

Over the last few years, he'd tried his hand at most things. He'd even turned bounty hunter for a while, which in turn gave him his reputation as a fast gun. But that was all behind him now. He was headed for Tombstone, a town out in the Arizona Territory. He'd been told a man could make a small fortune there if he had the right connections and enough cash to buy real estate. He dreamed of opening his own freight business, settling down and raising a family.

The saloon was full of life, and it felt good to be among people after spending days with just his horse for company.

As Angelo cut into the steak, he noted Turner looking over from the card table. He gave a curt nod and continued eating.

Turner stood and walked over. "I hope we can start afresh after our little misunderstanding."

"I didn't realize there was a misunderstanding."

Turner pulled out a chair and sat. "It matters not. I didn't catch your name."

"I didn't throw it. Call me Angelo."

"Would that be Mr Angelo, or just plain Angelo?"

"Angelo's just fine. But I'm not keen on the 'plain' bit."

Turner attempted a chuckle, but it didn't quite come off. "I wanted to say that the young cowboy, Joe Paxton, he meant no harm. He's just highly strung. When he gets in one of his moods, it's best to keep clear of him."

"What's this Joe boy to you?" Angelo licked his lips; the steak was sure tender enough.

"I know his father, Tom. I'm a banker, you see, and I do business with him. He owns a spread just north of here."

Angelo didn't respond.

Turner fidgeted with his tie. After a while, Turner said, "I must say, you're a man of few words."

Angelo looked hard into the man's eyes. "I'm eating, and I'd be obliged if I could eat the rest of my meal in peace."

Abruptly, Turner stood. "Certainly, I just wanted you to know there are no hard feelings." He turned and scurried back to his friends and resumed a game of cards. The remnants of their earlier meal cluttered the table. A dog lay on the floor next to them, chewing on a discarded bone.

Suddenly, Turner drew back his chair. "Dammit, Frank. I swear since that flea ridden piece of fur followed you in here, he's brought me nothing but bad luck." He stood and kicked the dog hard in the ribs. It yelped and ran off behind the bar. "Stupid mutt, I was doing fine till he showed up. He's jinxed me for sure. I ought to put the son-of-a-bitch out of its misery."

One of Turner's associates threw his cards in the middle of the table. "Will you sit down, Turner! It's not as if we're playing for high stakes here. It's only nickels and dimes."

Angelo watched as the dog sheepishly emerged and loped towards his table. "You hungry, boy?"

The dog responded by moving closer, ears down. It sat by his chair and held out a paw. "So, you're a jinx, eh? Okay, Mr Jinx, how'd you like the rest of this steak?" A low rumble came in answer. Angelo cut the meat into small pieces and placed his plate on the floor.

In a matter of seconds, the mutt had gulped down every morsel and licked the plate clean. He was an odd looking thing, mostly Canaan but with something else thrown in: a little wolf-like, but with a much smoother coat of creamy white, and a shorter snout with low-set erect ears and bushy tail. When he picked up his ears, a distinct 'u' shape was visible on the left one, where the point should have been. Angelo thought possibly a large caliber bullet had sliced through it.

Angelo rubbed the dog's neck with both hands. "Okay, fella. That's all I have for now." The mutt gave a little bark then ran out of the saloon.

"Seems like that stray has taken to you." Dixie sat next to Angelo. "Anything else I can get for you?"

"That was a real fine meal, ma'am. I think I'll have me another beer."

Dixie signaled to Marty with her long slender hand. "Hey, Marty, two beers over here, when you're ready."

A tall lean man in his fifties strode into the saloon and removed his Stetson from his short wavy gray hair. His dark brown continental suit lent extra brightness to the polished star on his chest. A walnut handled butt of an Army Colt .45 jutted out of the holster tied down to his right thigh.

"Who's the lawman?" Angelo asked.

"That's Sheriff William Hart," Dixie said. "A good man."

Sheriff Hart sauntered up to the bar and placed his hat on the polished surface.

Marty grabbed a glass from under the bar. "The usual, Sheriff?"

"You bet, Marty," Hart replied as he glanced around the room.

Marty poured a beer and placed it on the counter.

Hart reached for it and took a sip. "The stranger sitting with Dixie, is his name Angelo?"

"That's what I heard, Sheriff."

Sheriff Hart strolled over to Angelo's table, pulled up a chair and sat down. "I believe I ought to say thanks."

Angelo was taken aback. "For what?"

Hart removed a cheroot from his top pocket and rolled it between his thumb and forefinger. "For helping Buckskin with the runaway stage. He probably would've been killed too if you hadn't helped."

Dixie jumped to her feet. "What do you mean, *killed too*? What's happened?"

Hart held out a palm, lowering it. "Keep it down. I don't want all and sundry knowing, just yet."

Angelo stood and briefly held Dixie's arm. "The stage was robbed ma'am. With the exception of Buckskin, everyone else was killed."

Dixie's eyes filled up. "Travis?"

"I know the name, ma'am," Angelo said in a low voice. "Buckskin said he was the driver. He's dead – shot as he tried to get away."

"No!" Dixie lifted her skirts and ran towards the back room behind the bar. "Dear God, no!"

Hart lit the cheroot. "She'll be fine. Just a little shocked, is all."

Angelo sat down and took out his makings. "Was she close to Travis?"

"I do believe they were seeing each other. How serious was their relationship? Well, I wouldn't know."

The back room door slammed shut. "I guess tact isn't one of your strong points, Sheriff."

"What's that supposed to mean?"

"Go figure."

Marty stepped out of the back room and stood in front of the bar. "Okay, everybody, listen up!" he bawled. "Miss Dixie wants everyone to leave. She's closing the place for the day."

There was considerable muttering, and feet shuffled. The drinkers seemed reluctant to leave.

"If you don't move it, I'll throw you out!"

Accompanied by swearing and scuffling of feet, the drinkers moved to the swing doors – with the exception of Turner. Within a matter of moments, the saloon seemed very quiet. Turner took his time and finished his drink, fastened his jacket and stood.

"Not so fast, Mr Turner," Hart said. "I want you to stay awhile."

"I said *everyone*," Marty growled, "and that means you too, Sheriff."

Hart frowned. "Yeah, maybe so. But I have some unfinished business here that needs taking care of." He eyed Angelo. "I need you to stick around as well."

"I've nothing better to do, Sheriff, so why not?"

Turner joined Angelo and Hart at their table. "What's this all about, Sheriff?"

"All in good time, all in good time." Hart turned his gaze to Marty. "They tell me you gave a room to a stranger earlier today, besides our friend Angelo here. Is that right?"

Marty looked puzzled. "Yeah, what of it?"

"When a stranger comes to my town after the stage has been robbed, I figure I need to talk with him."

Turner gasped. "The stage has been robbed?"

"Don't act coy. Knowing you the way I do, you probably know more than any of us about the robbery."

"I take offense at that, Sheriff."

Hart gave a cold grin. "I doubt that."

"His name's Freeman," Marty said. "I put him in room six. Do you want me to go get him?"

"What do *you* think?"

Marty hurried up the stairs and out of sight.

Hart delved into his pants pocket and pulled out a steel spur rowel and put it on the table. "I found this inside the coach. Could be somethin' and nothin', but I thought you ought to know in case it was yours."

Angelo studied the object with interest. "Looks pretty new, but it ain't mine. I didn't step up into that charnel-house."

"I thought so." Hart nodded. "Seeing as Buckskin or any of the passengers would have no reason to be wearing spurs, I reckoned it might be worth hanging onto. I figure it belongs to the bandit who climbed in to steal the strongbox."

Marty strutted down the stairs closely followed by Freeman.

Fastening the buttons on his white cotton shirt, Freeman said, "What the hell is this all about? I have an appointment early tomorrow, and I was trying to get some shuteye."

Suddenly, Freeman's face lit up. "Angelo!"

Angelo smiled. "As I live and breathe, if it isn't Ned!"

"You know this man?" Hart asked.

"I should do, he's my cousin!"

Freeman pulled up a chair and sat next to Angelo. "Boy, it must be all of five years since we last saw each other."

"At least! How's your Ma and Pa?"

"They're fine. Did you know that young Sally got wed?"

"She did?"

"You betya. And a baby on the way."

Angelo banged his fist on the table. "Well, I'll be a son-of-a-gun. I'm starting to feel old!"

"Ah, I hate to break up this little family reunion," Hart said, "but I have more pressing matters at hand." He turned his attention back to Ned. "Appointment – who with?"

"My employer, Mr McAlister. What's it to you?"

"Plenty, Freeman," Hart said. "McAlister's dead."

"What? But how?"

Angelo cut in. "The stage was held up and, apart from the shotgun rider, everyone was gunned down."

Ned Freeman pursed his lips and shook his head. "Guess this has been a wasted journey."

"What about you, Mr Turner?" Hart said. "You're the banker around here. You must have known about McAlister and his money comin' to Gatlin."

Turner cleared his throat. "Yes, of course I knew! McAlister was carrying over twenty thousand dollars in cash and five thousand in gold coin. A small portion of it was to pay old man Paxton for his ranch and livestock. The whole kit and caboodle was up for sale as Paxton was in a financial mess."

"Old man Paxton was selling-out?" Hart asked.

"He had no choice," Turner said. "His debts kept mounting, until he was forced to sell. Paxton was happy to take McAlister's generous offer. His son Joe, on the other hand, was not so happy about his father's decision to sell. The ranch was his heritage."

"Joe Paxton. That was the cowboy in here earlier, right?" Angelo asked.

"That's right," Turner said.

"Sounds as if he had a motive for robbing the stage," Ned said.

Turner pulled a kerchief out of his jacket pocket and wiped the sweat from his brow and hands. "Yes – yes, that's all well and good." He pointed shakily at Ned. "If *you* had something to do with the robbery, you could have made the whole thing up about working for McAlister. After all, he isn't around to verify your story."

Angelo jumped. "Now just wait a doggone minute, Turner. This man's my blood and I tell you, he's no thief."

Sheriff Hart drew his six-gun and leveled it at Ned. "Turner here don't know dung from wild honey, but he's got a point. You being a stranger in town and turning up just after the hold-up, well, I'll have to treat you as a suspect."

"You're making a big mistake, Sheriff," Ned said.

"That's as maybe, but I'm taking you to the calaboose until I get this mess cleared up. If you're innocent, you've nothin' to worry about."

Angelo gave Hart a cold stare. "He ain't going anywhere."

"Don't be foolish," Hart said evenly. "I ain't got any beef with you."

"The way I see it, you point a gun at my cousin, you're pointing it at the both of us."

The sheriff shifted the angle of his six-gun to cover both Angelo and Freeman. "Okay, drop the gun-belt. Move!"

Angelo didn't stir.

"Didn't you hear me? I said move!"

A fearsome growl drew everyone's eyes. Hart slowly lowered his gaze.

Teeth bared, Mr Jinx had his snout level with Hart's crotch. The dog moved closer, and gripped the bulge of the sheriff's pants with its front teeth, all the while letting out a threatening sound.

Hart stood rigid and his cigar dropped to the floor. Beads of sweat formed on his forehead as he looked at Angelo.

"For some reason," Angelo said straight-faced, "seems like you've pissed off Mr Jinx."

Hart slowly moved his six-gun, as if preparing to hit or even shoot the dog.

Mr Jinx growled and tugged vigorously.

"I'd drop the weapon, if I was you," suggested Angelo.

Hart dropped the gun. "Doggone it, Angelo, c– c– call him off!"

"Nothing to do with me. I can't tell him what to do."

Turner jumped up and moved a hand to the inside pocket of his jacket.

Angelo drew his .45. "Don't do anything stupid. The dog might get the idea that you're trying to hurt him. Now whatever you have in that pocket of yours, I'd be obliged if you put it on the table next to me."

Gingerly, Turner pulled out between his fingers and thumb a .41 caliber Remington derringer, and then placed it carefully on the table. "You've got some nerve," Turner said as he stepped away from the table.

"Stop your griping," Angelo said. He picked up Hart's six-gun and handed it to his cousin Ned. "Cover Turner and the sheriff, will you?" Ned nodded while Angelo holstered his own gun and emptied the cartridges from the derringer and threw them across the floor.

Turner frowned. "You won't get away with this!"

Angelo raised his eyebrows. "Get away with what? I've done nothing wrong, and I ain't gonna sit in some hot stinking jail while Sheriff Hart here pussyfoots around trying to solve the crime."

"Can you please get your dog off of me?" Hart pleaded.

"Like I said, he ain't nothing to do with me."

"For God's sake, Angelo, call him off," Turner said. "You know darn well that the mutt will do anything you ask of it."

Angelo gave a little smile. "Here, boy, it's okay."

The dog released its grip and trotted over to him.

Turner headed towards the batwing doors. "I can't stand around here, I have a bank to run –"

"Stop whining," Dixie said as she stepped out from the back room with a large glass of whiskey in her hand. "I'm not working, so I might as well enjoy myself." She turned to Marty. "No need to hang around, you might as well go home."

Marty looked a little hesitant. "Are you sure?"

"Yes, go! I'll see you tomorrow."

Marty left through the back door.

The sound of jingling spurs echoed throughout the barroom. Joe Paxton entered, followed by Clay and Billy, two friends of his who pushed Turner to one side and strode up to the bar. Billy was of average height and build, with long greasy hair, small piggy eyes and buckteeth. Clay had tight red curly hair. His wiry frame stood four inches short of six foot. A pair of beady eyes was set close together on his pear-shaped face. They were both in their late teens.

"By the look on your face," Joe said to Dixie, "you'd think someone just died."

Dixie knocked back the whiskey. "You ought to know, you sniveling little coward." Tears streamed, her mascara trailing down flushed cheeks. "You said no one would get hurt!"

"If I were you, I'd keep my mouth shut," Joe said in a low voice. "I lost two of my best pals back there, one of them to some do-gooder with a rifle who also blinded Freddy with ricochet. If I ever get my hands on the son-of-a-bitch, he'll wish he'd never been born." His gaze drifted round the room and rested on Ned Freeman with a six-gun trained on the sheriff. "Well, well. Looks like you have a spot of bother there, Sheriff."

"Keep out of this, Joe," Hart said evenly. "Just a little misunderstanding, is all. Nothin' to be concerned about."

Joe leaned against the bar. "Seems like the stranger has a problem with being understood."

To one side now, Angelo stood beside the dog, lit a cigarette and watched.

"There was no misunderstanding earlier, when his cousin helped bring the stage in," Hart said, thumbing at Angelo. "If it hadn't been for him, Buckskin would've met the same fate as Travis and the passengers."

Joe's lip began twitching. "Is that so?"

"It sure is."

Joe moseyed up to Angelo. "You're quite the hero, huh?"

"Not really. I just did what had to be done."

Joe looked over to the bar where his two friends stood. "Did you hear that, boys? He just did what had to be done."

Angelo looked at Joe. "Did you lose something other than two friends today?"

Joe's eyes widened. "What's that supposed to mean?"

Angelo said over his shoulder, "Ned, cover those two cowboys at the bar with Hart's pistol."

"Huh?"

"Just do as I say. If one of them so much as moves a muscle, shoot him." He then picked up the steel rowel from the table and threw it at Joe's feet.

Joe looked down at his spurs: one of the rowels was missing. "I suppose it's no good denying that it's mine?"

Angelo shook his head.

"And by the look on your face," Joe added, "I can guess where it was found."

"Right on both counts, fella."

"Okay, Ned," Hart said. "Give me my gun, I'll take it from here."

As Ned handed the sheriff his pistol, Dixie poured herself another whiskey. "Travis is dead!" she yelled. "How'd you account for that?"

Joe grinned and grabbed the bottle out of her hand and took a large swig. "If the stupid fool hadn't tried to run, he'd still be alive. His choice." He'd moved fast, positioning Dixie between the sheriff's gun and him.

Dixie lunged forward with her arm extended, ready to strike him.

Billy the buck-toothed cowboy grabbed hold of her wrist before it could make contact with Joe's face. "Hey, missy, not so fast, eh! It'd be a pity to break that pretty face with my fist."

"Dammit, can't get a clean shot!" snapped Hart.

Angelo moved softly over the boards, to one side, unnoticed during the scuffle. Mr Jinx padded by his feet. Three youths, loaded weapons and a hostage meant trouble. He didn't want to invite any rash moves and hotheaded shooting.

Dixie tried to free herself from Billy's grasp, but the man was too strong for her. He pulled her close and began to lick her cheek, his tongue finding the contour of her lips. She struggled and spat in his face. Then her legs buckled as Billy's hand struck the side of her head. She staggered a little, tears filling her eyes.

"Enough!" Hart snapped. "I'm taking the three of you in. Let her go!"

Now Joe grabbed Dixie from behind and drew a knife from its sheath and rested the blade on her throat.

Mr Jinx growled at him.

"Keep that mutt of yours in check," Joe snarled. "Drop your guns, or I swear I'll cut her up!"

"Easy boy." Angelo rubbed behind the dog's ears. "There'll be time enough for play later," he said then removed his gun from its holster and dropped it to the floor.

Hart placed his gun on the table. "Don't be foolish, Joe."

Joe waved his knife at Ned and Turner. "What about you two?"

"Neither of us is packing iron," Ned said.

"OK, all of you sit down so I can keep an eye on you," Joe said, pointing to one of the tables. "Clay, Billy, go get the box. Keep it covered with the blanket so no one on the street gets suspicious."

"What are you going to do with us?" Turner asked.

Joe drew his six-gun and sheathed his knife. "That depends on our friend here." He pointed to Ned. "I take it by what I've been told, you must be McAlister's new foreman?"

"What of it?"

At that moment, Clay and Billy struggled through the doorway carrying the stolen strongbox. They put it down in the middle of the floor and removed the blanket.

"This is no ordinary box, gentlemen," Joe said as he rested his foot on it. "It's custom made. Instead of the usual clasp and padlock, it has two built-in locks. It's made of two-inch thick steel."

Angelo reckoned it was a good two and a half feet in length. Nothing short of dynamite could penetrate that strongbox.

"McAlister was no fool," Joe went on. "I knew he sent the keys on ahead so the box couldn't be opened till it reached Gatlin. Now I believe you have those keys," Joe said to Ned. "Hand them over."

"I have one key," Ned said. "I know nothing about a second one!"

"Maybe Clay here can help you remember where it is."

Ned took the key from his shirt pocket and threw it at Clay, who caught it. "If I had the second key, or knew its whereabouts, I'd freely give it. Since McAlister's no longer with us, I don't give a damn who ends up with the money."

Joe grabbed Dixie by her hair. "What else did Travis tell you, Dixie? He must have said where the other key was."

Dixie screamed and struggled to get free from Joe's grip. "I told you everything I know. He never mentioned a second key."

"Why don't you leave the lady alone?" Angelo said.

"And why don't you shut the hell up?" Joe let go of Dixie's hair. "Maybe you wouldn't be so accommodating towards this whore if you knew what she was really like."

Angelo fixed his gaze on Joe and took the makings out of his shirt pocket. He rolled himself a smoke. "Now that you've got my attention, why don't *you* tell me?"

Joe stood opposite Angelo, careful not to get too close to Mr Jinx. "OK, I'll tell you. I've nothing to lose. It was Dixie's idea to rob the coach. She got all the information from lover-boy Travis. He was such a trusting fool and look where it got him!"

"I don't believe it!" Turner exclaimed.

"Believe what you like, I don't give a damn. With my Pa losing my inheritance, I figured it only fittin' I should take what was rightfully mine, before he could spend it."

Angelo lit his cigarette and slowly exhaled the smoke. "You can't spend it either, if you can't open the box."

"I'll worry about that later. First off, I lost two good pals today. Now, I want to see if you're as good with a six-gun as you are with a rifle."

Turner made a move for the doors.

"Hold it, fat man!" Joe snapped. "Pick the hero's gun from the floor, and carefully put it in his holster."

Turner was shaking uncontrollably. "P– Please, Joe. Let me go. I won't say anything, I swear."

"Just do it!"

Turner picked up Angelo's pistol and slid it into the holster.

Joe smiled. "Good! Now everyone move to the side, and leave me and the hero here to have a little dance."

Dixie and Turner rushed towards the stairwell for cover, while Ned crouched down at the side of the bar. Sheriff Hart calmly sat in one of the chairs near to Angelo, his feet up on the table.

Beads of sweat trickled down Joe's brow as he held Angelo's steady gaze. He went for his gun.

Sheriff Hart retrieved his six-gun from the table as Angelo slid his own .45 smoothly from its holster, thumbed back the hammer and squeezed the trigger. Both Angelo and Hart fired in unison.

Joe took two hits to the gut and stumbled backwards against the bar.

In the same instant, Clay was hit in the chest. He fell backwards. Mr Jinx leapt and locked onto his arm. Keeping a tight grip, the dog shook his head vigorously, flesh and bone torn savagely apart. Clay screamed for help. His pleas were answered as a bullet tore through the side of his head and he reeled out of the doorway.

A couple of bullets pumped into the front of the bar, and a sliver of wood hit Billy in the eye. He screamed as blood and a gel-like fluid wept from the wound and trickled down his cheek. Another bullet tore a path through his flesh and shattered bone as it drilled into his left shoulder. He slumped to the floor, aiming his pistol at Hart.

Angelo saw the danger to the sheriff and fired. A little round hole appeared in Billy's chest; the bullet tore through his heart.

It was all over in a matter of seconds. The room seemed clogged with gunsmoke and the stink of black powder.

Angelo holstered his gun and looked over at the bar.

Joe coughed as blood filled his lungs. He spat some of the thick fluid onto the floor. "Sweet Jesus ... just look at me. I need a doctor."

"You need a priest," Angelo said.

Sheriff Hart walked up to Angelo. "I guess I'm in your debt again, big fella."

"I guess so, Sheriff. Let me open the box for you. Then Turner can deposit it safely in his bank until McAlister's kin-folk turn up to claim it."

A look of surprise showed on Dixie's face "*You* can open it?"

Angelo smiled. "Fetch me the key. It's on the floor next to the doorway, where Clay dropped it."

Hart walked over, picked it up, and handed it to Angelo. "This I've got to see!"

Angelo inserted the key in the keyhole on the left and turned it, then locked it back.

"Well?" Dixie said.

"Just give it time."

From inside the box there was a clicking noise. Angelo took hold of the lid and lifted it with ease.

"You son-of-a-bitch! All this time, and you had the other key," Joe gasped and took his last breath.

Turner frowned. "I don't understand."

"There was only ever one key," Angelo said. "If you were a bandit unlocking the box with the only key you had, it wouldn't make sense to lock it again. You'd try to find the second key."

"I still don't get it," Dixie said.

"By turning the key once more to lock it, it actually releases a mechanical device that unlocks the box after a couple of minutes. Clever, huh?"

"But how'd you work it out?" Ned asked.

"After the hold-up, McAlister was still alive. Barely, but he lived long enough to tell me the secret. I didn't understand it at first. One key, turn to unlock it, then turn to lock it ... wait two minutes and it'll open!"

Dixie slumped down on one of the chairs, a look of despair shadowing her face.

"Sorry, Dixie, but you're under arrest," the sheriff said, clipping a pair of handcuffs on her.

"Thanks for the meal, ma'am," Angelo said, "but I reckon I'll sleep on the trail after all. It'll be a mite quieter." He turned to his cousin. "Sorry, I can't stay, Ned. If you want to join me along and catch up with old times, you're more than welcome."

Ned headed for the stairs. "I'll just collect my things and I'll meet you at the livery."

"*Adios*, folks." Angelo walked out of the saloon and stood on the boardwalk. Dusk dusted the town with somber shadows.

Mr Jinx waited beside Clay's lifeless body, as if on guard. He gave a soft bark to greet Angelo.

"I guess you can leave him now, boy. I don't think he's going anywhere." He crouched down and scratched the dog behind his ears. "I reckon this is *adios*, Mr Jinx. I need to be moving on."

Angelo headed for the livery stables and Mr Jinx ran ahead and then sat wagging his tail.

He gave the dog a knowing look. "Let's get one thing clear. If you're gonna tag along, then you'll have to fend for yourself. I ain't got the time to wet nurse you, OK?"

Mr Jinx let out a loud bark.

"I guess that's a 'yes'." Angelo smiled. "Come on, then. What are you waiting for?"

CRIB GIRLS

Kit Churchill

Although born in South Wales, United Kingdom, Andrea Hughes, writing as Kit Churchill, has always been fascinated by America's Old West. Indeed, her great-grandfather was a pioneer to North America in the late 19th century. She has been an avid reader of westerns, particularly Black Horse Westerns, since her teens, and also enjoys gardening, music, and talking on the telephone. Her first western short story 'Desert Surrender' appeared in Where Legends Ride.

Erin brushed aside the tears, but she blamed herself. She wanted to live. That was her weakness. And this was the only way she could do it.

Lifting up a tiny hand mirror, one of her few possessions, she examined the purple blotches on top of old yellowed bruises. Her face was a mess. The bruises spread the length of her jaw, and darkened her cheekbone. Her lip was split, and oozed crimson blood that dripped down onto her dress. She glanced around the small tent: a chair, a crib one man's width. No need for wide beds here. No time, or desire, for cuddling. It was better this way. It was all that was needed. The musty odor of recently performed sexual acts hung in the air, and made her nose wrinkle.

She stood, and pulled down her faded yellow cotton dress, eager to get to the river and wash off the worst. Sometimes, when it was quiet, she went further upriver and stripped. Immersing herself in the pure icy water did more than just wash away the dirt. It made her feel clean. She gathered up her towel, soap and a small, tapestry purse. The purse and the mirror had been given to her by Mrs Yung, a Chinese woman who ran the town laundry. The vibrant purple hues of the tapestry were fading now, and some of the threads had come loose along the clasp, but she loved it as if it were finest silk.

Taking a deep breath, Erin pulled up the flap of the tent and peered out at the wakening day. Sounds carried across the river. The townsfolk were stirring. A dog's yapping pierced the morning stillness, but a rough curse curtailed its eagerness. She recognized the voice and willed the dog to keep barking. But the dog had learned, as she had learned. At first, she'd fought back against the beatings, thinking it was the only way to survive. She wasn't every drunken cowboy's punch bag! At first. Then she learned it was easier not to fight. The impulse still came, as it had last night, but the beatings were always worse. She couldn't afford too many of those if she was to stay alive.

A morning mist hung over the river, obscuring the view from the other side, as if a veil had been drawn. The railroad's arrival had brought with it fresh opportunities and the settlement had become a dropping-off point for cattle drives shipping their herds east. It was quiet today. The latest batch of cows shipped out yesterday and the cowboys had departed, for now anyway.

Barefoot, Erin picked her way through the line of tents alongside the river and wandered as far as she could go without being out of hearing range. She reached her usual spot, with overhanging trees and a narrow, sandy beach.

She pulled her dress over her head and draped it carefully over a mulberry bush that grew on the edge of the riverbank. As she stepped naked into the river, some of the pebbles hurt her feet, making her wince, but she ignored the pain and leant back into the cool water. Her long dark curls spread out fan like behind her. She closed her eyes as the water's healing touch soothed her aches. A near forgotten passage of a play from another world forced itself into her mind. Her father had insisted on reading her poetry and plays. Shakespeare, most of all. Her stupid dreamer of a father had thought the world would let her benefit from being cultured. That was fine as long as he was alive to protect her, but useless after he'd died and left her alone. As she lay here now, she wondered whether she'd be better off just letting the water take her, sink into its depths as Ophelia had done in *Hamlet*.

Still visible in the lightening sky, the stars winked at her from empty space. They were her friends, her confidantes. She told them about the men who used her night after night. There were the bad ones and sometimes, when she was lucky, the kind ones. But that didn't happen very often.

The sounds from the settlement drifted upriver and she closed her eyes, and immersed herself in the water. She wanted to forget. Why did ribald curses and harsh voices follow her even here? She held her breath under the water for as long as possible and then burst up, spreading a shower of droplets.

The realization that she'd taken too long made her hurry out of the water and struggle to dry herself. The grass and moss beside the river caressed her bare feet, feeling like nature's velvet. Her hair hung down her back in damp ringlets, and she pulled it into a rough ponytail, using a faded piece of scarlet ribbon her father had given her years before. Rushing to pull on her dress, the thin cotton ripped down the front and Erin cursed herself for being careless. Now she'd have to walk through the town holding her dress together and then spend precious minutes tonight sewing up this harlot's wear. She grabbed her meager possessions and gave a longing glance back at the water, wishing she could have stayed there, at least for another hour or so. But she knew it was hopeless and turned away.

Half running, she prayed she would get to her cabin before the town started on its daily routine. Daydreams in rivers had to be paid for in this place. This time, the price was the whispered insults from the respectable women, their eyes as hard and black as the tiny stones at the bottom of the river. She clutched her towel and purse to her chest, trying to hide the fact her dress was ripped, but groaned as she saw one of the worst of her "clients" stumbling toward her. He was half-drunk even this early.

"Hey, darlin'," the man slurred. "Where you goin' in such a hurry?"

Erin didn't look up from the dusty boardwalk, but could still see his scuffed, dirt encrusted boots.

"Hey!" The voice hardened. "Don't ignore me, bitch. You won't tonight." He guffawed, as if what he said was funny.

"Please," she said, "I want to get home."

"To what, whore? The Chinese shit you call friends? Well, shit finds shit." He laughed again, amused with himself, and walked off down the road, his belly wobbling in time with his chuckles. Holding her head high, she walked straighter now. She was not shit and neither were her friends. Most of her natural high spirits had been knocked out of her, but she still had pride, buried deep down.

She slept in a shack at the back of the Chinese laundry and always popped in to say hello. Mrs Yung was at the counter, as usual. Her ebony black hair held a little gray now and lines creased around the Oriental eyes, but they still shone with kindness.

"Mrs Yung, hi."

The old lady pressed a parcel of food into her hands then tenderly touched the bruises on her face.

"My girl. I'm so sorry. I wish you could work here, but we barely have enough as it is."

"No, don't worry. It's OK. You are so kind to me already." She didn't want to worry Mrs Yung. They had enough troubles of their own, enough persecution.

Erin forced herself to smile again and left the shop, eager to get to a bed on which she didn't need to do anything but sleep. The river's touch had calmed her aches some but they still pained her.

Her footsteps quickened at the sight of her little shack at the end of the alley, next to the laundry. It had been roughly built, thrown together for storage for the Yungs, but they had let her have it. Paint peeled from some of the boards, and there was only one window to let in light, but it was her refuge. Shadows from surrounding buildings cloaked it in semi-darkness most of the time, and hardly anyone came down the alley. She reached out, inserted and turned the key, but before she could go inside a voice stopped her. It was quiet but brutal.

"Where've you been, bitch?" Dobbs muttered. "I heard you'd left your tent half an hour ago. You know you're supposed to come to me first."

She hated that voice more than her clients' voices.

Turning, she saw him leaning against the Yungs' building, arrogance pouring from every inch of his body, an almost spent cigar clamped between yellow teeth. Dobbs stood straight then walked toward her with slow steady steps, his eyes holding hers. When he was close enough to touch her, he stopped.

"You know I like a report on the night." He threw the cigar down and ground it into the dirt with his boot. His gaze stayed on the still glowing end for a moment. "So?"

When she didn't answer, Dobbs glanced up. His eyes were as cold as his voice, as blue as the clear blue of the river she'd just bathed in, but far less welcoming. His garb was black, all black, signifying a wealth he didn't earn himself. Coat buttons shone, boots were polished. Even his hair was black, slicked back, smooth and fashionable.

She glanced down at her ripped dress.

"I was–" She was cut off when his hand shot up and closed round her chin, making her wince as his fingers caught the bruises on her jaw.

"I don't want to hear you're tired." His eyes were inches from hers and their contempt held her. The scent of pomade that covered his hair made her eyes water. "I own you, do you understand? Just because you're in those tents and not in a saloon, doesn't mean I can't see you and know everything you do."

His face twisted into a vicious grin. "Now don't you see how much better off you were in the saloon?" His grip tightened on her jaw. The pain intensified. "I usually put the older, uglier whores in those tents, but I wanted you to see how good you had it." His lips came down on hers, but as a punishment not a kiss. "Behave and I might take you back. Disobey me again and you'll get old in those tents. You hear?"

Unable to speak, she nodded.

"That's better." His body pushed further into hers and she recoiled at the smell of whiskey on his breath. "Watch your step, miss. Otherwise, those won't be the only bruises you'll get today."

Dobbs pushed her so violently she stumbled backwards against the door, which flung open. Catching a foot on the step to her room, she fell hard on the wooden planks.

His coarse laugh echoed through the alleyway as he sauntered back to the saloon.

Anger boiled within her, but there was nothing she could do now. She pulled herself up and with trembling hands extracted the key and banged the door shut. Sobbing, she leaned against the door and used the key to turn the lock.

She stood, her breath coming in violent gasps, as if she had been running.

The shack boasted a table, a chair and a makeshift bed without headboards or décor, but adorned with sweet-smelling soft linen, courtesy of the Yungs. She threw herself on the bed and held the softness close. Her fall had skinned her palms and she held them to her face, trying to ease the heat of the injuries.

She closed her eyes and the soft scents soothed her. While still wearing her torn dress, Erin drifted off into a deep sleep.

Heavy knocking intruded and for a moment Erin didn't know if it came from her dreams or from real life. The sound persisted and she sat up, rubbing the sleep from her eyes. The door shook as the knocks grew louder and more insistent.

Groaning at her bruises, she shifted herself out of bed and stumbled to the door. She unlocked it and pulled the door open.

"Oh, Mary," Erin whispered. The girl standing in front of her was about fourteen; too young to be here, definitely too young to be doing this work. Erin had grown to view Mary as her younger sister in all but name. Mary's upper lip was split and dried blood caked around her nose. One eye was almost closed, the puffiness marring the beauty of her blue eyes.

"Oh, Mary," Erin repeated and glanced around the shadowy alley.

She pulled the girl inside then slammed the door shut and locked it. Tears welled in her eyes as Erin put her arms around the battered and broken mess that used to be a young woman. Erin had been young herself only a few short years ago. Now, though only twenty, she felt she'd lived forever.

The sobbing started and Mary collapsed in her embrace. Erin soothingly stroked Mary's blond hair that was usually piled up behind her head, though now it tumbled over her shoulders. A sleeve was ripped from her dress and the bodice torn. Purple bruises traveled down from Mary's throat to her breasts.

Erin held her until the sobs quieted.

Finally, Mary pulled away, dabbing her eyes with the clean rag Erin had given her.

"Who did this?" Erin asked.

"Dobbs." Mary twisted the rag and sniffed. "He – they wanted me to – to do stuff I didn't want to do, so –"

"So, they beat you until you did." Erin went to the bucket at the back of the hut and dipped a cup into icy, fresh water. The Yungs supplied her with water drawn from their well, and once again she was grateful. She took the cup to the girl. "Here, drink this."

"I can't go back, Erin. I can't. But Dobbs said he'd kill me rather than let me go."

Erin gave a short laugh and tossed her head. "I've heard that one before."

The hut was cool, hidden in the shadows from the noonday sun. Erin went to the window and glanced out from behind the shabby, homespun curtain. The alley was empty.

"Erin, what can I do? I'm scared."

The tears were starting again and Erin sank down onto the bed. There it was. What could she do? What could any of them do? What choice did they have?

Erin had been a fighter. Her father always told her off after the troubles her high spirits got her into. He'd been a dreamer and a poet; he'd also believed in right and wrong and in adhering to the law. He'd be heartbroken at her *choice* of career, but it had happened and once in, she hadn't known how to get out. Now, with a fourteen-year-old girl relying on her, more of her father's principles would have to be broken.

"Tell me, honey." She grasped Mary's hand. "Would you be willing to leave this place with me?"

The light that shone in Mary's eyes was daunting and gave Erin doubts. Would she be taking her from one kind of bad life to another?

"I'd go anywhere with you."

"Then I'll tell you." Erin paced the floor of the shack, deep in thought. "There aren't that many things we can do on our own without a great deal of risk, but there is one thing I've been thinking about for a while. It won't be an easy life."

Mary stood up. "Anything – anything is better than this."

Erin nodded. "OK. You'll have to trust me. For now, stay here." She gripped Mary's shoulder and held it firmly. "I'll lock you in. If anyone knocks, hide so they can't see you through the window and ignore them."

"I promise."

"Well, Mr Dobbs..." Erin smiled thinly, a glimmer of hope taking hold. "I'm afraid you're going to be somewhat short on your takings tonight."

Now that she'd decided on her plan, Erin moved fast. There wasn't much time. Dusk would fall all too soon and Dobbs would come looking if they weren't where they were supposed to be.

The alley was still deserted, so she hurried to the back door of the Yungs' laundry. Her knocking brought Mrs Yung rushing to open the door, the worry lines around her eyes deep.

"Mrs Yung, I need to ask you for one more favor."

The woman smiled. "You know that anything we can do for you, we will."

"I need one of your guns."

Erin wasn't surprised by the shock on Mrs Yung's face.

"Erin, whatever you are thinking of... you must not."

"I'm sorry, but this time I must. Please?" Her plan depended on that gun. The Yungs had one behind the counter of the laundry and one upstairs. With the abuse and persecution they suffered daily from drunken cowboys, they needed them.

Mrs Yung shook her head. "I'm not sure we should. I must ask Lee."

"No. Please, you know I don't ask you for anything. But this is urgent."

Erin held her breath while waiting for the reply. The gun was essential, without it, her plan would be useless. After what seemed like an age, Mrs Yung shrugged, a tiny smile playing on her lips. "I suppose I don't tell Lee everything. But promise me." She rested a hand on Erin's arm. "Promise me, you will be careful."

"Oh, I can promise that."

While her friend hurried away to find the gun, doubts coursed through Erin's mind. She sat on one of the finely embroidered chairs by the back door and glanced at the elegant, understated décor of the Chinese culture. She'd miss this place.

Mrs Yung returned quickly with a small calico bundle.

"First, please tell me..." It was her nature to worry and they had become close, almost like mother and daughter. "You're not going to kill anyone, are you? I know you're having a hard time, but–"

"No, believe me. I just.... I just need it, that's all."

"Alright, then. Here." Mrs Yung handed her the calico bundle. "Be careful, it is loaded. Six shots, I think."

Erin hugged her. "Thank you. But I won't be able to return it, I'm going away."

"Away? Where?"

Erin laughed. "Who knows where? But I promise I'll be careful. And I promise, wherever it is, it'll be better than this place."

Tears formed in Mrs Yung's eyes and Erin held her again. Then, a sense of urgency made her release the old woman and kiss her cheek. "I have to go. Thank you for everything you've done. Thank your husband, too."

Mrs Yung waved her away; she seemed too overcome with emotion to say any more.

Erin glanced up as she hurried down the main street. It was around noon, but time would go by too quickly for her to waste it. She clutched the bundle to her. By the saloon, one of Dobbs's men was lounging on a chair on the boardwalk, a foot on the handrail. He studied her for the report he would no doubt make to Dobbs later. She was meant to be resting for the night ahead, not parading about on her own business.

As she neared the end of town, she prayed the liveryman would be having his afternoon nap. He often dozed in the shade by the side of the stable as the heat of the noon sun sent most of the residents scurrying inside. For once, luck was with her. A hat was over the man's face and an empty whiskey bottle stood beside his chair. She guessed he wouldn't wake without being shaken.

Inside, shafts of light found their way through gaps in the woodwork and dust motes danced in the sunbeams. Several horses were present, some for rent, some housed for visitors. This was the problematic part of her plan. Stealing was stealing. She'd always been loath to take anything that didn't belong to her. And there was the added worry of the death penalty if she was caught. Since she had no money, she was going to have to do things she didn't want to, so she'd gain freedom for her and Mary.

She chose two horses that had the finest saddles resting on the stall partitions. Anyone who could afford such saddles would probably be able to cope with losing their horses better than those with poorer saddles. She laughed at the irony of the excuses she was making for herself.

The horses were strong, their coats shining with health and they snorted a greeting as she approached them. She placed the gun bundle in one of the saddle bags that hung over the partition, and was just about to reach for a halter for the piebald, when the stable door creaked open. Loud voices sounded, obtrusive in the silence, and she ducked behind the horse, hoping it wasn't the owner coming to claim him.

Her heart hammered in her chest as the voices approached. Images flashed before her of what would happen to her and Mary if she were caught right now. Dobbs was not exactly a gentleman at the best of times. If they were caught trying to escape, a few bruises would be the least of their troubles.

The horse obscured her vision, but she glimpsed two heads over the stall. They were strangers, to her anyway. As they came nearer, Erin shifted position and pushed herself closer to the partition wall, praying she was out of sight. A small knothole in the wood meant she could still see a little of what was happening. The cowboys went into the stalls beside hers and saddled their horses.

"Hey, Jonesy." The nearest one chortled and clamped his hat on his head. His blond curls peeped out from underneath. "What you gonna do tonight, eh?"

"I reckon a visit to the saloon wouldn't go amiss. Hear tell there's a fine-looking whore in those tents now. Dobbs put her there as punishment 'cause she's too quick with her mouth."

The cowboy with the blond curls walked to the other side of his horse to tighten the girth. He was inches from her now, and she could just see his head above the partition. She bent her own head lower. Her hands became clammy with sweat; her breathing harder, and she prayed he wouldn't look down.

"Yeah." He chuckled. "Reckon a beating will teach her more of a lesson, but Dobbs said he'd tried that. Thought he'd stick her in the tents for a while. Let her see what rough really means."

Once they'd finished, the cowboys led their horses from the stalls and their voices receded. As they closed the main door, Erin let out the breath that she hadn't realized she was holding and leant against the piebald. His coat was silken and she let his warmth soothe her.

After a moment's respite, she saddled the piebald and a roan stalled nearby. She had cause to thank her father for many things, and teaching her to ride at an early age was one of them. She could out-ride anyone in this town; with what she had planned, that would come in mighty handy. She led the horses out of the rear door of the stables.

The stables were on the same side of the street as the laundry, so all she had to do was walk the horses down the back of the street until she got to her shack. At this time of day it was quiet there, most of the townspeople still enjoying their siesta, and she reached the shack with no problem.

A group of cottonwoods grew on the edge of town, behind the laundry, and she tied the horses to a low hanging branch. After retrieving the gun bundle from the saddlebags, she wiped the sweat from her forehead with the sleeve of her dress. She'd put on her only other dress before embarking on her mission and this reminded her of the pitiful lack of clothing that she and Mary possessed. Mary must take only the clothes she wore, as it would be too dangerous to go and pack. They'd need water and food, too. Water would be no problem, as canteens hung from the saddles. Food might have to wait, apart from the bundle Mrs Yung had given her earlier.

As Erin turned to her shack, she saw a washing line strung from the back of a building to the trees, two doors up. Clothing hung, drying in the heat. There were three pairs of canvas pants and three cotton shirts. She hesitated then ran to the line, checked all was clear, then snatched the clothes. They were too big, but could be adjusted and would be more sensible attire on the trail than flimsy dresses. She returned to the horses and stuffed the clothing into the empty saddlebags.

Now came the difficult part, and it scared her. She knocked on the shack's door, unlocked it then entered.

Mary stopped pacing the floor, anxiety creasing her bruised face. "Oh, Erin. I've been so worried. Where've you been?"

"Don't mind that now, Mary. Just do what I tell you to do, OK?"

Mary nodded, anxious to please her friend.

Erin pushed two canteens into Mary's hand. "Fill these up and take them to the horses at the back. Untie them. Mount one of the horses and hold the other. Be ready to ride the minute I yell, is that clear?"

"Yes, but what–?"

Erin held up a hand. "I'm sorry. There's no time to explain. You'll have to trust me."

The young girl nodded and Erin felt the weight of responsibility on her shoulders. What they were doing was wrong, but to stay here would mean an early death, used up by men too hardened to care, and lining the pockets of one who was too evil to care. Whatever they did, now or in the future, had to be better than that.

"OK, I'll go." Mary turned to head out of the doorway.

"Oh, and if I don't come back and you hear yelling, or if it's quiet and I'm not back soon, head out yourself and go anywhere. Find a town, ask someone for help. Anything is better than this."

"But I can't–"

"You can." Erin smiled and hugged the girl. "You have to. Now go!"

Mary nodded and hurried out of the shack, though a thousand questions must be burning in her mind.

Erin sighed and looked round the shack she'd soon be leaving. Worry still lanced her thoughts. When she'd been young, her father had prayed to God. He was not conventionally religious, hating the churches full of mostly hypocrites, but he believed in the Almighty. She felt a hypocrite herself, praying for help when she'd lived a sinful life and especially as she planned to be sinful again. But she felt the God her father had prayed to would understand.

As she headed onto the main street, her hands shook and she clamped tightly onto the bundle containing the gun. She studied the dusty boardwalks. For the most part they were still empty. Her gaze traveled to the saloon, hoping Dobbs's henchman wouldn't be there. She let out a sigh of relief. The chair was vacant.

The bank was three doors' down from the Chinese laundry and she reached it too quickly for her own liking. After a moment's hesitation, Erin pushed the heavy door open. She'd rarely been in here. She had no money to deposit. There were two customers, and panic threatened to seize hold as the possible bad outcomes ran through her mind. She held the gun in front of her, covered with the calico cloth.

Only one of two counters was manned and there was a sturdy iron safe against the back wall. A woman stood before Charlie the bank clerk; she turned round and tutted on seeing Erin out amongst decent folk. An old man was dozing in a chair as he waited for his wife to finish. His balding head dropped lower in the first throes of sleep. She liked him. He was one of the few townsmen who never visited the whores on the riverbank or the saloon.

"Come on..." Erin whispered to herself, the muscles at the back of her neck bunching with the tension. Beads of sweat formed on her forehead.

As Erin willed the woman to hurry, she studied Charlie. He was young, balding, with a nervous twitch in one eye. He wore thin wire glasses.

At last the woman gathered up her papers and nodded a stiff farewell to Charlie. She glared at Erin then collected her husband like so much baggage and left.

Charlie raised his eyes from his ledger and looked at Erin.

This was it. No return from here. She strode the final step to the counter, trying to hide the fact her hands were trembling, her mouth had suddenly gone dry. She swallowed.

"I wish to make a withdrawal."

Charlie laughed. They knew each other well, physically at least. "That is gonna be difficult. As I recollect, you don't have any money in this bank."

"No?" She smiled, quick and humorless. "I guess the money you gave to me every Saturday night never did go in my bank account, did it?"

"So?"

She whipped the six-gun out from under the cloth and aimed it at his face. His brow creased and humor fled from his eyes and mouth. Her hands trembled.

"I said I want to make a withdrawal."

"Hey!" His hands went up and his faded blue eyes widened. "What the–?"

"Put the money from the counter in that bag." Erin indicated a canvas bag lying on a table behind him. "And make it quick." Her voice shook, and her hands became slippery as sweat threatened to loosen her grip.

He didn't move and she cursed silently under her breath. Still keeping the gun trained on the man, she backed up to the front door and pushed home the bolt. Then she darted behind the counter and held the gun to Charlie's forehead.

"You won't use that." He seemed more confident now, as if the shock was wearing off. "You're just a whore. You haven't got the guts."

The old familiar rage came to her aid. She drew the gun back and pistol-whipped his ear, drawing crimson blood from the lobe.

"Listen, you son-of-a-bitch, I've had enough. So either you gather up that money or you'll find a gap where your face used to be."

"All right," he murmured. He pushed the money into the canvas bag. It was enough to see Mary and her through the next few weeks, but no more.

"What about the safe?"

"Whoa." He snorted a laugh. "I don't have the combination. There's no way you're getting into that."

"Oh, no?" Erin bored her gaze into him. "I learn things from my clients and I know Mr Walters has gone away for the week, and yet the bank's open. So either he's coming back from Washington every night to put the money in the safe, or you *do* have the combination."

She trailed the gun down Charlie's shirt towards his lap. Beads of sweat appeared on his brow then trickled down behind his glasses.

"I'm desperate," she repeated. She aimed the gun at his groin. "Hell, I might even be *crazy*." She grinned. "And I'm sick of being used every night and tossed away like a dirty rag. So either you open that safe or I'll take out on you all my disgust for all the men in this town."

She pulled back the Colt's hammer and ground the muzzle into his lap.

Fear widened his eyes. He swallowed, unable to move.

The power over him felt good. She wanted it to continue, but time was against her.

Charlie nodded, his Adam's apple working up and down. "OK! Just don't – just don't do anything stupid. I'll unlock the safe."

"Good." Erin stood back to let him vacate his chair, and he stumbled across the room.

She smiled as his fingers shook, grasping the dial, but within minutes all the dollar bills were inside the bag.

"You'll never get away with this."

"Oh, honey." She used her best hooker's voice, dripping with sarcasm. "It looks like I just did." Erin moved to the window. The street was still empty. She'd chosen her time well. Sheriff away, deputy sheriff snoring off the heat of the day in his office, bank owner absent, town at siesta, the lull after the storm of the visiting cattle drive. No one had expected any townsfolk would do this, least of all a whore. And only a whore would know all of a town's business.

She took out a rope she'd hid under the shawl. It was one that had been left behind after the Yungs moved their possessions out of the shack, and she'd guessed it would come in useful sometime. "Sit down."

He scrambled to obey her. A handkerchief was folded neatly in his pocket. It was the one he used to dab the sweat from his brow after his Saturday night "entertainment". Stuffing it into his mouth and tying rope around it felt good. She lashed him to the chair, fingers fumbling in her haste. Finally, it was done and she stepped back, satisfied.

Holding up the bag, she grinned. "Thanks for this, Charlie. From now on you'll have to get your kicks somewhere else Saturday nights."

Then she ran out the back door, elation and fear struggling for dominance. She couldn't believe it had gone so smoothly. Her head swam as she raced into the alley at the back of the bank and down to Mary waiting with the horses.

Astride the roan, Mary was about to speak when she saw the bulging bags. But Erin shook her head. "No time. I'll explain later." She pushed her hair away from her eyes and smiled. "We'll ride slowly out of town so we don't draw any attention." Erin slung the bags over the pommel and mounted up.

"Once we get out of sight, ride faster than you've ever ridden in your life, OK?"

Mary nodded, eyes bright.

Erin led them out of the deserted back alley to the end of the street. A quick glance told her no alarm had gone up yet.

As they approached the town perimeter, Erin cast a last look at the river. Beams from the late afternoon sun caught the ripples in the water and they shimmered, as if waving goodbye. It was the only clean thing about the place. Then her gaze went to the tent where she'd worked for the last month. Not any more, she thought and heady euphoria swept over her. She turned her horse away and Mary followed at a steady pace.

She was an outlaw. So was Mary, as an accessory to the bank robbery. But she'd never felt so free in her life.

"Come on, Mary." Digging her heels in, she urged her piebald to increase its pace and Mary confidently rode alongside her. "Let's get the hell out of here!" Erin pulled the ribbon that constrained her long dark curls and let the wind take them until they streamed out behind her. "We have a life to catch up on."

MAN OF IRON

Chuck Tyrell

Charlie Whipple is the co-editor of this anthology. He has the distinction of having two stories featured because the editor wanted to say thanks for all his hard work; besides, he's a damned fine writer. He is also a proud grandfather of 17 grandchildren and lives in Japan.

God, I wish I hadn't shot that woman.

She was Chiricahua, plain as day, and that meant only one thing. She was one of Massai's people, and he'd sworn to kill me on sight. But there she was, down and bleeding from my bullet, and almighty weak from bearing a baby boy.

What in heaven could I do with an Apache girl and a newborn babe, only a stone's throw from Hell's Gate?

For a while, I just stood there, rifle cocked and pointed at her belly. She stared back, not about to let me see how scared she was, and clutched the newborn to her. Her Sharps rifle lay on the ground, out of reach. A ways away, I could hear water chuckling over the stone streambed.

I studied the Apache woman's face. "You're Chiricahua," I said.

She tilted her head. Beads of sweat formed on her brow. I tried the same line again, this time in my border Spanish.

"*Si*," came the reply.

At least we could communicate. "Do you know who I am?"

She nodded.

"Then you know that I am not a man who makes war against women and children. Still, your shot almost killed me."

"No Apache bullet can kill *Mano del Hierro*," she said. "Nevertheless, I had to try. To protect my son."

Man of Iron, she called me. The corners of my mouth turned up ever so slightly. Over the years, Apaches had taken so many shots at me they'd come to the conclusion their aim wasn't that's bad, rather my iron skin turned back their bullets. So they gave me that crazy name. Our scrapping seemed almost a friendly dispute, until last fall. They'd shoot and I'd shoot back and no one got hurt, not seriously anyway. Then they stole some Butterfield stock, and I'm responsible for those horses. I run the stage station at Apache Pass.

I went hunting the horses and found them bunched up in a blind canyon near the mouth of Hell's Gate, not far from where I shot the Chiricahua woman. There were only two braves with the horses so I rode straight toward them, grinning, playing the game.

"Come for my horses," I said, and started rounding them up. The older Apache laughed and waved at me, but the youngster wasn't about to let me leave with those three mares. He came charging across the canyon floor on a little paint horse, yipping and yelling, set on lifting my yellow hair.

To cut down his target, I turned sideways and waited. I figured he'd shoot if he was serious. If he didn't, the charge was all for show.

He fired his old single-shot Springfield from about fifty yards away. Put a bullet through the loose folds of my shirt. By reaction, I shucked my old Remington Navy and shot him dead through the chest. How was I to know the kid was Massai's only brother?

After that, our dispute turned ugly. And now I'd shot one of his women.

The newborn looked somewhat strange, covered as it was with reddish creamy looking stuff. The little feller filled his lungs and bawled. The woman clamped a hand over his mouth and nose. He'd soon learn that crying brought a strong hand that cut off sound and breath. She'd tied off the baby's cord with two buckskin thongs, one near the navel, one a bit farther up. She motioned for me to cut the cord between the ties. I leaned the rifle against a boulder, pulled the Remington Navy and held it cocked in my right hand while I shucked my Bowie and did as I was told.

"I am going to carry you and the baby down to the creek," I told her, "but first I must search you." I patted her down for weapons. She had a little knife in the top of her *n'deh b'keh* moccasins, and a piece of flint and three Sharps cartridges in her medicine bag. I slid the knife into my own moccasin and threw the flint away. The cartridges I left in the bag. We wouldn't be taking her Sharps.

The gunshot wound in her left thigh oozed blood as I shouldered her, picked up the baby, and took them to the stream. Tiny little grunts were the only signs of her pain. When I put her down, I could see things had gotten worse. Her face had gone pale and she seemed semi-conscious, and we stood a hell of a long ways from shelter of any kind.

I whistled, and Pocoueno came trotting, though he didn't like the smell of blood, or of Apache for that matter. I got the makings from my saddlebags and within minutes had a tin of water heating over a hatful of fire. No telling where Massai's Apaches were, but it looked like they'd gone, expecting the woman to follow after the baby was born. They must have been in some hurry.

While the water was coming to a boil, I cut two ears from a prickly pear cactus, singed the spines off and split them. Then I pounded them to a pulp against an old log with the handle of my Bowie.

By the time I finished, the water was hot. I gently bathed the entry and exit wounds. The bleeding had stopped, and the holes were clean: no bits of bone to indicate that my bullet had broken her leg. I made poultices from the cactus pulp and pieces torn from an old flour sack I had. One went on the entry wound, the other on the exit, and I bound them in place with strips from the same sack.

She stirred and said something I couldn't catch. She tried to hike up her skirt. I helped, though I wasn't used to the nakedness of women. She pulled the skirt way up past her navel and then started pushing against her belly.

"Help," she pleaded.

Kneeling beside her, I pushed against her belly while her hands guided mine in stroking downward movements. There was a gurgling sound and a gout of blood and matter as the afterbirth slid from her. She sighed in relief.

"Bury it. Hide it from the animals," she whispered. "If they eat it, fate will bear ill for my son."

She stared at me until I nodded. Then she pointed at the pan of water on the fire and at herself. "Wash."

I wet the cloth I'd used to clean her wound and handed it to her, but she was too weak to do the job. So I did it.

All this time I was wondering what to do with her. I couldn't take her to the station. A troop of cavalry was there, up from their Mescal Creek camp. They'd spent the day before burying the Kings on their ranch down in San Bernadino country. Mescalero Apaches had killed them. Not prettily, either. Also, the fact that Mescaleros and not Chiricahuas had massacred the Kings didn't mean a thing, especially to Sergeant Lars Erikson, the topkick. He figured dead Indians were the only decent kind, mainly because his own parents had been killed on the way west while he was still in Sweden. In fact, the only reason he even came to America was to kill Indians: men, women, children. "Polliwogs turn into frogs," he always said. Taking that woman back to Apache Pass would be like putting my Remington to her head and pulling the trigger.

Then again, I couldn't leave her. In her condition, she wouldn't last three days. And I didn't want to spend the rest of my life wondering if I could have saved the Apache woman and her newborn child.

My mother brought me up right. I was only fourteen when I left home, but Ma's parting words never left me. "You're a man growed, Oliver Perry, and you're too restless for this farm. Just remember. Keep your own council. Trust no man. But treat every woman like a lady. She's someone's wife and mother... or will be."

Ill prepared as we were, we had no choice. We had to go up through *yahdesut*, Hell's Gate, and into *tsril kawa*, the great mountain, from whence the Chiricahua range gets its name. We had to find Massai. After that, if he wanted my life... I'd cross that desert when we got to it.

With the mother resting, I washed the baby and wrapped him in my blanket.

For the three of us there was one horse, a bit of jerky, some coffee and sugar, a lump of bread, and one canteen. Yet we had to go. There was no other way.

Box elder grew along the creek, tough as iron and about as easy to cut, but perfect for my needs. Still, it took me more time than I felt easy about to fashion a serviceable travois from long staves, lengths of lariat, and my oilskin slicker.

As the sun set, I boiled water again, this time slicing jerked beef into it to make a broth for the woman to drink. She took not quite a cupful before turning her head. Her brow was hot and dry, and she hadn't nursed the baby.

I rummaged in my saddlebags and brought out my coffee cup, a sack of beans, and a small packet of sugar. I poured a little warm water into the cup and added some sugar. Picking up the baby, I dipped the corner of a strip of flour sack into the sweetened water and trailed it across his mouth. Immediately the boy babe started sucking, slurping at the moisture in the cloth. He finally drank nearly half a cup. I knew he'd be better off with his mother's milk, but until she could feed him, I had to get something into his stomach.

It was a restless night. Pocoueno grazed along the banks of the stream, and I lay there planning the next day's journey. By dawn, we were well on our way.

Pocoueno didn't like the travois, but he pulled it. Up away from the stream we went, forsaking its life-giving water for the convoluted, fractured land beyond Hell's Gate. Somewhere to the south, in the high ranges of the Chiricahua Mountains, we'd find Massai. And if I could keep the woman alive, I might not have to die.

The pace was slower than slow, and the woman's fever didn't break. She made no sound except for her labored breathing. Twice I fed the kid on sugared water. Once, I had to put him back in his old blanket because he pissed in mine. I spread the wet blanket across Pocoueno's rump to dry; something he didn't seem too pleased about.

We walked, Pocoueno and me, through the turns and twists of that giant land of pillared stone, through the shards and slivers of rocks chewed by some mighty force in some pre-historic time.

The first night saw us making a dry camp, for there is no water near Hell's Gate, or in the Devil's Kitchen beyond, and all the water we had was in one canteen.

I wet my bandanna and wiped Pocoueno's mouth out. He'd have to wait for a drink. I checked the woman. She was unconscious, and her breathing was shallow. Her eyelids fluttered.

The kid had shit his blanket. Goes with kids, I reckoned. I used the blanket to wipe him, scraped the excess off with a stick, then rubbed the blanket around in the dirt and laid it out on a rock. This time I fed the kid plain water. Sugar was getting low and we still had a way to go. I took a small sip of water myself, then shook the canteen. A little more than half full.

We slept.

In the morning, the woman was no better. I wet her lips with water and she licked them. Eventually I got nearly a cupful down her, but it took time. We didn't start moving until the sun was too high for my liking.

By noon we'd climbed up and out of Hell's Gate. Far across the Devil's Kitchen lay Rustler's Cienega and a spring that never dried up.

I chewed grimly on a piece of jerky, partly for the nourishment, partly to keep the juices flowing in my mouth. The way was blocked by jumbled rocks as big as houses and columns of stone from some giant's coliseum. The dry air carried the acrid scent of the desert. To make a mile of southward progress, we twisted and switched back at least five times that distance.

Pocoueno started to labor and rumble deep in his chest. He couldn't go without water much longer.

The night dropped on us while we were still in the Kitchen. We had to stop.

The woman's eyes were open. I noticed wet spots on her calico blouse. She feebly held her arms out, motioning for the child. I gave him to her and she lifted the blouse and put him to a swollen breast. First time I'd ever seen a baby suckle its mother. I got a strange feeling, a kind of warmth in my chest. I blinked and watched some more. It was beautiful.

I rubbed Pocoueno down and wiped his mouth out again. "Sorry old man," I said. "Tough it out. We'll be into the Chiricahua tomorrow. We'll find water there for sure."

Pocoueno didn't answer.

I took the last of the jerky from my saddlebags and handed half to the woman. We had nothing to make a fire with, so she'd have to chew it.

My thoughts were on Massai as I started gnawing on my half. Was he looking for this woman? Did he know about the boy, a treasure among the Apache? Would he make good on his vow to have my long blond hair?

Again, we slept.

The third morning brought still harder going. Even Pocoueno was listless. Everything seemed to take extra effort. The woman's fever had not broken, either. Yet, she nursed her child. Vaguely, I wondered if there was anything in the fever that would hurt him, but soon discarded the thought.

To the south, I glimpsed the heights of the Chiricahua, our goal. To the north and west, once in a while I could see the twin peaks of Dos Cabezas. We plodded on.

The mountains were still a long way off when Pocoueno stopped, head drooping nearly to the ground. I got my arm around his neck and tried to look him in the eye. It was blank, fogged over like he was in another world.

"'Ueno. 'Ueno. Come on. It's only a little farther." I tried to cajole him into moving, but my voice cracked like a dry willow, and dark, thick blood oozed from the splits in the corners of my mouth.

It took me an age or two to get the saddle off Pocoueno. And another one to get the travois lowered to the ground and the saddle, blankets, bridle, Winchester, and everything stuffed into a cleft of a nearby rock. I figured I could come back for them when and if I was ever able. The woman watched, dark-rimmed eyes sad, resigned.

The canteen was empty, but I hooked it to one tree of the travois. "The horse can go no farther," I explained in Spanish. "I will pull the travois, but you must care for your son." She must have understood because she clutched the baby to her when I handed him over.

I heaved the travois to my shoulders and pulled. One step. Two. That's all it takes, I told myself. One foot in front of the other. I picked out a whitish rock ahead and made it my goal. After an interminable time, I reached it. Then I picked another goal. Time blurred.

I fell.

Got up.

Once I thought I saw 'Ueno following a long way behind.

Fell again.

Then crawled, dragging the travois after me, an inch at a time.

For a while, everything was black.

Then it was night. Cooler. I felt a little strength come back. I crawled some more. A few more inches... then a few more. I wouldn't... no, I couldn't leave that travois behind, yet I dared not look at the woman and child. I only hoped and prayed to God that they were alive.

The skin was gone from my hands and knees, torn away by the rock floor of the Devil's Kitchen.

Blood dotted the trail behind me where I'd clutched at rocks and shrubs to pull myself and the travois along. *Don't forget the travois. Thank God it's cooler. Move. Move!* Then there was nothing.

After forever in the darkness, light speared my eyes. I blinked and turned my head. *Where's the travois?* Blindly I searched behind me with my battered hands. *The poles are gone!*

A shadow crossed my face. I forced my eyes open, mere slits, and into focus. From high atop a pinto stallion, a stern face looked down. *Massai.*

Someone threw me face down across a horse and tied my hands to my feet beneath its belly. Then we were off, scrambling toward Massai's high mountain rancheria.

I reckon I passed out because I woke up in an Apache wickiup. A shriveled old woman peered into my face. Noting my open eyes, she grunted and hobbled out. I tried to raise my head but gave up when the effort sent bolts of pain through my skull.

Moments later, a dark shape filled the wickiup entrance. Dressed in a loose cotton shirt, *himper* kilt, knee-high *n'deh b'ken* moccasins, with his long hair bound back by a headband of red flannel, Massai looked like any other Apache man. His face was stern, not with cruelty but with forty years of life in the harsh desert of southern Arizona. Deep lines ran from his nostrils to the corners of his mouth, signs of his humiliation as a captive on the San Carlos Indian Reservation.

Massai spoke to me in Spanish. "Man of Iron," he said, his voice rasping like the wind of the desert. "You killed my brother. Now you have restored my wife and son, who otherwise would be dead."

They were both alive! I figured silence was the best answer, but I was surprised to learn the woman was his wife.

"Whooping Crane, the medicine woman, says Coo may not live. The wound in her leg from your bullet is healing, but she has the fever of birthing. The boy is strong. A woman who lost her baby cares for him."

Massai sat cross-legged across the fire from me, his black eyes hooded. Finally, he spoke again. "Man of Iron. I have sworn to take your life to avenge my brother. Now you have returned to me a more precious life, that of my son. From this day forth, my blood is yours and yours is mine." He drew a huge Greenriver knife from his belt and pricked first my palm, then his own.

We clasped hands and were blood brothers.

"We have a law, my brother," said Massai. He stood up. "If one among the People wounds or kills another, he must take that person's place. Coo lies in my wickiup, wounded by your bullet. You shall live here as an Apache in her stead until she is once more among us."

I nodded.

"I have said your life is precious. None of Massai's people will harm you. Still, you are Man of Iron." Massai lifted his arm and pointed at me. "While you are among us, all men shall be free to challenge you, hand-to-hand, but not for blood. You shall meet these challenges, showing us new ways to fight. And perhaps you can learn a few things from the Apache, too. But for now you shall rest. You will need your strength."

Massai turned toward the entrance of the wickiup. "Pray to your God that Coo lives," he said. "Anytime you think you can escape, you are free to leave. But the moment you do, you are no longer under my protection."

With that warning, he left.

The old woman came bustling in again, chattering to me with words I didn't understand. She carried a bowl full of green goo, which she proceeded to plaster all over the palms of my hands and any other place I was scraped or scratched. It was cool and soothing. Felt good. Found out later, she squoze the goo from aloe cactus.

There was nothing for me to do, so I rested, as Massai suggested. A man must rest and eat when he can, because he never knows when he's going to need extra strength.

I awoke to the smell of cooking. My stomach growled its complaint, wondering if my mouth was still connected to it. The medicine woman bent over a pot, muttering and stirring some concoction.

When she noticed I was awake, she ladled food into a bowl and brought it to me. I never ate tastier dog in my life.

As soon as I could walk, people started challenging me to fights. First it was kids. Out of deference for my weakened condition, I reckoned. But gradually the challengers got bigger and tougher, and I had to stretch some. More than once I found myself on my back looking at the sky with a Chiricahua brave hooting at my disgrace.

It wasn't all fighting. They'd challenge me to run, to throw, to jump. Man! It was like they were trying to make an Apache of me.... Maybe they were.

Coo didn't die. But she was a long time healing. One day about three months after we'd crossed the Devil's Kitchen, she limped to the wickiup I shared with the medicine woman.

"Man of Iron," she said. "But for you, my son and I would have joined the Great Spirit of which Nakanklini the prophet told us. Now I am whole."

With her healed, I thought Massai would come around to tell me I could leave. But he didn't, and I started getting antsy. While Bill and Maggie Stocks could take care of the stage station fine, they probably figured me for dead by now. With a good deal of back pay due, I was raring to ride home.

At dawn one fine Indian summer day, Massai entered my wickiup. "Today you run, my brother," he said. "It is the test of young warriors. They must run to the *Ojo del Muerte*, spit the pebbles from their mouths, and run back before the rising of tomorrow's sun. You are to run with them."

Ojo del Muerte, the spring they call the Eye of Death, lay twenty miles down and across the Mexican border.

Stripped to breechclouts and moccasins, six of us started out. Five youngsters who'd just turned fifteen, and me, who was fighting shy of thirty.

But I was lean and strong. The wind whipped my long blond hair as I matched them stride for stride.

Soon we scattered, each man to seek out his own route. Too many running together would be dangerous; a single Apache could run all day without being seen.

Not long after we scattered, I was startled by movement off to my right. I dropped from sight behind a mesquite thicket.

A minute or so later, a horse came trotting through the brush.

Pocoueno. The horse I'd named Little Good in bastard Spanish.

Then I knew I was free to go, if I could make it without water or food.

I whistled, and the horse came at once.

'Ueno hadn't forgotten me.

I caught his mane, swung aboard, and turned his head toward Sunset, fifty miles or more away. Later, when we were down on the shimmering desert floor and the sun was high overhead, I looked back toward the Chiricahuas. I fancied I could see the dark figure of my blood brother outlined against the sky, watching my back trail.

CASH LARAMIE AND THE MASKED DEVIL

Edward A. Grainger

Edward A. Grainger is the pen-name of David Cranmer whose fiction has appeared in Out of the Gutter, Powder Burn Flash, Yellow Mama, *and* A Twist of Noir. *He regularly updates his blog* The Education of a Pulp Writer *(http://davidcranmer.blogspot.com/), is the editor of BEAT to a PULP e-zine, and is currently working with Anonymous-9 on the novel* Hard Bite.

The horses were hitched and the deputies, Hayes and Reed, heaved two canvas bags filled with dollar bills and silver into the wagon. Under the corner streetlamp, Marshal Robert Boland glanced at his gold timepiece: ten-thirty p.m. The three lawmen planned to ride through the night and deliver the money to the Rawlins bank no later than noon tomorrow. After that, back to Cheyenne, where he'd ask Chief Penn for some well-deserved time off.

His buoyant thoughts were quickly dashed by the approach of drumming hoof-beats. A horned figure with a dark crimson face and glinting cutlass emerged out of the darkness, barreling down on the lawmen.

"It's the Masked Devil!" the deputies exclaimed.

Drawing his Colt, Boland pulled back the hammer with a ratcheting click and fired three shots at the oncoming apparition. Then he pitched to the side, his hat tumbling away, as the legs of the ghostly white horse came crashing down beside him. In an instant, the sword slashed off his left ear. He came up on one knee and clasped a hand over the wound. Blood threaded between his fingers; shaking the warm essence from his hand, he squeezed off two more shots while the devil circled and headed back at a full gallop.

"Fire, dammit, fire!" Boland snapped at his men.

Hayes, the thin deputy closest to Boland, snagged the barrel of his six-gun in its holster; Reed, the chunky one, just stood there, wide-eyed and frozen. The devil raised the cutlass high in his right hand, drew a Walker Colt with the other, and fired off wild shots in their direction. Hayes stumbled back, knocking Reed down. Reed fell unconscious as his head slammed into a wagon wheel.

Blood from the stump of Boland's ear coursed down into the straw colored hair that curled over his mackinaw jacket. He fumbled while reloading his Colt. The devil closed in and suddenly the sword sliced through Boland's neck, severed his head completely, and sent it somersaulting several feet away.

The Masked Devil reined his white horse to the severed head, pierced it with the tip of his sword, and held it aloft, shaking it at the citizens of Pleasance who cowered along the town's wooden boardwalk. He lobbed it at them and jeered as they gasped and jumped back from the head as if it was a stick of dynamite with the fuse lit.

The fiend tugged the reins. His white horse whinnied and reared up, then stormed west out of town. A haze of dust settled in wispy layers on Deputy Hayes as he fruitlessly fired after them.

From the shadows of the narrow alley between the livery and depot, a slouched figure crept out, stepped swiftly over the unconscious deputy, snagged the two canvas bags and slithered back into the cover of darkness with the money.

"A masked rider dressed like Beelzebub?" Cash Laramie asked, shrugging his broad shoulders that stuck up well above the Windsor armchair he was sitting in.

"According to spooked townsfolk, there's no 'like' about it. That rider was the devil in the flesh." Chief Deputy US Marshal Devon Penn interlaced his fingers and planted his hands down firmly on the desk. His bushy brows furrowed on his round face as he continued, "But *The Cheyenne Star* has a slightly different take. The paper's editorial speculates it may be the spirit of a dead Arapaho leader seeking vengeance."

Cash rolled his eyes. "Ghosts and goblins live in dime novels."

"That may be so. Anyway, Marshal Boland was transporting $85,000 from Blue Mountain, California to Rawlins when he encountered trouble near Salt Lake City. Rather than run any more risk, he wired ahead for help, asking that the extra men join him in Pleasance. So I wired the mayor and asked him to hire two deputies to accompany Boland the rest of the trip to Rawlins. Then this happens." Penn pointed to the newspaper on his desk. "The whole motley town of farmers, drifters, Negroes and Indians is terrified."

Cash snatched up the newspaper. The front page featured a crude sketch of Boland's head tumbling from his body while a satanic figure dressed in Arapaho garments danced in triumph beside him. The headline screeched, "Masked Devil Beheads Marshal."

"This can't be the first attack if the paper's already come up with a catchy name for the killer," Cash said.

"That's correct. He's struck half a dozen times before. Always been raids on the white folks' homesteads or businesses in and around Pleasance."

"Not so strange, if you consider who holds the purse strings." Cash fished a cheroot from his shirt pocket and stoked the end with a lucifer. Exhaling upward, he sent the smoke funneling out through an open window onto the

Cheyenne streets. Penn detested cigars and the battle over smoking in the office had been going on for years but, on occasion, when he needed Cash for a new job, he looked the other way.

"What I can't fathom is why a US Marshal was used to transport that $85,000," Cash said. "Unless it's federal money?"

Penn unlocked his fingers and tapped two together on his desk, as was his custom when the discussion turned to sensitive topics. "There are federal links, as it happens. The Cheyenne Historical Society finally sold that strip of land south of Cumberland ridge to a wealthy railroad entrepreneur from California—with government backing, I might add. The mission was meticulously planned. A decoy with plenty of flash left the day before Boland. The need for the secrecy was paramount because that piece of land is—"

"Highly controversial," Cash interrupted. He leaned forward, slapped the paper back down on the desk and dropped his cheroot's ash into the ornamental bronze spittoon. "I take it everything was done quietly so as not to further enrage the Arapaho Nation whose land was stolen?"

"Acquired. Remember, Marshal Laramie, we don't make the laws. We might not always agree but it's our duty to enforce them. I know you have a special bond with the Arapaho people but you may have to put it aside for this assignment."

"Still, a Wells Fargo full escort would have been the wiser choice."

Penn's eyes narrowed.

"Just stating a fact," Cash said, speaking around the stub in his mouth.

"Well here's a fact for you. You're on the three o'clock stage to Pleasance. Find out who killed Boland and get the money back." Penn reached into his top drawer and took out an envelope. "Here's your travel money. Marshal Miles will be heading back from Shoshone Indian Territory and will meet you in town."

Cash nodded and left. He was glad to team up with Gideon Miles again. A fast gun and the most reliable lawman he had worked with since joining the Marshal Service.

He studied the watch attached by chain to his vest. Just enough time for a whiskey and a poke, if Lenora wasn't already busy with a client. He smiled, withdrawing two dollars from the envelope. It was kindly of his boss to provide for expenses.

"I never saw nuttin' like it. Our lead passed clean through 'im," Slim Hayes said as he pulled a crooked leg inward. "Hell, I protected Davey best I could by pushin' him down and whatnot."

"Yeah, I don't remember that," Davey Reed added. "But I cain't forget them flaming yellow eyes—"

"You idiot. He didn't have no flaming eyeballs, but hisself was inpem...er... inpener...er –"

"Impenetrable," Cash finished the half-wit's sentence. Puffing on his cheroot, he wondered where Boland found these guys.

"Yep, to bullets," Slim said.

As he interviewed the two jaspers in the back room of the general store, Cash looked from one fool to the other. Boland got a nickel's worth of nothing for help.

"Where'd you meet Boland?" Cash asked, jotting down notes in his notepad as they spoke.

"At Dodge's Six –"

"Who's Dodge?"

"Farley Dodge," Slim answered. "He's the Mayor. Whenever a posse needs a roundin' up or sumthin' needs gettin' dun or whatnot, he's the one to see about it."

"And he also owns the bank," Davey chimed in, "and the saloon and pretty much everything else in town."

Slim shot Davey an aggravated glance over the interruption then carried on with his story. "So, we meets Marshal Boland at Dodge's Six Gun Saloon and was told about the money an' trip to Rawlins and whatnot. We swore oaths to be all-quiet, and then they told us to meet up with 'im later that evenin' at the livery to ride by night. After he was done talkin', me and Davey took our advance and went up to the bar fer a drink of Maryland Ale."

"And Marshal Boland?" Cash asked.

"Why, from the moment he walked into the Six Gun, Miss Carlene was all over him."

"Saloon-girl?"

"Yep and I kin tell ya not just any saloon-girl but a top-dollar whore. She beds just the rich fellers that pass through. The rest of us settle fer Molly Ann. She ain't a bad poke if you can get past the one leg and foul breath."

Davey scrunched his nose and nodded.

There was a quick succession of raps on the door and then it was opened by a short square man with a graying beard and a dark brown mustache. The newcomer extended a hand to Cash. "Hi – Mayor Dodge," he said.

The mayor's palm was sweaty. "Laramie. Deputy US Marshal Cash Laramie."

"Well, Marshal, I live a ways out of town but came as soon as I was notified you were here. I see you've met Slim and Davey. I hope you didn't rake them over the coals too much. It was clearly a savage masquerading as the Devil that killed Marshal Boland. The townsfolk are pretty riled and want to hang the lot of them redskins for what happened."

Cash reckoned Dodge talked too fast and said too much.

The mayor spied an Arapaho arrowhead hanging from Cash's neck on a leather thong and shifted uncomfortably.

Cash didn't like the plump politician, and he savored the mayor's uneasiness for a beat while he blew out smoke. Finally, he broke the awkward silence. "I'd like to see where this 'savage' cut Boland down."

Leaving Slim and Davey, the mayor led Cash outside and along the dusty street toward the livery stable. As they passed by the general store, Cash eyed a hunched-over black beggar dragging his belongings in a potato sack and humming *Amazing Grace*. The only other onlooker was a solemn Indian on the edge of town, about a hundred feet from the livery.

"This is it." Dodge pointed at faint spots of dried blood. "Yesterday's rain just about washed the signs away," he said.

"Interesting," Cash mused, his eyes flicking over the wider area.

"What is?" Dodge asked.

"The witness report I got said Boland emptied his cylinder and was about to reload when he died. But I don't see any empty shells lying around."

"Well young 'uns have a tendency to pick up such things and keep 'em as souvenirs," Dodge said.

"I see."

The beggar had wandered over and started to cackle with dubious glee.

"Now git!" Dodge rushed at the black man, flailing his arms.

The beggar stepped back a few feet, and huffed before resuming his stroll down the street with the potato sack.

"What's his story?" Cash asked.

"He's just a tumbleweed that blew in a couple of days ago. He's been gathering up the garbage around town, burning it to stay warm at night. He seems harmless."

"Wouldn't you like to think so," Cash said, dissecting the stray.

Dodge turned to the marshal and his gaze flicked to the arrowhead. "I didn't mean to offend you back there with talk about savages and all."

"Sure, no offence taken," Cash replied coldly.

The mayor quickly changed the subject. "Now, I know Slim and Davey don't seem like much, but they're honest and fair to accurate with a gun. When I was asked for some help with the money transport, I couldn't think of two better men in Pleasance for the job."

Cash noticed the Indian had vanished in the dust being kicked up by the wind. Dark rain clouds formed in the distance.

"I didn't question their integrity." Cash scowled, dropping his spent cigar and mashing it into the ground with the heel of his boot. He turned and walked away, leaving Mayor Dodge to follow after, scratching the bridge of his nose. Cash headed for the hanging shingle marked, *Art Bell—Minister / Coffin Maker / Undertaker.*

"I cleaned the body best I could but wasn't sure where to send it," said Bell. His words sounded flat, without intonation. His drawn face and angular posture reminded Cash of all the undertakers he had ever met: pallid replicas of their customers.

Cash examined Boland's head that was crated separately in a foot-square box. He pulled his notepad from his pocket and sketched the grisly sight for his report to Penn. The sword's entry through the soft tissue of the neck and exit point through the mouth had ripped the tongue and left it dangling. The detached ear lay in the box next to the head. Cash had met Robert Boland's wife, Emily, and he knew they had three children and one on the way. He cringed inwardly at the ghastly image that awaited them.

"Sew him back together best you can," Cash commanded, "and fit him with a high collared shirt that will cover the stitching."

"Pardon?" Bell asked in an exasperated tone. "I'm a small town undertaker – I just bury 'em."

Cash pulled twenty dollars from his wallet.

"Mister, I don't have the facilities to embalm or reconstruct like that. Besides, he's been dead near four days."

Cash pulled out another twenty.

The undertaker couldn't take his eyes off the money. His hand moved towards the bills. "Of course. It's not fitting that the family should lay their eyes on such horror."

Cash let Bell have the two twenties. "Pack him on ice and see he makes the one-twenty to Cheyenne tomorrow."

The Pleasance town hall was under siege by Mrs Maude Van Ettan's fiery tirade against everything from Reconstruction to whiskey. Mayor Dodge had hastily gathered the group in hopes of quieting fears but the forum had become a free-for-all as anger swelled among the town's privileged. One thing seemed clear to Mrs Van Ettan and her forum: Indians, Negroes and phantoms were the cause for every woe since Pleasance's founding.

Cash sat at a table near the window, listening to the gaggle of the crowd. His investigation had taken him to all the businesses in town but he garnered little information of any value, except the bank, where some sizable transactions had occurred. He must dig deeper into them. He looked through a grimy window streaked with raindrops from a steady afternoon drizzle.

Across the street, the old Arapaho he'd seen earlier now stood outside the blacksmith shop, watching. Then Maude spotted the Indian and the pitch of her voice went up an octave. "There, a red devil stands in the middle of town and no one lifts a finger. If only we had real men here, they'd take care of these godforsaken savages."

She lifted her sagging chin and huffed her way from the room. Men hung their heads in her wake.

Unnoticed by anyone there, Cash nodded to the Indian.

The Arapaho ambled past Maude. She stood with clenched fists tight against her sides and flung insults at him. The rain turned Pleasance into a mud bowl around her but she brazenly stood her ground like an old water buffalo staking its claim.

It wasn't easy talking in weather like this. They were under a rock that jutted out like a roof, protecting them from the now-driving rain that musically slammed the granite. Day was giving way to night. Two warriors stood nearby, holding a small arsenal of Winchester rifles and bows and arrows. Cash learned the old man was Little Wing, chief of a splinter group of Arapahos forced to relocate whenever the land they inhabited was deemed valuable to white men.

Cash was at ease among them. Peculiar, some might think, because when he was an infant, Arapahos had slain his family at the Battle of Fall Creek. Chief Lightning Cloud spared young Laramie's life and raised him as one of his own. Cash eventually learned the story of his murdered parents, which made him confused and bitter. He fled the only home he knew and lived off the land as his surrogate family had taught him to do. Cash returned the first winter only to run away again. He survived the next winter but not alone. His stepfather's protection was never far, always watching from a distance.

Little Wing was very much like Lightning Cloud, his stepfather. Strong and stoic. Cash still hadn't fully come to terms with his past, but when he did, he knew he would return to the Arapaho. He also knew, even before talking to Little Wing, that the Arapaho had nothing to do with the Masked Devil. The proud Arapahos would never play such games.

The beggar's eyes secretly scanned them in the dark. He cursed the rain that soaked his poncho but he remained focused.

When the marshal and the Arapaho finished their business and parted ways, the beggar followed the lawman.

She stood at the bar. Chestnut curls pinned up high on her head, ruffled black dress cut low and scalloped over her milk-white breasts. Cash wandered over, throwing two bits on the counter. "I'd like to buy the lady a drink."

The greasy barkeep looked up, glanced at Carlene. She nodded. He poured pale yellow ale into two spotty glasses.

"Much obliged," she said.

Cash carried his drink to the end of the bar and studied her closely. Indeed she was beautiful, maybe a little too beautiful, to be turning tricks in a small jerkwater town.

"I heard you were the place for excitement," Cash said, taking a swallow of his beer.

She turned her back to the bar's edge, resting her elbows on the rail, and thrust her breasts out. She eyed him sideways. "That's quite a way to frame it."

"No offense intended."

She watched his face as he broke into a warm grin.

"None taken. For $20, you'll have your answer."

"Lead the way."

They passed a lone drunk lying facedown on the table.

Cash laughed. "Another satisfied customer?"

"Nah, he's just a washed-up circus performer."

The man wearily lifted his bald head and opened one drunken eye to lecherously ogle Carlene's swaying hips as she led the marshal upstairs.

While Cash moved along the landing, he glanced sideways at the reflection in a big mirror at the far side of the saloon: the bartender wiped oily sweat from his forehead and slipped out into the street.

Carlene's room was sparsely furnished—a four-poster bed, a ladder-back chair, a bureau with a washbasin, and a nightstand with a lamp and two books: *The Bible* and *The Adventures of Tom Sawyer*.

"Interesting reading for a painted lady," Cash said.

"I was once a school teacher in Boston. Married a snake who dumped me here."

She stepped out of her dress, resplendent in her scarlet bustier and garter, and strolled over to him.

She kissed him on the cheek, fluttered a hand down his chest and across his lap. She lowered herself before him, unbuckling his belt. "But enough about me, let's see what you're packing."

He dropped his head back with pleasure as she went to work. Once more, he considered the nightstand. *The Bible?*

A bright sliver of first light peaked under the emerald curtain. The sound of a galloping horse came from the street. Then gunfire. Cash grabbed his belt and peered outside. "Beelzebub" had returned to Pleasance and delivered a stream of bullets into the dawn sky. Alarmed faces peered from windows and doorways as Cash strapped on his gun-belt.

"You better not leave me here like this, you son-of-a-bitch," Carlene said. Still wearing her bright red undergarments, she was spreadeagled on the mattress with her arms and legs tied to each bedpost.

"My apologies, ma'am." Cash grabbed a washcloth from the basin and stuffed it in her mouth. "We *will* continue this conversation."

A muffled scream escaped her as he headed out the door.

The horseman waited at street's end, where Robert Boland had fallen.

"Looks like it's your turn to face old Scratch's redemption," the beggar said. He squatted next to the horse trough, his poncho pulled tight around his neck to deflect the cold morning wind. "Yes-suh, seems it's your time to be pushin' up daisies," he sang and then let out a deep baritone laugh.

Cash gritted his teeth. "That'll be the day."

Little Wing and his men were in front of the funeral home cattycorner across from the livery. A small crowd emerged from the hotel and bank entrances. Maude Van Ettan shielded a young girl's eyes and hurried her inside, returning a moment later to observe the ensuing mayhem.

The rider pulled his shining cutlass from its sheath with theatrical flair and began galloping towards Cash.

Cash Laramie saw firsthand how this menace inflicted fear. Chalky hands gripped taut reins. A black cape flowed over blocky shoulders. Charred black holes peered through a red leather mask. Ebon-tipped horns jutted from the sides of its head. Unreal, as if the apparition charged straight from the heart of Hades's inferno.

Cash drew his Colt and stood steadfast, waiting until the rider was fifteen feet away and then tripped the hammer onto a cartridge that sunk a bullet smashing through the Masked Devil's throat.

The horseman doubled over his saddle horn. Cash grabbed the dangling reins and was pulled running a few yards before the white horse came to a halt. He lowered the masked rider to the ground and removed the hood.

The ex-circus performer gurgled foamy blood. His head reeled back with a lifeless stare.

More shots rang out. Cash dove to the ground and rolled. He came up behind the water trough as bullets from Slim's Remington .44 whistled from the second floor hotel window, rhythmically splintering the trough's wood. Cash kept his head down.

Before Cash could get a shot off, Slim lurched forward, a dark hole in his forehead. He plunged through the window, his rifle falling beside him.

The black beggar straightened up to full height, threw the poncho over his shoulder, so the hump disappeared. Spitting the paper wadding from his mouth, he flashed a smile at Cash, his Colt still smoking.

Newly ventilated, Slim lay motionless on the ground.

Cash started to speak when lead spurted from the Six Gun.

The bartender screamed an oath and thrust his shotgun over the saloon batwings. His shots sent Cash spinning around. He aimed and blew the left side of the man's skull away. The barkeep collapsed and the batwing doors swung back and forth above his body.

The marshal surveyed the town for further signs of danger but an eerie silence had settled over Pleasance.

"What took you so long?" Cash asked the black man.

"Is that all the thanks I get for saving your life again?"

"Again? I reckon it was the other way around."

The citizens who had flattened themselves on the ground alongside the town's buildings now slowly rose to their feet. They seemed perplexed at the anti-climatic showdown with the horseman. Cash was well aware that, as news of The Masked Devil's demise spread, the duel would become one of the West's great myths.

The mayor ran from his office wiping his brow with a handkerchief. "I don't understand," he said, looking at the beggar with the Peacemaker in his hand.

"Let me introduce you to my partner, Marshal Gidcon Miles."

Miles tipped the corner of his hat.

Dodge continued to stare at Slim and the bartender.

"They... I don't believe it... were responsible for—" Dodge stammered.

"Partly them, partly the lovely Carlene," Cash said, turning to Maude Van Ettan, who had wandered over to listen, "but mostly you."

She stepped back, startled. Then, as the crowd closed in, she seemed to regain her courage. "What's the meaning of this?" Maude demanded.

"Marshal Laramie, what do you base your accusation on?" Dodge said. "Why, Mrs Van Ettan is a leading citizen of this community."

"Miss Carlene gave you up after a little gentle persuasion," Cash said.

"What kind of persuasion?" Miles interjected, grinning.

Cash returned the smile. "No more than required."

"I'll bet."

"Ha! That's your evidence?" Maude Van Ettan guffawed, standing straight, dignified and haughty. "Who will believe the ranting of a whore?"

"You're right. It helps to have some evidence." Cash reached into his pocket and withdrew several empty cartridges. "Next time you ask someone to dispose of evidence, you ought to make sure she does."

Dread swirled across Maude's face.

"I couldn't quite figure out how an accomplished gunman like Marshal Boland could miss at such close range," Cash said. He bounced the empty shells in his hand. "Miss Carlene switched his bullets for blanks after she'd serviced him and he dozed off for a spell. While everyone was distracted by the Masked Devil's staged showdown with Boland, the bartender swiped the money."

"Where'd you find the casings?" Miles asked.

"Miss Carlene had a hollowed-out book on her shelf where she hid them. It seemed odd that a prostitute would be reading the Good Book so I took a gander at it while she was working."

Miles smiled. "She kept a little collateral on hand just in case someone tried to double-cross her."

"Or to siphon off a little more. Whatever the reason, a judge should find it thought provoking. Also, I inquired at the bank about any large transactions in the past week. There were two: Mrs. Van Ettan here and Carlene. Circumstantial perhaps, but with Carlene's confession and Marshal Boland's bullets switched for blanks, we have the makings of a solid case."

Cash turned to Maude. "Where's the money?" he demanded.

She swallowed, then swallowed again, as though her throat was dry. "At my house," she said. "There's a built-in safe behind the family portrait."

"A fire!" Devon Penn interlocked his fingers and placed his hands on his desk.

"Gutted Mrs Van Ettan's house," Cash said.

"None of the money was found?"

"Except what she'd paid the riffraff in cahoots with her."

Penn turned to Miles who nodded.

"Damn. That's not going to sit well with the town council and Historical Society. No sign of foul play?"

"None," Cash said. "It looked like Maude's chimney caught fire."

"What the hell are the chances?" Devon Penn leaned back in his chair, unlacing his fingers. "And what caused this Maude Van Ettan to take up a life of crime?"

"Not so far a stretch when you dig around Pleasance awhile for information," Miles explained. "Maude and her late husband amassed their wealth as carpetbaggers in Alabama before striking out for the great northwest where they lived a so-called pious life in Pleasance while occasionally dipping into fringe criminal activity."

"I see. Well, our part is done and it's up to the judge now."

Cash stood up and gathered his hat. "I also checked up on the dead circus performer. He used to be good with a saber. Could ride a horse and slice and dice a watermelon on the run."

"Sounds like a one-trick pony, to me," said Miles, also rising to his feet.

"Yeah, so he turned to booze. Then Mrs Van Ettan stumbled on him and offered him a few encores."

Penn shook his head and grinned. "Good job, men." He stood and shook their hands. "Both of you get some rest. First thing in the morning, you'll be tracking a couple of owlhoots that skipped bail." Penn waved his hands in the air. "And get that damn cigar out of my office."

*

Cash and Miles walked into the warm Cheyenne afternoon. Cash snagged a cheroot from his pocket as they meandered along the busy sidewalk. Miles joined Cash with a pipe.

"Amazing, that fire happening like that."

Cash leisurely blew smoke skyward as he spotted Lenora entering the Cheyenne's Beckett Hotel and Saloon. She looked over her shoulder, smiled and went inside.

"Amazing. I didn't even see any evidence of a safe or burnt money." Miles struck a lucifer on his pants leg and puffed at his pipe.

"Yep. Strange," Cash said rolling his cheroot to the corner of his mouth where it settled.

"Not to mention Little Wing leaving town with several bulging saddlebags."

Cash reached for the Arapaho arrowhead on its thong around his neck and rubbed it. He looked across the street, eyes fixed on Lenora's curtains, waiting to see her pull them aside.

"What are you suggesting, Marshal?" Cash asked.

"Only that a guardian angel saw fit to right a wrong."

Cash clasped Miles's shoulder. "Wouldn't you like to think so!"

DEAD MAN WALKING

Lee Walker

Lee Walker is the pen name of Ed Ferguson who lives in the picturesque Scottish market town of Lanark. His first western novel, Gun Law, *was published by Robert Hale in 2009 and he is now busy on the second one. Ed hopes one day to visit the places in America he writes about. Please visit him at leewalkerwesterns.blogspot.com.*

Ever since we'd killed Jimmy Leighton, I hadn't slept too well.

For the last two weeks, just before dawn, I found myself bolt upright on my cot, sweat-soaked and grabbing for air as though a rope was slowly tightening around my throat. I could still hear him: *"He'll get you! He'll get you all, you sonsabitches! You're all dead men walking...Every last one of ya..."*

I recalled the bang of the trap door as it fell away beneath him, the sickening crack of his neck, his few feeble kicks.

Unlike some lawmen, a hanging never sat easy with me and I considered that a good thing. If ever the time came when I'd take a man's life without a second thought, then I reckoned I'd be as bad as those I'd sent to a hemp necktie. So after a while I learned to live with it, knowing my conscience was clear. I never had a hand in helping a soul depart this earth that didn't deserve it.

I swung my legs out from under the coarse blanket and went out back of the house. The sun was starting to scatter the night sky and there was a cool breeze coming off the mountains. I pumped some water, splashed it over the back of my neck and face and heaved in a few deep breaths. I couldn't let people see things were getting to me.

Six years I'd been the sheriff of Westward, which was a good run in anybody's books considering most lawmen in these parts didn't wear their tin star for more than a year or so. Some handed it back. Most died wearing it. But I'd be a liar if I didn't admit those six years had taken a heavy toll.

I like to think I'm in good shape. I'm over six feet tall, still as slim at forty-three as I was in my twenties, and I guess I'm lucky that the muscles I got punching cattle in my young days hadn't all turned to flab. There aren't many things I can't handle, but even so, I'd been getting to thinking that maybe I was just too long in the tooth for law work and it was high time I handed the badge onto someone else. Someone younger and fitter with that fire in his belly I'd had when I first took the job. Someone who didn't suffer sleepless nights.

I sat on the edge of the water trough and watched the sun climb but couldn't keep my thoughts from turning to young Jimmy Leighton and his smooth, blue-eyed face. I saw him clear as day, every night.

Maybe it bothered me that he was a kid. He couldn't have been more than sixteen when we strung him up. Then I had to remind myself that although he was just a boy, he'd killed like a man.

He'd run with the Leighton Bunch. We caught up with them just after they'd held up a train not two miles north of Westward. Although nobody testified that Jimmy had actually pulled the trigger, a crowd of witnesses swore he was part of the gang that gunned down two unarmed engineers.

By the time I arrived at the head of Westward's posse, the Leighton Bunch had finished their bloody business, filled their saddlebags with cash and headed into the foothills. The gang probably knew we'd have no hope of tracking them once they got into the mountains, but we chased them anyway. Their head start might have put a lot of dust between them and us if a wild lucky shot from one of our boys hadn't caught Jimmy's mustang on the hind leg, bringing it down like a sack of oats.

We hauled Jimmy back to town, convened a court in the Wranglers Saloon and had no problem getting twelve upstanding citizens to form a jury. By the time the circuit judge arrived we were ready and it was virtually a done deal.

Five days later, Jimmy stood on a newly built scaffold and received his last rights from Father Mahoney. That was when he started screaming at the jury:

"He'll get you! He'll get you all, you sonsabitches! You're all dead men walking...Every last one of ya..."

"He" was Casper Leighton, Jimmy's older brother by a good four years and the head of the Leighton Bunch made up of the two Leighton brothers and their cousins, John and Ethan Carlton. Casper had a fearsome reputation in the territory as a killer, even before he formed his gang. The murder of the two engineers was just the latest in a killing spree spread over the last eighteen months. Casper was wanted dead or alive in nearly every state west of the Mississippi for a string of violent bank and train robberies. The last known tally of his victims numbered twenty-four. So when Jimmy Leighton said his older brother would settle a score with you, you'd be a fool not to take it seriously.

I knew Jimmy's words rattled the jurors. I saw it in their eyes – the way they glanced at each other nervously and shuffled their feet, as if wishing they could get the hanging over and done with.

As for me, I wish I had a dollar for every time someone said they were going to get even, so I didn't set much store by it – until, one by one, those jurors started dying…

The sun was now over the hills. It was too early to be up and too late to go back to bed so I went indoors, put on a pot of Arbuckle's and heated a pan of water for shaving. I was just finishing off, wiping the lather from my neck, when I heard the office door bang.

Through the dusty glass, I made out the anxious face of Gus McGrath. He was the proud proprietor of the Wranglers Saloon, President of Westward Town Council and, maybe something he didn't brag about too much now, Foreman of the jury that delivered the verdict that sent Casper Leighton's kid brother to eternity.

"Door's open!" I called.

Gus pushed against the door with his two hundred and fifty pounds and nearly fell into my sparse office.

"Coffee's hot," I said, nodding at the stove.

"I'm fine," said Gus quietly.

"You sure don't look fine." The morning was cool but there were beads of sweat across his brow. I couldn't help but notice puffy dark rings under his eyes and the patches of sweat below his armpits. "You alright?"

Gus flopped into the nearest chair and rubbed his eyes with his fingertips. "Ain't sleeping so good – and neither is anybody else since…since…you know…" His words trailed off. "What about you?"

"Like a baby," I lied. I buttoned up my red shirt and slipped on my leather vest. I took a while making sure my silver badge was sitting just right.

Gus watched me closely but didn't say a word. The silence got uncomfortable, so I broke it. "What can I do for you, Gus?"

"Sheriff Webb–"

"Gus – we've known each other for years, for God'sakes!"

He cleared his throat nervously and started again. "Hank, dammit. I need to know what you plan to do." He stopped and looked out into the street as though someone might be following him. Turning to me again, his podgy face crumpled like a baby's. I thought he was going to cry. "He's here…in Westward. Ain't he?"

"Who?"

"Casper Leighton, of course!"

"He ain't here, Gus."

"How d'you *know*? How can you be so goddamn *sure* of yourself?"

"I just know. Someone would've seen him by now."

"So how d'you explain what's happening to Jimmy Leighton's jury, eh? Dammit, Hank, we're dropping like flies!"

Gus stood up and started pacing. "At first I thought like everyone else, that Albert Coyne had poisoned himself by taking too much of that patent medicine he was so fond of. Then Sonny Smithson...well, that was tragic the way he blew his own brains out like that..."

"Accidents. Coincidence. Things happen..."

"...and that's what I thought too, until yesterday. I thought I was doing Abe Sutter a favor letting him stay in one of our rooms above the saloon. I felt sorry for the old guy. And then I go and find him lying in his bed with his throat cut wide open. For Chrissakes, Hank! There was so much blood! He musta drowned in it. ..."

"I know, Gus. It's never easy..."

"...but the thing is, Abe's death weren't no accident. He didn't slit his own throat, did he? That killer was in my saloon, in my home, a few doors down from my bedroom. It could've been me, Hank, it could've been me..."

I didn't like Gus McGrath. Never did. He was a blowhard and a bully who happened to be in the right place at the right time, running a poky sawdust-covered drinking hole when the cattle started coming through Westward with lines of thirsty cowboys playing loose and free with their pay, and Gus cashed in big time. He was like a lot of self-made men. They forget the part Lady Luck plays in their success and come to think they had it all planned right from the set off.

The cattle drives were now long gone but Gus still acted like a big shot, thinking that just because he'd got himself elected to the head of the Town Council, he owned the whole place. But I knew he found his big talk in a whiskey bottle and I knew how free and easy he was with his fists on his wife, Ruby, who'd started out as a percentage girl at the Wranglers.

Still, it was hard not to feel a little sorry for him. He was a wreck. I tried to reassure him. "It's not Casper, Gus. Sure, there's been some mighty strange goings on of late, but I'll get to the bottom of it."

"Well, you'd better!" Gus turned, his cheeks red. He stabbed a tobacco-stained finger at me. "I'm telling you, Hank. It's your job to protect this town but if you can't, then maybe we need to bring in somebody who *can*!"

There is nothing worse than watching a weak man pretending to be strong but I wasn't in the mood for an argument. His bluster petered out and then he left, banging the door behind him.

I may have felt nothing but contempt for Gus McGrath, but at the end of the day he was right. It *was* my job to protect these people and maybe I wasn't up to it. All I did know, I had to stop the rumors that Casper Leighton was cutting a swathe through the citizens of Westward right under my nose. And I had to do it quick.

I left the jailhouse and crossed the main street to the telegraph office. The sun was well up now and the town was busy as stores and offices opened for business. It was just another day in Westward; except for the fact there might be a killer prowling among us.

I greeted folk as they passed. I knew most by name but today I was looking for those I didn't know. I stared at unfamiliar faces, looking for anyone who might resemble Casper Leighton. Nobody fitted the bill.

A small bell tinkled above my head as I strode into the telegraph office.

"'Morning, Sheriff," called out Tom Saddler from behind his grilled counter, "what can I do for you?"

"Need to send an urgent message, Tom."

"Sure thing." He swung a Western Union form towards me. "Just jot it down there."

I lifted the pencil and printed: NEED WHEREABOUTS OF CASPER LEIGHTON STOP URGENT END OF MESSAGE.

I passed it to Tom.

He read it quickly then looked up. "Where's it going, Sheriff?"

"The Pinkerton's. Denver."

"Anyone in particular?"

"Old friend of mine. Name of Seth Brownlie. Owes me one."

"Sure thing. I'll get on to it straight away."

As I handed over the regular fee, I looked him straight in the eye. "It's real important no one knows about this here telegram, Tom – or what you get back..."

Tom nodded. "I'll deal with it personally and bring the reply straight to you when it comes in."

He was already tapping the Morse key before I left the office.

When I got back, the door to my office was open. As I walked in, I noticed the dark green shades had been drawn and in the gloom I saw a figure sitting behind my desk.

"Ruby?"

Even in the dark I would have recognized her. The long dress couldn't conceal her thin waist and full figure. Her brown hair was tied back with a pretty ribbon but I knew how it fell to her shoulders in long thick curls when released. The room filled with the smell of lavender.

I hurriedly shut the door behind me, threw the latch and walked over to my desk. As I raised the wick on the kerosene lamp, the light started to spread across her.

"You know, you shouldn't be here," I said, "if someone saw you, if Gus–"

Then she looked up and I froze. A livid deep purple bruise ran across her left cheekbone and down to her jaw. The edges were already starting to turn yellow. One of her beautiful gray-blue eyes was almost fully closed.

I didn't need to ask, but I did anyway. "Did Gus do this?"

"Oh, Hank..."

The next thing I knew, she was in my arms, her voice breaking with heavy sobs, her tears making a dark patch on my chest. As she clung to me, I couldn't help but hold her firm womanly body close to me.

"It was the usual thing. He'd had too much to drink. What with this Casper Leighton thing and then finding Abe Sutter... He's frightened, Hank. He thinks he's next. He's convinced Casper Leighton's going to wipe out the whole jury. I said the wrong thing and he just let loose on me. I've never seen him so scared. Oh, Hank, I don't know how much more of this I can take!"

I cradled her smooth, pretty face in my hands. "I'll stop it..."

"Who you gonna stop, Hank?" She looked into my eyes. "Casper or Gus?"

"Both. Leighton first –"

"So you *do* think it's him?"

I shook my head. "I don't know..." I turned away from her and put my hat on the peg by the door. I ran a hand through my hair. "To tell the truth, I ain't sure. I'm starting to think too many people on that jury are dead for this all to be a coincidence..."

She came up behind me, put her arms around my waist and leaned her head between my shoulder blades. "I'm frightened, Hank. We should just go. Get out of here together, tonight..."

"Ruby, I can't. I've told you."

She pushed away from me. I turned. Her face was flushed with anger. "Oh, I know, Hank. I've heard it plenty of times. You've got a job to do. You got no money for us to live on. You can't take another man's woman. I've heard all the excuses before–"

"They're not excuses!" I said, stepping toward her.

"*Don't!*" she said as she turned away. "You didn't say all them things the night we ended up in bed together, did you? That's not what you were whispering in my ear that night..."

"Ruby, you know it's not like that."

"Ain't it?" She walked to the door. "Tell me the truth, Hank. If I wasn't married to Gus. If we had enough money to set ourselves up. If you didn't wear that damn tin badge, would we be married?"

"That's way too many 'ifs' for a straight 'yes' or 'no'."

She looked into my eyes for what seemed an eternity. Finally, she said, "Oh, I think I got your answer, Sheriff Hank Webb." She turned and unlatched the door.

"Ruby, I promise. I'll fix things."

"Don't worry about me, Sheriff. I can take care of things myself! I always have."

She swung out into the daylight. I didn't try to stop her. I knew how it worked. We'd had words like this before. She'd cool down and we'd talk again in a day or two.

Meanwhile, I had a killer to catch.

I spent the rest of the morning staring at the wanted posters of Casper Leighton then, restless and preoccupied, walked up and down Main Street to see if I could spot someone who matched the only description I had. It seemed evil came in small packages. Five foot five, smooth complexion, blue eyes and so slightly built he'd once disguised himself as a woman in a bank raid.

By nightfall I was exhausted but didn't want to go to bed. I sat at my desk with the kerosene lamp turned low and sometime after midnight I must have dozed off.

At first, I thought I'd heard a gunshot in my dreams but with the second, I knew they were real. I yanked myself fully awake, rushed out onto the boardwalk and into the dark deserted street. The third gunshot shattered the silence and this time I was sure it had come from the rooms above the Wranglers Saloon.

I sprinted across the street and kicked in the front doors. In the darkness I weaved between tables and chairs then ran up the stairs three at a time. Behind a door at the end of the passage, another gunshot rang out. I ran towards it, charging at the door shoulder first, splintering the frame and taking the door right off its hinges.

The first thing I saw was Gus McGrath lying in the bed. My eyes fixed on the two bullet holes in the white sheets across his body, their edges blackened with gunpowder and starting to stain with red.

On the edge of my vision, something moved. I spun around. The long blue curtains shifted on the night breeze wafting through the open window. I rushed over and looked out.

A short, slim figure dressed in black from hat to boot slid easily down the slates of the lean-to porch at the back of the saloon.

I shouted a warning but the fugitive didn't stop. I drew my gun, fired twice, but missed both times. With a groan, I hesitantly climbed out onto the roof after the killer who by this time had jumped lightly from the roof to the alleyway and was mounting a horse tied in the back alley.

By the time I'd noisily clambered down the lean-to's roof and lowered myself on to the ground, the rider was at the edge of town. In frustration, I fired a couple of rounds at him then stared into the gloom long after the black rider was gone.

So he *was* here. Casper Leighton was in Westward and he was busy taking out his brother's killers one by one!

I realized some townsfolk had joined me, roused from their beds by all the noise. They looked at me, waiting for me to take charge. I called for one of them to go get Doc Smith and asked some men to follow me up to the room above the Wranglers Saloon.

Gus moaned softly as we gathered round him.

"Looks bad," said Bill Jeffries.

"Wonder who's next on Casper's list," murmured Jed.

"Quit crowding the man!" said Doc Smith as he hurried into the room.

Doc did a quick examination and declared we had to get Gus to the surgery before he lost much more blood. We made a stretcher out of the door I'd knocked off its hinges and lifted him as gently as we could down the stairs and across the street to Doc Smith's place. As soon as we laid him on the scrubbed wooden table, Doc waved all of us out of the room while he rolled up his shirtsleeves.

I waited outside.

After about an hour, Doc came out to join me on the boardwalk, wiping his hands on a blood-soaked towel.

"How is he, Doc?"

"In bad shape but lucky. One in the gut, one in the chest. Another inch would've gone through his heart."

"Will he make it?"

"I think so. Next twenty-four hours'll tell. I'll do my best."

"Thanks, Doc. I'll swing by later. See how things are."

I made to step off the boardwalk.

"Hank?"

I turned to face the old man.

"There's a lot of scared people in this town, you know," he said. "Talk is that Casper Leighton's gonna come back and finish off the job. Then he'll just keep going 'til there's nobody left who sat on that jury."

"I know, Doc. I'll stop him. Just need a little more time."

Doc wiped his hands thoughtfully and smiled. "I hope so. I was on that jury too, remember?"

I nodded and watched the old man shuffle into his surgery.

I wasn't a gambling man but I would have bet that if Casper Leighton paid a visit, this is where he'd call and get two birds with the same stone.

On my way to the office, I noticed a light in the Wranglers. I decided to check in.

Ruby sat by herself at the bar with an open bottle of red-eye on the counter. She held up an empty glass when she saw me. "Care to join me?" she said. Her words were slurred.

I shook my head. "Got a busy night ahead."

"So have I, Sheriff, so have I," she said, topping up her glass. "And how's my darling husband?"

"He's hanging in there. He's over at Doc Smith's. Wanna go see him?"

She shook her head and took another sip of whiskey. "Not me."

As I watched her reflection in the large gilt-framed mirror behind the bar, a sudden thought came to me. "Ruby, where were you when the shooting was going on?"

"I was in the next room," she said, staring into her glass, "Gus and I don't sleep together. Haven't for years – unless he gets the urge, if you know what I mean." She took another gulp of whiskey and wiped her mouth with the back of her hand. "When the shooting started I hid under the bed. By the time I was brave enough to come out, you'd taken Gus to the Doc's. I could guess what happened."

I waited until she finished. It was not so much what she said, but how she said it. Her husband was fighting for his life and she couldn't have cared less. I realized then, she was through with him. I decided when this Leighton business was done, no matter what happened to Gus, I'd call it a day as sheriff and ride out of here with Ruby by my side. There was no reason for either of us to stay.

"I gotta go now," I said eventually. "Will you be alright here by yourself?"

"Sure," she smiled. "Ain't me Casper's after. I wasn't no member of any jury."

"Casper Leighton won't be shooting no more jurymen. I'll make sure of it."

She raised her glass in salute. "Whatever you say, Sheriff. Don't try *too* hard though, will ya?"

Her drunken laughter taunted me as I pushed through the batwing doors and made my way to the office.

Four hours later, I sat motionless in a rocking chair in the small bedroom at the back of Doc Smith's surgery and waited in the dark. In the moonlight I checked my pocket watch. It was coming up for nearly five in the morning. For the hundredth time, I ran through my plans. If Casper Leighton came calling tonight, or any night from now on, I'd need to be ready.

After all the commotion, everyone in the town knew Gus McGrath would be bunked here at Doc Smith's place, so just after midnight, me and Doc carefully moved him out of the surgery, across the alley, and into the home of a local woman who sometimes helped Doc as a nurse and midwife. He assured me she was reliable.

I used the oldest trick in the book and put some pillows under the blankets. In the dark no one could tell it wasn't Gus. I'd spread the word around town that I didn't expect Casper Leighton to come back. In fact, I'd said I didn't believe it was Casper Leighton who shot Gus.

I'd picked eight men I could trust, swore them in as deputies, and put two at each end of town. If Leighton gave me the slip again, they'd be already mounted and ready to give chase. The other four were armed with rifles and hidden on the rooftops on either side of the street in front of Doc's place. These men had good vantage points and should be able to get clear shots if needed.

Now, there was nothing left to do but wait.

I glanced through the window. The moon was bright in the clear sky. I was sure Casper would come back tonight to finish off this loose end and then get on with dispatching more of the jury. The thought made me shiver. I had to stop this tonight.

There was only one window and one door. If he came through either, I'd have a clear shot. But first I wanted him in the room. I wanted him close, so I could take him alive. I wanted him tried by the survivors of the jury he was trying to kill off. I wanted to see him swing the same way I'd watched his younger brother swing.

Just when I thought I couldn't fight sleep any longer, I heard light footsteps outside the window. I slowly cocked my Colt .45 lying on my thigh and held my breath.

A figure was outlined against the moon. Dressed in black with a dark bandanna covering his face, he lifted the window sash and quietly stepped into the room. I watched as he calmly pulled his gun and pointed it at the pillows where Gus's head should have been.

Suddenly, a small circle of light moved on the intruder's body. I pushed myself back into the chair and the light traveled up to his shoulder, his cheek, and then flashed into his eyes. He raised his hand and swung round as I realized it was moonlight reflecting off my badge. I quickly covered it with my hand.

He saw my movement in the dark and, with lightning speed, swung his gun in my direction and fired before I could even raise my .45.

The bullet sliced some flesh off of my shoulder and the shock pinned me against the chair. I cursed loudly as my gun clattered on the pine boards.

Casper Leighton fired two slugs into the pillows on the bed and then, as lightly as a dancer, hopped back through the window. I scrabbled for my gun, rushed to the window, and fired three quick shots into the air to alert the men.

I stumbled from Doc's surgery into the street. Around me I heard gunfire, men shouting and the hoof-beats of horses.

"You alright, Hank?" came Bill's voice from the roof, his silhouette against the treacherous moon.

"Hit in the shoulder but it ain't serious. What's happening?"

He pointed to the east side of town. "That varmint got to his horse but Jed and Cliff are right on his tail. He ain't gonna get away this time, Sheriff!"

No thanks to me, I thought.

Dawn started to break as I stood in the middle of the street and followed Bill's gaze. The throbbing in my shoulder was like being hit by a blacksmith's hammer but I wasn't leaving until I was sure they'd got him.

After what seemed hours but was only minutes, Bill called out, "Riders coming!"

I shielded my eyes. Sure enough, three small black figures on horseback, silhouetted against the light. My deputies had him!

As I started to walk towards them, I couldn't help the smile that spread across my face. We'd stopped Casper Leighton! Soon, he'd be behind bars. In a few days, a judge and jury would do their work and he'd be dead and his kid brother's threats would be as harmless as a story in a dime novel.

"Sheriff! Sheriff! Hold up a minute!"

I turned.

Tom from the telegraph office was running towards me, waving a slip of paper in his hand. "Sheriff, you got your answer from the Pinkerton's!"

I let him catch up with me and get his breath back.

"Must've come during the night, Sheriff," he panted.

"Thanks, Tom, but I know where Leighton is. They're bringing him in now." I pointed to the three riders well inside the town boundary.

Tom shook his head. "That can't be Casper Leighton…"

"What d'ya mean?"

"Think you'd better read this, Sheriff."

He placed a neatly folded slip of paper in my hand.

I quickly opened it and read the few words. I *read* them, but I couldn't work out what they *meant*. Each word was like an arrow piercing my gut: CASPER LEIGHTON AND GANG DEAD STOP GUNNED DOWN BY PINKERTONS IN BANK RAID SEVEN DAYS PAST END OF MESSAGE.

"Sheriff? You alright?"

I saw Tom's lips move but I didn't hear most of his words above the roar in my head. I crumpled the telegram into a small ball in my fist.

If Casper Leighton was dead then who…?

The three riders reached us. I looked up but the sun's rays flashed in my eyes. I couldn't make out their faces.

I saw Jed dismount, walk round to the middle rider and roughly haul him out his saddle. He threw him at my feet.

I looked down and the pain in my shoulder pounded harder and harder until I thought I was going to pass out.

"I'm sorry, Hank..." Ruby looked up at me and started to sob. Her shoulders shuddered as tears rolled from those lovely gray-blue eyes.

I don't remember much after that.

Jed and Cliff took her to the jailhouse while Doc Smith patched me up. I was lucky. I needed some stitches but the bullet had only grazed me and was nothing that wouldn't mend. He told me I needed to rest but I discarded my sling and busied myself doing things that didn't need doing; anything to avoid going to the jailhouse.

Eventually I had to quit stalling.

Jed was sleeping in my chair when I arrived. I nudged him awake and told him he could go home. He didn't need telling twice. Near midnight, I brewed some coffee and took a tin mug in to her.

She was standing with her head pressed against the steel bars, still wearing a dusty black shirt and pants. I offered the cup but she shook her head.

I turned to leave, and then she whispered, "I did it for you, Hank. I killed them all for you."

I moved back to the bars. I thought I hadn't heard her right. "What d'ya mean, 'all'? You ain't killed nobody. Gus is still alive. Doc says he's gonna make it."

She shook her head slowly. "I don't mean Gus. I mean the others."

"The others?"

"Don't you see, Hank? I had to kill them so I could get to Gus. So we could have each other."

"I don't know what you're saying, Ruby..."

She gripped the bars so hard, her knuckles turned white.

"I couldn't take it from Gus anymore but I couldn't see a way out. If I'd walked out on him, he woulda killed me. And I wasn't about to leave behind everything I'd helped him build up over those years. I wanted what was rightfully mine!" She looked into my eyes. "And I couldn't leave you, Hank. I had to find a way of getting Gus out the way, keeping the Wranglers *and* you!"

I stared at her, struggling to take in what I was hearing.

"Then the day Jimmy Leighton was hanged it came to me. I stood in that crowd and listened to him threaten everyone with Casper. I saw how scared the jury was – especially Gus. They *believed* Casper Leighton would come back. All I had to do was make them think he had."

She gripped the bars tighter, crying. "Don't you see, Hank? If everyone thought Casper Leighton had killed Gus, I'd be in the clear. More than that, I'd be a victim too. I'd just be poor Gus's widow. But to make it ring true, if Gus was to die, others would have to die as well. And it nearly worked, Hank. I nearly got away with it!"

She slid to the floor and sat sobbing, her face pressed against the steel bars.

"Don't you see, Hank? I did it all for you. I love you, Hank! I love you!"

I could hardly breathe as I walked into my office and closed the door on her.

I lay awake the rest of the night, listening to her calling out my name and then at first light I got up, wrote my letter of resignation and swore in Bill Jeffries as acting sheriff of Westward.

I didn't see Ruby again until the day she climbed the scaffold.

I knew her last cries would haunt my nights the way Jimmy Leighton's once had, but I waited in the crowd and watched until she was still. I looked over at the stony faces of the jury. Gus McGrath was foreman. They could all sleep better now.

As Father Mahoney's prayers filled the silence, I left unnoticed. My shoulder ached some, but I was glad to feel some pain. As I led my horse up the deserted main street towards the town limits and took a last look at Westward, my heart was solid and cold.

I was numb.

Empty.

Like a dead man walking.

AFTERWORD

Nik Morton

For over forty years I've been editing submitted material and I'm pleased to write that I still enjoy that sense of anticipation when a new story arrives on the doormat or, as is most likely these days, in my email inbox. Sometimes, I've read a story and have been convinced I've found a new voice, someone who is going to go far; that's a great feeling.

Indeed, every one of this latest selection of Old West tales for *Express Westerns* tells a story which drew me in. I wanted to know more; I wanted to find out what was going to happen next. This should be true of any short story, whether a western or another genre, including so-called mainstream.

Speaking for all writers in this anthology, we're honored that James Reasoner agreed to write the Introduction. If you haven't read any of his quite substantial work – over 200 novels – then I recommend you do so soon. He has written ten books in the Civil War Battle series, is renowned for the mystery *Texas Wind* and his latest two books are *Death Head Crossing* and *Gabriel Hunt at the Well of Eternity*. Visit him at his blog http://jamesreasoner.blogspot.com and also at www.jamesreasoner.net.

I'd like to thank my co-editor, Charlie Whipple, for his tireless help and encyclopaedic knowledge of the Old West. If any factual errors remain, lay them at my door, not his. My appreciation also to Jennifer Smith-Mayo for the wonderful cover design.

It's refreshing to read humorous western tales, whether that's the dark irony of Ian Parnham's story or the off-the-wall slapstick of Evan Lewis's Crockett saga. As these two stories testify, the western can be many things and long ago escaped its straitjacket of men in white and black hats shooting it out. Of course, there's gunplay and death, but that was an aspect of the Old West. Yet the tales within these pages contain so much more.

Revenge is a sure-fire motive for a western and there have been scores of books and films that have dealt with the subject. Derek Rutherford and Ben Bridges go down this route but with unexpected consequences.

The West was not tamed solely by men, of course. Women played their significant part and it's a pleasure to feature three tales from female writers. What's also interesting is that several stories have female protagonists, not least Chuck Tyrell's endearing 'Big Enough', Peter Avarillo's tale, Kit

Churchill's strongly felt exploration of prostitution 'Crib Girls' and also my 'Visitors'.

While several authors in this collection are established, the western, like any genre, needs new blood and this collection sheds some. It also has the distinction of featuring a story from a sixteen-year-old young lady, Chantel Foster. I think we shall be hearing more from her as the years go by. Other relative newcomers include Cody Wells, Edward A Grainger, Lee Walker and Jack Martin, the latter having sold a phenomenal number of copies of his début western, *The Tarnished Star*.

As was proven in the previous anthology, *Where Legends Ride*, and reiterated by James Reasoner in this book's Introduction, the western can cover all manner of storylines relevant to today's readership. And this collection endorses that belief in spades. Lance Howard always produces challenging stories and his featured tale is no exception. There are hints of the supernatural from Courtney Joyner, faction from old hand Jack Giles, a couple of tales about doctors with a difference from Gillian Taylor and Bobby Nash, and, inevitably, a few lynchings, not least from the editor of the previous anthology, Matthew P Mayo.

I don't know, I'm guessing, but perhaps five characters you meet in these pages will go on to bigger things, maybe featuring in series volumes. If so, remember, they appeared in print here first: Cash Laramie, Bloodhound, Morgana Darke, Angelo and Dave Crockett...

I hope you have enjoyed this varied exposure to the characters, the land, the dangers and the splendor of the Old West and will want to come back for more in future volumes.

Adios, amigos!
San Fulgencio, Alicante, Spain

CALLING ALL WESTERN FANS!

If you like what you've read here, be sure to visit the following websites for more Old West action:

The Official Home of Black Horse Westerns:
www.halebooks.com

The Official Watering Hole of Black Horse Western Writers on the Web: **Groups.yahoo.com/group/blackhorsewesterns**

The Black Horse Express:
www.blackhorsewesterns.org

Black Horse Extra
The quarterly newsletter about westerns and BHW books and writers:
www.blackhorsewesterns.com

Recently there has been an explosion of interest in westerns on many Internet blogs. Here is a sample selection:

http://blackhorseexpress.blogspot.com/
http://westernfictionreview.blogspot.com/
http://meridianbridge.com/
http://www.lamourproject.com/
http://spurandlock.blogspot.com/
http://westernsfanclub.blogspot.com/

And don't forget to request the best in Western storytelling at your local libraries and bookstores.

Keep a sharp eye on the horizon – EXPRESS WESTERNS will be back!

Some of our authors' books available in Robert Hale hardback:

SILVER EXPRESS
Gillian F Taylor
Robert Hale Black Horse Western: ISBN-13: 9780709087816
No one needed to tell Sheriff Alec Lawson that thousands of dollars in silver bullion had been stolen from a train on the Northern Colorado Railroad: he was on the train at the time. Now he and his deputies had to search the mountains and mining camps for the thieves. The more he looked into the robbery, the more Lawson was convinced that it was not just a simple theft. The desire for money was at the root of it all: bribes, bounties, social status and death. The Sheriff and his men were risking their lives for other people's money, and death seems very close when you're riding on the roof of a runaway train.

THE $300 MAN
Ross Morton
Robert Hale Black Horse Western:ISBN-13: 9780709087502
What's a life worth? $300, maybe. Half-Mexican Corbin Molina lost a hand during the Civil War but he has adapted. Now he's on a mission to Walkerville. On the way, he prevents a train robbery and finds an old friend. Corbin always carries $300, which is significant, since that's what he was paid as substitute soldier for the Union. When Corbin starts asking questions about Walkerville's law and administration, he discovers that the Walker family, who seem to have bought and paid for loyalty and position, dominate the townspeople. Inevitably, Corbin's questions attract plenty of trouble. And his past emerges to confront him during a tense showdown that threatens not only him but also his newfound love.

RIDERS OF THE BARREN PLAINS
I J Parnham
Robert Hale Black Horse Western: ISBN-13: 9780709087687
Jeff Steed rode into Carmon looking for work, but when he got caught up in a bank raid he found himself running from both Sheriff Cassidy Yates and the bank raider Blake Kelly. To escape from the net that was inexorably closing in on him he assumed the identity of a dead man. But as that man was the leader of a supply convoy, he had to undertake a hazardous journey across the Barren Plains to the silver miners at Bleak Point. With the convoy being escorted by the lawman who had been trying to catch him and the bandit he double-crossed hiding out in the Barren Plains, can Jeff ever hope to survive?

THE TARNISHED STAR
Jack Martin
Robert Hale Black Horse Western: ISBN-13: 9780709087618
All Sheriff Cole Masters wants is to raise a family with the woman he loves. However upholding the law in an era when gunfire speaks louder than words can be a risky business.Cole makes an arrest for the brutal murder of a saloon girl but the killer is the son of a wealthy rancher and it is clear the old man will do anything to see his son set free. Soon the peace of the small town is shattered with deadly force and Cole finds himself a lawman on the run for murder.The rancher wants Masters dead and the two deadly gunmen on his tail are sure they can do it. Soon blood will run as Cole Masters attempts to reclaim his tarnished star.

WAR SMOKE
Michael D George
Robert Hale Black Horse Western: ISBN-13: 9780709087250
Marshal Matt Fallen was faced with a series of horrific murders in the town of War Smoke. Yet these were not like others killings in the history of the remote Nevada settlement. Someone was brutally clubbing innocent men, women and even children to death with their six shooters. With so many strangers in War Smoke it was impossible to find the culprit yet Fallen was determined to get to the bottom of the slayings. Who was the murderer? A body had been discovered each night for two weeks. As the sun set the marshal vowed to get his man. A showdown was brewing. Fallen was ready.

GUN LAW
Lee Walker
Robert Hale Black Horse Western: ISBN-13: 978-0709088349
As a boy of fourteen, Jake Chalmers saw his parents callously murdered by two drunken cowboys in the street. Now a young man, he is determined to protect himself, even if he has to use his gun to do so. On the run after killing in self-defence, Jake arrives in Sweetwater, a boomtown growing rich on cattle drives. His plans to keep a low profile soon go awry as he finds himself in the middle of a feud between the ruthless businessman, Jordan Carter, and an elderly sheriff, Luke Gardner. Finally, Luke is murdered by one of Carter's henchmen and Jake must choose between the law of the land and the law of the gun.

Keep checking the Hale website as new books appear monthly:
www.halebooks.com

Express Westerns presents

WHERE LEGENDS RIDE

New tales of the Old West

This first collection from Express Westerns is filled to the brim with 14 tales of hot lead, cold hearts, and more leather-slappin' action, adventure, and outright edge-of-the-seat danger than you'll find in any other Western collection roaming the Badlands today.

The writers who penned these tales—themselves all lovers of ripping Western yarns—run the gamut from seasoned, professional Western scribblers to backroom pen slingers. And most are responsible for a whole passel of novels under the Black Horse Westerns imprint by Robert Hale Books of London, one of the few publishers worldwide to continue to publish that most venerable of bookrack institutions: the Western novel.

From high-noon showdowns and shade-tree lynchings to raging prairie fires and scrub-country manhunts, Express Westerns' *Where Legends Ride* is a collection that will grab you by the vest front and won't let go until long after you've surrendered to the posse. Are you up to the challenge?

Saddle up . . . it's time to go *where legends ride!*

Here's what the press has to say about some of our authors:
"...In truth, no one writes the Western series novel any better than David Whitehead!" —Link Hullar, *Horizons West*

"I.J. Parnham's fast-paced story . . . won't fail to delight." —*Booklist*, the American Library Association magazine

"Lance Howard is the Master of Westerns." —*All About Murder Reviews*

"Gillian Taylor's [writing is a] splendid evocation of the Old West. . . . the denouement is fast and furious. . . " —*The Portsmouth and District Post*

Order from any good bookstore or direct from:
http://stores.lulu.com/expresswesterns

Made in the USA
Lexington, KY
22 April 2010